THE HEAT OF PASSION

"Don't you know the boy's half in love with you?"

"I'll talk to him about his feelings for me, explain he's only infatuated with me because I'm his teacher and—" Her voice trailed off under the intensity of his dark eyes.

He let his gaze drift slowly over her, and she felt an absurd urge to cover herself. A heat she blamed on embarrassment crept up her neck and then swept over the rest of her. When his dark eyes found hers again, the heat settled into the pit of her stomach.

"No wonder he thinks about you that way," he said, his voice husky.

"I've never encouraged him," she insisted, oddly breathless.

"You don't have to. All a man has to do is look at you to be encouraged." His gaze was like a caress. Her heart slowed to a dull thud, and the breath caught in her throat.

"Sam . . ." She meant it as a protest, but it sounded like an invitation.

He reached for her. His mouth found hers unerringly, seeking the sweetness she could not deny him.

His arms crushed her to him . . .

HISTORICAL ROMANCES BY VICTORIA THOMPSON

BOLD TEXAS EMBRACE (2835, $4.50)

Art teacher Catherine Eaton could hardly believe how stubborn Sam Connors was! Even though the rancher's young stepbrother was an exceptionally talented painter, Sam forbade Catherine to instruct him, fearing that art would make a sissy out of him. Spunky and determined, the blond schoolmarm confronted the muleheaded cowboy . . . only to find that he was as handsome as he was hard-headed and as desirable as he was dictatorial. Before long she had nearly forgotten what she'd come for, as Sam's brash, breathless embrace drove from her mind all thought of anything save wanting him . . .

TEXAS BLONDE (2183, $3.95)

When dashing Josh Logan resued her from death by exposure, petite Felicity Morrow realized she'd never survive rugged frontier life without a man by her side. And when she gazed at the Texas rancher's lean hard frame and strong rippling muscles, the determined beauty decided he was the one for her. To reach her goal, feisty Felicity pretended to be meek and mild: the only kind of gal Josh proclaimed he'd wed. But after she'd won his hand, the blue-eyed temptress swore she'd quit playing his game — and still win his heart!

ANGEL HEART (2426, $3.95)

Ever since Angelica's father died, Harlan Snyder had been angling to get his hands on her ranch, the Diamond R. And now, just when she had an important government contract to fulfill, she couldn't find a single cowhand to hire on — all because of Snyder's threats. It was only a matter of time before she lost the ranch. . . . That is, until the legendary gunfighter Kid Collins turned up on her doorstep, badly wounded. Angelica assessed his firmly muscled physique and stared into his startling blue eyes. Beneath all that blood and dirt he was the handsomest man she had ever seen, and the one person who could help her beat Snyder at his own game — if the price were not too high. . . .

Available wherever paperbacks are sold, or order direct from the Publisher. Send cover price plus 50¢ per copy for mailing and handling to Zebra Books, Dept. 2835, 475 Park Avenue South, New York, N.Y. 10016. Residents of New York, New Jersey and Pennsylvania must include sales tax. DO NOT SEND CASH.

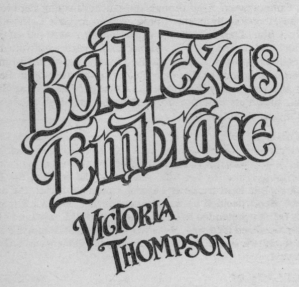

Bold Texas Embrace

Victoria Thompson

ZEBRA BOOKS
KENSINGTON PUBLISHING CORP.

Also by Victoria Thompson:

Texas Treasure
Texas Vixen
Texas Triumph
Texas Blonde
Angel Heart

ZEBRA BOOKS

are published by

Kensington Publishing Corp.
475 Park Avenue South
New York, NY 10016

First printing: December, 1989

Printed in the United States of America

Chapter One

"I know it's not nearly as fancy as you were used to back east," Twila Shallcross said apologetically.

Catherine glanced around the room that was to be her new home. It was furnished with what were undoubtedly the castoffs from many families—an iron bedstead, a chifforobe, a small stove, and a table with mismatched chairs—but everything was spotlessly clean and the faded curtains stirring in the afternoon breeze had been carefully starched and pressed. "It's fine, really," Catherine assured her. "And you must not think I lived in a mansion back in Philadelphia. Our home was quite modest."

"Pshaw," Mrs. Shallcross scoffed. "We all know your pa was a famous painter."

"Hardly famous," Catherine said with a pang, thinking of the paintings she'd had to give away because no one would pay a cent for anything by James Eaton, not even after he was dead and gone. "Mostly he was a teacher, and we all know how poorly paid teachers are," she added with a smile.

Mrs. Shallcross touched Catherine's arm, her expression still apologetic. "You know we'd pay you more if we could, but after we bought your train ticket to Dallas, the town just didn't have much money left for the schoolmarm's salary."

"I knew what the salary would be before I agreed to take the position," Catherine reminded her gently.

"And we'll make things as pleasant for you as we can," Mrs. Shallcross continued as if she had not heard. "You'll stay here during the week while school is in session, of course. We built this room onto the schoolhouse especially so the teacher wouldn't have to worry about traveling when the weather was bad. But on the weekends, you'll board with the families of the children, and when school is out, you'll spend the summer with my husband and me."

Mr. and Mrs. Shallcross ran the general store in Crosswicks, and Mr. Shallcross served as mayor and chairman of the school board as well. Twila Shallcross looked exactly as one would expect the mayor's wife to look. She bore her forty-odd years with dignity, styling her graying brown hair sedately and choosing clothing that was stylish but not ostentatious. Only her work-roughened hands betrayed the years of labor she and her husband had invested in their present prosperity.

Catherine had corresponded with them frequently during the past few months since she had applied for the job as schoolmistress in Crosswicks. She had learned to like them long before meeting them, but she had her own ideas about where the teacher should board.

"I intended to discuss the matter of the weekend visits with you. I really see no need for me to impose on the families, and I'd much rather—"

"Oh, you wouldn't be imposing! In fact, they'd be

insulted if you didn't stay with them. Keeping the teacher has become sort of a tradition around here, and the womenfolk are especially eager to visit with you. The last couple of teachers we had were men, and a new woman in town, especially one from so far away and from a big city, has everybody stirred up. We all want to know about the latest fashions and such like."

"Oh" was all Catherine could manage. As a spinster of twenty-three who had never so much as shared a bedroom with another person, she was appalled at the thought of moving in with a different family of strangers every week. Had she known how important this aspect of the job was, she might not have accepted it with such enthusiasm. But of course Mrs. Shallcross was not the final authority on such things. Catherine would ask Mr. Shallcross about it at the first opportunity. Perhaps she should tell him she was not as poverty-stricken as they seemed to think and would not need to have so many of her meals supplied by the families. She hadn't told anyone about the legacy her father had left her, for fear they wouldn't hire her if they knew she didn't really need to earn her own way.

"Yes," Mrs. Shallcross went on, "even with you in mourning, I can see you've got an eye for fashion. I'm kind of surprised you're still in black, though. Hasn't your pa been gone for more than a year now?"

Catherine nodded, reluctant to speak of her tragic loss even after all this time. "But my mother died more recently." It was a poor excuse. The period of mourning for her mother was over, too, if she would only admit it. Wearing black had become a comfortable habit that insulated her from burdensome social obligations.

"Oh, I'm sorry. I'd forgotten about your mother.

7

You're so pretty, it seems a shame you can't wear colors. But even in black, you'll put the rest of us in the shade, I'm afraid.''

Catherine smiled politely. No one had ever accused her of being pretty. She knew she had an interesting face, the kind an artist would find challenging. But *pretty?* No, not by anyone's definition.

Oblivious to Catherine's thoughts, Mrs. Shallcross rattled on. ''You'll be the belle of the ball tonight, too, I'll wager. There's something about blond hair and blue eyes that men just can't seem to resist. The boys haven't been able to talk about anything else all week—''

''Excuse me, Mrs. Shallcross, but what's this about tonight?'' Catherine asked with renewed apprehension.

''Oh, surely I didn't forget to tell you about the dance? What a featherbrain I'm getting to be!''

''No, you didn't mention it.'' Catherine could have groaned aloud. First the business about boarding with the families and now a dance on her first full day in town. She'd spent far too many hours as a wallflower at far too many other dances to enjoy the prospect of attending one where she would not know a soul except for Mr. and Mrs. Shallcross. But surely she could beg off. She was still quite fatigued from the journey, having arrived late the day before and having only awakened a few hours earlier. They couldn't expect her to . . .

''It's in your honor, of course. People are coming from miles around just to make you welcome,'' Mrs. Shallcross explained happily.

This time Catherine did groan.

''Is something wrong, dear?''

8

"I—I have a little headache, I'm afraid."

"Then I'd better leave you alone so you can rest. We want you to be feeling fine by the time the dance starts tonight. If you need anything, you know where I am. Come over to the house around seven for a late supper." She paused at the door and looked back with a small smile. "Maybe you could forget you're in mourning just for this one night and wear something pretty." Then she was gone.

Catherine sighed as she watched Twila disappear around the corner of the building. The schoolhouse was located at the very edge of town, and the door to this room faced the "river" beside which Crosswicks had been built. A few willow trees struggled for purchase beside the thin trickle of water that would have barely qualified as a creek back in Pennsylvania. Beyond them stretched a barren expanse of nothingness, broken only by an occasional hill or clump of vegetation.

From this angle, Catherine might have imagined herself alone in the universe. She shivered slightly at the thought and reminded herself the entire town lay just out of her range of vision. Mrs. Shallcross's house, the largest in Crosswicks, was only a short walk away, and beyond it was the main street with its row of businesses. There, people walked and talked and laughed and lived, and now she was part of their lives, too.

Isn't that what she'd wanted? A new life, completely different from the one she had known and as far away from the Philadelphia art world as she could get? Yes, she told herself sternly, laying a hand over the nervous flutter in her stomach. She simply hadn't expected it to start quite so suddenly or so publicly. Classes would not begin for several days yet, and she had pictured those days passing quietly as she accustomed herself to this stark new land and the startlingly friendly people in it.

Perhaps she could excuse herself from the dance early. Yes, that's what she would do. Surely, after she had been introduced, no one would miss her. Comforted by the thought, Catherine moved over to the iron bedstead and tested the mattress with her hand. A feather tick, she noted with surprise. And the quilt covering it was brand new, probably pieced by the ladies in town especially for her.

She was surprised to note the headache she had invented earlier had begun in earnest. Succumbing to the temptation of the bed in front of her, she lay down, feeling only mildly guilty for resting when she should have been unpacking her belongings and settling into her new home.

She had fallen into a light doze when a noise startled her awake. At first she did not recognize the unfamiliar surroundings, but just as memory returned, the door to her room opened and a man walked in.

Not a man, really, she realized, jerking upright on the bed in alarm. Although he was tall, he was not more than fifteen or sixteen. He turned at the sound of her movement, and she saw he was as startled as she and twice as mortified.

He uttered an agonized sound and bolted from the room.

The fright she had first felt instantly gave way to outrage at the intrusion. Without conscious thought, she scrambled off the bed and started after him.

"Wait a minute, young man!" she called in her best schoolteacher voice.

The boy stopped dead in his tracks, halfway to the horse he had tied to one of the straggly willow trees.

"I think you owe me an explanation," she informed him, marching up and grabbing his arm. She jerked him around to face her.

He stood a good half foot taller than her own five feet two inches, but from the terrified expression in his bright blue eyes, he was unaware of his physical advantage. He was, her artist's eye noted, quite handsome, almost pretty in fact. His features were finely molded, bordering on aristocratic. Lashes as long as a girl's fringed his beautiful eyes, and the hair visible beneath his Stetson was the color of spun gold.

"Who are you, young man?" she demanded.

"I—I—" His tanned face flushed scarlet. "My name's David Connors, and I—I didn't know you was in there, miss. I swear to God!"

Although she had no reason to, she found she believed him. "Even still, why would you have been sneaking into my room?"

His embarrassment increased tenfold. "Not to steal nothing, if that's what you think! I was gonna leave this."

He thrust a roll of paper into her hands. She recognized it instantly as sketch paper, carefully tied up with string.

"What is it?"

"It's . . . Mrs. Shallcross told me . . . she said it would brighten up the place, and I should . . . But I only finished it this morning and I thought—I thought you was still at Mrs. Shallcross's house."

Totally confused, Catherine pulled the string loose and began to unroll the paper.

"Oh, no, don't—" David's protest died as Catherine examined the drawing.

It was a sketch of the schoolhouse, which he had

colored in with watercolors. Her trained eye immediately recognized his natural ability, and she marveled at the accuracy of perspective and design. He had improved the aspect somewhat, making the straggly spring grass a lush green, filling out the willows, and adding other trees where none grew. The trees themselves were amazingly realistic. Trees were among the most difficult things to capture correctly on paper, but David had done an admirable job.

"This is very good work, David," she said, glancing up to catch his look of apprehension.

"Thank you, miss, but you don't have to . . . I mean . . ."

"I'm not being polite," she assured him with a smile. "Surely you must know how well you draw."

"I . . . uh . . . everybody always says so, but—" He shuffled his feet.

"Well, *I* don't just say so. In fact, I'm somewhat of an artist myself."

"You are?" His eyes lit up like sparklers, and Catherine couldn't help smiling at his excitement.

"I'm not very gifted," she said, surprised that for once the admission did not hurt, "but I've had a lot of training. In fact, I used to teach art back east."

"You did? Gosh, Miss—Miss—"

"Eaton. Catherine Eaton," she said, giving him her hand. He shook it gingerly, making her smile again. "Why don't you come inside for a few moments, David, so we can talk about your work."

"My work?" he echoed, following her obediently back into her room.

"Yes, your art work. I can see you've had some training." Catherine pulled out one of the chairs at her table and motioned for David to take the other one.

"Mr. Simmons—he was the teacher here a couple years back—he taught me how to get things to look right," David said, pulling off his hat and taking the chair Catherine had offered. "You know, if they're far away, they look smaller."

"Perspective."

"Yeah, that's it. I always forget the word. Anyway, he showed me that and lots of other things. I'd do a picture, and he'd show me how to do it better. But he got a job keeping books for a store in Dallas, and he had to leave."

"I'm glad you didn't get discouraged and quit when you lost your teacher."

David shrugged self-consciously. "I just couldn't quit drawing," he admitted reluctantly.

His confession touched a chord within her. How many other young people had confessed the same thing to her through the years? The proof of her own deficiency was her ability to pack up her paints and not touch them for a whole year. Still, she understood only too well the driving need of which he spoke. "I know what you mean. You see, my father was an artist, a really good one. He said it was like an obsession. He couldn't have quit even if he'd wanted to."

"Yeah, that's what it's like," David agreed eagerly. "I keep seeing pictures in my mind, and I have to put them down on paper. Was your father somebody famous?"

"No, I'm afraid not," Catherine admitted, her smile feeling slightly strained. "His work was never . . . appreciated." She marveled at her choice of words and how easily she was able to speak of the injustice that had embittered her life. Her father had been a genius, a man ahead of his time, yet his peers had ridiculed

13

his work out of jealousy. They had allowed him to teach but had never given him the recognition he had earned. "My father was a well-known teacher, though. He taught at the Pennsylvania Academy of Art."

David's eyes widened. "You mean they've got schools where you can just learn art?"

Catherine managed to conceal her astonishment at his ignorance. "Yes, they do. Not many, of course, and most of them are in Europe, but we do have a very good one in Philadelphia."

"Gosh! I'd give anything to go to a school like that."

Catherine blinked at the sting of tears. What a tragedy. She, who had no talent at all, had been handed such an education as a result of her birthright, while David, who had the talent, possibly even the genius to make use of it, didn't even know the school existed.

From some distant part of her brain, a memory stirred. Someone had once again refused to pay for a portrait her father had painted because it did not flatter the subject. It wasn't fair, she had told him. They thought he was good enough to teach but not to paint. Her father had comforted her, and she could almost hear him speaking the words.

"It doesn't matter, Cathy. I don't paint for them, anyway. I paint for myself, and I teach for myself. I was given a gift and teaching is the way I share it with others. They won't accept my paintings, but they'll have to accept my students, and thus the gift gets passed on. You have a gift, too, Cathy."

She'd thought he was being kind since she well knew she was not as gifted as he. She hadn't understood then, but now she did. She might not be able to paint the way her father had, but she could certainly teach the way he had.

14

"You know, David, we could start a branch of that art school right here in Crosswicks. Even though I'm not the artist my father was, he taught me everything he knew, and he allowed me to instruct the female students at the Pennsylvania Academy. How would you like to be my first student at the Crosswicks Academy of Art?"

"I—" His joyful expression froze and then faded into dismay. "I don't think I can."

"Don't worry," she said, patting his hand. "I'm only teasing about opening an art school. But I could tutor you after school a few days a week, and you wouldn't have to worry about paying me, either. I'd consider it an honor to instruct such a talented pupil."

But David was shaking his head. "It ain't that, Miss Eaton. It's . . . I don't think I'll be coming to school at all."

"Not coming? Why not?" She studied his face again, wondering if she had misjudged his age. "How old are you?"

"Fifteen."

"Do you think you're too old for school?"

"Oh, no, ma'am. It's Sam. He says I've already had almost five years of school and that's plenty for anybody. He says it's time I was learning how to run the ranch."

"Who's Sam?"

"My brother. My half brother, really. He's a lot older than me and—"

"What do your parents say?"

"They don't say anything. I mean, they're both dead. It's just me and Sam and has been for a long time. He's always taken care of me, and I can't buck him on this."

"But, David, surely he won't object to your getting an education."

David made a helpless gesture. "He figures it's more important for me to learn how to run the Spur."

"The Spur?"

"Yes, ma'am. That's the name of our ranch. Our brand is the shape of a spur, so that's what we call it."

"Oh." Catherine considered the situation for a moment and decided she would simply have to change Sam Connor's mind. Her visually oriented imagination began to picture what David's brother would look like. The brother who was a *lot* older than he. She resisted the urge to ask exactly *how* old he was. Surely Sam Connors would be twenty-five or thirty. Her artist's eye could easily imagine what handsome young David would look like in ten or fifteen years. And her heart could imagine how his sensitivity and brightness would be improved by a decade of maturity.

Suddenly Catherine was quite eager to make the acquaintance of Sam Connors. That is, unless . . . "Perhaps if I spoke to your brother's wife, she would help us change his mind."

"Sam ain't married," David said, as if wondering how she could have thought such a ridiculous thing.

Catherine resisted the feeling of anticipation. After all, what were the chances Sam Connors was as wonderful as she imagined him to be? On the other hand, what were the chances she would find a talented art student on her very first day in Texas, either? "Well, then, I suppose I'll have to speak to your brother myself." Anticipation tingled over her again, but David's frown squelched it.

"I don't know if you oughta try that. I mean, he's

got pretty set ideas about how things oughta be, and he don't like folks to argue with him."

"I have no intention of arguing with him," Catherine assured the boy with a smile. "I plan to *persuade* him. I'm sure when he understands how important it is to you, he'll change his mind."

"I don't know," David muttered.

"David, the school term is only three months long. Surely your brother won't object to your delaying your training for such a brief period. No one is *that* unreasonable."

"I—I guess you're right," David allowed, but he was still doubtful. It took Catherine a few more minutes to imbue him with her confidence, but by the time he left, he was smiling.

He had an absolutely beatific smile, and Catherine had no trouble at all picturing it on a much older man. As soon as David was gone, she opened the trunk she had been so reluctant to unpack a short time earlier. Perhaps it *was* time she ended her mourning and began wearing colors again. Somewhere near the bottom of the trunk was a perfectly lovely gown of robin's egg blue, the exact shade of her eyes. As she dug for it, she wondered idly whether Mrs. Shallcross had been right about Texans liking women with blond hair and blue eyes. She only wished Twila had been correct in calling her pretty.

The dance was being held in the Shallcross's barn. Twila explained that dances were held at the school when the teacher was not in residence, but in deference to Catherine, the barn had been selected instead.

"Your dress is just lovely," Twila said as they left her house and started for the barn.

Catherine fingered the low neckline self-consciously. It wasn't daringly low, since she had no cleavage to display, but it did reveal her shoulders and left her arms bare. The smooth sateen had pressed up very nicely, and Catherine felt at least presentable. "It's a little out of fashion, I'm afraid. I haven't had anything new in quite a while, not since my parents died."

"It surely was a tragedy, both of them dying so close together."

"Yes, it was." Catherine felt no need to explain the special relationship that had existed between her parents. She hadn't fully understood it herself until she heard her father tell her mother on his death bed how glad he was to be the first to die, since he could never have continued to paint without her by his side. When he was gone, her mother had faded almost visibly. Robbed of her reason for existence, she had simply ceased to exist.

"We'll make you forget all the sadness," Twila said with a comforting smile. She took Catherine's arm and led her into the barn.

The first thing Catherine noticed was the disproportionate ratio of men to women. At all the dances she had ever attended, the numbers had been roughly even, and since she had often sat out the festivities with other unclaimed females, she suspected in most cases the women had actually outnumbered the men. Not so in Crosswicks. Here the women—including those old enough to have seen their great-grandchildren and those young enough to *be* the great-grandchildren— were outnumbered at least ten to one.

As Twila Shallcross introduced Catherine to each and every female in the room, the young woman quickly determined another amazing fact: No female over the age of sixteen was single unless she was an elderly widow. Every woman near her own age held a baby on her hip and had at least one other child clinging to her skirts. Most of them also had children whom Catherine would be teaching in school.

And *all* of them expressed their eagerness to board her in their homes. Catherine felt her precious privacy slipping away already.

"I'm not even going to try to introduce you to all these men," Twila said as she steered Catherine toward a vacant bench near the edge of the dance floor. "They'll be on you like a duck on a june bug just as soon as the music starts, anyway, and I figure they can introduce themselves."

"But where are all the other single women?" Catherine whispered in dismay.

Twila grinned knowingly. "Ain't none. A woman's got her pick of men out here, so none of 'em stays single very long unless she's got a mortal fear of marriage. I only hope you'll be able to hold off your suitors until the school term is up."

Catherine absorbed this information in wide-eyed amazement as they seated themselves on the bench. By moving to Texas, she had hoped to achieve many things—escaping the cloistered society of the artists who were her only friends in Philadelphia and the unhappy memories of her father's rejection associated with them, finally obtaining some measure of independence, and developing an identity of her own separate from her father's. In achieving those things, she had never dreamed she might also be deluged with potential suitors. Nor did she find the prospect appealing.

"You don't need to worry about me," she told Mrs.

Shallcross. "I have no intention of getting married—now or ever."

"What kind of crazy talk is that?" Twila wanted to know. "Every woman wants to get married."

"Not every woman I know. I had lots of female friends in Philadelphia who were single by choice. They still managed to lead interesting and fulfilling lives."

"With no husband and no children? Humph!" Twila scoffed. "You can bet your life they'd marry in a minute if the right man offered for them. That's what it is, you know. They just never got an offer from a man they really wanted."

Twila's words stung. Catherine remembered far too well the pain of watching the men whom she found attractive pass her over for women with more beauty. "Unfortunately, there are far too few men really worth having," Catherine observed bitterly.

Twila's eyebrows lifted, but she had the good manners not to probe. "Maybe that's true back where you come from, but out here you'll have your pick of men. I have a notion you'll find at least one you can get excited about."

Catherine realized with some surprise that she was already excited about one of them, one whom she had not even met. She scanned the gathering crowd for sight of David Connors and, more specifically, a grown man who looked like David Connors. Before she could locate either of them, however, she noticed with some alarm that the gathering crowd was all male and that every one of them was staring directly at her.

"Here they come," Twila murmured. Nearby, two fiddlers were tuning up, and the crowd pulsed and swelled like a living thing. At last, three men broke free and made for Catherine. Amid much elbowing as

20

they jostled for preeminence, they managed to murmur their names and request a dance. Instantly, Catherine found her first three dances claimed by a rancher, a cowboy, and a farmer. She barely had time to consent before the first song began and the farmer pulled her out onto the floor.

As soon as her first partner released her, the next claimed her, and he was followed by a steady stream of men whose names soon began to run together in her mind. Far from being the wallflower, as she had been at most of her previous dances, Catherine was indeed the belle of the ball. By the time the musicians took their first break, her feet were aching and her head was spinning.

She sought refuge amid a group of women gathered around the punch bowl. Twila Shallcross was holding forth for several other matrons. They all laughed when Catherine rolled her eyes and thirstily gulped down a glass of punch.

"Wearing you out, are they?" one of the women asked.

Catherine nodded wearily. Searching her memory, she recalled the woman was Lulie Nylan, mother of four of Catherine's future pupils. She looked far too old to have recently given birth to the infant on her hip or even to the two toddlers wrestling with her skirts, but Catherine supposed having had so many children had aged her beyond her years. Another reason to avoid marriage, Catherine thought grimly.

"Miss Eaton?"

Catherine whirled at the sound of the familiar voice and found David Connors standing behind her. His face was rosy with chagrin as he avoided the curious gazes of the other women.

"David, how nice to see you." In all the excitement, she had almost forgotten her eagerness to meet David's brother. She forced herself not to look around for the man she had been thinking about all afternoon.

"My—my brother's outside if you still want to—to talk to him." David wrung his hands in an agony of embarrassment. His golden hair had been slicked down close to his head and he wore a brown nankeen suit with a boiled shirt and a string tie, obviously his Sunday best.

"Of course I do," she assured him gently. "By all means, bring him in."

David's Adam's apple bobbed as he swallowed loudly. "I'll be right back."

Catherine watched him go with an indulgent smile. The poor boy was scared to death she wouldn't be able to convince his brother.

"You're going to meet Sam Connors?" Lulie Nylan asked sharply.

"Yes," Catherine said in surprise, turning back to face the other women. Their smiles had turned to concern. Even Twila looked troubled. "Is something wrong? Is there something I should know about him?"

"Of course not," Twila said too quickly. "He's a fine young man."

Lulie made a rude noise. "A fine young man who fenced off his water so his poorer neighbors couldn't get to it."

"Now, Lulie, he didn't do anything illegal. . . ."

"Maybe not, but that don't mean what he did was right."

In an obvious attempt to change the subject, Twila asked Catherine, "What are you going to talk to him about?"

"About David coming to school. It seems Mr. Connors thinks his brother is too old for any further education."

Twila's expressive eyebrows lifted, but she only said, "If anyone can convince him, you can. Oh, here he comes now."

Catherine's stomach did a little flip, and she took a moment to compose herself before turning to greet David and his companion. She heard the other women discreetly withdrawing as she looked past David for a tall, blond man with the same blue eyes as his brother's.

David cleared his throat nervously. "Miss Eaton, this here's my brother Sam."

Startled, Catherine glanced up at the man David indicated. Up and up. He seemed like a giant, and when she finally encountered his eyes, she thought vaguely of the old saying, "The difference between night and day."

If David Connors was day, then Sam Connors was night. The eyes glaring down at her seemed black in the lamplit room, as black as the ebony hair carelessly pushed back from his forehead and curling at his shirt collar. While David's features were fine, this man's were sharp, as if the relentless Texas wind had scoured all traces of softness from him. His powerful shoulders and massive chest would have made him imposing under any circumstances, but the tension radiating from him, the tension reflected in his closed fists and his stiff-legged stance, made him positively terrifying. Even his black suit contributed to his sinister air, and she saw he was older than she had guessed, probably in his early thirties.

"How do you do?" Catherine managed, feeling a trifle breathless. Why on earth was he so angry?

"Miss Eaton, I think we need to talk," he said. His voice was as huge as the rest of him, rumbling like an avalanche.

She tried smiling, but her face resisted the effort. "Of course," she murmured.

Connors cast his brother a meaningful look, and the boy mumbled something unintelligible and darted away. The poor thing was terrified! She could easily understand why, being terrified herself, but outrage was rapidly replacing her own fear. Who did this fellow think he was? Catherine Eaton had once told off one of the most powerful art critics in America for failing to recognize her father's genius. Why should she quake at the wrath of an unimportant Texas rancher? And why should she let him terrorize poor David?

At that moment, the musicians struck up the next dance, a waltz. Catherine lifted her chin in an effort to more squarely meet Sam Connor's glowering gaze and said, "Perhaps you'll ask me to dance."

She'd surprised him, and she saw him preparing to refuse, when the would-be partners she had been expecting began to swarm around them.

At least Connors wasn't stupid, she noted with some relief. He quickly comprehend the situation and used his bulk to block his rivals for her attention. "Miss Eaton promised this dance to me, boys," he said, with enough authority to make the others back off.

"I've got the next one!" someone shouted, but someone else disputed his claim and an argument broke out.

"Good God," Connors muttered as he led her out to the dance floor, away from the ruckus. He pulled her awkwardly into his arms, and she saw at once he was no dancer. Or perhaps his anger made him clumsy. At any rate, he merely walked her around the floor, making no attempt to follow the music.

Standing as far from him as she could manage and yet appear to be his partner, Catherine still felt the power of his physical presence. His shoulder was rock hard beneath her hand and his callused palm abraded hers with disturbing intimacy. She'd never found the smell of any man particularly attractive, but the musky scent emanating from Sam Connors was almost enervating and annoyingly pleasant. She didn't want to like anything about him, particularly not the way he smelled.

Resolutely, she ignored the various messages her senses were sending her and tried to read the stony expression on his sun-darkened face. When he did not speak, she finally said, "You wanted to talk to me?"

"You're some kind of artist, aren't you?" The words were an accusation. She'd judged his mood correctly: He was furious.

"I used to teach art back in Philadelphia," she said, refusing to sound apologetic.

"If you're an art teacher, why'd you take the job here?"

She was tempted to tell him it was none of his business, but she squelched the urge and said, "I'm trained to teach in all subjects, and I got tired of teaching only one."

"Davy don't need to go to school anymore. He can read and write and cipher just fine, and he's too old."

Blinking at his vehemence, Catherine quickly gathered her arguments. "I'll have several students just as old or older than David. And I'm sure there are many things he has yet to learn. Besides, I've offered to help him with his art and—"

"He sure as hell don't need to learn to draw. He already does that just fine, for all the good it'll ever do him. What he needs to know is how to run a ranch, and it's time he learned."

"Perhaps it is, but the school term is only three months long. Surely he can delay his education in ranching for such a brief period."

"Perhaps he can," Connors said, mimicking her. "But there's no reason for him to, and I want him on the ranch."

"And you're used to getting your own way, aren't you?" she asked, recalling what Lulie Nylan had said about him. "Aren't you the one who fenced off your water so your neighbors couldn't get to it?"

His dark eyes narrowed contemptuously. "I see you've been gossiping already. Tell me, Miss Eaton, are you one of those 'free-grassers'?"

Catherine had no idea what a free-grasser was and decided she had better change tactics quickly. "Mr. Connors, do you have any idea how important art is to David?"

Instinctively, she had struck the right nerve. Connor's jaw flexed and his nostrils flared, betraying his reaction although he said not one word. "I can see you care a great deal for your brother," she went on ruthlessly. "His happiness surely is important to you. I saw his face this afternoon when he talked about art to me, and I know how happy it would make him to learn the things I could teach him."

"But why does he need to know those things?" Connors demanded. "No man ever made a living drawing pictures."

26

"Some do," she insisted, not letting herself think of her father's failure to sell his work.

"Not many, I'd reckon," he sneered. "And not much of a living, either."

"So you'd deny him the opportunity to try? To do what he loves most in this world?"

He drew in his breath with a hiss and let it out in a disgusted sigh. "I told you, I need him on the ranch."

She looked him up and down in mock amazement. "Do you expect me to believe you can't run the Spur without the help of a fifteen-year-old boy?"

His ears reddened, but he bit back whatever reply he might have been considering. "You've got a tongue like a viper, Miss Eaton," he said after a long moment.

Ignoring his barb, she said, "You're a rancher, aren't you, Mr. Connors?"

"You know I am," he said, instantly wary.

"Did anyone force you to become one or did you choose that profession for yourself?"

"My father owned the ranch. I just naturally fell into it."

"But you love it, don't you?" she pressed, certain she was right.

He nodded, grudgingly conceding her point.

"Suppose someone bigger and more powerful than you—your father, for instance—had forbidden you to become a rancher and had forced you to do something you hated instead."

"Davy doesn't hate the ranch," he protested.

"But it isn't his first love, not the way it's yours. It isn't fair of you to force him to give up art when—"

"Miss Eaton, who put you in charge of Davy's life?" he asked through gritted teeth.

"Who put *you* in charge of it?" she countered.

But he had her there, and his sudden grin reflected his triumph. "God or fate or whoever you believe is in charge of those things, Miss Eaton. I'm his brother and his legal guardian. Whether you like it or not, Davy is my responsibility."

"Then God or fate or whatever you believe in had better protect you when he realizes how you've cheated him!"

For one awful moment she thought he might actually do her physical harm. His hand tightened around hers and his eyes sparked with the black fires of pure hatred. Then, suddenly, they were surrounded by men clamoring for the next dance, and Catherine realized the music had stopped.

She and Connors jerked apart, and he turned abruptly away to disappear into the crowd. She stared after him for what must have been too long, because she incurred the displeasure of her would-be partners for her inattention. Numbly, she selected someone to honor with the next dance and moved through the steps of the reel mechanically, her heart leaden as she became more and more certain her unbridled tongue had forever ruined things for David.

Sam Connors strode outside into the coolness of the evening. Avoiding the crowd of men gathered around the whiskey barrel, he sought the privacy of the deeper shadows on the side of the Shallcrosses' house. There he tried to regain some semblance of control over his temper before he had to tell Davy how his conversation with the remarkable Miss Eaton had gone.

She was even worse than he had expected. Not only was she tiny and frail, the kind of woman this land chewed up and spit out in no time at all, but she was a shrew into the bargain. And damn her soul to hell,

28

she was right about Davy. The boy did love art more than he loved cattle, although for the life of him, Sam couldn't understand how anyone could prefer sitting inside the house with a piece of paper when he could be outside on the back of a horse.

Davy was just like his mother, Sam thought bitterly. Not only had he inherited Adora's delicate blond beauty, but he had also inherited her love for delicate beauty. But Davy was a Connors, too, and he was a man. He had a place to fill that didn't include pictures and drawings, and damnit, Sam was going to make sure he filled it.

"Sam? Is that you?"

Davy materialized out of the shadows. Sam didn't need to see his face to know how anxious he was, and the knowledge made the rancher's heart ache.

"Did you like Miss Eaton?"

Like her? What a ridiculous notion, Sam thought, but he said, "We didn't get to know each other real well. We mostly talked about you."

"You weren't too hard on her, were you?"

Sam almost laughed aloud. "Maybe you oughta ask her if she was too hard on me. That woman could draw blood on a rawhide boot."

"Miss Eaton?"

"I don't reckon she showed you that side of her," Sam allowed wryly. Then he sobered. "She seems to think you'll curl up and die if I don't let her teach you to draw."

Davy glanced away and shifted uneasily. "Sam—"

"Davy, you don't need no woman to teach you anything. You already draw better than anybody I ever knew, and why would you want to be cooped up in school when all your friends'll be out riding the range?''

"It's only for a few months, and Sam, she used to teach in a school where they don't teach anything *but* art. She must know all sorts of things I don't and—''

His voice trailed off as he sensed Sam's resistance to the idea, but he hesitated only a moment.

"I'll work on the ranch after school. I'll work twice as hard as anyone, and when school is over, I'll do whatever you want me to, I swear. Sam, please . . .''

Sam swallowed around the lump of dread forming in his throat. Davy was just like Adora, and just like her, he could get his brother to agree to anything, no matter how wrong Sam knew it was. "You're going to be a rancher. You know that, don't you? We're partners, you and me. The Spur is half yours, and Pa wanted—''

"I know, I know,'' Davy said impatiently. "I'll be a rancher for the rest of my life. Why can't it wait for three more months?''

Because, Sam thought, I'm afraid of losing you to that woman, that woman who is so much like Adora it makes my blood run cold. He closed his eyes and sighed wearily. "All right, Davy. Three months, but when school's out, you're going to be a rancher.''

"Oh, thanks, Sam, thanks!'' he exclaimed, grabbing Sam's arm and shaking it. "I can't wait to tell Miss Eaton.''

The next instant he was gone, off to see his precious Miss Eaton. Sam fought the tide of despair that threatened to overwhelm him. "You won't get him, Adora,'' he whispered to the night sky. "You won the last time, but this time he's mine.''

* * *

Catherine could hardly believe her eyes when she looked up and saw David motioning to her. She missed a step and stumbled as her partner swung her around. When she caught sight of David again, he was grinning from ear to ear. Her breath snagged in her chest when she recognized that triumphant grin as the same one Sam Connors had given her a few minutes earlier. It was, she decided, the one and only similarity between the brothers.

And it could only mean one thing. Connors must have relented! Somehow she managed to finish the dance without doing herself or anyone else bodily harm, and as soon as it was over, she left her partner with unseemly haste and met David as he hurried toward her.

"He said I could come to school!"

"Oh, David, that's wonderful! But what about my tutoring you?"

"That too. And I know you said you wouldn't charge me anything, but I've got my own money. Sam's been paying me wages for a long time and . . . well, anyway, I'll pay you, and—"

"Don't worry about it, David. We can discuss it later," she told him, feeling almost weak with relief. "The important thing is your brother said yes. I was so afraid I'd ruined everything. I was unspeakably rude, but when I saw how scared you were of him, I went a little crazy. . . ."

"Scared? I'm not scared of Sam," he said, obviously puzzled at her assessment.

"But I thought . . . I mean, you seemed so nervous, and when he just looked at you, you went running off. . . ."

"I was nervous because I didn't think you could convince him, and I was afraid he might be rude to

31

you. Sam's manners ain't . . . aren't the best. He don't . . . doesn't have much truck with ladies, and I thought he might offend you."

Catherine had indeed found Sam Connor's manners offensive, but hers had been none too exemplary, either. "Why did you run off?"

"Sam said he'd talk to you but only if I didn't hang around. I reckon he knew I'd be on him about the way he treated you."

Catherine smiled at the thought of gentle David chastening his formidable brother's behavior. "Neither one of us behaved well, I'm sorry to say. Perhaps I should apologize to him. I said some terrible things."

David shook his head doubtfully. "Maybe you oughta just leave well enough alone."

"I suppose you're right. No use tempting fate." She winced as she recalled how she had threatened Sam Connors with the wrath of the fates. Whatever had possessed her? On the other hand, he had been no better than she. "By the way, David, what is a free-grasser?"

"Did you call Sam that? Gosh, no wonder he got mad!" David replied, but before he could explain the meaning to her, her next partner appeared at her elbow and drew her back to the dancing.

Oh, well, she thought, she could always find out later. She'd be seeing a lot of David now. And she would probably be wise to make peace with the brother if for no other reason than to ensure he didn't change his mind again.

The idea was a sound one, but when she tried to think of a way to implement it, she failed. How did one make peace with a devil like Sam Connors?

* * *

32

Sam left the shadows and joined the men gathered around the whiskey barrel Mathias Shallcross had thoughtfully provided. He drew himself a drink and tossed it back, hoping to kill the bitter taste in his mouth.

Inside, the music started up, and the other men drifted away, leaving Sam alone with his host.

"I saw you dancing with the new schoolteacher," Mathias remarked.

Sam grinned mirthlessly at the older man. "Yeah, I did. I don't reckon she'll have any trouble keeping the kids in line. She took a strip of hide off me a yard wide."

Mathias chuckled. Tall and gangly, he looked the part of a storekeeper, with his bald pate and middle-aged paunch. "Don't tell me you got out of line with her."

"Never got the chance. She lit into me right off about Davy. She wants to teach him how to draw." He snorted his disgust at the idea.

"Davy's a very talented boy. You shouldn't deny him the chance to learn."

Sam raised his hands in mock surrender. "Hold it! I already gave him permission. Good God Almighty, everybody in town must be in on this," he grumbled. Drawing himself another drink, he sought to change the subject. "Say, when's my wire coming in, anyway?"

Mathias's good humor vanished. "I expect it'll be in this week sometime. . . . Sam, do you think it's a good idea to put up more fence just now?"

This time Sam sipped the whiskey. "Don't tell me you're turning into a free-grasser, too, Mathias."

"You know me better than that, but feeling is running pretty high right now. What'll it hurt if you hold off for a while?"

"I'll tell you what it'll hurt: I've got a fortune invested in breeding stock. I almost lost my shirt in the drought last year, and now my only hope is to upgrade my herd. What happens if my bulls get loose or somebody else's bull gets to my cows?"

"I know, I know," Mathias soothed him. "But you've got most all your range fenced already. Would it hurt to wait awhile before fencing that section you just leased?"

"Sooner or later, folks have to face the fact that barbwire is here to stay."

"They might accept it easier if you didn't ram it down their throats."

Sam sighed gustily, but his lips twitched into a reluctant grin. "I guess you're right. I can wait a few weeks till folks cool down a bit. But I'm not going to stop fencing. We both know it's the best thing ever happened to this country. It's the only thing that'll save us from another summer like last year."

"You don't have to convince me," Mathias said. "Just remember, barbwire may be the best thing, but it's like medicine: Being good for you don't make it any fun to take."

"Are you suggesting I sugarcoat it a bit?"

"It's worth a try."

Sam shook his head, but his grin was back. "Did you ever consider becoming a preacher, Mathias? You got a real gift for making converts."

Mathias did not smile. "Just be careful, Sam. I don't want to see anybody get killed over this wire."

"Neither do I, Mathias, neither do I."

34

Chapter Two

David Connors was the first student to arrive at school on Monday morning. He rode in on a big bay gelding, looking proud and tall and demonstrating that his concern for artistic impression extended beyond the pictures he drew. Catherine could barely suppress a smile when she saw the cut on his chin that proved he had shaved the down from his cheeks this morning.

His face was alight with the same suppressed excitement she felt at the prospect of not only starting her new job but of having her first session with her new art student.

Soon more children began to arrive. The next group came on foot and consisted not of four but of *five* Nylans. Lulie had told her the eldest, Jessica, would not be attending, but there she was, herding her younger siblings into the yard.

"Jessica, what a nice surprise," Catherine greeted her. "I thought you'd be staying home to help your mother."

"I was going to, but then I heard Davy was coming,

and I figured if he wasn't too old, then I wasn't, either, since we're the same age.''

From the look Jessica shot David, Catherine decided the girl was older than her fifteen years and that she had her rapidly maturing eye on the Connors boy. Jessica wasn't particularly pretty. Her face was plain and her hair was a nondescript brown and worn in an unflattering braid, but her fully mature body strained provocatively against the buttons of her bodice. The smile she gave David was equally provocative, and although he frowned and turned away, his gaze slid to her breasts before he did so.

Catherine sighed, thinking she would have her hands full keeping David's attention in class and knowing she would have none of Jessica's.

The other children began to arrive, some on horseback and some walking, and soon the schoolyard was filled with youthful shrieks and laughter. Catherine almost hated to ring the bell and end their fun. Some of the younger children had never been to school and did not know the significance of the clanging bell. Thinking she had found a use for Jessica, she asked the girl to help round them up and get them in line.

Only too happy to take on a position of leadership, Jessica masterfully got all the children organized and marched them inside. She even helped seat them, informing Catherine of each one's age and abilities. Catherine spent the morning calling each age group up and testing them on their progress. By lunchtime she had begun to realize what a formidable task it would be to teach twenty-two children ranging from five-year-old Tommy Nylan, who did not recognize a single letter, to fifteen-year-old Jessica Nylan, who knew lots of things she shouldn't.

Catherine had made herself a cheese sandwich from the stores in her room behind the school, and she went out to join the children eating their lunches in the shade of the willows by the river. As they finished eating, they got up and began to run off their excess energy, leaving Catherine, David, and Jessica alone.

"I appreciate the help you gave me this morning," Catherine told the girl.

"I'm used to helping," she demurred. "I've been taking care of kids my whole life. Ma thinks I'm too old to be coming to school, but that's just because she got married when she was my age."

"What!" Catherine could hardly credit it.

"Yeah, and she was just turned sixteen when I was born," Jessica continued matter-of-factly.

Catherine didn't know which was more surprising, hearing of such a youthful bride or learning that Lulie Nylan, who looked old enough to be Catherine's mother, was only eight years her senior.

"I reckon she thinks I'll be married soon, too," Jessica was saying, "but I figure I'll wait another year or two. I want to have some fun before I settle down." She flashed David a meaningful smile, which made him squirm.

"Davy! Davy! Draw us a picture!" Several of the older boys raced up and fell on David en masse. "Draw us a picture! Please!"

Obviously pleased by the request, David made only a halfhearted protest before going for the paper and pencils he had brought for his afternoon class.

When Catherine and Jessica were alone, the girl turned to her curiously. "How come you're not married yet, Miss Eaton? I mean, you must be at least twenty."

"I'm twenty-three," Catherine said, shocking the daylights out of poor Jessica.

"Oh dear, did your sweetheart die or something?" she asked in dismay.

"I've never had a sweetheart." Catherine tried not to sound defensive. Having never been courted was certainly no disgrace, but from the expression on Jessica's face, it was the greatest tragedy imaginable.

Then her expression suddenly lightened. "So *that's* why you came here! You want to find a husband."

Before Catherine could protest such an outrageous assumption, Jessica scrambled up and said, "I'll check on the kids." In an instant, she had made her way over to where David was sketching something for a group of fascinated onlookers.

Catherine watched in amused admiration as the girl expertly diverted David's attention to herself time and again. While she watched, she also brooded over Jessica's remarks. Did everyone think Catherine had come to Texas to find a husband? How annoying. Well, they'd soon find out that a husband was the very last thing she wanted, especially now that she knew from her run-in with Sam Connors what overbearing creatures Texas men could be.

When Catherine dismissed her class later in the day, Jessica Nylan lingered at the door, watching David and apparently waiting for him to leave, too. When he made no move to do so, she said, "Why don't you walk with us, Davy? It's on your way."

"I'm not leaving yet," he told her, obviously uncomfortable with her attention. "Miss Eaton is going to help me with my drawing."

Jessica digested this information and frowned thoughtfully. "Oh," she said in disappointment. The look she flashed the schoolmistress as she left was far from friendly, and Catherine hoped she had not made an enemy.

"Jessica seems like a nice girl," Catherine remarked, trying to judge David's opinion.

His cheeks colored slightly, and he refused to meet her eye. "She's all right, I guess, but she can be a pest."

"I think she likes you."

His color deepened, and he glanced up in alarm. "Who told you?"

"Nobody," she assured him. "I figured it out for myself."

"Well, I don't like her. Jessie Nylan's only interested in getting a man with some money, and Sam says—" He caught himself and turned away.

Catherine was dying to know what Sam said, but she decided not to press the point. Instead, she invited David to go for a walk with her until they found something interesting to sketch. They selected the Shallcrosses' house and found some shade a comfortable distance away from which to observe it.

David positioned his sketchbook and gave Catherine a questioning glance.

"Go ahead and start. I want to see how much you already know. I'll watch and give you some pointers as you go along."

He hesitated a moment and then began lightly sketching in the basic outlines of the building. Catherine had brought her own book, and she began a drawing of her own, glancing up at her companion's striking profile from time to time to make sure she was getting it right.

"You don't look much like your brother," she observed after a few moments.

"Everybody says that," David said with a grin that belied her statement. "He looks like our pa, and I look like my mother. We've got a picture of her, and she sure was pretty."

"You don't remember her?"

"No, she died when I was three, but Sam says she was even prettier than the picture. She was young, too, not much older than Sam. She was only twenty-four when she died."

"How tragic," Catherine said, thinking how sad it was David's mother had not lived to see what a fine young man he had become. "Do you know how she died?"

"Sam said she was always sickly. She just got weaker and weaker until she died." He paused, deep in thought. "I never could figure out why she—"

"Why she what?" Catherine prompted.

"Why she left home and married my pa. I mean, she was from a rich family in New Orleans, and he was a lot older and—" He shrugged.

"Perhaps she loved him," Catherine suggested.

"That's what Sam always says, too." David returned to his drawing.

"This line is too straight,' Catherine pointed out. "See the way it seems to slant away from us?"

David studied the house and then nodded. "Yeah, I see." He made the correction and concentrated on the picture for a few minutes.

Catherine debated whether to broach the subject of Sam with David, but she knew if she ever wanted to understand the boy, she needed to understand his relationship with his brother.

40

"You and Sam are very close, aren't you?"

David's expression showed he had never given the matter much thought. "I guess so."

"I suppose your father died when you were very young, also."

"I was eight, but even when he was alive, Pa never had much time for me. He was pretty busy running the ranch and everything, but Sam played with me. It always seemed like he was my father even before Pa died, and after—" David shrugged again, as if Sam's devotion to him were the most natural thing in the world.

She smiled. "You were right to warn me about how stubborn he can be."

David's quick frown showed his concern. "Sam means well, but there's some things he just doesn't understand, like about my drawing. He says I get that from her, too—from my mother, I mean."

"Was she an artist?"

"She made a lot of pictures. I have them all at the house. They're mostly of flowers, but they're not like any flowers I've ever seen. Sam says they grow back in New Orleans, where she came from."

Sam says. Catherine had been right to suspect Sam Connors was the moving force in David's life. She supposed David's willingness to defy his sainted brother on the matter of art classes proved the boy's driving need to express himself. She also knew Connors's permission could be withdrawn at any time, and if she wanted to ensure his continued cooperation, she would be wise to come to terms with the man. She would never like him, of course, but that didn't mean she couldn't learn to be civil to him. At least she hoped she could.

When David had finished his sketch of the house, Catherine critiqued it for him. Then he gave her his familiar grin and said, "Now, let me see the one you did so I'll know how bad I really am."

"Oh, I didn't draw the house," she explained, handing him her book. "I drew something else."

"Wow! It's me!" he exclaimed in amazement. "How did you do that? Every time I try to draw a picture of a person, it never looks anything like them."

"There's a secret to it. I'll show it to you, and then you'll be able to capture a likeness, too."

" 'Capture a likeness,' " he quoted in wonder, as if the words were some mystical chant. "Do you really think I can?"

"If *I* can, anyone can," Catherine assured him.

He frowned his confusion. "Why do you keep telling me you aren't much of an artist? You draw a lot better than I do."

"I'm technically better because I've had more training, but I don't have the genius it takes to rise above the ordinary," she said, once again amazed to find she did not mind admitting her deficiencies to David.

"How do you know?"

"I—I just do," she hedged, thinking about all the futile hours she had spent trying unsuccessfully to re-create on paper the magnificent pictures she saw in her mind.

"What about me? Do you think I'm 'above the ordinary'?"

"Yes, I do, or I wouldn't waste time with you. Now, it's getting late. I'd better send you home or your brother will never let you stay for another lesson."

Walking slowly and stopping occasionally to discuss a potential site for future sketching, they made their way back to the school. Catherine had just noticed the strange horse in the yard when David yelled, "Sam!" and waved a greeting.

The figure sitting on the front steps rose and waved back. Sam Connors was larger than she remembered and twice as forbidding, even in ordinary range clothes. He took a final drag on his cigarette and dropped it, grinding it out with the heel of his boot before moving to meet them halfway.

"I was wondering where you two got off to. I was in town and thought I'd ride home with Davy." His mouth was smiling politely, but his black eyes were wary and guarded, as if he expected a fight. Determined not to start one, Catherine smiled politely back.

"I took David over to town to do some sketching," she said.

"See if you can tell what this is," David said, producing his drawing.

Connors examined it closely. "The saloon?" he guessed, with what Catherine could only have described as a twinkle.

"Sam!" David protested, punching his brother in the arm.

"It's the Shallcrosses' house," Connors admitted with a chuckle that startled Catherine with its warmth. "And it's damn good."

"Sam, you shouldn't swear in front of a lady," David said, but neither Catherine nor Sam heard his chastisement.

Connor's gaze had settled on her in silent challenge, and she could not look away. "See how good he draws?" Connors said. "I told you he doesn't need any lessons."

"Oh, but I do, Sam," David insisted. "Miss Eaton, show him what you drew."

Catherine reached into her sketchbook, pulled out the drawing of David, and handed it to his brother.

"See, Sam, it's me. Isn't it good? Miss Eaton said she can teach me how to draw people, too. Hey, maybe I'll do a picture of you."

Connors stared at the paper for a long time, so long that Catherine began to wonder if he saw something there she had not. His dark eyes were bleak when they lifted to her again, and then she understood. Even in his ignorance, Connors had recognized the superiority of her work over David's.

The grin he gave David was slightly sad. "Don't waste your time on me, Davy. If you ever learn to draw this good, you'll want a pretty model. Maybe Miss Eaton'll let you do her picture."

A compliment? Catherine decided not to analyze it too closely. "You underestimate your brother, Mr. Connors. David will be doing much better than that in no time at all." This time her smile was genuine, but he didn't look at her. Instead, he glanced back down at the drawing he still held. Now she was sure. He *did* see something there, something no one else saw. After another long moment, he seemed to recall himself and reluctantly handed the paper back to her.

"Oh, keep it if you like," she said, wishing she dared ask why he found the portrait so fascinating. Of course, he doted on the boy. Perhaps he'd never seen a picture of him before. It might be nothing more than that, but Catherine didn't think so.

"Thank you," he said, his voice a little husky. His eyes were wary again, although why he still found her threatening she could not guess.

"Gee, thanks, Miss Eaton," David said, taking the paper from Sam and slipping it safely into his own sketchbook. "Can you show me how to do this tomorrow?"

Catherine watched Connors for a reaction, but she saw none. He seemed to be waiting for what she would say. "I think your brother only gave you permission to come two days a week. Don't you want to space them a bit?"

David's face fell, and he turned beseechingly to Sam.

"You can't take up all Miss Eaton's time, boy. She's got other things to do besides teaching you."

"No, I don't," Catherine contradicted, knowing she would gladly spend all her free time instructing David. "I don't mind teaching him as many days as you can spare him."

"Sam, please," David pleaded.

Connors wasn't happy, but for some mysterious reason he seemed unable to deny David's request. He sighed in defeat. "You can have him as many days as you can stand him, but only if you let me pay you for your time."

She was going to protest that she didn't want any money, but she knew he needed to salvage his pride in some small way. She'd beaten him in everything but this, and she did want to make peace. "All right. How about a dollar a week?"

"How about a dollar a day?" Connors countered. "Or don't you think your time is worth that much?"

Again she met his silent challenge. "Whatever you think is fair," she conceded. She would spend the money on art supplies for David, anyway.

He nodded his agreement. "Just don't let him wear you out. He'll do that if you let him." Connors's tone

45

was grim, but his eyes held a teasing glint when they shifted to David.

"I've never been able to wear *you* out," David protested.

Connors lifted his eyebrows in amazement. "You're getting art lessons, aren't you?" Without giving the boy a chance to respond, he added, "Come along now. You've taken up enough of Miss Eaton's time." He touched his hat brim and gave Catherine a little nod. " 'Afternoon, miss."

"Good-bye," she murmured to his back as he strode off to his horse.

"Thanks for everything, Miss Eaton," David said, beaming his triumph. "I'll see you tomorrow."

"Yes, tomorrow." Catherine waved as they rode off, and she stood in the yard watching for a long time, until they disappeared from sight. She should have felt pleased. She and Sam Connors had made a peace of sorts. At least they had conversed civilly, and both had made concessions. Still, there was something about Connors that disturbed her.

Perhaps it was his overwhelming physical presence that made her ill at ease. When he was near, she felt the unevenness of the match between them. His size and obvious strength made her feel weak and helpless. She knew she was being ridiculous, especially considering she had been victorious in their confrontations. Her feelings of weakness were only an illusion.

But she wasn't foolish enough to imagine he couldn't be invincible if he set his mind to it. She would simply have to make certain he never set his mind against *her*.

By the time the first week of school had ended, Catherine and the children had settled into a routine, and the school was running smoothly. David proved himself as able as he was enthusiastic in improving his technique, and Catherine had to watch herself so she wouldn't be tempted to keep him far too late each day.

When Friday came, she had to tell him with regret that they could not have a lesson at all.

"I'm supposed to stay with the Nylans this weekend, so I'll be walking home with the Nylan children," she explained as the students filed out at the end of the day.

"You can walk with us, Davy," Jessica offered, having at last found a way to entice David into going with them. Apparently, she had come to school with the idea of having David Connors walk her home each day, and she had let Catherine know her displeasure at the situation. Now it seemed all was forgiven, and she included Catherine in her gracious smile.

"All right," David agreed, although he still seemed wary of Jessica's attention. Whatever Sam Connors had told David about the girl had been enough to counter the obvious attraction he felt for her feminine charms.

As they walked, Jessica asserted her powers of conversation, but David resisted, showing a strength of will Catherine thought must be another trait he shared with this brother. When he turned off toward his own ranch, Jessica fell silent, no longer feeling obligated to be charming.

Catherine knew a sense of foreboding the instant she caught sight of the Nylan ranch house. Knowing the building housed eight children and two adults, she wondered first how so many bodies could be accommodated in such a small space. Then she wondered where on earth *she* would be expected to sleep. Why hadn't she been firmer in her refusal to board with the families on the weekends?

Lulie Nylan's enthusiastic greeting made Catherine regret her negative thoughts. The woman was obviously delighted to have an adult woman visitor, and Catherine guessed she must be starved for female company.

"I'm sorry we ain't got a room you can have all to yourself," Lulie said as she escorted Catherine inside, "but the two younger girls'll sleep on the floor in our room while you're here, so you and Jessie can have the girls' room all to yourself."

"I'm sure that will be fine," Catherine said, relieved to see the Nylan home was spotlessly clean in spite of its small size and numerous occupants. The house consisted of one main room that served as kitchen, dining room, and parlor, and three smaller rooms that had been added as the family grew. Lulie and her husband Augustus shared one and the boys another, while the girls occupied the third.

Catherine was instructed to put her carpetbag in the smallest bedroom, which held only one bed. She had to assume all three girls normally shared it. The prospect of sharing it with Jessica was far from inviting.

Putting on a brave face, Catherine returned to the main room to help Lulie with supper, but all the children had fallen to the task, each performing a separate duty with the competence of long practice.

"Let's sit outside a spell so we don't get in the young-uns' way," Lulie suggested, shifting the ubiquitous baby on her hip and leading Catherine onto the porch, where several weathered ladder-back chairs stood.

"Jessie just loves school, and so do the rest. They can't wait to get there every morning," Lulie remarked as she sat down and settled her baby on her lap.

"I'm glad. I'm enjoying it, too." Catherine took the chair beside her, smiled at the baby, and received a gurgle in response.

"Jessie says you're teaching the Connors boy to draw."

"Yes, that's right. He's very good."

"Always did like to draw, that one. I'm a little surprised Sam's letting him do it, though. He's never cared much about Davy's pictures. What'd you say to him to change his mind?"

"I . . . nothing really," Catherine hedged, unwilling to recall the argument she and Connors had had at the dance. "David must have done the persuading."

"Looked to me like you and Sam weren't getting along at all last Saturday night. You never did say what you thought of him."

Catherine remembered Lulie had expressed her dislike of Sam Connors. What had she accused him of? Oh, yes, of fencing in his water. "I barely know him. I haven't really formed an opinion."

Lulie snorted. "You don't need more'n a minute to get an opinion about Sam Connors. Are you one of them ladies who don't like to gossip?" she asked archly.

Catherine could make no such claim, although she still wasn't ready to confide in Lulie. "What do *you* think of him?" she asked with a conspiratorial smile.

Satisfied, Lulie leaned back and returned the smile. "I think he's a no-good son of a bitch. Now, don't look so shocked. When I tell you some of the things he's done, you'll think so, too."

"I'd be fascinated to hear all about him," Catherine replied, leaning back in her own chair.

"Well, like I told you, he was one of the first around here to put up fences. Cheap as barbwire is, it still costs a pretty penny to run it all the way around a ranch, so only the bigger ranchers can afford it."

"Surely no one can fault him for fencing his own property," Catherine argued, wondering what all the fuss was about.

"He didn't only fence his own property. He fenced public land, too."

"Public land?"

"Yeah, land owned by the state that everybody'd always used for free," she said bitterly.

"Isn't that illegal?"

"Oh, he leased it. Paid all of fourteen cents an acre for it, but that's not the worst. He closed in his water, too. Everybody'd always shared their water before. Lots of water holes dry up come summer, and those folks lucky enough to have reliable water always let the rest use it. But no more. Now them with the money to do it have put up fences, and our cattle dies of thirst, bawling for water outside the wire."

"How awful! Hasn't anyone protested? Surely, if you went to Mr. Connors and explained—"

"You think he don't know what he's doing to us? He knows, all right. He *wants* to drive us out, all us little ranchers and the farmers, too. Then he'd take our land and be even richer than ever."

So Catherine had been right to mistrust Sam Connors. He was even more cruel and ruthless than she had feared. Some men covered such things with a veneer of charm, but Connors apparently felt no need to conceal his true character. Everyone who knew him must surely know what kind of man he was, so why should he bother with the customs of polite society?

The only thing she could not figure out was how sweet, sensitive David could be the man's brother.

Lulie continued her tirade against Connors, listing his many sins and shortcomings, but Catherine barely heard. She was too busy thinking how closely she had courted disaster. She had been a fool to challenge Connors so directly on their first meeting. Now she remembered the worried looks from the other women when she'd told them she was going to meet him. Her only salvation had been his soft spot for David. She would have to be very careful in the future not to upset the delicate balance she had established with Connors.

A little while later, Augustus Nylan came ambling over, wondering aloud when his supper would be ready. He was, Catherine realized, probably not much older than his wife, but he was already bent from poverty and hard work, his skin tanned and toughened like leather from the relentless Texas sun, his pale blond hair thinning. How different he seemed from Sam Connors, who was about the same age and who certainly must work every bit as hard. She had never given much thought to the factors that aged people, but now she determined poverty and disappointment must somehow accelerate the process. Connors's success seemed to have sealed him against the forces of time that had ravaged his neighbors.

"Is Lulie telling you all about Sam Connors?" Augustus asked, his eyes bright with a bitterness she could easily understand. "He's a bad one, all right, though he ain't the worst of 'em, not by a long shot."

"Are you gonna defend him?" Lulie demanded.

"Not hardly, but at least he only fenced his own land. Amos Pettigrew didn't even bother to lease the land he fenced. He just took what he wanted and shut the rest of us out. Even closed off the road so his neighbors couldn't get to town.''

"Why don't they take him to court?'' Catherine asked. She couldn't believe such corruption could go unpunished.

Augustus chuckled at her naiveté. "When you got money, you got nothing to fear from the law, either. We complain, and the judge says he don't see anything wrong.''

"That's outrageous!''

Lulie nodded sagely. "Now you see the way things is around here.''

"And since she does,'' Augustus said, "let's talk about something else. I don't want my digestion ruined. Come on, woman, and get my supper on the table.''

Huffing indignantly, Lulie stalked into the house, her baby squirming on her hip. Catherine followed, hoping to be of some help.

Obediently, Lulie did not mention Sam Connors again, but that night when Catherine and Jessica had settled into bed, the younger girl brought up the other Connors brother.

"Davy really likes you, Miss Eaton.''

"I like him, too. He's a very sweet boy.''

"He's rich, you know. He owns half the Spur. Old man Connors left it to both boys equal.''

"So I've heard,'' Catherine murmured.

"Davy ain't much more'n a boy, and you're a woman grown.''

Catherine rolled over and tried to make out the girl's face in the dark. "What are you getting at, Jessica?''

She sighed gustily. "I'm getting at you and Davy. Do you have your eye on him or not?''

"What?" Catherine sat up in outrage.

"You're making an awful big fuss over him, and any fool can see he's crazy for you," she accused, sitting up, too.

"David and I are *friends,* nothing more," Catherine insisted.

"Friends?" she mocked. "Is that why he follows you around like a lovesick puppy?"

"He loves what I'm teaching him," Catherine tried, wondering how on earth she could explain David's obsession to this ignorant girl.

"And what exactly are you teaching him?" she asked snidely.

"To draw," Catherine replied, hating the defensive tone in her voice.

"And what have you been telling him about *me?* He used to like me before you came along."

"I haven't said a thing about you. If his attitude has changed, it's none of my doing." She wondered whether she should warn Jessica she had a much more formidable adversary than Catherine Eaton, one whose opinion David trusted far more and whose influence was much stronger. But Jessica gave her no chance.

"Well, his attitude is going to change right back again, and pretty soon, too. Davy Connors is mine, and I'm going to be living on the Spur before the year is out."

With that, she flopped back down, giving Catherine her back. Catherine thought someone should probably point out to Jessica that while fifteen-year-old girls might marry, they seldom married fifteen-year-old boys. Certainly Sam Connors would have something to say about the match, and Catherine didn't think it would be anything good. Poor Jessica was overmatched, but Catherine didn't think she would appreciate any advice from the person she considered her rival for David's affections. With a resigned sigh, she lay back down and closed her eyes.

The next day Jessica gave no sign they had ever had their bedtime conversation. She was perfectly pleasant to Catherine, at least in front of other people, and in private she simply ignored her. Catherine passed the day playing games with the children and listening to Lulie's well-formed opinions on every subject. That night Jessica feigned sleep when Catherine came to bed, and the next morning the whole family piled into the wagon to go to church.

By rights, Catherine should have been the Nylans' guest for Sunday dinner, too, but she persuaded them it would be much more convenient to simply drop her off at the school after church rather than to make another trip to town with her after dinner.

She was already eagerly anticipating the hours of solitude ahead of her when they pulled up to the church, but when she saw the hostile crowd gathered in the yard, she forgot everything else.

She spotted Sam and David Connors in the group gathered around another rancher whose name Catherine could not recall. He was red-faced and angry, speaking belligerently to those around him, although Catherine could not make out his words.

"Wonder what's got old Pettigrew in an uproar?" Augustus muttered as he reined in and got down from his wagon. The children began to pile out of the back, and Nylan helped his wife and Catherine down from the seat.

"Hey, Nylan," Pettigrew shouted from across the

yard. "Somebody cut my fence last night. What do you know about it?"

"What you just told me," Nylan replied. Lulie laid a restraining hand on his arm, but he shook it off. He strode over to face the furious rancher.

"Everybody knows you're the head honcho of all the small ranchers and farmers," Pettigrew said. "Nobody cuts a fence without checking with you first."

"I don't tell anybody what to do," Nylan said, his face growing as red as Pettigrew's. "If somebody cut your fence, I don't know nothing about it."

"You lying little bas—"

"Pettigrew!" Sam Connors's commanding voice cut him off. "Do you have any proof Nylan was involved?"

Amos Pettigrew was a large barrel-chested man, but he looked small beside Connors. "The bastards who cut my fence didn't leave a calling card, if that's what you're asking, but we all know Nylan's their leader."

"You don't know no such thing!" Lulie Nylan shouted. "Augustus was home all night last night. Miss Eaton was staying with us. Ask her!"

Everyone turned to Catherine, who stood speechless at the edge of the crowd. Although several dozen people were staring at her, she was aware only of Sam Connors's expectant gaze. For a long moment no one spoke, and then Connors said, "I doubt Miss Eaton can vouch for Gus's whereabouts *all* night."

Someone snickered, and Catherine felt her cheeks burning. "He was at home when I retired around ten o'clock," she volunteered, knowing such testimony would hardly help but compelled to say something.

Connors's eyes flickered, perhaps in annoyance, but before he could speak, Augustus said, "I got no reason

55

to cut your fence, Pettigrew. It's not my land you've got blocked off.''

"It's not anybody else's land, either. Spencer and Riley don't have any legal right to live there.''

"But they been living on that land for years," Augustus said, and a chorus of voices agreed with him.

"Then they should've laid claim to it before somebody else did. It's public land, and I've got as much right to it as anyone.''

"Do you think you got a right to their cattle, too?" someone wanted to know. "We hang rustlers around here.''

Pettigrew turned his fury in the direction of the voice, but Connors clamped a hand on his shoulder to restrain him.

"We can't solve anything this way, Amos. The fact is, you got no idea who cut your fence and you ain't likely to find out.''

For an instant, Catherine thought Pettigrew would turn on him, too, but the irate rancher managed to regain control of his temper. He shook off Connors's hand in irritation, but he said, "You're right, Sam, but I'll give you all a warning. From now on, my men'll be patrolling at night, and if they catch any fence cutters, they'll shoot them where they stand.''

Catherine's gasp was lost amid the roar of disapproval from the crowd. Pettigrew stomped off toward his horse, and in a few moments he and what Catherine guessed must be his crew rode away. She stood where she was as the crowd coalesced into various groups. One group clustered around Augustus Nylan, who was muttering furiously while Lulie tried unsuccessfully to soothe him. Another group gathered around Sam Connors. She could hear the deep vibration of his voice as he urged them to something, but she could not make out the words.

In a few minutes David broke from the group and made his way over to where she stood. "I'm sorry you had to see this, Miss Eaton. It's a sad thing when you can't even go to church in peace."

"Yes, it is," she said. "I had no idea how serious the fencing problem was. Would Mr. Pettigrew's men really shoot someone?"

David glanced uneasily down at his boots. "I—I reckon they would, but they won't catch anybody," he hastened to assure her. "I mean, the ones who do the cutting don't never get caught."

"I guess that's some comfort." She glanced at the men to whom Connors was speaking. She could see some of them were ready to resort to violence, too. Would Connors condone shooting?

David followed the direction of her gaze and said, "Sam didn't mean to embarrass you by what he said."

Catherine doubted that, but she decided not to argue the point. "He was only stating a fact."

David nodded vigorously. "And he was trying to keep you out of it."

"How very considerate of him," she said, but David missed the sarcasm in her voice.

"Yeah, Sam's a little rough, but he's a good man. Not like Pettigrew and some of the others."

"Isn't your ranch fenced, too?" she pointed out.

David's expression told her he did not consider it the same thing at all. "We only fenced our own land, and we put up a gate so folks could use the road."

"And what about your water?" she challenged.

Before David could reply, the church bell began to ring. Catherine thought it had a desperate sound to it, and one look at the Reverend Fletcher's face as he pulled the rope confirmed her impression. He was obviously trying to break up the conclaves being held in his churchyard, and Catherine hoped his sermon that morning would soften a few of the hearts.

Hoping to encourage the others, she took David's arm and started for the church door. A few of those who had also been mere onlookers in the morning's drama followed, and soon the larger groups broke up and began to move toward the church.

Inside, Catherine and David took a seat near the back on one side, but she quickly saw the earlier animosity was still holding. Augustus and his people sat on one side, and Connors's friends sat on the other. Catherine and David were on the side of the big ranchers, and she did not even want to know if the black look Jessica Nylan gave her was because she was on the wrong side or because she sat with David.

The entire service as a disaster. Hardly anyone sang during the hymns, and by the time the Reverend Fletcher got up to preach, he actually trembled with apprehension. Fletcher was a short, stout man with a bald head and a tendency to sweat profusely. To give him credit, he made a valiant effort. He chose the Sermon on the Mount as his text, and he expounded at length on Christ's promise of blessing to the peacemakers. Unfortunately, Catherine did not think one in ten of those present heard a word he said.

By the time they rose for the closing hymn, the clapboard building was fairly crackling with tension. Grateful she had already begged off having dinner with the Nylans, she excused herself from David the instant the service was over and made her way outside to find Lulie.

The older woman was already surrounded by the wives of the farmers and smaller ranchers. Catherine laid a comforting hand on her arm and said, "I wanted to thank you for your hospitality and tell you how sorry I am for what happened this morn—"

"You see how it is? I told you about Sam Connors, didn't I?" Lulie said. "He's their ringleader, too, just like they accuse Augustus of leading our group. It was probably his idea to shoot the fence cutters."

Although Catherine had no cause to like Sam Connors, she felt Lulie painted him a little too black. "Mr. Connors seemed to be trying to calm Mr. Pettigrew down."

Lulie's pale brown eyes flashed. "Whose side are you on, anyways?"

"I'm not on anyone's *side*. I simply want to see everyone treated fairly," Catherine insisted, turning to the other women for their support.

Twila Shallcross jumped to her defense. "Miss Eaton is new here. We can't expect her to get involved in our battles."

"She can see who's right and who's wrong, can't she?" Lulie asked. "If it's fairness she wants, she won't be on Connor's side for long."

Catherine sighed in frustration, but before she could reply, Augustus called. "Lulie, get the kids together. We're leaving."

"Come on, Miss Eaton. We'll drop you at the school," Lulie said.

"There's no need to trouble yourself. It's out of your way, and I'd enjoy the walk," Catherine said, eager to get away from the Nylans as quickly as possible. "I'll just get my bag out of the wagon."

Catherine thanked her again, but Lulie was too dis-

59

tracted to notice as she called to Jessica to help gather the rest of the children. Catherine slipped away without further incident.

The school was on the opposite end of town, but that was not a long distance. Catherine chose the shady side of Main Street, and the sound of her heels on the wooden sidewalk as she walked past the shuttered businesses was loud in the mostly deserted town.

"Miss Eaton!"

She turned to see David riding down the street toward her. Behind him, hanging back, rode Sam Connors, astride the most magnificent horse she had ever seen, a black stallion with a white blaze. Riding this horse, wearing his black suit and with his face shaded by an even blacker Stetson, Connors looked to Catherine's artist's eye like the perfect metaphor for evil. She shivered slightly at the thought.

David reined up beside her and jumped down from his horse. "Aren't you going to the Nylans for dinner?"

"No, I'm going back to the school. I told the Nylans I had some work to do and excused myself from Sunday dinner."

Sam Connors came up and reined his stallion in. "Didn't they offer to drive you over to the school on their way home?"

"Yes, but I told them I'd rather walk."

His dark gaze was faintly disbelieving, and David said, "Sam don't believe in walking. He'd saddle up to go from the house to the barn if he could." The boy ignored his brother's glance of reprimand and added, "Here, I'll carry your bag for you."

He snatched the bag from her before she could refuse and started off, leading his horse with his free hand.

Catherine glanced uncertainly at Connors, who muttered an imprecation and then swung resignedly down from his own mount with a creak of saddle leather. Covering a smile, Catherine fell into step beside David. In a moment, Connors came up on her other side, leading his restive stallion.

He wasn't really a giant, she told herself as she tried to judge his height out of the corner of her eye. He probably only stood a little over six feet without those high-heeled riding boots. Still, he was rather broad. In the shadows stretching out before them, she looked like a little girl next to him. She had always known she was petite, but never before had she felt insignificant. To make matters worse, she was afraid the illusion of evil about him wasn't just her overactive imagination.

Connors's dark eyes glittered down at her, and she tried in vain to read the emotion in them. "Davy said I should apologize for what I said this morning."

She frowned at his ungracious tone. Determined to mind her own manners, she said, "There's no need."

"That's what I told him," Connors replied with irritating unconcern. "I figured you'd be glad I tried to keep you out of it."

Glad? She didn't feel remotely *glad* about anything that had happened this morning, but she remembered with whom she was dealing and bit back her sharp reply. There was no use in jeopardizing David's art lessons for the small pleasure of putting this man firmly in his place.

They walked on for a little way while Catherine cast about for a neutral topic of conversation. "That's a beautiful horse, Mr. Connors."

His eyebrows rose skeptically. "Are you a judge of horseflesh, Miss Eaton?"

61

"One needn't know much to recognize such quality," she countered. "But I probably know more than you would ever suppose.

His dark gaze flicked over her disdainfully, making her feel smaller and more insignificant than ever. "If you know anything at all, it would be more than I'd suppose."

"Sam!" David chastened. "You promised."

Connors's lips tightened, and Catherine wondered exactly what he'd promised. "Your brother has a right to be skeptical," she said generously. "I know I don't look like an authority, but as an art student, I had quite a bit of experience dissecting horses and other animals, too."

"Dissecting?" David asked, puzzling over the unfamiliar word.

"Yes. You know, cutting them up."

"You butchered livestock?" Connors scoffed, plainly amused at such a preposterous idea.

"No, of course I didn't *butcher* livestock. I cut them up to examine the muscle and bone structure."

"What in God's name for?" Connors demanded incredulously.

"So when I drew or painted pictures of them, I could use my knowledge of anatomy to make the animals look as real as possible."

"Gosh!" David exclaimed. "Maybe that's why my animals don't look any better than my people do."

"Your people are getting much better, David," she assured him.

"You better not let Miss Eaton draw your picture again, Davy," Connors said dryly. "She might want to cut you up to make sure she gets it right."

David laughed good-naturedly, although his eyes asked her a silent question.

"No, I don't cut up my models," Catherine said, giving Connors a disgruntled frown, "but I have studied human anatomy, too. In fact, my father taught anatomy at the Pennsylvania Academy, and he made all his students attend lectures at the Jefferson Medical College."

"Next, you'll be telling us you really did cut people up," Connors said in disgust.

She had, of course. The study of human anatomy included dissecting cadavers, but Catherine would never admit such a thing to Sam Connors. He probably wouldn't believe her, anyway.

David was shaking his head in wonder. "There's a lot more to being an artist than I ever thought," he said.

Now Connors frowned, and his sharp gaze went from David to Catherine and back to David again. "Don't worry about it, Davy. You're going to be a rancher, remember?"

Catherine thought his tone held a warning, but if David heard it, he gave no sign it disturbed him. "Oh, sure, I remember," he said. "I'd just—I'd like to learn as much as I can."

"Well, you're lucky you have Miss Eaton, then," Connors said slyly. "Seems she knows everything there is to know already."

Catherine scowled at him, but he only grinned that maddening grin of his, the one that made him look like David, which made her even angrier.

Trying to remember she had vowed not to cross Sam Connors again, she managed a semblance of her sweetest smile as they stopped in front of the school.

"Your brother is right. I do know *almost* everything, and I'll do my best to pass my knowledge along to you. We'll even dissect some animals, if you like." She turned to Connors and looked him up and down with the same disdain he had used on her. "We might even cut up a person if the opportunity presents itself."

Connors's dark eyes narrowed, but David hooted with laughter. "Now *you'd* better watch out, Sam, especially if you see Miss Eaton with a skinning knife."

The expression in Connor's eyes was murderous for a moment, but only for a moment. Then the triumphant twinkle she had come to hate returned. His gaze slid over her small figure with insulting thoroughness. "I'm not too scared," he decided. "She'd have to wrestle me down first, and I think I have the advantage."

Catherine's cheeks flamed, but too many other parts of her also burned for her to blame simple embarrassment. She had the uncomfortable feeling he had examined her and found her lacking as a woman in some elemental way. She did not like the feeling at all.

"Come on, Davy. Miss Eaton said she's got some work to do, and we're keeping her from it." He touched his hat brim, then turned the stallion and mounted.

The stallion was restless from being led, and Sam let him dance away a few dozen feet before checking him to wait for Davy. From this safe distance, he let himself look back and watch the boy return her bag and say good-bye to her.

God, she was a pretty little thing, all sunshine and light. Her skin was as white as milk, and her hair gleamed like gold in the morning sun. He could still remember how soft her hand had been the night they'd danced. The rest of her would be soft too, and he knew just what she would look like under those prim clothes. Her small breasts would tilt upward, the tips as pink as her lips and straining to be touched. He would be able to span her tiny waist with his hands, and then he'd trace the flare of her hips and her long, slender legs.

He knew just how she'd be in bed, too—quiet and submissive, absorbing his passion, draining him until he was as weak and as helpless as a babe. Oh, yes, he knew all about women like Catherine Eaton.

Did she think she could cut him up, *dissect* him, like one of her animals? Well, she had another think coming if she did. Sam Connors had been cut up by an expert, and now he was immune to women like her.

And if he sometimes dreamed about her golden hair drifting across his chest and her white body pressed against his, no one but he would ever know about it.

Chapter Three

Catherine smiled as she watched David sketching a portrait of Tommy Nylan. The five-year-old squirmed, fighting the desire to look over and see how the picture was coming. At last David finished and handed it to the boy for his approval.

"Wow! It's me! Look, everybody, Davy drew a pitcher of me!"

Tommy took off at a run to show his prize to the rest of the children, who were playing in the schoolyard during their noon break. The first morning back to school after the incident at church had been uneventful, and Catherine had finally begun to relax in the knowledge that the tensions between the adults had not carried over to the children.

David's gaze sought hers, and he grinned smugly. "It really does look like him," he told her.

"I know. See, I told you all you needed was a little practice. Of course, you realize what you've done, don't you? Now all the children will want you to do a picture of them."

"I won't mind," he was saying when the sounds of

an altercation drew their attention. Tommy was arguing with his older brother Jimmy.

"You see, it's started already," Catherine said in resignation as she hurried over to break up the fight.

"Pa'll throw it in the fire when he finds out who drew it," ten-year-old Jimmy was saying. "He told you not to have any truck with Davy Connors."

"No, he didn't," Tommy denied, but his voice trembled and tears brimmed in his eyes. "He won't burn my pitcher!"

"What's going on?" Catherine demanded, although her stomach already churned at what she had heard.

"Pa told us to stay away from Davy and his kind," Jimmy said, but one of the other boys grabbed his arm and swung him around before Catherine could reply:

"Whadda ya mean, 'his kind'?" Billy McCoy yelled. "You're nothing but a bunch of lousy free-grassers."

"Am not!"

"Are too!"

Before Catherine could think, the two boys were on the ground, thrashing in the dust. "Stop it!" she cried, but to no avail. "David, help me!"

David grabbed Billy while Catherine seized Jimmy and tried to smother his struggles. She hardly felt the small elbows and heels that resisted her efforts until, at last, both boys surrendered to their captors. Only their red faces and raspy breaths gave evidence of their continued fury.

"Fighting is not the way to settle anything," Catherine insisted, but she could see from the expressions of the children gathered around they did not believe her. "Come inside, everyone, and we'll talk about this."

Hoping her impulse to try solving the problems

through discussion wasn't just wishful thinking, she conducted all the students back into the schoolroom. Her mind was racing ahead, trying to think about how to handle the situation, and she decided an informal approach would be best.

"Don't take your seats. Come up front, all of you. Bigger children take the benches and smaller ones on the floor." She arranged the reading benches into a V and had the younger children sit down between them. Then she pulled her own chair up in front of them.

"First of all, will someone tell me what a free-grasser is?"

Her question broke the tension. The children could not believe her ignorance, and a few even laughed openly, although no one volunteered to explain.

"Jimmy, will you tell me?" she asked.

Jimmy's face was still red from the fight, but he blushed even redder. "It's someone who—who thinks there shouldn't be no fences at all."

"*Any* fences," she corrected. "Then why were you so angry when Billy called you a free-grasser? I thought your father didn't believe in fences."

This remark brought a howl of protest from both sides.

"Only a damn fool thinks there shouldn't be any fences at all!" Billy McCoy declared to another howl in reaction to his profanity. "Well, that's what my pa says."

"Then you should tell your father to watch his language," Catherine said sternly. "And you should, too. Getting back to our discussion, now I'm totally confused. If everyone thinks fencing is a good idea, why are they fighting about it?"

"Because it's not fair!" Jimmy shouted, and for a

68

few moments everyone talked at once until Catherine could get them settled down again.

"One at a time, please," she said. "Why isn't it fair, Jessica?"

Jessica glanced up in surprise. She had been observing the whole process with contempt, and Catherine was determined to get her involved.

"Because not everybody can afford to fence their land," she said, giving David a challenging look. "And them who can take advantage of them who can't."

"How?" Catherine asked, inspiring another general outburst that she had to quiet. "Alice, can you tell me?"

Alice Tate was a small, shy girl who seemed overwhelmed by the arguing. She looked around uncertainly. "Well, because some people fence other people off their own land."

"That's not true!" Billy and his friends protested, but Catherine shushed them.

"What do you mean, Alice?"

"They—they put fences across the roads so people can't get to town or anything."

"And what about Mr. Riley and Mr. Spencer?" Jimmy Nylan wanted to know. "They been living on their land a long, long time, but Mr. Pettigrew come along and claimed it was his and put a fence around it so they couldn't get to it no more."

"That land didn't belong to Spencer and Riley," Billy McCoy argued. "They been using it, but they never owned it legal. Mr. Pettigrew had every right to claim it."

"But it wasn't fair!"

"How about them that cut Mr. Pettigrew's fence. They wasn't fair, neither!"

When Catherine had once again quieted the children, she said, "I'm new here and I don't own any land, so maybe it's a little easier for me to see both sides of the issue. In any case, it seems to me that there is right and wrong on both sides."

"You're right, Miss Eaton," Jessica said, her plain face alight with triumph. "The only problem is that when you've got money, nobody cares whether you're right or wrong. You win anyway."

Catherine glanced at David, concerned because he hadn't said a word yet. His startlingly blue eyes met hers, and she could see the anguish he felt over Jessica's charge. "Not all the big ranchers are cheating people," he said.

"Just 'cause they didn't break no laws don't mean they ain't cheating," Jimmy insisted. "If there's another drought this summer, is your brother gonna take down his fences so everybody can use his water?"

David had no reply, and Catherine felt his pain at not being able to defend his beloved brother. She sighed in defeat. She had hoped this discussion would help the children see how foolish their parents' disagreements were and enable them to get along with each other in spite of what was going on in the community. Now she knew the disagreements ran far deeper than she had imagined. If she hoped to make peace in her classroom, she would have to begin in the homes of her students.

Suddenly, the idea of boarding with the families on weekends began to seem more like an opportunity than an ordeal. Surely the other women were as appalled by the violence as she. She could talk to the mothers, who could then work on the men.

Of course, David Connors had no mother, and from what she had seen of Sam Connors yesterday, Cath-

70

erine suspected his cooperation would be vital to the cause of peace. But Catherine had the ear of someone equally as influential. She would reach Connors through David.

That afternoon as she and David sat sketching under the willows, Catherine tried to decide how best to approach the subject. Before she could, David startled her with a muttered imprecation. He wadded up the paper in front of him and threw it down in disgust.

"Is something the matter?" she inquired wryly, picking up the discarded page and smoothing it out. David had been trying to draw her face but without much success.

"I didn't have any trouble drawing Tommy this morning," he complained.

"Tommy's not your teacher. Maybe you're trying too hard," she suggested with a smile.

"Maybe," he grumbled, refusing to meet her eye.

She studied the botched picture to determine where he had gone wrong. "Give me your hand," she said, laying the picture and her own sketchbook aside.

Puzzled, David placed his hand in hers, and she lifted it to her face. "Feel where my cheekbones are . . . and here, where my jaw curves around. . . ." She let him trace all the contours, and when he was finished, he withdrew his hand slowly, his cheeks flushed and his eyes wide.

"Your skin's so soft," he marveled.

"That's because I'm a woman," she explained easily. "Women's bodies are different from men's."

"I—I know," David murmured in an agony of embarrassment.

"Oh, I'm sorry," Catherine said with an apologetic laugh. "I wasn't talking about *that*. I'm sure you know the differences between males and females. What I meant was that women's bodies are softer than men's because women have a layer of fat under the skin. It makes us smoother and rounder. Look, roll up your sleeve.''

David obediently did so as Catherine turned back the cuff of her shirtwaist to reveal her own forearm. She held it next to David's. ''You see the difference? How your muscles are more pronounced and my arm is smooth and round?''

''Yes,'' he said, enthralled. He stared at the two arms for a few moments, then said, ''Is that what *anatomy* is? Studying bodies?''

''Yes,'' she said in surprise. She'd never dreamed he wouldn't be familiar with the word.

''I was too embarrassed to ask you yesterday,'' he explained. ''Is this the kind of stuff they teach you at art school?''

She nodded. ''They have lectures using live models for demonstration, and in life class they use live models for you to draw from.'' She signed with regret. ''It's too bad you can't go to the Academy. I doubt we'd be able to find you a model in Crosswicks who was willing to pose nude.''

''*Nude?*'' David echoed incredulously. ''You mean *naked?* With no clothes on?''

Catherine winced. She tended to forget how inhibited people outside the insular world of art were about nudity. She had obviously shocked David to his core. ''Yes, but it's all very properly done. Some of the models wear drapes, and of course we have female models for the female students and male models for the male students.'' And photographs of each for the other, although she didn't think she would tell David that for the time being.

"Where do you get people who'll pose with no clothes on?" he asked, still not able to completely believe such a shocking thing.

Catherine briefly considered lying. If David were to carry this wild tale home to his brother, heaven only knew what his reaction would be. "Well, we hire people whenever we can, but . . ." Should she mention that they were reluctant to hire prostitutes, the only females generally willing to pose, because the only prostitutes willing were those too old and ugly to earn much money at their chosen profession? No, she wouldn't tell him. David had been educated enough for one day. ". . . but mostly the students take turns posing for each other."

"Did *you* do it?" David asked with a glimmer of adolescent lechery.

Catherine realized with alarm that the conversation was taking a decidedly dangerous turn. "Well, yes," she admitted reluctantly, but hastened to add, "but I only posed for the other girls . . . and there are limits to how much I am willing to teach *you.*"

He blushed furiously. "I didn't mean—"

"I know exactly what you meant," she said tartly. "I'll teach you what I can about anatomy, but I'm afraid you'll have to do without a live model . . . except for faces."

He thought this over for a moment, and then he grinned. "Can I at least touch your face again?" he asked hopefully.

"You're stretching your luck," she warned with mock sternness. "Now get another piece of paper and try your sketch again."

He cheerfully did so and made a great show of hiding his work from her until he was finished.

While he worked, Catherine made a few idle sketches of her own as she mulled over her conversation with David. She would have to warn him not to mention anything about nude models to his brother. She felt certain Sam Connors would not approve of her corrupting this innocent boy with tales of the immorality of the big city.

She pictured Connors's outraged disapproval and found her pencil tracing the outline of a square-jawed face with wide-set eyes and heavy brows. A few more strokes supplied his blade of a nose, and then she colored in the ebony hair curling to his collar. She paused over the mouth, trying to decide what expression he should be wearing. To her own amazement, her fingers chose a smile, the smile that was so much like David's. She wondered vaguely how an expression she had seen so seldom could have lingered so vividly in her mind, but she had no trouble recalling it exactly. The eyes crinkled slightly at the corners, and the lines by his nose deepened.

Her pencil flew across the page as memory supplied more details, and when she was finished, she stared down in surprise. Her portrait of Sam Connors was one she barely recognized as the man she had come to know. Was her drawing mere wishful thinking, or could there be a man like this beneath his harsh exterior? If so, he would be an invaluable ally in her peacemaking efforts.

"That must be some picture," David remarked, startling her back to reality.

He had obviously been watching her for some time, and she wondered what her own expression might have revealed. "Are you finished?" she asked, striving for lightness.

"Yeah, but you can only see it if you let me see yours."

Catherine resisted a childish urge to conceal her work. She had nothing to be ashamed of. It wasn't as if she had drawn Sam Connors nude, for heaven's sake. While few of the female students studied male anatomy, Catherine's father had thought such strictures ridiculous, and the male nude held no mysteries for her. She realized with some surprise she would have had little trouble imagining what Connors's powerful body looked like beneath his devil's black suit.

Feeling the heat in her cheeks at the thought of Sam Connors nude, she handed David the picture and accepted his in return. His was of her face, her lips pursed, her brow furrowed in concentration. Good heavens, had she looked so engrossed?

"Wow! It's Sam. Wait'll he sees this!"

"Oh, don't . . ." She caught herself. What excuse would she give for not wanting him to see it? "It's really not very good," she tried.

"It's great," he contradicted. "It's the best I've ever seen you do."

"A labor of love," she muttered miserably. Oh, well, maybe the picture would soften Connors's heart of stone a little. Maybe it would even inspire him to smile more often.

Now that Catherine was looking forward to her next weekend visit, the week seemed to drag by. The tensions between the children eased somewhat after their discussion, but the conflict was never far from anyone's mind, and Catherine noticed the children separated into two groups for play in spite of her efforts to unite them.

She was next scheduled to visit little Alice's home. The Tates were cotton farmers who had been hurt by the drought the summer before and who sided with the smaller ranchers in the fight against indiscriminate fencing. Catherine remembered Mrs. Tate as a soft-spoken woman who she hoped would be more reasonable than Lulie Nylan.

Her well-laid plans collapsed, however, when Alice came in to school on Friday morning.

"Miss Eaton, my ma said to tell you she's real sorry, but she's too sick and she can't have you this weekend."

"Oh, I'm sorry, Alice. How sick is she? Should I tell some of the other ladies to go out to help her?"

"They already comed. Ma's sick in bed, and I heard 'em say she'll be there for two weeks."

Catherine recalled that Alice's mother had been showing with an early pregnancy, and she feared some problem with miscarriage. She would inquire of Twila Shallcross as soon as school was out.

"She said we should change with somebody else," Alice was saying.

"What, dear?" Catherine asked absently.

"Ma said somebody else should take our turn with you, and you can come another time."

"That really isn't necessary. . . ."

"I'll take your turn," David offered, having overheard the conversation.

Alice gave him a grateful smile. "Thanks. Ma was real worried about losing her turn with Miss Eaton."

David grinned back at her. "I'll draw you a pretty picture at lunch for you to take back to your ma."

76

While they discussed what type of picture it should be, Catherine considered the situation. As unfortunate as it was, Mrs. Tate's illness might be providential. Now Catherine would have whole two days in which to convince Sam Connors he should adopt the cause of peace.

"But Sam said not to bring you out to the ranch," David told her that afternoon when she asked how he planned to transport her.

"But you said . . . I thought . . ."

"I'll take care of your meals. That's what we're supposed to do, but Sam already told me when it's our turn, I'm supposed to stay in town and take you to eat at the hotel. Because you're a woman and we don't have a woman at our place, it wouldn't be proper for you to stay out there."

"You don't have any women at all at your ranch?"

"Well, there's Inez."

"Who's Inez?"

"She's married to one of our men, and she keeps house for me and Sam, but she's not—"

"Could she serve as a chaperone?" Catherine asked, unwilling to give up her plan if there was any possibility of carrying it through.

"I don't know. . . ."

"Oh, I don't suppose you have a place where I could sleep, either," Catherine said, beginning to see the magnitude of the problem.

"Sure we do. There's Pa's old room, and now that I think of it, Inez and Pat could sleep in the house, too. There's a room where the cook can sleep off the kitchen. I don't guess Sam thought of that!"

"Then everything would be completely proper."

David's triumph faded a bit. "But how would I get you out there?"

Catherine considered a moment. "I know! We can rent a wagon at the livery. We'll use the money your brother paid me for your lessons." She felt like rubbing her hands together in anticipation of the coming confrontation, but she didn't want to frighten David with her enthusiasm. If he even suspected her plans for his brother, she knew he would never take her out to the ranch at all. "Just think, David, we can work together all day tomorrow."

His eyes brightened. "Sam won't even know we're there!"

On the way out to the Spur, Catherine got her first close look at barbed wire. When David stopped the rented wagon to open the first gate, Catherine climbed down, too, and went over to examine the cause of all the controversy.

From a distance, the thin strands of wire looked incapable of retaining anything stronger than a jackrabbit, but up close she could see the sharp barbs that gave the wire its name. She touched one gingerly, imagining how painful it would be to have one's body impaled on a section of such a fence. No wonder it worked so effectively in restraining the animals within the enclosure.

"Has your brother had much trouble with his fences being cut?" she asked when they were on their way again.

"Not yet," David said, unconsciously expressing his fears for the future. "Oh, we lost a few sections, but we figure it was mostly for devilment. Some fellows

78

think it's great fun to go out at night and snip a few wires.''

"I don't suppose they'll think it's much fun if someone starts shooting at them.''

"I just hope the threat of it keeps them at home," David replied grimly.

Catherine hoped so, too.

The Spur was by far the most impressive ranch she had seen thus far in Texas. The buildings were arranged neatly around a center square, and all of them were large and in good repair. Spreading cottonwood trees shaded the house and the extensive corrals, and the well-tended stock gave evidence of good management.

The house itself was massive, stretching along one side of the square and sprawling back from it in a series of wings. The basic structure was of squared logs and adobe, and porches lined every side, shading all the windows against the merciless Texas sun.

David said, "It's early. I doubt Sam and the men have come in yet.''

Catherine let out the breath she hadn't realized she had been holding. She would have time to settle in and compose herself before facing Connors.

David stopped the wagon in front of the house and helped Catherine down. An olive-skinned woman stood on the porch, drying her hands on an apron stretched over her faded calico dress. She was short, shorter even than Catherine, and almost as broad as she was tall. Her raven hair was pulled back in a bun, accentuating her strong features and her disapproving expression.

"Who is this lady?'' the woman wanted to know. Her dark eyes took Catherine in from head to toe, and the schoolmistress got the distinct impression the woman did not approve of what she saw.

"This is Miss Eaton, the schoolteacher," David said with forced cheerfulness. Inez might only be the housekeeper, but apparently her opinion carried enough weight to make him wary.

"Why is she here?"

Catherine managed a friendly smile. "It's the Connors's turn to board me this weekend," she said, mounting the few steps to the porch and extending her hand. "I'm pleased to meet you, Mrs.—?"

"Kelly," the woman said. She took Catherine's hand, but her eyes were still suspicious. "Mr. Sam did not say she was coming."

"He didn't know," David hastily explained, mounting the steps behind Catherine. "She was supposed to go to the Tates, but Mrs. Tate is sick, so I thought—" He shrugged.

Inez apparently did not agree. "Mr. Sam will not like it."

David ignored her remark. "I figured she could sleep in Pa's old room," he continued doggedly. "And of course you and Pat'll have to sleep in the house tonight to be chaperones."

Inez's eyes narrowed, and she spoke rapidly in Spanish. The boy colored and glanced at Catherine. Relieved to see she had not understood, he said, "I'll fix things with Sam."

"*Madre de Dios,*" Inez muttered in exasperation, and then she seemed to recall herself and turned to Catherine with a grudging welcome. "Do you have a bag?"

"Yes, I—"

"I'll get it," David offered, jumping off the porch.

"Come inside," Inez said, shaking her head. "I do

not know what that boy is thinking sometimes. Imagine, bringing a lady here."

Catherine began to wonder if she had been foolish to come. "Perhaps I should have David take me back to town. I don't want to cause any problems."

Inez shook her head again. "That is for Mr. Sam to say. If he does not want you here, he will tell you. Come, I will show you where you will sleep."

The front room was enormous and furnished with a curious combination of furniture obviously shipped in from the East and other pieces that were just as obviously homemade. Braided rugs made colorful patches on the floors, and various animal trophies and hides hung on the walls. The whole place had a decidedly masculine feel about it, all except for the portrait that hung over the huge fireplace.

There, framed in gilt and staring down at her with soleful eyes, was one of the most beautiful young women Catherine had ever seen. She knew instantly this was David's mother. The resemblance was unmistakable. In fact, she looked as if she were hardly any older than David was now. Probably the painting had been done before her marriage back in Louisiana.

Catherine gave it a critical examination. The pose was traditional and uninspired, but the artist had put something of himself into the painting. Probably, he was enamored of his subject, Catherine thought with a small smile. And who could blame him? If the girl had been half as lovely as the artist had portrayed her, she was exquisite.

"That is Señora Connors, Davy's mama," Inez explained.

"I can tell. She was lovely."

Inez made a snorting noise and looked away. "Your room is this way."

Puzzled, Catherine resisted the urge to question Inez. It was considered bad manners to question servants about the affairs of the family, and Catherine had no reason to believe the housekeeper would confide in her, anyway. She had best concentrate on making friends with the woman instead, since her opinion might influence Sam Connors into letting her stay.

Inez led her down a long, cool hall in one of the wings of the house. A door opened into a large bedroom in which the furniture was covered with sheets, giving it a ghostly appearance.

"I will have to open this room and make up the bed . . . *if* you stay," Inez added.

"Do you think there is a possibility I won't be staying?" Catherine asked frankly.

Inez crossed her arms over her ample bosom and looked Catherine up and down again. Refusing to flinch, Catherine lifted her chin and looked down her nose at the shorter woman. After a moment, Inez's skeptical expression slid into a grin.

"I think Mr. Sam will not like it, but I think you will stay. Help me take off these covers."

An hour later, Catherine and David were sitting in the front room on a velvet sofa left over from David's mother's brief reign at the Spur, when they heard Sam Connors and his men returning to the ranch. In a few minutes, Connors mounted the front steps and came through the front door.

He paused a moment as he allowed his eyes to become accustomed to the interior dimness, and Catherine rose unconsciously to her feet, her breath lodged somewhere in her chest in anticipation of his reaction to her presence. He was dressed in ordinary range clothes and wore the bat-wing chaps that she found so picturesque. His clothes were dusty and his shirt clung damply to his body. He removed his hat, wiped his brow with his forearm sleeve, and sighed wearily.

Then, sensing her presence, his gaze swung to where she stood. In that one unguarded moment, she saw his initial surprise, but it hardened almost instantly into anger. He took her in from head to toe, much as Inez had done earlier, and then he turned to David, who stood beside her.

"What's she doing here?" Connors demanded.

"She . . . it's our turn to board the teacher," David said with false bravado.

"That's not true."

"You're right, Mr. Connors," Catherine said, rushing to David's rescue. "I was supposed to stay with Alice Tate's family this weekend, but Mrs. Tate is ill." Twila had confirmed Catherine's theory about the miscarriage and assured the schoolteacher that Mrs. Tate was recovering. "David generously offered to take Alice's turn."

Connors turned back to David implacably. "I told you to stay in town and feed her at the hotel."

Catherine knew a flash of irritation at his refusal to address her directly, but she squelched it, reminding herself she was on very thin ice. After all, she had forced David to bring her here against his better judgment and without his brother's knowledge. Her conscience pricked her, but she couldn't give into it, not if she wanted a chance to discuss the fencing situation with Connors. "Please don't blame David. I'm afraid I insisted on coming out here."

Again he looked at her, and his eyes smoldered with

an anger far greater than her social indiscretion merited. "Why?"

"I—I feel it's important for me to see my students in their homes," she improvised. "I can't understand them completely unless I know what their family life is like."

"And just where were you planning to sleep?" he inquired snidely. "With Davy or with me?"

"Sam!" David cried.

Catherine felt the heat rising in her face but refused to respond to Connors's attempt to fluster her. "Your housekeeper has opened up your father's bedroom for me, and she has also agreed to serve as chaperone."

Connors turned to David in exasperation. "Didn't you explain to her that a Mexican woman isn't a suitable chaperone?"

"I—I—" David stammered, casting Catherine a beseeching look.

Oh, dear, what had she gotten herself into? Hadn't David tried to explain something to her earlier, something she had dismissed as unimportant?

Sensing her uncertainty, Connors made a visible effort to control his anger and become reasonable. "You're taking a chance with your reputation, Miss Eaton, bunking in with two bachelors. But don't worry, Davy'll take you back right now, before any harm is done."

"Nonsense," she replied with more confidence than she actually felt. "I'm sure my reputation won't suffer from my staying here. After all, Mrs. Shallcross made it very clear to me that boarding with the families was part of the teacher's duty."

"It's the teacher's duty to do as she's told," Connors snapped, all traces of reason gone. "And I'm telling you you've got no business here. Davy, take her back. Now.''

"Sam, I invited her here!" David protested.

"Then *un*invite her. If she wants to make a scandal of herself, she can do it with somebody else.''

Catherine was trembling with suppressed rage, and her voice was far from steady when she said, ''I find your concern for my good name rather touching, but totally unnecessary. I do, however, know when I'm not wanted. David, please fetch my bag from my room. It's obvious your brother doesn't want me to know what's going on around here. . . .''

"What? What are you talking about?" Connors demanded fiercely.

Startled at his vehemence, Catherine could not for a moment realize what she had said to cause such a reaction. "I—I told you, I only came to see what David's home life is like, but if you have some deep, dark secret you don't want me to know—"

"Where'd you get an idea like that?"

"From you."

"I never said any such thing."

Realizing she had accidentally touched on a sensitive subject—even though she wasn't exactly sure what the subject was—she played her advantage. ''I have no wish to pry into your private affairs. David, if you'll get my bag—"

"Wait a minute," Connors said as the boy started for the hall. With difficulty, Connors got control of his temper and managed a semblance of calm. "We don't have anything to hide.''

"I'm sure you don't," she said, as if she were not sure at all, then turned to David. "I'm ready to go whenever you are.''

"Sam!" David pleaded.

"All right, she can stay," Connors said through gritted teeth.

Catherine did not even acknowledge him. She crossed her arms and kept her gaze expectantly on David. Connors muttered what might have been a curse and then sighed gustily. "Miss Eaton," he began with exaggerated formality, "we would be greatly honored if you would remain here as our guest."

Her conscience pricked her again. She was being abominably rude by insisting on Connors's hospitality. Maybe he did have something to hide, something she would be far better off not knowing. She felt the fight drain out her at the thought. Her hands fell to her sides, and she turned back to Connors with a sigh of defeat.

"I'm sorry, Mr. Connors. I'm being terribly rude. If you think it's for the best, of course I'll let David take me back to town."

His eyes widened in surprise, then instantly narrowed suspiciously, not trusting her sudden docility. "Oh, no, you don't. You're staying here now, whether you want to or not. I won't have you carrying stories back to town about how I was ashamed to have you here."

"I assure you, I have no intention of—"

"You're staying and that's that. Davy, sit down here and entertain Miss Eaton while I get cleaned up, and don't let her out of your sight." With that he stalked off, disappearing down another of the hallways leading out of the room.

Catherine stared after him in wonder. She had won. Why did she feel so defeated? She sank down wearily onto the sofa.

"I'm sorry, Miss Eaton," David said, sitting down beside her. "Sam don't mean to be rude. I guess he's just worried about stirring up more trouble. He's always telling me how a person's good name is all he has. I reckon he don't want to hurt yours none."

Catherine nodded, although she would have bet her life that Sam Connors's disapproval of her visit had nothing whatsoever to do with whether she was adequately chaperoned. In any event, anyone who had seen her and Connors together for more than thirty seconds would know there was nothing improper in their relationship. The very thought was preposterous.

Sam stopped off in his bedroom to pick up some clean clothes and regain his composure. What in the hell was Catherine Eaton doing here tonight of all nights? Did she know what was going on?

No, he told himself, she couldn't possibly know. But if she didn't, what had she meant when she accused him of hiding something? She must surely suspect or she wouldn't be here. He didn't for one minute believe all that bull about her wanting to see her students in their homes.

Shaking his head, he continued down the hall to the bathing room Adora had insisted upon installing. It was, he conceded, one of her better ideas, few though those had been.

As he stripped for his bath, he mentally replayed the scene with Catherine Eaton. Seeing her had given him quite a turn. It had been a long time since he had seen a blond-haired woman in his house, and for a moment the years had slipped away. . . .

But only for a moment. No one could possibly mistake the acid-tongued Miss Eaton for the sweetly submissive Adora. Imagine Catherine coming out here and moving into his house without so much as a by-your-leave. Poor Davy hadn't stood a chance of convincing her otherwise once her mind had been made up.

Sam shook his head in disgust. What was she up to? Well, whatever she hoped to accomplish, he would put a stop to it. He'd make sure she was in bed and fast asleep long before midnight. She'd learn nothing from her visit here.

When the tub was filled with water from the boiler in the adjacent room, Sam sank down into it gratefully and once more his thoughts drifted to Catherine. This time he allowed himself to recall how cute she looked when she was angry. She reminded him of a cat, sleek and soft but ready to spit and hiss and bare her claws at the slightest provocation.

Sam closed his eyes and imagined all her fire turned to passion. Maybe he'd been wrong to assume she would be submissive in bed. Catherine Eaton didn't seem the type to be submissive anywhere, and Sam decided he wouldn't mind at all if she sank her claws into him.

Whose idea had it been to put her in his father's old room, anyway? He smiled at the thought of having her in his bed tonight. Of course it was only a thought, and he had no intention of doing anything more than thinking, but wouldn't little Miss Eaton head back to town at a dead run if she could read his mind?

The sight of Sam Connors all freshly scrubbed, his face cleanly shaven, his raven hair slicked back, and his skin still flushed from his bath, was slightly unnerving. Catherine tried not to picture him stretched out naked in the tub Inez had shown her earlier, but her vivid imagination kept flicking tantalizing images in her mind's eye.

The thin cotton shirt and close-fitting Levi's he had chosen to wear weren't helping, either. She could easily see every bulge of muscle beneath them. Even trying to keep her eyes on his face didn't help, since she was fascinated by the way his dark whiskers shaded his jaw even after a shave.

He had been standing in the doorway for several moments, studying her the way she had been studying him, until David cleared his throat to break the tense silence. "Inez said supper is ready."

Connors nodded and, to her complete surprise, smiled quite pleasantly. "I wonder if anyone considered the fact Miss Eaton might not enjoy eating with the men down at the cook house."

"We all did," David hastily assured him. "Inez set the table in the dining room for us."

"You should feel honored, Miss Eaton," Connors said with what Catherine could only call charm. "Inez only lets us use the dining room on Christmas."

"So David tells me," she replied, rising to her feet as he approached. She tried to tell herself the strange flutter in her stomach was caused by her astonishment at his sudden change in manner. After the way he had treated her, she should be immune to his charm, shouldn't she? Maybe she was only reacting to his overwhelming physical presence.

The silence fell again as everyone seemed to be waiting for someone else to do something. Finally, Connors said, "Davy, why don't you escort Miss Eaton in to supper?"

David brightened at the prospect and, with a flourish, offered Catherine his arm. Slightly surprised to discover the boy knew at least the rudiments of mannerly behavior, Catherine wondered vaguely where he'd learned them. Surely not from his obnoxious brother. As if he could read her thoughts, the obnoxious brother shot her a knowing grin just before she turned away.

Sam fell in behind them as they made their way into the other room. He couldn't keep himself from a silent appreciation of Catherine Eaton's trim figure. She was dressed, as usual, in something plain and sensible, but she still couldn't disguise the feminine curves lying beneath the simple skirt and shirtwaist. Beside her petite form, Davy looked like a grown man. Skinny as he was, the boy probably outweighed her by thirty pounds. Which meant Sam himself would make two of her.

The very thought of her fragility compared to his strength made Sam's body tighten in response. Easy, he told himself sternly, a rattler looks fragile, too, until it bites you. The analogy had the desired effect, so by the time they reached the table, Sam's more lecherous thoughts were in abeyance.

"A tablecloth," Sam muttered in amazement as he waited for Davy to seat their guest. Sam took the chair at the head of the table, leaving Davy to sit at his left, across from Catherine.

The dining room was built on the same massive scale as the rest of the house, and the table could have easily seated twenty people. Catherine felt rather grand as the only guest and noted the fine china and silver that had been set out in her honor.

In a moment, Inez bustled out of the kitchen and set a platter of fried steaks on the table.

"I could get used to this, Inez," Connors told her with a grin.

"Humph," Inez replied disdainfully. "If you want

to live like a gentleman, you will have to act like one
. . . and get yourself a wife, too," she added slyly,
earning a frown from her employer, which she ignored
as she sashayed back to the kitchen.

David was grinning, and Catherine looked quickly
down at her lap rather than be caught doing the same.
At least she now knew Sam Connors wasn't anywhere
near as fierce as he pretended to be. David felt free to
laugh at him, and even his hired help was not afraid
to sass him to his face. Perhaps beneath the bluster was
a reasonable man after all.

"Sam really liked the picture you did of him, Miss
Eaton," David said when Inez had carried in all the
serving dishes and vanished again.

Catherine felt the heat in her cheeks once more, but
she noticed with relief that Connors seemed equally ill
at ease. "Yes, it was . . . real good," he said lamely,
studiously avoiding meeting her eye.

"At first I let him think I did it," David explained,
"but that was a mistake, 'cause he started saying I sure
didn't need lessons anymore."

"It's difficult to do a sketch from memory," she lied,
remembering how easily she had recalled Connors's
features. "I was surprised David even recognized
you."

"Oh, I recognized him, all right," David said slyly.
"Only thing was, I couldn't figure out how you knew
what he looked like smiling."

"I have a good imagination," she replied, unable to
resist. This time Connors's glower did not intimidate
her.

"Some potatoes, Miss Eaton?" Connors asked,
handing her the bowl in a pointed attempt to change
the subject.

Catherine accepted both the bowl and the attempt. All three of them fell silent as they filled their plates and began to eat. Like true westerners, Sam and David ate with a singleness of purpose that excluded such amenities as conversation. Catherine respected their silence, although she found herself gulping her food in order to keep up with them. Still, she was not quite finished when their plates were clean, and they waited politely for her to finish.

After a brief internal debate, Catherine chose to introduce the subject that she had come to discuss. "Your friend Mr. Pettigrew was very upset last Sunday morning," she remarked.

She could almost feel Connors's instant wariness. "Any man whose fences have been cut would be upset."

"You did an admirable job of trying to make peace."

"I wasn't trying to 'make peace.' I was trying to prevent a riot."

"You succeeded," she said, trying a smile. "I got the feeling you could put a stop to *all* this trouble if you set your mind to it."

Connors frowned. "What trouble do you mean?"

"Why, the trouble with the fencing, all the inequities—"

"Inequities?"

"Yes, the children have been explaining to me how some of the larger ranchers have fenced off public roads and blocked their neighbors from their own land and—"

"Nobody's broken any laws. The Land Act of '83 gave us the right to fence land we lease, and that's what we've done."

"I understand Mr. Pettigrew took over land that belonged to someone else."

Connors sighed impatiently. "Those men never filed legal claim. Pettigrew was within his rights to fence them out."

"You can't really believe that," she insisted.

"It's the law, Miss Eaton, whether I believe it or not."

Catherine tried a different tack. "Then you can't believe it's *fair*, even though it might be legal."

"Who's to say what's fair?" he replied stubbornly.

Fighting her frustration, Catherine managed a semblance of her conciliatory smile. "It isn't fair to let other men's cattle die of thirst when you have more than enough water."

"Is it fair to give them the water I worked so hard to get? You act like water is free, but I assure you, Miss Eaton, it isn't, not in this country. I built those windmills out there with my own hands. If I don't have to worry about the drought, it's because I made plans and worked hard. Why should I give my water away to those who didn't?"

"But surely you don't think it's—" She groped for a word.

"Fair?" he suggested. "Life isn't fair, Miss Eaton. The strong survive, and the weak get along the best they can."

"But if the strong help the weak—"

"Why should they? And who says I'm one of the strong ones? Last year my cattle was worth twenty-five dollars a head—that's up seven dollars from three years ago—but what's going to happen this year? The range burned up last summer, and we were overstocked because we got greedy. A lot of the grass was ruined, and a lot of cattle died. This year I might go broke, and who's going to help *me* out?''

Catherine had no answer.

Seeing he had silenced her, Connors rose from his chair. ''If you'll excuse me, I'll go outside to smoke.''

Catherine sighed in dismay as she watched him leave.

''I'm sorry, Miss Eaton,'' David began, but she stopped him with a wave of her hand.

''Stop apologizing for your brother, David. I'm not nearly as offended as I pretend to be, anyway,'' she assured him with a smile. ''I find him particularly irritating because he's so close to being right most of the time.''

David looked a little startled. ''Then you agree with him?''

''Of course not, but his arguments are hard to refute. I must confess, I came to your ranch with the intention of persuading your brother to side with the small ranchers, but now I see that the larger ranchers have right on their side, too.''

''Do you think what Jessie said is true? That if you have money, you can do what you want?''

''Well, that's usually true, but in this case it seems as if even those with money are at the mercy of the elements.''

Catherine was beginning to see her noble crusade as a futile effort. How could she hope to make peace when even the forces of nature were united against her?

Inez came in and looked around in surprise. ''Where is Mr. Sam?''

''He went outside for a cigarette,'' David said.

''Is he still mad with you?'' she asked Catherine.

Catherine smiled ruefully. "I'm afraid he's upset about something else now."

Inez snorted her disapproval. "You will be here two days. Are you going to let him stay mad the whole time?"

Catherine sighed. "Two days is a long time to be at odds, isn't it?"

"*Sí,* it is. Maybe you should find him and try to make up."

"That's a good idea," David said, jumping to his feet. "I'll go with you."

"No," Inez said. "She will go alone."

Catherine winced. She would much rather have David beside her to cry, "Sam!" whenever Connors got too outrageous, but she knew Inez was right. She would have to do this alone. "Where is he?"

She found him on one of the side porches, staring off into the west, where the sunset had streaked the sky with shades of pink and turned the land to molten gold. Catherine still was not used to the magnificent way the sky and land seemed to stretch on forever out here. "I wish I were a better artist so I could do justice to this," she said as she approached.

He glanced up in surprise, and she could see him brace himself in anticipation of another argument. She stopped a respectable distance away—she refused to think of the distance as "safe"—and tried a friendly smile. His eyes darkened with suspicion.

"I think I owe you an apology," she said.

"Why?"

"Shouldn't you be asking, 'For which offense?' It seems to me I've done several things for which an apology would be in order," she said archly.

95

His lips twitched grudgingly into a grin. "I suppose that's true."

"If you were a gentleman, you'd deny it."

"I think you already know I'm not a gentleman."

"I think you've been trying very hard to convince me you aren't."

"Have I succeeded?"

"Admirably," she replied.

"You've been a bit shrewish yourself," he countered.

"Have I?" she asked innocently, pleased to note he was enjoying this as much as she was.

His expression told her he had no intention of answering her question, so she said, "I've been very concerned about Mr. Pettigrew's threat to shoot any fence cutters. I thought perhaps you could help prevent the violence."

"Don't give me too much credit, Miss Eaton. Nobody tells a Texan what to do, not even another Texan."

"So I'm learning. I still plan to speak to some of the women, though. I'm hoping they can influence their husbands and prevent any shooting."

"I wish you good luck." His eyes said he thought she'd need it.

Satisfied they had established some camaraderie, Catherine gazed out at the breathtaking sunset again. "Someday David will be able to capture all this beauty on canvas." He did not respond, so she said, "David thinks he inherited his artistic ability from his mother."

"I reckon he did. Adora was always drawing pictures of one thing or another."

"*Adora?*" she asked in disbelief.

"Yeah," he said. "Hell of a name, isn't it?"

His dark eyes challenged her to reprimand him for using profanity, so she chose not to. "Yes, it is."

"It suited her, though. Everyone adored her."

Surprised at the bitterness in his voice, she said, "You don't sound as if you did."

His grin was mirthless. "I was only seventeen when she came here. I didn't know any better."

"What was she like?" Catherine asked, remembering Inez huffing in disapproval at the mention of Señora Connors.

His eyebrows rose. "I thought you had no intention of prying into our private lives," he chided.

"I need to understand David completely if I hope to teach him," she replied.

He conceded her point and considered for a moment. "She was like you—small and pretty and useless."

"Useless!" she echoed, stung.

He was unrepentant. "Yes, useless. Look at your hands." He took one of hers and spread her palm open in his. His fingers were rough against her delicate flesh, and his touch sent a jolt of alarm coursing through her. "These hands prove you've never done a day's work in your life."

"That isn't true!" she exclaimed, but looking down at her smooth, white skin contrasted with his sun-darkened hand, she could see how he would think so.

"You're a hothouse flower, Miss Eaton, just like Adora. You belong in a city with houses all around and friends coming to call and stores on every corner. You need parties and theaters and art galleries, or you'll wither up and die. Adora did. I watched her, and it wasn't a pretty sight."

"I—I'm not like that," she said, suddenly breathless

97

and vitally aware of his fingers wrapped around her wrist. The touch of his callused palm sent tingles of warning up her arm, although she could not have said exactly what she feared.

His eyes smoldered, but for once the emotion in them was not anger. "This is a country for men, not for women, especially not women like you."

She knew a desperate need to retaliate. "And what about boys like David? He's sensitive like his mother was."

"No!" Connors denied, but his fingers tightened painfully on her wrist.

"Yes, he is. Is he going to wither up and die out here, too? Look at *your* hands, Mr. Connors." She twisted out of his grip and spread his palm open. "Look at these calluses. If David's hands get like this, he'll never be able to draw another picture. His talent will be lost forever."

"What will it matter?" he demanded, jerking his hand free. "Davy's going to be a rancher."

"Is that what *he* wants or is that what you want for him? If you think Adora's death was ugly, wait until you watch David dying a little every day because you killed his dreams."

"What do you know about it?" he asked furiously.

"Enough to know I'm right. David needs things he can't get here, too. He needs a city, and a school, and people who appreciate his talents, and—"

"No, you won't get him, not this time," he shouted, and then caught himself.

"Not this time?" she repeated in confusion.

He shook his head as if to deny he had said the words. More calmly, he said, "Davy isn't going anywhere. This is his home, and he's not a fragile little girl. He's a man, and he's strong. I'll make him strong, and he'll survive."

"But will he be happy?" she asked, desperate to make him understand David's driving needs.

"Happy? How many people are ever happy? Are you? I doubt it. If you had been, you wouldn't have traveled over a thousand miles for a three-month job that pays twenty-five dollars a month."

He was right, of course, making her even more furious. "Mr. Connors, you don't understand!"

"No, Miss Eaton, *you* don't understand. We all have a place in this world, and Davy's is here. Maybe you ought to go back to *your* place and leave us alone."

"Sam? Miss Eaton?" David's voice startled them both. They whirled around to find him standing in the doorway, frowning worriedly. "I thought you were going to make up."

Catherine glanced at Connors, who had wiped all trace of fury from his expression. She tried to match his nonchalance and hoped David had not heard too much of the conversation. "We did make up, David, but I'm afraid we started fighting again."

"Yes," Connors said with his rueful grin. "Some people just can't seem to get along, and I guess me and Miss Eaton are two of them. But don't worry about it. Neither one of us has drawn blood."

"Yet," Catherine whispered for Connors's ears alone.

"Don't tempt me," he replied, and then to David he said, "I'm going out for a little ride. You'll take care of our guest, won't you?"

Before the boy could answer, Connors was off the porch and striding across the neatly raked yard toward the corrals.

99

"Miss Eaton, I'm—"

"Please don't say you're sorry, David. It was all my fault, anyway," she admitted sadly. Now she'd really done it. As usual, her tongue had run away with her, and she had managed to alienate the one person whose influence she would need. Not that she cared a fig what Sam Connors thought of her as a woman, although his judgment of her still rankled. No, what mattered was whether he would continue to let her teach David. After the conversation they had just had, she was certain he would not. He would probably even take David out of school completely.

Not wanting to upset David, she did not share her fears with him. The two of them passed the evening looking at his mother's paintings. Catherine had no trouble picturing the lovely young woman in the portrait sitting at her easel and creating the delicate works David proudly showed her. Adora had had talent, but she had lacked emotional depth. The watercolors Catherine saw were pretty, but they evoked no response in her.

Catherine wondered about the woman and recalled Connors's assessment. "Everyone adored her," he had said, but obviously she had cared for nothing and no one in return. She could not even put feeling into her art.

David was indeed blessed to have inherited his brother's emotional intensity. As infuriating as Sam Connors was, at least he had feelings. Too many feelings, she thought with despair.

It was early when Catherine excused herself for bed. Connors was not yet back from his ride, and she hoped to avoid seeing him again that night. She did not feel up to another confrontation.

Still worrying about the harm she had done, Catherine found herself unable to fall asleep. If only she'd stayed in town as David had suggested. Her plans to get Sam Connors to make peace among the ranchers were nothing but pipe dreams, and she had probably lost David as a student forever by alienating his brother. When would she ever learn?

After lying in bed for several hours, she got up and began to pace the large room, hoping to wear herself out. She guessed the time to be around midnight, and the large house was as still as a tomb. Not bothering with a light, she walked to the window and looked out, enjoying the view of the moonlight bathing the ranch buildings in a golden glow. From here, she could see some of the corrals and a corner of the bunkhouse. She'd been standing there a long time before she realized what was wrong with the scene.

Someone was moving around outside. Not just some*one,* either, but several people. After a few minutes, a horseman rode in and disappeared behind the bunkhouse. Then two more rode in and spoke softly to those in the yard before following the first rider out of sight.

Soon Catherine had counted over twenty riders. Why on earth would so many men be out at this time of night? She tried to think of all sorts of explanations, but none of them were satisfactory. Finally, she was left with the conclusion that they had come here for a reason, for a meeting of some kind. With growing apprehension, she recalled how eager Sam Connors had been to get her away from here until she had accused him of hiding something.

Was this what he had been hiding? A clandestine

meeting? And what could they be discussing that could not be planned in the light of day?

Catherine didn't know for sure, but she intended to find out.

Chapter Four

Hidden in the shadows of the front porch, Sam leaned back against the house and took a deep drag on his cigarette as he watched the riders gathering in the yard. He really should be over there to greet them, but he couldn't shake the feeling he needed to stay close to the house just in case Miss Catherine Eaton woke up.

At least he'd had the foresight to warn everyone to be quiet lest Davy hear them. He hoped their care would keep the woman from being disturbed, too. God only knew what trouble she would cause if she found out about his meeting.

When he judged that everyone had arrived, Sam took one last pull on his smoke, ground the butt out beneath his heel, and left his hiding place. He'd heard not one sound from the house to indicate his visitors had roused anyone.

Moving silently across the yard, Sam smiled to himself, thinking how surprised Miss Eaton would be if she knew what he had planned for tonight. She was so anxious to make peace between the large and small ranchers, and she was so damn sure he was the man who could do it. God, he only hoped she was right.

From her hiding place along the side of the house, Catherine watched Sam Connors hurry away. Luckily, she had seen the glowing tip of his cigarette just in time to duck back out of sight before he noticed her skulking around.

She shivered slightly as the night wind whipped at her skirt, and she pulled her shawl more closely around her shoulders. She had thrown on her skirt and shirt-waist over her nightdress in her haste to get outside, remembering only at the last moment that her white top would make her all too visible in the moonlight. The shawl had been an effort at disguise, but now she was glad she had worn it.

When Connors had joined the others on the far side of the bunkhouse, Catherine stole around the corner of the house and darted across the open space to the bunkhouse. The building was perfectly quiet, and she assumed its occupants were also attending the meeting.

Briefly, she considered how she might get close enough to hear what was going on without being seen, and she decided the most logical observation point would be from inside the bunkhouse. From there she could listen at a rear window while remaining safely out of sight. Unfortunately, if someone reentered the building, she would be caught. To avoid such an incident, she would have to take care to slip away before the meeting broke up.

On tiptoe, she crossed the bunkhouse porch and darted inside. The large room smelled of horses and leather and men's sweat, but she wasted no time turning up her nose. Feeling her way in the darkness, she found a rear window that had been opened to the night air.

Flattening herself against the wall beside it, she went completely still, willing her heart to stop pounding so she could hear what was being said outside.

At first, she heard nothing in particular. Everyone seemed to be talking at once in hushed voices, then gradually they fell silent. Catherine had no trouble picturing Sam Connors drawing everyone's attention to himself.

"I reckon you all know why I called you here tonight. Everybody knows we can't settle this fencing business by shooting each other."

Catherine covered her mouth to smother her gasp of surprise. Could that really be Sam Connors speaking? Perhaps she had mistaken his voice.

"We don't plan to shoot *each other*, Sam," someone said. "We're only gonna shoot them what cuts our fences."

"And who do you think is doing it, Enoch? There ain't any strangers in this fight. We're all neighbors, and we were friends before anybody started stringing up wire."

"*I* was never friends with any of them sodbusters, nor any of them bastards who run a three-cow outfit and call themselves ranchers, neither," Enoch claimed. "They been living off our beef for years, and I for one am ready to put a stop to it."

The murmur of assent sent a cold chill up Catherine's spine, and she clapped both hands over her mouth to keep from crying out in protest.

Sam spoke again. "Your fences'll protect what's yours. You've got no call to worry anymore, not if you treat everyone else fair."

Fair! Catherine almost choked as she recalled how he had ridiculed her plea for fairness. Was it possible her feeble arguments had changed his mind? She sincerely doubted it. More likely, Sam Connors had simply been provoking her by pretending indifference to her pleas. She leaned closer to the window so she could catch his every word.

"It won't hurt anybody to put in some gates so the roads ain't blocked anymore."

"How about if we hang out a sign telling the rustlers they's welcome, too," a voice asked sarcastically. Catherine recognized it as Amos Pettigrew's.

"If you're worried about the gates making things too easy for rustlers, post some guards. It's sure as hell easier to watch a few gates than to patrol twenty miles of fence, Amos."

"Even if we do put in gates, what's to keep 'em from cutting the fences anyway?" someone else asked.

"Nothing, until we talk this thing out with them and find out what's really stuck in their craws. That's why we need to pay Gus Nylan a visit. We know he speaks for all the small ranchers and the farmers. We'll find out exactly why they're all mad. . . ."

"We know why they're mad!" someone protested.

"Then we'll ask him what it'll take to make them stop cutting fences," Sam replied.

"I ain't lettin' Spencer and Riley back on my place," Pettigrew shouted.

"Then let 'em have their cattle back," Sam said. Catherine smiled at the impatience in his voice. It was the same tone he had used with her on more than one occasion. "It's called a compromise, Amos. Each side gives a little so nobody has to surrender. We all keep our pride, and nobody gets hurt."

"Are you afraid of getting hurt?" Pettigrew accused. "So far, you've got off easy. Maybe you're already in cahoots with 'em."

"If you think so, you can leave now." Sam's voice rang like steel, and once again Catherine shivered. She held her breath as she waited, but she heard no sound to indicate Pettigrew had accepted the invitation.

"How about the rest of you? Does anybody doubt which side I'm on?"

Catherine heard only the rustle of booted feet shuffling in the dirt. After what seemed an eternity, Sam spoke again.

"All right. First off, we need to send somebody to see Nylan. I don't think we should all go. We don't aim to scare him to death, just put the fear of God into him."

The crowd chuckled uncertainly at this attempt at humor, and Catherine could sense their tension easing.

"I need about five men to go with me." He called some names, a few of which Catherine recognized as parents of her students. She noticed he did not include Pettigrew in the group.

"Six guns ain't many," Pettigrew pointed out in annoyance.

"I don't expect I'll need any *guns* at all. I said, we're going to *talk*. We'll meet here tomorrow night, as soon as it's dark. I don't want any of Nylan's friends to see us and get the idea we're going to burn him out or anything."

"What happens then?" someone asked.

"I'll send word around about what he says. I think he'll see reason once he knows we don't want any trouble. If he agrees to stop the cutting, we'll all put in gates."

"And if he don't?"

"Then we'll meet again."

There was more discussion, but Catherine could tell they had accomplished their main purpose. Soon they would mount up and be on their way. Quickly, before they could, she snuck out of the bunkhouse and retraced her steps back to the shadows of the porch. She was almost to her window when she heard the first riders drifting by.

She froze, turning her back to them so the whiteness of her face or her shirtwaist would not betray her. Her heart hammered in her chest as they came closer, and to her horror they pulled up directly across from where she stood.

"What do you think, Amos?" someone she did not know asked.

Pettigrew snorted. "I think Sam is a damn fool for trying to reason with those bastards."

"What are you going to do?"

"Oh, I'll give Sam his chance, but I've already sent to Dodge for some gunmen. Anybody tries to cut my fence is in for a big surprise. And if that don't scare 'em, maybe a little night riding will. Nothing like burning somebody's house down around his ears to 'put the fear of God into him,' like Sam says."

Pettigrew's nasty chuckle turned Catherine's heart to stone. She had no doubt he meant exactly what he said, and all she could see was the Nylan house going up in flames while those innocent children slept peacefully in their beds. Once again, she covered her mouth to prevent a cry from escaping as Pettigrew and his companion at last rode away.

The instant she judged it was safe, she climbed back in through her window. Her trembling legs could no longer support her, and she sank down onto the floor by the window, hugging her shawl around her to ward off a chill that had nothing to do with the night air.

What was she going to do? The question buzzed in . her head as she considered various alternatives and just as quickly discarded them.

Perhaps she was simply too shocked to think clearly, she reasoned. She could not seem to reconcile in her mind the Sam Connors she had come to know with the man she'd heard speaking outside just now. She had been right to believe he was the one who could bring both sides together, but why had he acted like such a scoundrel when she had suggested it to him?

Her head swam as she recalled how he had used all the same arguments on his friends that he had scorned when she had presented them to him. Unfortunately, she had far more to consider than Sam Connors's unexplainable behavior. There was also the matter of Amos Pettigrew's hired gunfighters and his threats to burn out innocent settlers. She should go to Sam immediately and warn him of Pettigrew's plans.

But how would she explain how she had come to overhear them? If her previous conduct had not already convinced him to remove David from her influence, he would probably put the boy under lock and key if he found out she had been sneaking around and spying on him.

And she couldn't be perfectly sure Sam would or even *could* stop the violence. No, when she thought it over, she realized the most logical thing to do was to warn Augustus Nylan, since he would be the first victim of any violence. If he were expecting the trouble, he would be ready for it, so even if no one could stop

Pettigrew from carrying out his threats, the Nylans would have a chance to protect themselves. And if Mr. Nylan knew Pettigrew's plans, he'd have an added incentive for cooperating with Sam.

Yes, she would warn Mr. Nylan, but she would have to do so tomorrow, since Sam was planning to visit him tomorrow night. That meant she would have to find an excuse to leave the ranch in the morning. David would be disappointed, but she imagined Sam would be relieved to be rid of her.

The thought sent a stab of longing through her. As foolish as it was, she suddenly wanted Sam Connors to desire her company. He was, of course, the most infuriating man she had ever met. Imagine him trying to convince her she was wrong when he agreed with everything she had said to him! Yet the very fact that he had taken such delight in tormenting her touched a responsive chord within her.

Here was a man who wasn't afraid of taking an unpopular position, whether his adversary was an unimportant schoolteacher or the most powerful man in the county. He enjoyed the conflict, too. Why else would he have pretended to disagree with Catherine?

She smiled at the memory of their arguments. He was, by far, the most exciting man she had ever known. And she hadn't forgotten he had said she was pretty. Twice.

But how could she change her attitude toward him without making him suspicious? Perhaps she could convince him she was only being reasonable for David's sake. She wouldn't have to let him know she knew the truth about him.

Why did everything have to be so difficult? she wondered irritably as she forced herself to rise and retire once more to bed.

Catherine slept much later than she had intended to once she finally drifted off. By the time she was up and dressed, she found that Sam and David had already eaten and gone about their business.

Inez gave Catherine's puffy eyes a curious glance, but the housekeeper was tactful enough not to question her on how she had slept.

As soon as she had finished her breakfast, Catherine asked, "Do you know where I can find Mr. Connors?"

"*Sí*, I think he is in his office." Inez gave her directions and sent her off with a knowing grin. Catherine assumed Inez expected her to try to make up with Mr. Sam again. Catherine only hoped she could.

Sam's office was located on the opposite side of the house, down the third wing, and also opened onto one of the many side porches. Sam Connors was seated at his desk, hunched over a large book that contained long rows of figures. The room's furnishings reflected the masculine tastes of its occupant. The ancient rolltop desk, scarred by cigarette burns and spur scratches, faced the far wall. The two stuffed chairs by the stove were worn and comfortable-looking, and a moth-eaten bearskin rug covered the floor. A cool breeze blew in the partially opened outside door and ruffled the pages of the ledger book. It also ruffled the black hair curling over Connor's collar.

Catherine placed a hand over her stomach where her breakfast was churning dangerously. Taking a deep breath to steady herself, she knocked on the open door.

Connors glanced over his shoulder in surprise and then rose from his chair. His dark eyes were guarded, but he managed a small smile. "Good morning, Miss Eaton."

"Good morning. May I speak with you for a moment?" she asked, glad her voice did not reflect the uncertainty she felt.

"Sure, come in."

Catherine toyed with the doorknob a moment, debating whether or not to shut the door. Impulsively, she did so, lest David overhear them and come rushing to her rescue again. This was one conversation she did not want interrupted.

"Mr. Connors, I said some things last night which I had no right to say. I'm afraid I have an alarming tendency to speak without thinking, and if I offended you, I am truly sorry."

She held her breath as she waited for his response. His eyes narrowed, but his mouth twitched in reluctant amusement. "Do you think that if you apologize to me often enough, I'll take the hint and apologize right back?"

Catherine smiled in spite of her nervousness. "You can't blame me for trying, now, can you?"

"No, I reckon I can't." He studied his boots for a few seconds. "Since you've put me on the spot, I guess I said some things last night I'm sorry for, too."

How could such an ungracious apology please her so much? She should give him the edge of her tongue, but oddly enough, she no longer wanted to. "Are you saying you really don't think I'm useless?" she asked, unconsciously taking a step toward him.

Useless? Sam thought as he watched the graceful way she moved. No, not entirely. He could think of many interesting and satisfactory ways in which he could use her. He let his gaze flick over her and pretended to consider her question. "Well, I doubt you'd be much help punching cows," he concluded.

"And you wouldn't be much help at the Pennsylvania Academy of Art, either, unless—" she looked him over consideringly, too, "unless you wanted to model."

He threw back his head and laughed.

"Oh, you'd be a wonderful model, Mr. Connors," she assured him. "You're so—" She caught herself just in time.

"So what?"

What on earth could she say? Certainly not what she was thinking, that his body was so blatantly masculine she was tempted to ask if she could see it. Certainly not that his changing expressions intrigued her so much she longed for the time to study each and every one of them at length.

"What am I, Miss Eaton," he prodded, coming closer. "And why are you blushing?"

"I'm not blushing."

His eyebrows lifted skeptically. "Then you must have a fever." His eyes were laughing at her, and when one of his hands came up to test her forehead, she captured it in self-defense.

"Really, Mr. Connors, if you aren't careful, you'll have to apologize again," she said in annoyance.

Sam grinned. This was what he'd been waiting for, the sparkle of anger in her eyes. The feel of her hands on his wasn't too bad, either. "I haven't said anything insulting, but I think you were about to."

"I was not!"

"Then why can't you tell me what you were going to say?"

"I can't remember now," she lied.

113

When she would have released his hand, he clasped her wrist and held on, not tightly, but she would have had to use force to free herself. She chose not to.

"My God, you're tiny," he said, measuring her wrist with his fingers.

"Small and useless, isn't that what you said?"

"I believe I said, 'small and *pretty* and useless.' "

She'd remembered, of course, and she was unaccountably delighted that he did. "Are you trying to soften my heart with flattery?"

"Could I?"

His voice was soft and deep, and suddenly she realized the fluttering in her chest wasn't caused by nervousness at all. His fingers still encircled her wrist, the rough skin sending sensation streaking up her arm, and he was so close she could actually feel the heat radiating from his body. Or maybe she was only imagining it. Maybe she did have a fever after all.

Sam gave her wrist a tug, bringing her a step nearer so he could smell the freshness of her skin and her hair. How long since he'd been so close to a woman like this?

Never, he admitted reluctantly. He'd never *known* a woman like Catherine Eaton before. She fascinated him in ways he'd never imagined.

She infuriated him, too, he reminded himself, but somehow that didn't matter when she was here, close enough to touch. Close enough to . . .

Catherine saw his face coming down toward hers. She read his intent in the depths of his eyes, but she didn't move away, *couldn't* have moved away even if she'd wanted to. And she didn't want to, not at all.

His fingers tightened on her arm, as if he were afraid she would escape, and then his mouth touched hers.

Not the least bit tentative, he drew her into his arms. Catherine rose up on tiptoe, instinctively clinging to his shirt as he embraced her and pulled her flush against his solid strength.

The feel of her breasts flattened against his chest unleashed a riot of sensation that sent her blood roaring. His hands slid over her back, molding her to him, and a groan started deep in his chest, vibrating through her.

Somehow her arms were around his neck, her fingers buried in the thick, dark hair the wind had teased moments ago. He cupped her buttocks, lifting her into the cradle of his thighs where she could feel the hard evidence of his desire. Something deep within her contracted in response, and need flared to life.

"Sam?" David's voice was muffled. "Sam, are you in there? Why is the door closed?"

They broke apart instantly. For one second they stared at each other, aghast at what had happened, before Sam turned away. The door opened, and David said, "Have you seen . . . Oh, I'm sorry, Miss Eaton. I didn't mean to interrupt. Inez said you were awake, and I've been looking all over for you."

Catherine couldn't seem to catch her breath. She had the oddest sensation of having fallen from a great height. Somehow she managed a small smile. "Here I am," she said, although she barely recognized her own voice.

"Is anything wrong? You two haven't been fighting again, have you?" David asked in dismay.

"Oh, no," she hastily assured him. "I . . . we . . ." She gave Sam a desperate glance, but he still had his back to them. She supposed he wasn't in any condition to face David just yet. Catherine drew a steadying

115

breath and ransacked her brain for something to tell David. "I was just explaining to your brother that I've decided he was right about my not being properly chaperoned here. I think I should go back to town today."

She felt as much as saw Sam's startled reaction, but she did not dare look directly at him, not yet. Her heart was still unsteady, and simply being this close to him was unnerving her.

"But you said we could work together today," David protested.

"Maybe Sa—your brother would let you stay in town so we could." Her voice sounded almost normal now. If only her lungs would begin to work without her conscious effort. She hazarded a glance in Sam's direction.

His expression revealed nothing. If he still felt a reaction to their kiss, no one would ever know. "Do you really have to go?" he asked. She wished she could read the emotions glittering in his dark eyes.

"I—I think it's best," she replied, thinking she now had another reason to get away besides having to warn the Nylans.

"Maybe it would be best," Sam replied thoughtfully. He turned to David at last. "You can stay at the hotel and take Miss Eaton there to eat."

"Oh, boy! Just give me a minute to get my gear together," David said, and disappeared from the doorway.

With David gone, Catherine felt vulnerable. She looked up at Sam, and the air seemed to crackle between them.

"Don't look so scared," he advised. "I'm not going to grab you again."

"I'm not scared," she lied. In fact, she was terrified, not of him but of her own reaction. No other experience in her life had left her so shaken.

He drew in a long breath and let it out slowly. "I guess now I have to apologize again."

Catherine wrapped her arms around her waist in an unconsciously defensive gesture. "I didn't exactly scream for help."

He muttered a curse and turned away, pacing angrily around the room. "I know you don't think much of me, but I don't want you to think I make a habit of grabbing women and forcing myself on them."

So, he did care what she thought of him after all. Somewhat reassured, she said, "And I don't make a habit of letting men kiss me."

"I never thought you did." He looked genuinely distressed, reminding her of the man her heart had seen even before she had heard him speaking up for justice last night.

"Well . . ." she began, not knowing what to say. She'd known she found him attractive, and after last night, she'd also begun to like him, but all this was too much, too soon. How did a lady explain she didn't mind if a gentleman kissed her so long as he waited until she was ready? And how did a lady say she would probably be ready again very soon.

"Well?" he replied expectantly.

"I . . . thank you for your hospitality," she said lamely.

His eyebrows rose, but he made no comment. Grateful for his silence, she hurried out.

Catherine had a little trouble getting rid of David long enough to allow her to walk the few miles out to

117

the Nylan place. Anxious for the lessons she had promised, he left her with ill-concealed reluctance when she explained she wanted a few hours alone to do some personal chores before noon. They arranged to meet at the hotel restaurant later for a meal.

As soon as David was out of sight, Catherine set out for the Nylan ranch. The walk seemed interminable, and Catherine had plenty of time to rehearse what she would say to Mr. Nylan. Above all else, she wanted him to understand Sam wanted peace. If the two of them could work together, the violence Pettigrew had threatened would not be necessary.

The younger Nylan children were playing in the yard and heralded her approach. Lulie came out on the porch juggling the baby, and she waved a welcome.

"Miss Eaton, this is a surprise. What brings you here on a Saturday morning?"

"I need to speak to your husband. Is he around? It's very important," Catherine explained breathlessly.

"He's out in the barn," Lulie replied, frowning. "Tommy, go fetch your pa."

When the boy had scampered away, Lulie invited Catherine in for something to drink, an offer the schoolteacher gratefully accepted.

Augustus Nylan apologized for his appearance. He had apparently been doing a laborious job out in the barn and was soaked with sweat and covered with dust.

"I'm sorry to take you from your work," Catherine said as he took a seat at the kitchen table opposite her, "but it's very important. Do you suppose you could send the children outside?"

Sensing Catherine's urgency, Lulie shooed them right out. Jessica was the last to leave. She sent her teacher a venomous look as she closed the door behind

118

her, but Catherine had more important things to worry about than Jessica's sensitive feelings.

"Mr. Nylan, I spent last night out at the Spur and—"

"Glory be, Miss Eaton. What were you doing out there?" Lulie wanted to know.

Impatiently, Catherine explained about Mrs. Tate's illness and the change in plans.

"You shouldn't of gone out there alone," Lulie chastened, but her husband silenced her with a look.

"Go on," Augustus said.

"Well, around midnight I was awakened by a commotion outside, and I saw several riders coming into the yard. I counted more than twenty, and I naturally assumed Mr. Connors must have called a meeting of some kind. He was very upset when he found out I was staying at the ranch and tried to make me leave, which makes me think he was afraid I might learn of the meeting. At any rate, I snuck outside and eavesdropped."

"Do you know who was at the meeting?" Nylan asked.

"I didn't see any faces but I recognized a few voices, and Mr. Connors called some of them by name." She told him who they were. "Please understand, Mr. Connors does not want any violence. He was trying to convince the others they should install gates and treat their neighbors fairly. He and a few others are coming over here tonight to talk with you about ways to settle the dispute."

"Coming here? Tonight?" Nylan sounded alarmed.

"Please don't be worried. They don't mean to cause you any harm. They only want to talk this thing out

119

so it can be settled. I know if you give them a chance, you can work everything out. But if you can't—''

"What?''

Catherine swallowed and chose her words very carefully. "If you can't, Mr. Pettigrew has sent for some gunmen from Dodge. I assume he meant Dodge City. The others don't know about this. I overheard him telling another man after the meeting broke up. If you and Mr. Connors can't come to terms, Mr. Pettigrew is going to turn his hired guns loose. He even mentioned night riding and burning people's homes.''

"Sweet Jesus,'' Lulie murmured, absently jostling her fussy baby. "Gus, I warned you. I told you if you didn't—''

"Hush up, woman. I sure thank you for telling me all this, Miss Eaton. I'll be ready for Connors when he comes tonight.''

Catherine didn't like the angry glitter in his eyes. "Mr. Connors does not mean you harm, Mr. Nylan. He's trying to do what's best for everyone concerned.''

Nylan smiled mirthlessly. "I'll remember that, Miss Eaton.''

Catherine couldn't think of anything else to say. Surely she had made herself clear, but if so, why did she feel so uneasy?

"Won't you stay for dinner?'' Lulie asked. "I'll have it on the table real soon.''

"Oh, thank you, but I'm supposed to meet David Connors at the hotel at noon. I don't want him to know I've been out here.'' She rose from the table, hoping the Nylans would offer to carry her back in a wagon. The long walk out had exhausted her, and she had learned even the early spring sun could be fierce in Texas.

120

"I'll get Jimmy to take you back to town," Nylan said. Catherine had barely begun to sigh in relief, when he added. "You can ride up behind him on the mare."

Catherine arrived back at the schoolhouse much the worse for the jostling she had received clinging to Jimmy's saddle. She barely had time to get cleaned up before meeting David. As the afternoon passed, Catherine's sense of unease increased. She told herself she was only concerned about the meeting tonight, but she knew she was fooling herself.

David noted her distraction more than once and commented on it. She explained she had slept poorly the night before and asked him to excuse her right after supper. Alone at the school, she watched the sunset with none of the elation she usually felt at the magnificent display. Soon Sam Connors would be riding out to the Nylan place. She tried picturing the meeting in her mind, imagining Sam using his powers of persuasion on Mr. Nylan the way he had on Pettigrew and the others last night. Nylan would be willing to cooperate. After all, that had been Catherine's sole purpose in warning him.

At long last, the sun disappeared below the horizon and darkness blanketed the sky. Her body ached with weariness, but she couldn't bring herself to go to bed, not while she knew Sam was out there with Nylan. She waited, as if her vigil could somehow influence the outcome of the meeting. Only when her lapel watch told her the meeting was most certainly long over did she finally change into her nightdress and seek the comfort of her feather mattress.

This night Sam met his visitors in the yard, his horse saddled and ready to go. He'd chosen a big bay gelding, since the stallion would be too skittish to be dependable. Sam had just finished cautioning the other five men when Pettigrew and two of his cowboys rode up.

"You weren't invited to this tea party, Amos," Sam said, managing to hold the major portion of his annoyance in check.

"I told you I didn't think you had enough guns. What if Nylan starts shooting?"

"Why would he shoot? He's got a wife and kids in that house. He's not going to take any chances."

"Maybe not, but the more there are of us, the less likely he'll be to cause trouble, so we're riding along with you."

Sam sighed in disgust. "Suit yourself, but you'd better keep those guns in your holsters, or when *I* start shooting, I'll be aiming your way."

Amos spit a stream of tobacco to show his contempt for Sam's threats, but Connors noticed Pettigrew cautioning his cowboys when he thought Sam wasn't looking.

The men rode swiftly, the pounding of their horses' hooves the only sound in the night air. Above them, stars twinkled crystal bright and the moon rose higher in the sky to light their way.

Sam stopped them just as the Nylan place came into view. "Remember what I said. No shooting. We're going to ride in and call for Nylan to come out and talk. Anybody who pulls a gun will have to answer to me."

Pettigrew grunted. "The place looks awful quiet to me."

"They're probably asleep, like most honest folks," Sam snapped. "Let's go."

He kicked the bay into motion and the others followed, going into the ranch yard at a lope. Sam reined in, his horse dancing as the others closed ranks around him. "Gus Nylan! Wake up! We've come to talk—"

Something flashed inside the house and a gunshot shattered the stillness. Instantly, the night exploded as a dozen guns spit fire at the riders. Horses screamed in terror, and the bay reared. Sam fought to control him as he tried to decide whether to fire back or run. The others took the decision from him. Someone to his left cried out in pain, and Pettigrew shouted, "Let's get out of here!"

A horse on Sam's right bumped the bay and sent it reeling again. Sam struggled with the reins as a bullet streamed past his ear. He was half turned when something struck him in the chest, taking his breath and turning the dark night even blacker.

Catherine awoke with a start, the sun bright on her face. For a moment she could not think why she felt alarmed, and then she remembered the meeting of the night before. She scrambled out of bed and looked outside. Everything was as still and peaceful as one would expect on a Sunday morning in Crosswicks.

How on earth would she find out what had happened? she wondered, and then castigated herself for being an idiot. It would surely be the main topic of conversation at church this morning. She was pulling her hair out of its nighttime braid before she even finished the thought.

Catherine fairly ran as she made her way down the wooden sidewalk of Main Street. Twila and Mathias Shallcross caught sight of her and waved a greeting, which she returned. David came out of the hotel up ahead and waited for her.

"Good morning," he said cheerfully, and Catherine wondered how he could be so happy, until she remembered he knew nothing of Sam's plans for the previous evening. "Did you sleep all right last night?"

"Just fine," she lied, deciding not to mention how late she had sat up worrying about his brother.

The church bell clanged, startling her. Unconsciously, she quickened her pace.

"That's just the first bell," David said with a laugh. "No need to run."

Catherine felt every need to run, but she consciously slowed her pace so she wouldn't have to explain her hurry to David. He would find out soon enough, and she didn't want him to suspect she already knew.

"Wonder where everybody is this morning," David said as the church came into view. Usually by this time, the churchyard was full of the wagons and horses of the outlying ranchers and farmers. This morning only a few were lined up at the hitching rails.

Catherine fought down a wave of apprehension and searched in vain for sight of Sam Connor's tall figure. The Shallcrosses reached the small crowd gathered in front of the church before Catherine and David did, and one of the men began talking rapidly to Mathias, gesturing wildly with his hands. This time David did not question her hurry as they both rushed over to hear what he was saying.

". . . an ambush! Nylan must've had twenty men inside, and as soon as they rode up, they opened fire."

Catherine felt the blood draining from her head and grasped David's arm for support. Fortunately, he was too preoccupied to notice.

"Who opened fire on who?" he wanted to know.

The man turned to David and his expression fell. "It was your brother. Sam and some other ranchers was going to make peace talk with Gun Nylan, but he must've gotten wind of it somehow, and he'd set up an ambush."

"With all those children in the house?" Mrs. Shallcross said in disbelief.

"He sent his family over to the Smiths," the man explained, then turned back to David, his homely face awash with sympathy.

Catherine's heart turned to stone even before she heard the words.

"Like I said, as soon as Sam and the others rode up, Nylan's men opened fire. Didn't even give a warning. One of Pettigrew's men took a bullet in the leg, and Sam was hit, too."

"How bad?" David demanded.

"Catherine, are you all right?" Twila cried, rushing to take Catherine's other arm.

"I'm . . . yes . . . fine . . ." she managed around the constriction in her throat. "How bad?" she echoed David's concern.

"Coulda been real bad. He got it in the chest, but the bullet hit a rib and skidded off. He's torn up some, but he'll be all right. I reckon you oughta get on home"

David was already running toward the livery stable for his horse. Catherine had actually taken a step to follow him, when common sense reminded her she had no right to go to Sam Connors. She really had no right to be upset at all, except to feel guilt for having caused this disaster.

"Catherine?" Twila put an arm around her waist.

"I know this must be a shock to you, you being from the East and all, but—"

"I saw him just yesterday," she said inanely.

"Yes, I've been meaning to talk to you about that." Twila's voice held a strong note of disapproval. "You should have told me you planned to go out to the Spur. I never would've—"

"Twila, shouldn't someone go out there now? Some of the women, I mean, to make sure he's all right?"

"Al just told us he's all right," Twila pointed out.

"I mean, that he's being well taken care of. Men are so—so lax about those things," Catherine improvised.

Twila's eyes narrowed speculatively. "Fancy that. I didn't think you and Sam got along too well."

The blood came rushing back to Catherine's face. "I'd be concerned about anyone who'd been shot . . . anyone I knew," she corrected, remembering someone else had been wounded in the attack, too.

"Of course, Sam has Inez to take care of him," Twila reminded her, "but she probably wouldn't mind if we brought her some food. Things are probably pretty hectic out there today. Would you like to go along?" she added in an innocent tone.

"Yes, I would," Catherine admitted, ignoring her burning cheeks and Twila's knowing grin.

Twila quickly organized the ladies into a relief effort, explaining to the Reverend Fletcher that sometimes doing Christian charity was more important than attending church. The good Reverend readily agreed and even offered to go with them.

It took a few hours to prepare the food, and by the time they were ready, Catherine was feeling close to frantic. What if Sam was more seriously hurt than Al

126

had indicated? What if he had been trying to spare the boy's feelings? And no matter how serious Sam's wound was, Catherine was personally responsible for it. She could not be more responsible than if she had fired the gun herself.

She carried her guilt like a leaden lump on the long ride out to Sam's ranch. With her guilt came the knowledge she must confess to Sam and beg his forgiveness for meddling in his affairs. Sooner or later, he was bound to hear about her part in all this. Better he hear it from her—or at least that was what she kept telling herself. Either way, he would be furious and would probably hate her. Better he not think she was a coward on top of everything else.

Her plan to tell him seemed difficult enough without considering the added complication of trying to speak to Sam alone. A single woman simply did not hold private tête-à-têtes with men. How could she possibly manage to do so under the watchful eyes of her half-dozen companions?

Sam lay sprawled on the sofa in the front room when he heard the wagon in the yard. He figured one of his neighbors had come to see how he was doing, so he muttered a curse and took another swig of the whiskey the doctor had recommended for the pain.

He glanced down at the jeans and the bandages wrapped around his bare middle, which were all he wore. It was hardly proper attire for greeting guests, but whoever was out there would have to make do, since Sam had no intention of aggravating his wound by moving.

He took another swallow of whiskey and set the bottle on the floor beside him. It wouldn't be proper to drink in front of company, he decided with a bleary grin. He figured he must be a little more than half drunk. As soon as his company left, he'd finish the job.

Davy had gone to meet the visitors, and Sam could hear his voice raised in outrage as he recounted the events of the previous night. Sam had been trying not to think about it, because whenever he did, he got so furious he could hardly see straight. Since he wouldn't be able to take any action for a few days at least, he tried not to dwell on it. The whiskey helped—or it would if people didn't keep interrupting his drinking.

He shifted very carefully to a more comfortable position when he heard the sound of footsteps on the porch.

"Look who came to see you," Davy said, coming through the door and stepping aside with a flourish to reveal Catherine Eaton.

The sight of her hit him like a lightening bolt, stunning him so he did not even feel his body's painful protest when he jerked in surprise. She was all decked out in her Sunday best, something blue that hugged her tiny figure with disturbing faithfulness. Getting shot had wiped the memory of their kiss from his mind, but now it came flooding back in a hot rush that tightened his loins and stopped his breath. Some distant part of his mind registered her stricken expression, and he was vaguely aware of several other women crowding in behind her.

"Hello, Sam," Twila Shallcross said, frowning down at him with motherly concern. "Catherine here thought we should come out and see you, but from the look on her face, I don't think she expected to see quite so much of you."

Suddenly, Sam became aware of his indecent state

of undress before this gaggle of ladies. Ignoring his body's renewed protests, he struggled to get up and flee to the privacy of his bedroom, but Twila stopped him at once.

"Don't you dare move. Davy, go get your brother a shirt, will you?" Twila scowled at Sam in disapproval. "You should really be in bed, you know."

"It got lonely with nobody to keep me company," the whiskey in him said.

Someone tittered, and Twila clucked a reprimand. She reached down and picked up the whiskey bottle, holding it high so she could judge the level of the contents. "How much have you had of this stuff?"

"Not enough," he replied, resolutely refusing to look at Catherine again.

Twila shook her head and set the bottle down. "Well, don't you worry. We've brought you some hearty beef broth to build your blood up again."

Sam made a face, but Twila pretended not to notice. Just then, Davy came racing back into the room with a shirt for Sam. Davy helped him sit up, making Sam sorry he hadn't finished off the whiskey, and held the shirt for him. It took Sam three tries to get his arm in the sleeve. When he glanced up self-consciously at his audience, he saw with some relief they had turned discreetly away—all but Catherine, who still stood staring at him as if she were transfixed.

Catherine had thought hearing about Sam's wound was awful, but actually seeing the bandages and watching him in pain was infinitely worse. Someone spoke to her and took the bowl she held from her nerveless fingers, but she hardly noticed. Mesmerized by the sight of Sam Connors's bare shoulders and the way the dark hair on his chest curled around the starkly white bandages, she couldn't seem to tear her gaze from him.

Then, still struggling with the shirt, he looked up and caught her staring. His eyes glowed like black fire, and the heat from them reached across the room and scorched her. Did he already know what she had done? she wondered frantically.

"Do you have any idea who warned Gus Nylan you were coming?" Twila asked, making Catherine tremble.

At last Sam managed to get his arm in the sleeve and began trying for the other. "Not yet, but I figure he'll be bragging about which one of the big ranchers turned on us."

"What makes you think it was one of them?"

Sam slipped his arm into the other sleeve and sank back against the sofa in exhaustion. Or maybe he was in a drunken stupor. He was too inebriated to know exactly. He gave a brief thought to buttoning the shirt, then abandoned the project as too complicated. "It had to be one of them. Nobody else knew what we were planning."

Catherine went weak with relief. He didn't know yet, thank heaven. Maybe she could make him understand. Maybe he would forgive her. Maybe . . . Then common sense took over, and Catherine realized understanding and forgiveness were completely out of the realm of possibility. She would consider herself lucky if he didn't murder her on the spot.

She cleared the hoarseness from her voice. "How— how badly are you hurt?"

He looked up at her again, his eyes more guarded this time, although she thought they still looked over-bright. Perhaps it was just the whiskey. Or maybe he had a fever. Had anyone checked?

"I was lucky. The bullet ricocheted off a rib. It took off about a pound of hide, but I'll live."

She wanted to check his temperature but reminded herself she had already exhibited quite enough interest in Sam Connors's welfare. She would speak to Twila or Inez about it privately.

The other women were moving off toward the kitchen, carrying the food they had brought. Catherine lingered as long as she could and then had no choice but to follow the others.

Just as she started after them, David said, "I guess it's a good thing you didn't stay over last night."

Catherine winced and managed to mumble, "Yes" before she hurried from the room. If she had remained there last night, none of this would have happened. Sam Connors's meeting would have been peaceful and possibly even successful, and he certainly wouldn't be sitting in there swathed in bandages. Because of her interference, he might have been killed!

The thought sent the blood rushing from her head again, but she didn't dare faint. She didn't deserve the oblivion it would offer.

Inez seemed overwhelmed by the women who had descended on her kitchen, and she shot Catherine a desperate glance when she came in the room.

"Has Mr. Connors been running you ragged this morning?" Catherine asked, forcing herself to smile pleasantly.

"Si. He does not want to eat, and he will not stay in bed. I tell him he will catch a chill or get infected, but he does not listen."

Twila clucked her tongue again. "He'll listen to me.

I'll see he's put to bed before we leave. Don't worry about a thing, Inez. Just sit down and rest while we put this food away." She turned to Catherine. "Maybe some of you should go keep Sam company."

The others picked up on Twila's matchmaking efforts instantly. "I'll go with you," one of the women, a Mrs. Price, offered, leaving Catherine no choice.

Certain Sam did not feel up to entertaining visitors—especially when one of them was going to confess her betrayal to him—Catherine walked back to the front room on leaden feet. How on earth would she ever speak to him alone?

Sam was lying down on the sofa again, and they caught him taking a swig from the whiskey bottle. "Doctor's orders," he explained. Catherine noticed his speech was a little slurred. Perhaps being under the influence, he would be less likely to fly into the rage to which he was entitled. The thought comforted her somewhat.

Her companion took a chair near the sofa, so Catherine followed suit, carefully refusing to look directly at Sam.

"I'm so glad Enoch didn't go with you last night," Mrs. Price remarked.

Enoch. Catherine remembered the name from the meeting and made the connection. Enoch was Enoch Price, one of the large ranchers. The Prices' children were grown, so Catherine did not know them very well.

Sam only grunted, and a lengthy silence fell as everyone tried to think of something neutral to talk about. Catherine noticed David fidgeting, and she got a sudden inspiration.

"David, have you finished the picture you were working on yesterday?"

132

David gave her a blank look.

"If you have, I'd like to see it." She rose and moved toward where he sat on the arm of the sofa at Sam's feet.

His expression reflected his confusion. "I don't—"

"Don't be shy," she said, giving him a wink and praying he would take the hint.

Still looking baffled, he stood and started off with her down the hallway that led to Sam's office. As soon as they were out of sight, Catherine pulled him to a stop.

"What picture are you talking about?" he wanted to know.

She shook her head and waved away his question. "I need to talk to Sam alone. It's very important. I have to tell him something about last night."

David's eyes widened. "You can tell me. I'll—"

"No! I have to speak to Sam and no one else."

He gave her a disgruntled frown. "Where? When?"

"Now, as soon as possible, and anywhere we won't be interrupted. Can you get him away?"

"Sure, but how'll you follow?"

"I'll pretend I'm going outside to the necessary."

David considered her plan for a moment, then nodded. "All right." Before she could ask him what he was going to do, he turned on his heel and left her standing there. By the time she caught up, they were back in the parlor.

"You know, Sam, Mrs. Shallcross was right. You oughta be in bed," he announced.

Catherine winced again. She couldn't meet Sam Connors in his bedroom!

But David was giving her no choice. "Come on, I'll help you up." He lowered Sam's bare feet to the floor while he was still blinking in surprise. "I'm sure Mrs.

Price will understand. She thinks you oughta be in bed, too, don't you?''

"Oh, yes,'' Mrs. Price agreed, although she also seemed a little taken aback by David's forceful attitude.

David helped Sam sit up, jarring a moan from him and earning a black look. Catherine bit her lip to keep from crying out in protest at David's rough treatment. "Be careful,'' she warned through stiff lips as David hauled Sam to his feet.

Sam wobbled a bit, and Catherine wondered if he were in pain or simply feeling the effects of the liquor. "Excuse me, ladies,'' he said as David led him away. "Don't forget the bottle.'' David scooped it up and took Sam's arm to steady him.

"Oh, my,'' Mrs. Price murmured when they were gone.

"I suppose we should tell the others he has retired,'' Catherine said.

Mrs. Price nodded absently and followed Catherine back to the kitchen. There Twila had organized the women into a work party that was preparing meals for several days so Inez would be spared the labor while she cared for Sam. Catherine knew she should help, and she would, as soon as she had accomplished her mission. Without a word, she ducked out of the kitchen and headed for the central wing of the house.

David closed the bedroom door behind him and lowered Sam carefully onto his bed.

"Thanks, Davy,'' Sam murmured, reaching for the bottle.

"Not yet,'' David said, holding it away. "And don't lay down. Miss Eaton's coming in to see you.''

134

Sam shook his head in an attempt to clear it. Surely, he hadn't heard Davy right. He must be drunker than he'd thought. "What did you say?"

"Miss Eaton told me she needed to talk to you alone. That's why I brought you in here."

Sam opened his mouth to remind him a man didn't entertain ladies in his bedroom, when someone with delicate hands knocked on the door. David hurried to open it, and Sam pushed himself to his feet, cursing his wound for hurting and the whiskey for making him so dizzy. Appearing before Catherine Eaton in his bedroom, half dressed and shot to hell, was bad enough without the liquor making it worse.

At least this time he was ready for her. She seemed even smaller and more fragile than ever here where he had spent so many nights dreaming about her. What on earth could she want to talk to him about that made her willing to come to his bedroom?

She flashed Davy a look of entreaty, and he headed for the door. "I'll wait outside in case anybody comes along."

Catherine literally held her breath until the door latch clicked. Then she let it out in a shaky sigh. Sam Connors looked big and fierce enough to make her wonder how far he might go when enraged. She knew he would be enraged in just a moment.

"You wanted to talk to me?" he asked when she didn't speak.

"I . . . yes, please, sit down. I know you must be in pain."

His eyes darkened suspiciously, but he sank wearily down onto the bed again, cradling his side, and waited patiently. She tried not to stare at the expanse of bare chest or the bandages revealed by his unbuttoned shirt.

135

"There's something I have to tell you, something I'm not very proud of, but you're going to hear it anyway, sooner or later, and I wanted to be the one to tell you."

He blinked, and she hoped she hadn't gone too fast for him. At last he nodded. "Well?"

"The other night, when I was here?" He nodded again, and Catherine's stomach quivered. "I—I overheard your meeting."

This time his eyes narrowed dangerously. *"Overheard?"* His voice was hard, the soft blur from the whiskey gone.

"Yes," she admitted, forcing herself to go on. "I couldn't sleep, and when I saw all the riders, I went out to investigate."

"You mean you spied on us."

The quiver in her stomach became a searing pain. "As you will. At any rate, I heard something you didn't. When the meeting broke up, Mr. Pettigrew told another man that he had sent for some gunmen from Dodge City. He was going to let you have your chance, but if things didn't go well, he would do some night riding and even burn people's houses if he had to."

"Damn!" He considered her words for a few seconds and then said, "That's it! He's the one who warned Nylan. He wanted trouble so he'd have an excuse to—"

"No, he didn't," Catherine broke in, speaking with difficulty now that the time had come to make her confession. "I did. I'm the one who told Mr. Nylan."

"What?" Sam lunged to his feet and instantly grabbed his side. He bit back a moan, but he grimaced in agony. Instinctively, Catherine reached for him, but he shook her hand off contemptuously. *"You* told Ny-

136

lan? What in the hell were you trying to do, get me killed? That's pretty stiff revenge for stealing a kiss."

"I was trying to *prevent* violence!" she cried. "I thought if Mr. Nylan knew what Pettigrew planned, he'd understand he simply *had* to cooperate with you. Don't you see? I was trying to help!"

"I'm glad you didn't 'help' any more than you did. I'd be laid out in a pine box by now!"

"Sam, please! I'm so sorry. If I'd known Nylan was going to ambush you, I never would have warned him, but all I could think about was Pettigrew burning down the Nylans' house with all those children inside. I couldn't let that happen. I had to do something!"

"Why didn't you tell *me* what Pettigrew was planning?"

His eyes were terrible, as hard as flint and full of scorn. She had no trouble recalling her reason. "I was afraid to."

"Afraid?" he scoffed. "Of what?"

"Afraid you'd be furious, just like you are right now. Afraid you'd forbid me to teach David anymore!"

"And what makes you think I'd let you near him now?"

"N . . . nothing," she said hoarsely, tears of regret welling in her throat. She wanted to weep for Sam's pain and David's wasted talent and her own foolishness, but she couldn't, not yet, not until she was alone. "I'm sorry. If I could change the past, I would."

She didn't know what else to say, and Sam didn't seem disposed to listen, anyway. She turned and started for the door. Her hand was on the latch when he stopped her.

"Catherine?"

Warily, she turned back to face him.

"Why did you tell me all this?" He looked genuinely puzzled.

"I knew you'd hear about it sooner or later. I wanted you to know my reasons."

"You can't be all that scared of me then." His eyes glittered with an emotion she couldn't name.

She sighed. "I knew I'd already lost David. I had nothing else to lose."

Chapter Five

Sam shifted in the saddle, trying to ease the ache in his side. Inez had been right about it being too soon for him to go out, but seeing how his men were coming along with the new fence was too important for him to waste another day in bed. He'd lost almost a week already.

Since Gus Nylan's bunch had thrown the first lead, Sam no longer gave a damn about how anybody reacted to his fence. He'd tried to keep the peace; now he'd protect what was his.

He reined up and watched his men stringing the glistening wire for a few minutes. Then one of them, a tall Negro who went by the name of Black George, came sauntering over. "A couple more days and we'll be finished, boss."

"You're posting guards at night?" Sam had put George in charge of the fencing job.

"Sure am. The boys are hoping somebody tries to cut it. We're all pretty hot about the way they threw down on you the other night."

Sam smiled grimly. "I'm pretty hot myself, although I did feel a little better when I heard Pettigrew had taken some revenge.''

A few days after the ambush, Nylan's barn had mysteriously caught fire and burned to the ground. No one had any proof, but it was generally believed Amos Pettigrew was responsible.

"Well, it don't seem enough to make up for taking a bullet," George said, "but it was pretty fine, all the same.''

Sam nodded, and George went back to work. In the time he had spent laid up, Sam's fury had cooled somewhat. Now he could even grudgingly acknowledge Gus Nylan's right to protect his home. Apparently, Nylan had not believed Catherine's tale about Sam wanting to make peace and had taken appropriate measures in the event Connors and his men rode in shooting. In Nylan's shoes, Sam probably would've done the same thing.

Common gossip said the shooting had started because one of Nylan's guards, a young boy, had panicked and fired too soon, setting the others off. It could've happened that way, Sam reasoned, but while he could understand Nylan's act, he'd taken a bullet that could easily have caused his death, so he wasn't inclined to forgive.

Sam kicked his horse into motion and drifted along the fence, inspecting the work. As he rode, his thoughts drifted, too, and as always, they came around eventually to Catherine Eaton.

Try as he would, he couldn't forget the way she'd come to him and confessed what she had done. And try as he would, he couldn't help admiring her. She had a lot more guts than he would've ever suspected.

Imagine her facing him down and telling him she'd almost gotten him killed. She was quite a woman.

While part of him still wanted to strangle her, another part of him was intrigued. He supposed he should have more common sense, but then again, what was the harm in thinking about her? After what had happened, she'd certainly never come within ten feet of him again. Even if she did, she was a lady, which meant he wouldn't dream of carrying out any of the numerous fantasies he'd had concerning her. No, Catherine Eaton was the kind of woman you married first and bedded after, and marriage to Catherine Eaton simply wasn't in Sam's plans.

With a sigh, Sam turned his horse back to where the men were working. His side was burning like hellfire, and he knew he'd better head home soon. Inez would berate him for disobeying her orders, but he'd be willing to put up with her just for the relief of lying down somewhere soft, he realized with chagrin.

Catherine walked slowly down the street, head lowered and lost in thought. The week following the ambush had been a nightmare. First, only a handful of children had shown up at school, just those who lived in town. Then the Nylans' barn had burned. The tension was palpable, and Catherine felt personally responsible for it all.

She hadn't even had a chance to apologize to David. After her conversation with Sam, she had hurried back to the other women, who had finished their work and left shortly afterwards. Catherine knew she should have explained everything to David, but she simply couldn't. She'd exhausted all her courage facing his brother, so she took the coward's way out and left it to Sam to tell David why he was taking him out of school.

No one had yet spoken directly to Catherine about her part in the disaster, and she supposed they were simply too disgusted with her. She'd seen hardly anyone all week, anyway, preferring the privacy of her room behind the school to the talk circulating in town.

The children whose family was supposed to board her over the weekend had not come to school all week, so Catherine had stayed at the school. Even now she hated to venture out of her sanctuary, but she had run out of food.

The town was relatively deserted for a Saturday afternoon, and Catherine supposed the violence was keeping people close to home. She paid little attention to the two strangers standing on the corner outside the Shallcrosses' store, until one of them spoke.

"Hey, ain't she a pretty one?"

"Hush up, Floyd. Don't bother the lady."

Catherine glanced at the two men slouching against the store wall, appalled at how filthy and menacing they looked. They wore ordinary range clothes, but they each had two pistols tied down to their thighs. The one called Floyd grinned at her, his eyes holding a maniacal gleam that sent a chill down her spine. His long, greasy hair and dirty, stubbled face repelled her, and she felt a frisson of fear.

Quickening her step, she hurried into the store.

"Who are those men outside?" she asked Twila.

Twila rolled her eyes in disgust. "The Taggert brothers. Gus Nylan and his friends hired them. They let me know they were the terrors of Dodge City before they came here."

"Good heavens! I thought Mr. Pettigrew was the one hiring gunfighters."

"He did, only his are a lot cleaner, I'll give him that. As soon as Gus got wind of Pettigrew's plans, he fired off a telegram, and what you saw outside is the result."

"Oh, dear," Catherine murmured, feeling sick.

"What are you doing here, anyway? I thought you'd be gone to someone's house."

Catherine forced herself to smile. "No one invited me."

"Landsakes, why didn't you say anything? You can always stay with us. No use spending any more time in that school than you have to."

"I don't mind, really. Besides, I've been ashamed to show my face after what I did."

Twila grinned conspiratorially and leaned across the counter so she would not be overheard. "You don't have to be embarrassed. I reckon I'm the only one who figured out you sneaked off to see Sam alone the other day. Everybody else thought you went to the necessary."

Catherine's cheeks flamed. "I—I didn't meant that. I meant about telling Mr. Nylan."

"Telling him what?"

Catherine stared at her in astonishment. "Don't you know? I was the one who warned him Sam . . . Mr. Connors was coming to see him."

Twila's mouth dropped open. "Does Sam know?"

"I . . . yes, I told him when—when I sneaked away to speak to him the other day."

Twila muttered something unintelligible.

"I can't believe you didn't know," Catherine said. "I was so sure Mr. Nylan would tell everyone."

143

Twila shook her head. "If he did, nobody told me, and I hear *everything* standing behind this counter all day."

"Then why didn't the children come to school? I thought the parents must be blaming me for the trouble."

"I reckon they're just playing it safe until they see how bad things get. I'll speak to Reverend Fletcher and have him say a few words from the pulpit tomorrow about putting the kids back in school. I expect you'll see most of them on Monday."

"I hope so," she said, thinking forlornly of one she would never see in her classroom again.

"Now, what brings you shopping this morning?"

Catherine gathered up the foodstuffs she would need for the coming week, and when she had paid for her purchases, Twila told her to wait until Mathias returned so he could walk her home. "No sense in letting you walk past them Taggerts alone again. You should've heard some of the things they've been saying out there. They keep it up, they're likely to get themselves shot before they can even draw their first month's wages."

Mathias walked her back to the school, and as they passed where the Taggerts still lounged on the sidewalk, the one called Floyd grinned at her again, displaying a set of rotting yellow teeth. Catherine quickly looked away, but his bray of laughter followed her and haunted her dreams that night.

Almost everyone in the community showed up for church the next morning, although Catherine watched in vain for the Connors brothers. The Reverend Fletcher encouraged the parents to send their children back to school, and the next morning Catherine was relieved to see most of them gathered in the yard.

Even the Nylan children came, although Jessica's cold stare warned Catherine not to make any friendly overtures. Surely Jessica knew of Catherine's role in all this, and she would have no reason to keep the secret. Why had *she* not spread the word?

Fighting her frustration, Catherine had just reached for the bell rope when she heard yet another horse approaching. Squinting into the morning sun, she made out a rider, and her heart did a little lurch in her chest. It couldn't be, and yet it was! David Connors rode into the yard, waving in acknowledgment to the greetings of the other children.

Why had he come? What did he want? Refusing to let herself hope, she waited breathlessly as he dismounted, turned his horse loose in the fenced enclosure, and sauntered over to the school.

" 'Morning, Miss Eaton," he said cheerfully. "I'm real sorry I had to miss last week, but I didn't want to leave Sam while he was laid up and all. I knew you'd understand and . . . is something wrong?"

"What? Oh, no, nothing at all. I'm just . . . I'm glad to see you," she stammered, unable to make sense of all this. "Did your brother say you could come?"

"He was after me all last week to get along to school. Said I was underfoot and a nuisance," David reported with a grin. "I could tell he was glad for the company, though. Sam's a bear when he's stuck indoors. Once we had a blizzard, lasted three days, and—"

Catherine barely heard the story. Sam hadn't told him! And Sam hadn't forbidden him to come back to her. Could this mean he had forgiven her? For some ridiculous reason, she wanted to laugh and cry at the

same time. Instead, she smiled at David. "I was thinking maybe we could start working in oils."

"Oils?" he echoed, delighted.

"Davy, help me get the kids lined up," Jessica
purred, sidling up to David and immediately capturing
his attention. She came so close that her well-developed
breasts brushed his sleeve. "Please?"

"I—" He swallowed loudly. "Sure. Excuse me,
Miss Eaton."

Catherine sighed, thinking her oils were going to
have some stiff competition.

Jessica's dour mood lifted the instant David appeared, and her good humor lasted until she left him
at the schoolhouse door that afternoon. The departing
frown she gave Catherine seemed to carry a silent message, and the schoolteacher recalled only too well Jessica's accusations. But she wouldn't worry about
Jessica, not today.

When all the children were gone, Catherine turned
to David and smiled mysteriously. "Come into my
room. I have something to show you."

Intrigued, David followed, and she pointed out a
large crate that stood in one corner. She handed him a
hammer and gestured for him to open it.

"What's in it?" he asked suspiciously.

"Something you'll like, I hope."

He made short work of the lid and brushed the packing straw away to reveal the first of several flat, square
packages carefully wrapped in brown paper.

"Open it."

He did, ripping the paper away eagerly. Catherine
held her breath. She did not know what worried her
most—David's reaction or her own.

"My God! Oh, I'm sorry, Miss Eaton, but I never

146

saw anything like it." David stared at the painting in awe. Seeing his response gave her the courage she had lacked until now, and she approached where he knelt on the floor. "Did you paint this?"

"Oh, no," she hastily assured him, looking at the masterfully crafted landscape he held. "My father did. I could only bring a few of his paintings with me, so I chose my favorites."

Seeing the reproduction of a spot where she and her father had spent countless hours together, sketching and painting, brought the sting of tears to her eyes. She blinked resolutely and managed a small smile. The memories are happy, she told herself sternly. Don't spoil them by remembering the bad things.

"Look at the way he did the trees and—Oh!" He grinned up at her sheepishly. "I guess you already know how he did the trees."

"Yes, I do." Gently, she took the painting from his hands and set it aside. "Open the rest of them."

He did so eagerly, tearing into each wrapping as if it contained a gift for which he had waited all his life. In a way it did, she acknowledged, her heart swelling as she watched his expression grow progressively more wondrous. She was opening a whole new world for him, a world in which she had once lived and which she had once loved.

Don't remember the pain, she told herself. Don't remember how shattered your father was when, time after time, the critics derided his work and his peers refused to recognize his genius. He was beyond pain now, and she would be foolish to feel it for him.

If the world's most famous critics had not recognized her father's talent, David Connors certainly did. The paintings spoke to him in some elemental way, and when he looked up, his eyes were moist. "Tell me about them, Miss Eaton."

So she did. The landscapes were easy, and she recounted some incidents to give the scenes life. The portraits were a little more difficult. She began with the easiest one. "This is me, of course."

David chuckled. "I figured. You were awful young."

"Thirteen, but I was vain enough to put up with hours of sitting in order to have my portrait painted by the man I considered the greatest artist in the world. I was a little disappointed, though. He didn't make me look pretty."

"You aren't pretty!" David exclaimed ingenuously. Catherine gave him a look of dismay, so he hastily corrected himself. "You're not *pretty,* you're *beautiful!*"

"Don't lie to try to get out of trouble," she scolded.

"But you are! Your eyes are so . . . and your mouth . . . and your cheeks . . ." He gestured helplessly, not knowing how to describe what he saw in her.

"Oh, I see. As an artist, you find my face interesting."

The concept puzzled him for a moment, but then he brightened instantly. "Am I really an artist?"

Catherine glared at him in mock annoyance. "Well, you certainly aren't a diplomat."

"What's a diplomat?"

Ignoring him, she reached for the next picture. "This is my mother."

She stared for a long moment at the soulful eyes and the plain face her father had captured so vividly. How many years had slipped by during which Catherine had only been marginally aware of her mother's existence? The woman had lived on what Catherine considered

148

the periphery of their lives, a shadowy figure of no consequence. How wrong she had been.

"I thought *this* must be your mother," David said, picking up a picture of an older woman who bore an uncanny resemblance to Catherine.

Catherine set her mother's portrait aside and examined the one David held. "No, that's me."

"Don't tease. Who is it really?"

"I told you, it's me."

"But this lady is *old*. Look at those wrinkles."

Catherine had, many times. She smiled. "My father painted it to show me how I'll look when I'm an old woman."

David's expression clearly showed his confusion.

"My father was an expert on human anatomy," she explained. "He could look at a person's face and know exactly where the wrinkles would form."

David's eyes widened, and he examined the picture again. "Gosh. He didn't make you pretty here, either."

Catching the twinkle in his eye, Catherine swatted at him and plucked the portrait from his hands. She set it alongside the others, which were lined up against the wall of her tiny room. "Now I'm going to teach you how to paint like this."

David's dismay was almost comic. "I could never paint this good, and I'd be afraid to use oil paint. What if I make a mistake?"

"You'll be happy to know that oil is much more forgiving than the watercolor you have been using. With oils, you can paint over something you don't like, and you can use texture and colors you never imagined and—Oh, come on, I'll show you how to mix it."

Still uncertain, David followed her for his first lesson in oil painting.

Sam leaned over his horse's neck, hoping to reduce the pounding he was taking as the animal raced along. He muttered curse after curse at the man who had shot him and the men who had made this ride necessary. At last he saw the small group of cowboys for whom he was looking, and he slowed his horse to a trot.

Black George waved and shouted something he did not catch. George had sent one of the men to fetch Sam when they had discovered the mischief someone had perpetrated the night before.

"Damn it to hell," Sam said, looking at the curls of twisted wire. His fence had been cut in between every pair of posts for as far as he could see, but even more infuriating was what the cutters had left behind. "A coffin," he said in disgust, swinging down from his saddle and ignoring the shaft of pain the motion caused.

The plain pine box gleamed in the mid-morning sun. "They left a note, too," George said, handing him the scrap of paper that was obviously a page torn from a tally book. On it, someone had scrawled, "Keep fencing and you'll need this." Sam wadded it up and threw it down. Rage boiled in him until he thought he might choke from the force of it.

When at last he could speak, he said, "Let's get a buckboard. I think I'd like to pay Gus Nylan another visit."

Sam timed his visit to coincide with the noon meal. The older children would be at school, and no one would be expecting trouble in broad daylight. He and his men rode up to the Nylan house at full gallop, the buckboard clattering loudly.

Nearby, a pile of blackened timbers marked the former location of the Nylans' barn and gave testimony to Gus's reason for wanting revenge.

Nylan and his men spilled out of the house, but before they could gather their wits, Sam and some others held shotguns on them. Lulie and her younger children hovered in the doorway, watching the proceedings with fearful eyes.

"I brought you a little present, Nylan," Sam said, gesturing to the driver of the wagon, who climbed over the seat and shoved the coffin out. It landed with a crash, and Mrs. Nylan uttered a startled cry, making the children howl.

"What's this all about?" Nylan demanded.

"You know what it's about. Your hired guns cut my fence last night and left me that, along with a warning to stop fencing. This is my warning to you: Next time, I'll bring it back with your men in it!"

"My men didn't cut your fence!"

"Then who did?"

"I don't know, but my men were only hired to *protect* us from you."

Sam glanced over the half-dozen men he was holding prisoner and quickly spotted the Taggerts, recognizing them from their description. One was apparently simpleminded, if Sam could judge by his vacant grin, but the other seemed perfectly calm and even cocky. "Maybe you'd better ask them if they've been obeying your orders to the letter."

Nylan frowned uneasily and turned to look at the Taggerts, who met his questioning gaze unflinchingly. "I didn't tell anyone to cut your fence. There's a dozen men around here who've got good reason. Why pick me?"

151

"Because you're the one with the hired guns, Gus," Sam told him with a cold smile.

Nylan's face reddened, but he bit back whatever reply he wanted to make.

"Come on, boys," Sam told his men, but before he could turn his horse, Lulie Nylan yelled, "Stop!"

He turned his questioning gaze on her, noticing her for the first time.

"You aren't going to leave that thing here, are you?" she cried pointing at the coffin. Her face was white, and the baby on her hip squalled pitifully.

Sam looked at the coffin and then back at her.

"The children . . ." she said, gesturing helplessly.

She made a pathetic picture in her faded calico, her limp hair drooping in its bun, a baby clutched to her sagging bosom.

Sam remembered her as a young bride, still pretty and full of hope. None of this was her fault. His conscience pricked him.

"Load it up," he told the man driving the wagon. "I think I'll keep it as a souvenir."

When the coffin was back in the buckboard, Sam started to turn his horse, but Gus Nylan called his name.

Sam looked back warily.

"I—I never meant for anybody to get shot the other night. I was only trying to protect my home."

"And see what it got you," Sam replied, gesturing toward the ruins of the Nylans' barn. "I didn't set that fire, but so help me God, if my fences are cut again, you'll wish your parents had never even met."

"Your fences are safe," Nylan said, with a meaningful glance at the Taggerts.

Sam jerked the reins and kicked his horse into motion. He and his men left the Nylans' yard in a cloud of dust. They weren't even out of sight when Lulie said, "That bastard! Who does he think he is, coming in here and—?"

"Shut up!" Gus snapped. "Get in the house."

With a disgusted snort, she obeyed, shooing the bawling children in before her and slamming the door.

Nylan turned to the Taggerts. "I told you I didn't want any trouble."

Floyd Taggert giggled and wiped some spit from the corner of his mouth with the back of his hand. Will Taggert blinked his rheumy, colorless eyes and said, "You leave things to us. We'll take care of Connors."

"I don't want you to 'take care' of anybody."

"There's some other folks think you should."

"They don't pay your wages. I do, and I give the orders."

Will's loose mouth stretched into a mirthless grin. "Then maybe we'll take our wages from somebody else." Floyd giggled again.

Nylan glanced at him impatiently. "Maybe you'd better. I'll pay you what you're owed, and you can ride out."

"Fine with us."

Nylan stomped into the house to get the money. The instant he came through the door, Lulie said, "I warned you Sam Connors was up to no good. He's nothing but a low-down—"

"Shut your goddamned mouth!"

Lulie gasped, and the children began to howl again.

"I'm sick of hearing you bitch about Sam Connors. What's he ever done to you?" Gus demanded.

"I—I—" Her face became mottled, and she closed her mouth with a snap and glared defiantly at him.

He muttered an imprecation and went to get the Taggerts' wages. The sooner he was rid of those two, the better off he'd be.

Sam and his men rode back to their ranch in silence. When they had finished putting their horses away, George approached Sam. "You wanna burn that coffin?"

Sam considered the box still sitting on the buckboard. "You think it'd hold water?"

George studied the coffin with narrow-eyed concentration. "I reckon it would."

"We could use a new watering trough, now, couldn't we?"

George's smile made a white slash in his dark face. "Wouldn't that be fine? Everybody who came could see it setting there."

"Just what I was thinking. Let's get it down."

Catherine never ceased to be amazed at the speed with which rumors spread in this country. Stories went from house to house and ranch to ranch as if carried by the gritty Texas wind. She heard about Sam's new watering trough the next morning at school. David was boasting about his brother's boldness, but the other children had already heard of the incident.

"A coffin? Where on earth would they have gotten it?" Catherine asked, rubbing her arms against a sudden chill at the thought.

The children looked at her as if she were simpleminded, and one of them said, "They made it." With chagrin, Catherine realized she had been thinking like a city dweller for whom coffins were supplied by the corner undertaker. Here such things were handmade when the necessity arose.

"Oh," she said lamely, and called the children inside for class. She took some comfort from the incident. At least this proved Gus Nylan had not told anyone she had warned him of Sam's visit. If he had, the news would have spread all the way back to Philadelphia by now.

And Sam hadn't told anyone, either. The thought caused a funny little flutter in her stomach. How odd of him. He had every reason to hate her and to want her vilified throughout the community. Instead, he had kept her secret and even sent David back to school. Would she ever understand what went on in his mind?

David kept her posted on events at his ranch. Sam mended his fences, and his nightly guards patrolled to keep cutters away. Gus Nylan had fired the Taggerts but they were still around, camped out somewhere or so the story went.

That weekend Catherine stayed with Billy McCoy's family, prosperous ranchers who had only good things to say about Sam Connors. On Sunday morning she saw him at church, looking remarkably fit and seeming no worse for his experience.

The sight of him set her heart to pounding. She told herself it was only apprehension over his certain anger at her and not the memory of his lips on hers.

Catherine found no opportunity to speak to Sam, although she longed to thank him for sending David back to school. When he tipped his hat as he walked by after the services, she smiled, hoping he could read the gratitude in her eyes. His eyes held no discernible expression at all. The blankness of his look haunted her for days.

* * *

"Where's Davy?" Sam asked.

Inez looked up from her cooking and frowned at Sam's intrusion into her kitchen. "He is not home yet. Every day he stays longer with Miss Eaton. Someday I think he will not come home at all."

Sam fought down an irrational surge of irritation. Why did the thought of Davy spending time with Catherine annoy him so much? He still didn't approve of the boy's interest in art, of course, but he really didn't mind the lessons. And Catherine had been right about Sam not needing Davy's help at the ranch. Why then did he feel like spitting nails?

He turned on his heel and stomped back out to the parlor. From the front window, he could see the road to town. No sign of his brother yet. Shoving his hands into his pockets, Sam began to pace. What was wrong with him? He felt like he was going to explode. Or hit something. Or somebody.

It was the waiting, he decided. Not knowing when Nylan and his bunch would strike again was driving him crazy. No wonder he felt so edgy.

Unfortunately, that didn't explain the dreams he'd been having lately, the ones in which Catherine Eaton played such an interesting part. Sometimes in the dreams, he remembered how angry he was at her, but the anger never lasted very long. As soon as he looked into her eyes, it flamed into desire.

Even now his body hardened in response. Damn her to hell. What right did she have to haunt him? Didn't he have enough ghosts to contend with already?

His gaze moved involuntarily to the portrait over the fireplace. Ordinarily, he never even noticed Adora's picture anymore, but now he studied the painting as if seeing it for the first time. Odd, he thought, how blond hair and blue eyes made some women look frail and others . . . Well, no one would ever think Catherine Eaton was frail.

He could still feel the jolt she'd given him on Sunday morning. Every time he remembered the look in her eyes, his blood quickened. No wonder his sleep had been so troubled.

In exasperation, he turned away from Adora's perfect insipid beauty. Suddenly, he knew an overwhelming urge to see Catherine's face. He couldn't go to her, of course, but if only he had a picture of her . . .

The thought formed with lightning swiftness. *Davy* would have a picture of her. He'd done dozens of sketches of her face. Without a second thought, Sam strode down the hall and burst into Davy's room.

The place was a mess. Clothes were strewn over the unmade bed and the floor, and broken bridles lay mingled with sketchbooks and boxes of paints. The only neat portion of the room was the corner where Davy's easel stood. The afternoon sun streamed in the window, shining directly on the canvas resting there.

For some reason, Davy had covered the picture he was working on. Sam recalled how the boy had sequestered himself all weekend, painting furiously on something. Curious, Sam walked over and lifted the piece of sheeting protecting the work.

"Catherine!" He spit the word out like a curse and followed it with a stream of profanity. What kind of a woman was she? And he'd sent Davy right back into her clutches!

Snatching up the painting, Sam strode from the room, wrapping the sheet around it as he went lest anyone else catch a glimpse of it. He'd been a fool and a jackass, but he'd correct his mistake right now.

Catherine was closing the classroom windows for the day when she heard a horse running into the yard. Alarmed, she started for the door and was halfway there when Sam Connors stormed into the room carrying some sort of bundle.

"Where is he?" he demanded, looking around.

"David? He's gone," she replied, alarmed by his obvious fury.

"I didn't see him on the road." The words were an accusation, as if he suspected her of something untoward.

"He left a few minutes ago. He can't have gotten far." Now she realized he was holding a canvas wrapped in what appeared to be a ragged sheet. "Is that one of David's paintings?"

"Yes," he said, and his lips stretched into a feral grin that sent a chill over her. "Would you like to see it?"

Catherine wasn't at all sure she did, but she didn't dare let him see how he was frightening her. "Certainly," she said, feigning cheerfulness.

He closed the distance between them in a few quick strides and presented the canvas, whipping off the sheet to reveal a perfectly ghastly portrait of her. A *nude* portrait.

"Good heavens!" she gasped, laying a hand over her heart.

"Good heavens?" Is that all you've got to say?"

"What do you expect me to say?" She couldn't seem to take her eyes from the painting. Its very vulgarity fascinated her.

"Oh, I figured a fancy educated woman like you could think of something," he said sarcastically. "I've been paying you to give Davy lessons, and now I want to know just exactly what you've been teaching him."

Catherine gasped again, this time in outrage. "What are you suggesting?"

"I'm suggesting Davy seems to know a lot more about you than he should."

Catherine had actually raised her hand to slap his insolent face, when she saw the warning glitter in his black eyes and thought better of it. "How dare you!" she said instead, looking at the picture and then back at him. "You can't think I *posed* for this?"

"No, because he's been working on it at home, but I figure he must know his model by heart by now. How long have you been *teaching* him? Three weeks? Four?"

Catherine glared at him, wishing looks could kill. What a pompous, evil-minded, idiotic . . . Words failed her. She looked at the painting again. How could he possibly think? . . . She looked more closely. Oh, dear, it was even worse than she'd thought the first time. "May I?" she asked, offering to take the canvas from him.

He surrendered it grudgingly. She carried it over to the window, where the light was better, conscious of Sam Connors's disapproving gaze. The more closely she examined the painting, the more amazed she became. Suddenly, she wasn't outraged at all. In fact, she was beginning to find the whole thing quite amusing. She looked up to find Connors scowling fiercely. Oh, this would be such fun!

"Mr. Connors, I know you are a bachelor. Does that mean you are unacquainted with female anatomy?" she asked sweetly.

His scowl deepened. "What do you mean by *female anatomy?*"

"I mean, do you know what a naked woman looks like?"

"Hell, yes!" He reddened, but Catherine didn't bother trying to decide if he were embarrassed or simply angry.

"Would you step over here please?"

Suspiciously, he moved closer, his gaze darting from her to the picture and back again. She laid the canvas down on a nearby desk where the light could strike it fully.

"Since you are so obviously a man of the world, I'm surprised you didn't notice the . . . shall we say *imperfections* in the painting," she began smugly. "Surely you must recall that women have nipples."

He started, and Catherine supposed no woman had ever spoken the word *nipple* to him before. Determined to shock him thoroughly, she smiled. "And of course there is hair on . . . ah . . . certain places that seems to be missing from this portrait."

Wide-eyed, he stared, first at her, then at the picture, and then at her again.

"You were correct in recognizing my face, of course. David has a lot of practice capturing my likeness, but my hair isn't nearly that long," she continued, indicating the flowing tresses cascading down past the very ample hips of the female in the picture. "And, of course, I'm not nearly so . . . *voluptuous* as the woman in the portrait." She crossed her arms beneath her small breasts and grinned at him in triumph.

Sam could hardly believe his ears! Never in all his thirty-two years had he ever heard such shocking things come out of a lady's mouth. She knew she'd shocked

160

him, too, and the little hussy was gloating! Mortified, he managed to dredge up the remnants of his rage and rake her slender form with a scathing look. "Yeah, now that I notice, you *are* too skinny to be the woman in the picture."

There now, they were even, and she didn't like it one bit. Not giving her a chance to reply, he said, "What I want to know is where he got the idea for this."

Still smarting from his insult, Catherine needed a moment to comprehend his question. "He . . . ah . . ." She felt the color coming to her cheeks at the memory. What a horrid thing to have to confess to Sam Connors! "I guess he got the idea because I told him we used nude models at the Pennsylvania Academy."

"Nude? You mean they don't wear clothes?"

Catherine winced. She'd known what his reaction would be, hadn't she? "It's not what you think."

"Then what is it?" he challenged.

"It's all very proper. Mostly, the students pose for each other and—"

"Students? Did *you* pose?"

"Well, yes . . ."

"And you told Davy all this?"

"Yes, but—"

"Good God!"

"You must believe me, I didn't do anything—"

"You didn't have to! Don't you know the boy's half in love with you?" She shook her head in frantic denial, but he ignored her. "He's with you every day. He *worships* you, for God's sake, and he's almost a man, so naturally he—" Sam made a vague gesture toward the painting.

161

Catherine bit her lip, knowing he was right. She'd seen the signs and tried to pretend she didn't. "I'll have a talk with him."

He snorted in disgust. "Oh, fine. Tell him all about how you posed naked. . . ."

"No! I'll talk to him about his feelings for me, explain he's only infatuated with me because I'm his teacher and—" Her voice trailed off under the intensity of his dark eyes.

He released his breath in a long, weary sigh and let his gaze drift slowly over her again. She knew he was imagining what she looked like without her clothes and felt an absurd urge to cover herself. A heat she blamed on embarrassment crept up her neck and then swept over the rest of her. When his dark eyes found her again, the heat settled into the pit of her stomach.

"No wonder he thinks about you that way," he said, his voice husky.

"I've never encouraged him," she insisted, oddly breathless.

"You don't have to. All a man has to do is look at you to be encouraged." His gaze on her breasts was like a caress, and her nipples hardened in response. Her heart slowed to a dull thud, and the breath caught in her throat.

"Sam . . ." She meant it as a protest, but it sounded like an invitation.

He reached for her, and she did not resist. His mouth found hers unerringly, seeking the sweetness she could not deny him. She opened her lips, and his tongue found hers.

His arms crushed her to him, lifting her to her toes and into the cradle of his thighs, where the hardness of his desire met the heat of hers. Need spiraled through her, taking her breath, and she clung to him desperately.

One of his hands slid down to her hip and pressed her to him, while the other found the curve of her breast. It swelled to fill his palm, and she moaned as sensation streaked over her and convulsed between her thighs.

"Cat," he breathed against her lips, and just before she surrendered once again to his kiss, some foreign sound tugged her back to reality.

"Wait," she whispered.

He would have ignored her entreaty, but then he heard it, too. Tearing his mouth from hers, he swore just as David's voice called, "Sam? Are you in there?"

"That boy's getting to be a nuisance," Sam muttered as he and Catherine untangled.

He turned away from her as David came through the door.

"What're you doing in town?" the boy asked, but he didn't wait for a reply. "I stopped at the store to ask Mrs. Shallcross to order me some more canvas, and somebody said they saw you. I figured you was looking for me and— What's wrong?"

"Nothing," Sam said gruffly, not looking at Catherine. "Come on, let's get on home. Inez'll be mad if we keep her supper waiting."

For an instant, Catherine thought David would obey, but then he saw the portrait she and Sam had forgotten about. "What's that?" he asked, stepping closer. His curiosity turned instantly to horror as he recognized the painting. His face blanched with the pain of betrayal and the humiliation of discovery. *"Sam!"* he protested in anguish.

For a moment all three of them stood frozen, then David whirled and bolted from the room.

"David!" Catherine cried, starting after him.

Sam caught her arm. "Wait! He's too embarrassed to face you right now. I'll talk to him."

Annoyed, she shook free of his grip. "You should have talked to him *before* you came riding in here making your ridiculous accusations!"

"Well, I'll talk to him *now*. He'll be all right."

"You'd better apologize to him for invading his privacy!"

His dark eyes flared with renewed anger. "Catherine, I raised him. I know how to handle him."

"Do you?" she challenged, thinking how little he really understood the boy.

He made an exasperated noise and then reached for her again, sliding an arm around her waist and pulling her to him. His kiss was swift and hard, and it left her breathless.

"I'll handle Davy," he said with assurance. "And then I'll be back to handle you."

Catherine might have kicked him for his arrogance, but he left too quickly. By the time she recovered from the shock of his kiss, he was already riding away after his brother. Trembling with rage and reaction, she sank down in the nearest desk and covered her face with her hands. She didn't know which had unnerved her more, seeing David's humiliation or experiencing Sam Connor's kiss.

The man was definitely a menace. Reluctantly, she glanced at the portrait again and winced. She couldn't really blame Sam for being upset, she supposed, but how could he possibly suspect her of seducing a fifteen-year-old boy?

164

Probably because of the way she'd let him kiss her, she told herself ruthlessly. No lady would submit to a man the way she'd surrendered to him that day in his office. She should have struggled and slapped his face. And what about today? Good heavens, she'd let him touch her breast, and instead of protesting, she had moaned with pleasure!

Her nipples puckered at the memory, and she moaned again, this time in dismay. What must he think of her? No worse than she thought of herself, certainly. When she remembered how she had reacted in his arms, she hardly recognized herself at all.

What made her act so wantonly with him? Unbidden came a distant memory of a girl she had known in Philadelphia, a fellow art student who had taken one of the male art students as a lover. Catherine had been shocked by her friend's confession.

"You must love him beyond reason," Catherine had supposed.

"Love?" she had replied, honestly puzzled. "I don't know whether I love him or not, but I can't deny the passion I feel for him. Oh, Cathy, you can't understand unless you've felt it yourself. I'll simply die if I can't have him."

Catherine had thought her friend insane to throw away her good name and her virtue for the sake of lust. Now, of course, she was beginning to feel slightly insane herself. How could cool, logical Catherine Eaton have let passion overrule her good sense?

She certainly wasn't in love with Sam Connors. They had nothing in common except a concern for David, and their ideas on what was best for him could not have been more different. No, the only thing between them was a strong physical attraction. Catherine would do well to remember that lust was hardly the basis for a relationship, at least not the kind of relationship she would demand before surrendering herself to any man.

Davy was riding hell-bent, so it took Sam a while to catch up to him. The boy ignored his brother's calls, but Sam saw him wiping his face with his sleeve and figured he was preparing himself for the inevitable. At last Davy slowed, allowing his horse to blow and giving Sam a chance to catch up.

"I reckon I acted like a jackass," Sam said, gratified to see the boy's head come up in surprise. "Miss Eaton said I had no right to invade your privacy."

"She's right," Davy replied tightly after clearing the huskiness out of his voice. "Why'd you go snooping around, anyhow?"

Sam hesitated. He couldn't very well confess he'd been desperate for the sight of Catherine Eaton's face. "I'd been wondering what you were working on. I didn't figure it'd hurt anything if I took a peek."

"But why'd you show it to *her?*" he wailed.

"I told you, I'm a jackass. When I saw it, I thought—"

"You thought what?"

"I thought maybe she . . . maybe you and she . . . maybe you were painting from memory."

Davy swore eloquently. "Are you *crazy?* Miss Eaton's a *lady!*"

Sam had his own ideas on that point, but he managed a sheepish smile. "Don't worry, she straightened me out."

"Now I'll never be able to face her again!"

"She's not mad," Sam assured him, only to earn a contemptuous glare.

"Sam, I painted her *naked*. She'll know I—I—"

"That you're in love with her?" Sam guessed. Davy nodded miserably. "She already knew. She said it's only natural for you to feel that way because she's your teacher and you're so grateful to her."

"That's not why!"

Sam smiled wisely. "No, I reckon it's not. She's a fine-looking woman, even with her clothes on. Any man would notice, and you're a man."

Again Davy started in surprise, then shook his head. "I'm not man enough for Miss Eaton, though. God, I wish I was older!"

Thinking how glad he was Davy *wasn't* older, Sam reached out and laid a comforting hand on his shoulder. "There'll be other women. You just gotta be patient."

Davy made a rude noise, and Sam chuckled sympathetically.

"But I ain't going back to school," Davy said. "I can't never face her again."

Sam lifted his eyebrows skeptically. "You want her to think you're a coward, too?" Sensing the boy's indecision, he added, "She blames me for the whole thing, anyway. I told you, she ain't mad, and I figure she understands what made you do the picture. She won't hold it against you. Don't worry, when we get home, I'll help you figure out what to say to her."

Davy nodded, the picture of abject misery again. They rode the rest of the way in silence, giving Sam a chance to consider what had happened between him and Catherine back at the school.

He'd been a fool about a lot of things lately. Even after Catherine had let him kiss her the first time, he'd still thought her innocent until he'd seen the portrait.

167

For one wild, insanely jealous moment, he'd actually believed her capable of seducing a young boy, but even as he'd accused her, he'd known it wasn't true. The whole thing had been nothing more than an excuse to see her again.

Then he'd gotten the shock of his life. Who would expect a woman like her to have a past? When he envisioned her flaunting her perfect little body in front of a roomful of men, his loins tightened with desire but his soul filled with rage. If the thought of Catherine with David had infuriated him, the thought of her with countless other men made him crazy. The bitter gall of jealousy was a familiar taste in his mouth, one he'd sworn never to experience again.

But on the other hand, he had no reason to be jealous. He sure as hell wasn't in love with Catherine Eaton. He wanted her, nothing more, and now he knew she wanted him, too. That's what she'd meant by the look she'd given him in church, and just now she'd shown him beyond a shadow of a doubt. Why should he care how many men had come before him so long as he was the next?

And he would be the next.

Chapter Six

Catherine lay awake, staring at the ceiling. Moonlight bathed the room in a golden glow, and she blamed its brightness for her inability to sleep. All evening visions of Sam's confrontation with David had haunted her. Did he truly know how to handle the boy, or would he further humiliate him? What if they quarreled? What if David ran away? What if? . . .

A dozen possible outcomes occurred to her, each one worse than the last. Her only consolation was knowing Sam loved the boy even more than she did and wouldn't purposely hurt him. If only he didn't hurt him accidentally.

She rolled over, punching her pillow in a vain attempt to get more comfortable, and then she heard a noise outside. Peering beneath the curtain, she had no trouble making out the rider disappearing into the shadow of the willows by the creek. Her nerve ends prickled in warning. She waited for the rider to emerge again, but when he did, he was on foot, walking toward the school!

Catherine sat up in alarm, squinting to recognize the

man. When she did, her alarm turned to dread. Why would Sam Connors be coming here at this hour? Something must have happened to David! She bolted from the bed, grabbing her robe as she ran.

Sam glanced around, relieved to note all was quiet. The town was dark, and likely, no one had seen him ride in. He hated sneaking around, but he'd promised Catherine he'd come back and he intended to keep his promise before another day went by. He'd wasted enough time already.

No light shone in her room, and he figured she'd already gone to bed. So much the better. He lifted his hand to knock, but the door flew open before he touched it.

"What's happened? Where's David?" she asked.

She stepped back automatically, allowing him to enter. He closed the door behind him and tried to make sense of her question. "He's at home, in bed." He pulled off his hat and tossed it on the table.

Catherine stared at him, trying to make out his expression in the darkness. "Then why are you here?"

"You know why. I told you I'd come." He reached for her as he had that afternoon. This time, all the warning alarms she had previously ignored began to sound and she tried to resist, but he was having none of it.

"Sam, I don't—"

His mouth smothered her words, and his arms crushed her to him. Through the thin fabric separating them, she could feel his heart thundering against hers. His kiss drained her strength, leaving her weak and trembling, and her hands slowly relaxed from fists into a caress, until she was clinging to his broad shoulders.

His hands moved over her urgently, tracing the

170

curves of her body through the fragile barrier of her nightclothes and scorching her wherever he touched. He cupped her breast, then lowered his head to mouth the puckered nipple through the cloth. She cried out as his gentle sucking sent a spasm of desire quaking through her.

Her cry seemed to startle him, and he jerked away. "No, not like this," he murmured, pulling out of her arms. Drawing a shaky breath, he backed toward the table and sank down in one of the chairs.

Catherine fought for her own breath, hugging herself to stop her trembling. She still didn't know why he had come. "Wh . . . what happened with David?"

His eyes glittered in the darkness. "We talked. I told him you weren't mad." He bent over, muffling his words, and Catherine had to strain to hear. "He's got a speech all ready for tomorrow. All you have to do is listen to it and tell him to behave himself from now on."

"Did you apologize for taking the painting?"

"Yes," he said impatiently. Catherine finally realized he was taking off his boots, then suddenly, he stood up and stripped off his vest.

"What are you doing?" she demanded in renewed alarm.

"I'm getting undressed." He pulled his shirt over his head as Catherine watched, stunned.

"Why?" she asked, her voice slightly shrill.

He tossed the shirt onto the table and began to unbuckle his gunbelt. "I figured you'd like it better that way."

"Like what?" she asked, although she was very much afraid she knew. Instinctively, she backed away.

His gunbelt hit the table with a clunk. "I—I think you'd better leave now, Sam."

"Don't be afraid," he said, capturing her easily. "I'm not one of your fancy artist friends, but I'll make you happy, Cat. You won't be sorry."

His words made no sense, but she understood him all the same. He was going to make love to her—or at least he thought he was. "Sam, you can't—"

But he could, and he did. This time when she struggled, she encountered bare flesh, hot and silken and inexorable. His tongue plunged into her mouth, and her fingers relaxed against his chest, burrowing into the mat of hair she found there. He pulled her robe loose and stripped it from her arms, then hauled her back against his chest with only her nightdress separating them.

The musky male scent and taste of him engulfed her, weakening her defenses. As if of their own accord, her arms encircled his neck in a futile attempt to get closer to him. She couldn't really let him make love to her, but this was so wonderful that she would enjoy it for another moment or two. He wasn't a rapist. He'd stop when she insisted.

His skin felt warm and vibrant, and she could sense the tensile strength he held so tightly leashed. Beneath her stroking hands, a groan began, deep in his chest. She coaxed it with teasing fingers until it became her name breathed fervently against her lips.

In the next instant, he lifted her high against his chest. His mouth never left hers, giving her no chance to protest, and then he lowered her onto the bed. New warnings screamed in her mind. She'd never intended to let things go this far.

"Sam, no, stop . . ."

Her voice was no more than a whisper of sound, and when his hands touched her naked flesh, the sound became a purr of pleasure.

"I'll make you forget the others, Cat," he said against her throat just before he slipped her nightdress over her head.

What others? she wondered, but then his mouth found her breast, and nothing else mattered. His hungry lips closed around one nipple, tugging gently while his fingers found the other and teased it to a tight bud. Desire coiled into white hot need.

She had to stop him, but she couldn't end this yet, not yet. His mouth moved lower, pressing stinging kisses down her belly, while his callused palms traced the curve of her hips. She shifted restlessly beneath him, needing something, wanting something for which she had no name.

Gently, he parted her thighs, abrading the sensitive inner flesh with the tips of his fingers and soothing it with his kiss. Her whole body ached with emptiness, an emptiness only he could fill, and her body wept the tears of need that dewed her womanhood.

"Sam?" The word was only a strangled cry, but he responded. She groaned when he left her, but he was only tearing away the last of his clothes. When he came back, nothing separated them. His flesh touched hers everywhere, his glorious weight crushing her, closer, closer, until he was almost close enough.

Almost, but not quite, not yet, not enough! She opened to him instinctively, offering what she had never considered giving another man.

"Cat, my sweet Cat," he breathed against her cheek, then his pulsing hardness touched her, probing, pushing, straining. She lifted at his urging, seeking fulfillment for the need that had become an agony.

Encountering resistance, he hesitated, muttering something she could not understand. She couldn't wait, not another minute. Wrapping her legs around his, she grasped his flanks. With a groan, he broke the barrier of her innocence.

The pain tore through her, wrenching a cry from her throat. Above her, he jerked in reaction. "Cat? Cat, I didn't know!"

She hadn't known, either. Tears stung her eyes, but already the pain was receding, leaving behind the glorious sense of fulfillment she had sought. He loomed above her, a shadow in the darkness, but she wanted him closer. She snaked her arms around his neck and pulled his mouth to hers. His kiss was sweet and infinitely tender, but she wanted his passion now.

She parted her lips, and his tongue sought hers. His skin grew damp beneath her palms, and she traced the powerful muscles of his back, reveling in his nearness.

And then he moved away!

"Don't go," she pleaded.

"I'm not going anywhere," he whispered back, burying his face in the curve of her neck as he slid back into her velvet depths.

She gasped at the sensations, lying perfectly still while he showed her another dimension of pleasure. He slipped his hands beneath her hips and taught her the ancient rhythms, too, until they moved together.

"Purr for me, Cat."

And she did, tiny sounds of abandon born in the deepest part of her where wants and needs coalesced. Her blood raced, roaring in her ears and shutting out all the world except the two of them, straining together until pleasure itself became a painful need for something more.

Each thrust brought her closer to the edge, and she teetered on some precipice, fighting the plunge into the unknown yet knowing she must fall. She clung to him, no longer sure where his body ended and hers began, holding back for one last second. And then she could resist no longer. With a cry, she yielded, shuddering with spasms of pure joy.

From far away she heard his voice, "Yes, Cat, yes." Tiny shocks still rippled through her when she felt his body convulse with his own release. A strangled cry escaped his lips, and she held him close, cradling him against the storm.

Afterward, for long moments, they lay still, gasping for breath. Finally, he rolled off her without letting go, still holding her in his arms. She rested her head against his shoulder, dazed, then she realized he was asleep, his regular breathing at first a comfort to her.

Gradually, however, sanity returned, and with it came the shock of what she had done. She was lying naked in Sam Connors's arms! Her eyes flew open as the magnitude of her act struck her. She stared at his profile, barely visible in the moonlight. He looked oddly young and vulnerable, and not at all like a man who would come to a woman's home and ravish her against her will.

Of course, she hadn't really resisted, not for more than a moment. Her whole body burned with shame when she recalled how eagerly she had surrendered to him. What must he think of her? But what must he have thought to have come here in the first place?

Carefully, she let her memory pick its way past the mind-numbing ecstasy she had experienced to recall what had come before. The senseless things he had said then now made perfect sense. He would make her forget the others, the fancy artists whom he believed had been her previous lovers! He'd thought her a loose woman, little better than a whore! The knowledge chilled her, mortified her, but when she tried to draw away from him in horror, he tightened his embrace, refusing to release her even in his sleep.

Catherine shuddered. She had given herself to a man she barely knew, a man she certainly didn't love, and a man she wasn't even sure she liked. True, he wasn't as bad as she had once thought. He had tried to make peace over the fencing issue, he had forgiven her betrayal, and he had even allowed David to continue his lessons. Still, every time she began to think well of him, he did something outrageous, like accusing her of seducing his brother!

No, she couldn't possibly love him, but why had she responded so passionately to him? Surely mere lust could not explain her reaction. And how could she ever face him again? Even though he knew she had been innocent, her eager surrender had proven his low opinion of her. What could she say to him?

He stirred, sending her into a panic. She slammed her eyes shut, knowing she was being a coward but unable to summon a shred of her usual courage.

Sam woke with a start, instantly aware of an overwhelming feeling of awe. How long had it been since he had made love to a woman? Oh, he had paid for the privilege of release and had taken his pleasure when it was freely offered, but to actually make love . . . The memory was dim and distant and infinitely painful, so he blotted it out.

He glanced down at Cat's tousled blond hair and

instantly remembered her cry of pain. Oh, God, what had he done to her? Guilt was like a knife in his vitals. He had behaved like a man possessed. How could he possibly make amends? Should he apologize? Should he *propose?*

He actually winced at the prospect of proposing to Catherine Eaton. What would a woman, a *lady,* like her want with Sam Connors, a man who had just forced himself on her, ignoring her protests? Oh, God, she *had* protested, too, but he'd been too dead set on having her to pay her any mind.

Gingerly, guiltily, he released her from his embrace, watching her lovely face for any sign she was awakening. "Cat?" he whispered.

No response.

"Cat?" he said a little louder.

She did not move, and he suddenly realized she wasn't really asleep. Her failure to respond was deliberate. She didn't want to face him, and who could blame her? Surely, she must despise him now.

The thought sent a spasm of agony through him. Of course she'd hate him, hate and fear him, and he had no right to expect anything else. His guilt burgeoned as he considered his options. He could force her to talk and risk an ugly emotional scene that might alienate her forever, or he could honor her wishes and steal away into the night, leaving the confrontation for another time when they were both more rational.

He really had no choice. He couldn't add cruelty to his sins by forcing her to talk about his violation when she plainly didn't want to. Still, he felt far more cowardly than considerate as he slipped from the bed and found the jeans he had so hastily discarded. When he had them on, he turned back. Catherine's perfect body seemed to gleam in the moonlight, and renewed desire hit him like a wave, taking his breath.

He wanted her all over again, but he'd had no right to take her the first time. How humiliated she must be, lying there naked, knowing he was looking at her but not daring to cover herself. Quickly, he reached for the sheet tangled at the foot of the bed and drew it up.

Catherine tensed when she sensed him moving toward her. She could hardly believe it when the cool sheet settled over her, covering the nakedness she had found so mortifying. Then she heard him walk away and finish dressing. He paused for a long moment, as if uncertain exactly what to do. She imagined him trying to wake her again, wanting to talk, but mercifully, he moved toward the door. In another minute she heard his footsteps outside, carrying him toward where his horse was tied in the willows.

Only now did she give way to the emotions churning inside her, the shame and embarrassment and confusion. A strangled sob escaped her. He'd covered her up! It was the act of a kind and gentle and considerate man, the type of man she'd never let herself believe Sam Connors to be. Clutching the sheet to her bosom, she tried to smother another sob.

Had she misjudged him? Was he more like David than she had imagined? He *had* to be, she realized in despair. After what had just happened between them, he simply had to be.

Once away from town, Sam rode fast and hard, as if he could escape his thoughts. Finally, though, he had to slow down or risk riding his horse to death, and his thoughts easily caught up with him again.

He'd hoped being away from Catherine would help

him see things more clearly, but now he was more confused than ever. Nothing made sense anymore. In spite
of all her scandalous talk, she'd been a virgin. He
hadn't let himself think much about the previous lovers
he'd imagined, since the very idea of their existence
had sent him into a towering rage. He'd wanted to
murder every one of them. He'd wanted to be the only
man alive who knew her body.

And now he was.

Oh, God, what a fool he'd been. And now he'd ruined any chance he might have had to win her.

Or had he? A woman who had lived the life Catherine had and still held onto her virginity would not
take its loss lightly. In the cold light of day, she'd begin
to realize the implications of her act . . . and the possible results. *Sam might have given her a child.*

A child, *his* child, a baby he could claim as his own
and a baby who would be part of Catherine. The
haunting need he had suppressed for so many years
surged suddenly to life again, and he knew he had
found his dream at last.

He had just begun to consider all the ramifications,
when his horse looked off to the right, its ears pricked.
He reined to a stop and listened, the possibility of danger wiping all the happy thoughts from his mind. He
heard nothing, but trusting the horse's instincts more
than his own, he waited for several minutes.

Then he saw a tiny pinpoint of light, a match being
struck by a man way off in the distance. It might be
one of his own men, of course. He still kept a few
riding fence at night, but something told him it wasn't
one of his men. He turned the horse and kicked it into
a trot, keeping his eyes trained on the spot where he
had seen the match flare.

The moon was still full and bright, a Comanche moon. Years ago settlers would have slept with one eye open on a night like this, expecting the Indians to swoop down, using the light to raid and slaughter. The Comanche were all safely ensconced on reservations now, but new raiders had taken their place, raiders who carried wire cutters instead of arrows.

He stopped again, listening, and then he heard the soft murmur of voices carrying clearly on the night air. His horse shifted restlessly, sensing others nearby. He gave the animal its head and allowed it to move toward the voices.

Then he heard the sharp snap of wire being cut. Once, twice, again. Sam drew his pistol. Soon he was close enough to see their horses grazing peacefully and the silhouettes of two men working on his fence.

One of their horses lifted its head and whinnied a welcome. The two men froze. "Who's there?" an unfamiliar voice asked.

Sam responded by pulling back the hammer of his pistol with a resounding click. "Hold it right there or I'll shoot."

"Jesus, it's Connors!" one of them said.

In the next instant, a gun spat flame and Sam ducked, leaning close to his horse's neck. Luckily, the shot went wild, and before Sam could still his dancing horse to take a shot of his own, the others were running toward their own mounts. He fired after them.

One of the men howled in pain.

"Floyd, you hit?"

Floyd swore viciously and snapped off another shot in Sam's direction, before flinging himself into his saddle. Sam fired back, but his horse was rearing now, panicked by the gunfire, and he missed.

The two men were galloping away, firing as they went. Sam shot back, kicked his horse into a gallop, and leaned low in the saddle. He couldn't let these two get away. The ground beneath him blurred as his horse stretched out, straining in the chase.

They ran for a mile or more, spitting shots at each other until their guns were empty. Then Sam felt his horse falter. He threw his weight forward, but his horse was already tired from the earlier run. Even in the dark, he could see he was losing ground, but he kept up the chase until he sensed his horse couldn't go on any longer. Swearing, he slowed to a walk, listening with growing frustration to the fading sound of their hoofbeats.

Well, he could trail them if nothing else. Sam was one of the best trackers around, and from the way these fellows were going, they'd leave prints a blind man could follow. But even Sam couldn't track them in the dark, and only an idiot would try it alone. Sighing with defeat, he turned toward the ranch. At first light, he'd be on their trail, and his men would finally get their chance to go after some real live fence cutters.

Once Catherine finally fell asleep, she slept too long, waking up with only minutes to spare before her students would begin to arrive. She threw on her clothes and hastily smoothed her hair into its customary style. She had no time for breakfast, but her stomach wouldn't have tolerated food in any case.

When she'd finished with her hair, she stared at her reflection in the mirror, wondering how she could still look exactly the same when she felt so changed. Well, what had she expected, a brand on her forehead? An *F,* perhaps, for "Fallen Woman"?

Bracing herself, she drew up the bedclothes without looking at the crimson stain on the bottom sheet, the evidence of her folly. She didn't need the visual reminder, because the unfamiliar aches in her body would not let her forget. How would she endure the coming day, trying to act as if nothing had happened? How would she face the children?

And David! Dear heaven, he would be coming to apologize to her for the painting. How could she deal with this? She had no time to decide. Her students were already beginning to arrive, cheerful and enthusiastic and wrapped in slickers against the morning drizzle. Perfect weather, she thought morosely, peering out at the scudding clouds and massaging her pounding temples.

Catherine waited nervously for David to appear, but when the time came to ring the bell, he still had not arrived. Now new fears assaulted her. Had Sam lied about having settled things with David? Or worse, had David found out about her and Sam? Knowing she could not dwell on such thoughts, she started the youngest children on their recitations, hoping they would provide sufficient distraction.

The morning dragged by, and more than once Catherine found herself staring out at the road, as if mere yearning could make David appear. His absence portended all sorts of unpleasant things, and Catherine couldn't bear thinking about any of them.

Ironically, it was after she had given up hope that he finally rode in, drenched and disheveled, just as she told the children to get their lunches. Hearing his horse, they ran to the door. Everyone sensed he had some important news to impart, and he was surrounded the instant he came in.

"I . . . I'm sorry I'm late, Miss Eaton," he said breathlessly. He flushed scarlet, perhaps thinking of the humiliation of their last meeting, but Catherine gave him what she hoped was a reassuring smile.

"No need to apologize. I'm sure you have a very good reason."

"Yeah, well, Sam saw some fence cutters last night. There was some shooting, but they got clean away and—"

"Shooting?" Catherine interrupted, feeling the blood drain from her head. "Was Sam hurt?"

"Oh, no, but he thinks he hit one of them." Catherine went weak with relief and barely heard the rest of the story. "He chased 'em, but his horse gave out, so he came back to the ranch and got some of the men together. They went out at first light. Sam, he can track a butterfly across solid rock, so they figured they'd catch up with no trouble, but then this blasted rain started and—" He shrugged his frustration. "Anyways, he told me to get along to school, since there wasn't anything else we could do."

The children bombarded him with questions while Catherine stood silently, gathering her wits. Sam had been shot at *again!* The thought sent a wrenching pain through her, and she blinked at the sting of tears. If anything happened to Sam, how would she bear it?

The thought stunned her, and at that moment she began to understand that she was falling in love with Sam Connors. Standing there, surrounded by children, listening to David's explanations, she suddenly realized why Sam had become such an important presence in her life, why his opinions mattered so much, and most of all, why she had surrendered to him last night. It hadn't been mere lust at all.

183

But how could she *love* a man like that?

She noticed David was staring at her, and she imagined her churning emotions must be reflected in her expression. Luckily, Jessica chose that moment to call David's attention to herself.

"Davy, you'd better take off your wet things before you catch a chill."

"Oh, yeah," he muttered, noticing the puddle forming beneath him. While he shrugged out of his slicker, Catherine composed herself.

"Have you eaten?" she asked, noticing he wasn't carrying a lunch pail.

"Uh . . . no, I . . . in all the excitement, I reckon I forgot."

"I'll make you a sandwich," Catherine offered, glad for the opportunity to escape, however briefly. But her room held far too many memories, she realized when she saw the hastily made bed. Turning to her makeshift kitchen, she pulled out the bread and cheese and began to slice, vitally aware of Sam's haunting presence in the room.

He must have encountered the fence cutters on his way home last night. Did anyone know where he had been? Did David suspect? The boy still seemed awkward around her, but maybe he was only embarrassed from yesterday.

"Miss Eaton?"

She jumped, glancing up to find David standing in the doorway leading to the classroom.

"Can I . . . I mean, I'd like . . . I need to talk to you a minute," he said, looking furtively over his shoulder lest any of the others overhear.

"David you don't have to explain anything."

"But Sam said—"

"You don't have to do *everything* Sam says!" she snapped, instantly sorry when she saw his bewildered expression. She consciously softened her voice. "I told Sam he had no right to take the painting from your room. I was quite angry with him, but certainly not at you. In fact, I'm proud of your creativity. Trying a nude without a model shows great courage."

His face flushed scarlet, and he glanced over his shoulder again. "I never meant it to be you," he whispered, "but your face was the only one I could do from memory."

"Of course," she replied, managing to maintain her nonchalance. "I never thought otherwise."

He blinked in surprise at her calm acceptance of his obvious lie. Catherine wondered if he could see how her hands were trembling. She finished up the sandwich and handed it to him, smiling benignly. "You'd better eat up before the others start asking you questions again."

David obediently took a bite.

Catherine started to clean up the mess, thinking she should probably make herself a sandwich but knowing she couldn't have swallowed a bite of it. "You said Sam wasn't hurt?" she asked, hoping she still sounded normal.

David swallowed. "No. It's pretty hard to hit anything when you're running for your life, like they were. It was dark, too."

Briefly, Catherine debated asking a dangerous question, but she needed to know how much Sam had told David. "What was Sam doing out so late?"

"He said he had a hunch something was going on, so he went out looking."

David's expression never flickered. He didn't know

185

about her and Sam! She felt almost giddy with relief. She wasn't even annoyed when Jessica sidled up beside David and batted her eyes provocatively. "Did you go after the fence cutters, too?"

"Well, no," he reluctantly admitted. "Sam sent me out to tell the neighbors so they could join in the hunt, but by the time we met up, the rain had already washed out the tracks."

Jessica slipped her arm through David's and skillfully drew him away, asking another question Catherine did not hear. Catherine slumped down in one of her kitchen chairs and sighed wearily, overwhelmed by a sudden need to see Sam.

How ridiculous. Last night she'd seen more of him than she'd ever expected to, and then she'd been too cowardly to exchange two words. Now, in spite of everything, she wanted nothing more than the opportunity to hold him close for one instant.

She must truly be in love, she thought in despair. What else could explain such bizarre emotions?

The afternoon dragged even more slowly than the morning, the rain and David's news making the children restless and cranky. Only when she had released them for the day did she remember it was Friday. She was scheduled to stay with the Redferns this weekend. Little Eli was barely five, one of her youngest students. His father was the town's blacksmith. For a moment she entertained thoughts of begging off, until Eli approached her with a radiant smile.

"You're staying at *my* house tonight," he announced proudly.

She simply didn't have the heart to disappoint him. "Yes, I am. Just give me a minute to get my things together."

Opal Redfern was about Catherine's age, a plain-faced woman who had grown plump with childbearing. Eli Junior was the oldest of three, but Opal seemed to thrive on the demands of caring for a houseful of little ones. Grateful for the confusion, Catherine allowed Opal to think her distracted attitude was the result of being overwhelmed.

Somehow Catherine managed to go through the motions of living that evening. The worst moment came when she held Opal's baby for a few minutes and suddenly realized she might, at that very moment, be carrying Sam Connors's child.

Panic seized her. What on earth would she do? Would Sam even care? Of course, she wasn't dependent on Sam Connors, she told herself sternly. She had the legacy her father had left her. She didn't need a man to take care of her or her child. But the prospect of bearing and raising that child alone and unloved loomed large and foreboding.

Her fears must have shown on her face because Opal asked if she was feeling well and took the baby from her arms.

That night, lying alone in the bed little Eli and his brother had vacated for her, Catherine stayed awake for a long time, trying to make sense of her feelings. Whether she loved him or not, she had been insane to surrender to Sam. He had treated her like a whore, and she had no idea if he felt remorse for having done so or if he were simply proud of his conquest.

And how did *she* feel? Humiliated, certainly, and guilty for having participated so eagerly in her own debasement. How could she have cast aside every principle of her life for a few moments of pleasure? How could she have risked creating another life for which she would be responsible? Hugging herself against the pain of her own emotions, she asked herself a hundred questions, but she had no idea what the answers were.

Saturday went by in a blur, with townspeople dropping in to exchange news about Sam's fence being cut. Catherine listened numbly, trying not to show any reaction to hearing him spoken of so casually. On Saturday night she slept poorly, bothered by nightmares of Sam getting shot again.

On Sunday morning she dressed carefully for church, in a blue sprigged muslin, and wrapped a shawl around her shoulders against the morning chill. The Redferns lived in town, only a short walk from the church, and Catherine spotted Sam standing in the church yard long before they reached it.

The first sight of him made her heart leap, and she lowered her eyes, not daring to stare lest everyone guess her guilty secret. She tried to tell herself she was only frightened at the prospect of seeing him again, but she knew her fears did not completely explain her reaction. For some reason she still found this dark, impossible man attractive, and no matter how much she wanted to, she couldn't forget she loved him. Catherine wanted to groan aloud in despair.

Sam took a deep drag on his cigarette and squinted through the smoke, watching her approach. He'd wanted to go see her the very next night, to get things settled between them. When he'd realized the next night was Friday and she'd be staying at someone's house, he'd been wild. Davy hadn't even known where she was. Sam was almost grateful for the fence cutters.

Everyone attributed his irritation and short temper to his encounter with the Taggert brothers.

God, she was even more beautiful than he remembered. Or maybe he was just seeing her differently now, recalling how sweet her kisses had been and the way she had melted in his arms. Whatever, he was hard-pressed to stand where he was and not run right over and take her in his arms. He should have been good at dissembling. He'd had plenty of practice, God knew.

But, he reminded himself, he didn't have to dissemble this time. No one would be the least bit shocked if he expressed an interest in Catherine Eaton. Of course, he had his work cut out for him. She wouldn't so much as speak to him the other night, and she wouldn't even look his way this morning. But she was with Opal Redfern. Opal had always liked him and Davy. All Sam had to do was drop a hint or two, and he'd be spending the whole afternoon with Catherine. And afterwards . . .

The church bell rang and Sam threw down his cigarette, watching Catherine move into the church. He'd sit behind her so he could watch her, he decided, feeling a surge of anticipation.

Catherine felt Sam's eyes on her through the entire service. She went through the motions in a daze—standing, sitting, singing, listening—all the while acutely aware only of the man whose gaze was like a warm hand on the back of her neck.

What was he thinking? How would he treat her? What would he say to her? What would *she* say? Her head spun with questions, and when the service ended, she left the building feeling mingled anticipation and dread.

Outside, the buzz of conversation swirled incomprehensibly around her. Someone asked her a question to which she responded automatically, while her heart did a flip in her chest as she saw Sam approaching.

" 'Morning, ladies," he said pleasantly. His greeting included Opal and the other women of the group, but his black eyes never left Catherine's heated face. The others returned his greeting, but Catherine couldn't force any words past the lump in her throat. Finally, he turned to Opal. "Do you still make the best lemon cake in Texas, Opal?"

"Why, Sam Connors, anybody'd think you were hinting for an invitation to Sunday dinner," Opal chided with a knowing grin.

Sam grinned back, and Catherine's heart jerked to a halt. "I figured a kindhearted lady like you would take pity on a poor, lonely bachelor."

To Catherine's dismay, his gaze flickered back to her. Why on earth was he looking at her like that? Now *everyone* would know what they had done!

"Bachelor, is it?" Opal teased. The other women chuckled and looked at Catherine. "Well, you're a little late. Some other bachelors have already put in their bids."

Sam's head came up with a jerk. "Who?"

"Tom Riley, Ed Spencer, and one or two others, I forget just who. Of course," she added slyly, "we've always got room for one more . . . or two more if Davy's feeling like a lonely bachelor, too."

Catherine would have sworn she couldn't have felt any more embarrassment, but this new information proved her wrong. Three or four other men had already finagled an invitation to the Redferns' Sunday dinner in order to be with her! The prospect of spending the afternoon in Sam's company was horrifying enough without an audience of eager would-be suitors to observe them. How would she ever endure it?

But endure it she did. Opal had the men set up a

makeshift table in the backyard. They were all quite eager to help, and they gave Catherine the impression of exuberant puppies falling all over each other. Catherine hid in the kitchen as much as she could, pretending to assist Opal and ignoring her hostess's commands to "go on outside and talk to the men."

At last the meal was ready and on the table, and Catherine had no further excuse for not joining the rest of them. When she went outside, she saw the only vacant seat at the table was on the end. Little Eli Redfern sat on one side and Sam Connors on the other. How had Sam engineered it? she wondered, feeling flattered and panicked all at once.

Sam jumped up to pull out her chair, making her blush even more furiously, and she took her seat without looking at him, murmuring her thanks. David, who was sitting on Sam's other side, caught her eye and gave her a quizzical smile, obviously puzzled by his brother's sudden interest in her.

Mr. Redfern sat at the far end of the table, opposite Catherine, and he started passing the various serving bowls. "Say, Sam, what makes you so sure it was the Taggerts who cut your fence?"

Catherine paused in the act of scooping a potato from the serving bowl she held, shuddering a bit as she recalled her initial reaction to seeing the Taggert brothers.

"One of them called the other one Floyd," Sam explained, relieving Catherine of the potato bowl.

"But don't they—" she blurted, before she could stop herself. She had intended to avoid talking to Sam. All eyes turned to her, and her face grew hot again. She forced herself to finish her question, pretending to look at Sam while actually looking somewhere over his shoulder. "I thought the Taggerts worked for Mr. Nylan."

"Gus fired them after they cut my fence and left the coffin."

She longed to ask another question but didn't want to risk drawing Sam's attention to her again. She dropped her eyes and pretended an interest in her food. Luckily, one of the other men voiced the question in her mind.

"Why do you reckon they stayed around after Gus fired them?"

"Maybe they're working for somebody else, although nobody'll claim 'em right now," Sam said.

Catherine passed a platter of ham to Sam, still not daring to meet his eye. She had just picked up her knife to cut her own meat when Sam's knee touched hers beneath the table.

The nudge sent a jolt of electricity through her and the knife jumped from her hand, clattering onto her plate. She jerked her knee away, tucking her feet beneath her chair in hopes of avoiding any further contact. Now she felt hot all over, and she wondered miserably if her face could possibly be as red as it felt. She didn't dare raise her head.

Sam's voice startled her again. "It's time we called in the Rangers."

"Rangers?" everyone echoed incredulously.

"Would they come?" Opal asked.

"Of course they'd come," Sam said. "Private property's been destroyed. There's been shooting."

"What do we need the Rangers for?" David asked. "We can take care of a couple of fence cutters."

"We've already tried, and look where it's got us," Sam replied. "All we've done is stir up more trouble.

It's never a good idea for people to take the law into their own hands, and especially not when the law's ready and willing to help out."

Some of the others murmured their disagreement, apparently feeling like David that the problem wasn't too big for them to handle.

"I still say lynch law and Judge Colt are the quickest way to settle this," one of the men argued.

"And what if 'Judge Colt' executes the wrong man, Tom?" Sam countered. "What if *you're* the one who goes down next time?"

Tom had no answer, and Catherine felt her respect for Sam Connors growing. He had more reason than anyone to seek his own revenge, but he was willing to bow to the proper authority. Underneath all that bluster, he really was a reasonable man.

The next time Sam's knee brushed hers, she glanced up to find his dark eyes upon her. The touch had been deliberate, and although she knew she was being foolish, she didn't mind—or at least not very much. She pulled her leg away, but slowly. Some emotion flickered in his eyes and was gone, but his lips twitched slightly, as if he were holding back a smile. Suddenly, she wished they were alone. She wanted to see that smile.

Unfortunately, the other "suitors" were not about to allow Catherine a moment alone with any of their rivals. They lingered all afternoon, and for a while Catherine feared she wouldn't even be able to go to the outhouse by herself.

Only Opal's not-too-subtle hints finally drove them away, and none of them would leave unless all the others did. Catherine found herself bidding Sam good-bye under the close scrutiny of half-dozen pairs of eyes. If she wasn't mistaken, he shared her frustration. The knowledge gave her some hope that he really did care about what had happened between them.

"I hope I'll see you again soon," he said, taking her hand.

The callused roughness of his palm sent chills racing over her as she recalled his touch on other, more sensitive parts of her body.

"Yes, soon," she replied inanely, wondering if the others could see the fire in his eyes and if her own were equally as bright.

Reluctantly, he released her hand and turned away. David said something she only half heard and to which she responded absently. Then the others filed by, said their adieus, and left.

"Well, well, well," Opal said smugly as she closed the door behind them.

Catherine gave her what she hoped was a puzzled look.

"You and Sam Connors. I never would've guessed."

"Wh—what do you mean?" Catherine stammered, feeling the heat rising in her cheeks for what seemed like the hundredth time that day.

"You know what I mean. The man's smitten, truly smitten. I declare, I don't recollect Sam ever taking an interest in *any* woman before now. Did you know how much he liked you? I mean, has he courted you any before today?"

Courted? What a quaint euphemism for what she and Sam had done. Catherine wondered whether Opal would agree but decided not to ask her. "No, not really," she hedged. "I mean, we've talked on several occasions about David's art lessons, but never about anything personal."

"You stayed out at his place, didn't you?" Opal prodded.

"Yes, but he barely spoke a civil word to me the entire time." Catherine didn't mention the way he had kissed her at the end of the visit.

"Well, I'd say he's willing to be *more* than 'civil' now."

"How come you're making such a fuss over poor Sam?" Mr. Redfern asked his wife in disgust. "There was some other fellows here, too, you know, and they all had eyes for Miss Eaton, same as Sam."

"Yes, but Miss Eaton didn't have eyes for any of them *except* Sam, now, did you, Catherine?" Opal asked. Luckily, she didn't wait for a reply. "Any fool could see the two of them didn't even know the rest of us was around. The other men knew it for sure. You noticed they wasn't about to let Sam get a second alone with her."

Catherine had certainly noticed and been grateful. As much as she longed for some time alone with Sam, she also dreaded the moment when she learned whether her worst fears were true and he saw her only as an easy conquest, a woman who had been more willing to submit to him than any decent woman should have been. Perhaps his interest in her was nothing more than eagerness to return to her bed.

As soon as she could politely do so, Catherine thanked the Redferns for their hospitality and returned to the school. Would Sam visit her tonight? And how should she treat him if he did?

Sam slowed his horse to a walk, straining to see through the darkness and listening for the faint echo of hoofbeats he had been hearing ever since leaving the

195

ranch. Yes, there it was again. Someone was following him.

Even as his nerves prickled to attention, he swore in frustration. He wanted nothing more than to get to Catherine, and now he had to deal with more trouble.

He guided his mount off the road, finding a deep shadow near a rock in which to hide and wait. When he heard the faint clip-clop of hooves growing louder, he pulled out his pistol. The horse and rider materialized out of the darkness, and Sam cocked the gun.

"Hold it right there, partner."

"Sam?" Davy squeaked in surprise. "God, Sam, you scared me to death!"

"Damnit, what're you doing out here? You could've got yourself killed." Sam shoved the pistol back into his holster and walked his horse over to Davy's.

"I—I was following you."

"What on earth for?"

"I thought you might run into trouble and need some help."

Sam opened his mouth to ask what kind of help a fifteen-year-old boy could provide, but he bit back the words. Davy was only doing exactly what Sam would have done in his place. The two of them had always stuck together, and now Davy was showing how much he loved his brother by following him into the night. Suddenly Sam felt cherished, as if someone had pulled him close in a gentle caress. He had to clear the hoarseness from his throat before he spoke.

"I appreciate it, Davy, but I doubt the Taggerts'll strike again this soon. I won't be gone long. Why don't you get on back to the house now."

"I—I thought maybe you'd like some company."

"No," he said too quickly, thinking of Catherine, who'd be waiting for him.

"Oh, well, then," Davy said, hurt thick in his voice.

"Wait, I—I'm sorry. I didn't mean—" Sam swore silently. Even if he sent Davy back, the boy would probably disobey and keep on following him, anyway, and he couldn't let Davy see him go to the schoolhouse. He forced a laugh. "Hell, I guess all this trouble has me spooked. For some reason I keep thinking you're still a kid and should be home in bed."

"I'm not a kid anymore," Davy said defensively.

"Of course you aren't. Come on, let's find us some fence cutters." He kicked his horse into motion and Davy fell in beside him, his grin a white slash in the darkness.

A vision of Catherine, her hair loose, her arms reaching for him, appeared before Sam's mind's eye, but he forced it away. Tomorrow, he promised himself, and he'd wait until Davy was asleep before he left the house.

Catherine waited up until late, reading by the poor light of the lamp until her head ached. Then, with unsteady hands, she undressed and prepared for bed, brushing her long, golden hair one hundred strokes and leaving it loose around her shoulders.

She lay awake for a long time, starting at every sound. When at last she could resist no more, she fell asleep, awaking at dawn to a profound sense of both disappointment and relief.

On Monday afternoon, Catherine took David outside to sketch some trees, thinking this would be safer than jumping back into the oil painting lessons. She could tell he was still embarrassed by the nude painting, but she treated him as casually as she always had and he soon loosened up.

"Tomorrow we'll start an oil of these trees," Catherine said as they sat sketching the straggly willows and the stream that ran beneath them. The willows where Sam had tied his horse the night he . . . Pushing that thought quickly away, she continued, "Maybe we should study some animal anatomy. Then you could do pictures of horses or cows or—"

"Anything except naked ladies," David concluded with a sheepish grin.

Catherine grinned back, relieved he could see some humor in the situation. "Exactly. I'm afraid you'll have to go to Paris if you want to draw naked ladies."

"Paris? Paris, France? Do ladies go around naked over there?" he asked eagerly.

"Of course not!" Catherine chided, wanting to bite her tongue for having mentioned the subject. "However, the art classes in Paris are mixed and they use nude models of both sexes, but if you ever even *mention* it to your brother, I'll never speak to you again!"

"I won't say a word, I promise!"

Catherine could have groaned at the lustful gleam in his eye. Perhaps Sam had been wrong about David being in love with her. Perhaps it was just his normal adolescent interest in sex that had inspired the nude and nothing personal with her at all.

"Of course, you might try to find a man or a boy who'd pose for you shirtless. That would be a start."

David nodded thoughtfully. "Not nearly as interesting, though," he said after a minute, earning a swat from Catherine.

They sketched for a while in silence, and then David said suddenly, "Do you think Sam likes you?"

Catherine's heart jumped up into her throat, but she swallowed it resolutely back down again. "I'm sure he doesn't *dislike* me," she said carefully.

"No, I don't mean that. I mean, he's been acting kind of strange lately, like the way he was so eager to eat over at the Redferns yesterday. He never did nothing like that before."

"*Anything,*" Catherine corrected, hoping to distract him.

She failed. "Anything like that. And he's been asking me lots of questions about you."

"What kind of questions?"

"Oh, he wanted to know whose house you'd be visiting last weekend, and whether you ever talked about him and—"

"And what?" she asked when he hesitated.

"It was the funniest thing. He asked me if I thought you liked flowers."

"Flowers?"

"Yeah, we was . . . were riding fence last night, and I said how the rain had brought out the wildflowers, and he asked did I think you were the kind of woman who'd like flowers."

Fascinated, Catherine could think of nothing to say for a whole minute. "I . . . did you say you were riding fence last night?" she managed finally.

"Yeah. Sam was going out alone again, but I made him take me with him. I figured he wouldn't get into any more shooting scrapes if I was along."

"Oh." So Sam had tried to get away last night and David had prevented him. But he'd been thinking of her. Flowers! Just imagine.

Did he plan to bring her some the next time he came to her?

Chapter Seven

Sam reigned up beneath the willows and sat silently concealed in the deeper shadows. All his ferocious need had suddenly evaporated, leaving him feeling like an awkward kid about to pay his first call on a girl.

He was certainly more than a little worried about the reception he'd receive. He and Catherine hadn't parted on the best of terms the last time he'd come here, and yesterday Cat had been as skittish as . . . well, as a cat. She was certainly mad at him. And probably scared, too. If folks knew she'd slept with him, her reputation would be ruined. They'd fire her from her job and run her out of town. She'd be at his mercy, and if he chose to turn his back on her . . .

But, of course, he had no intention of turning his back on her. Instead, he was wondering whether she'd turn her back on him, just as the only other woman he'd ever wanted had done.

Adora. He'd worshipped her, and he'd been so certain she loved him in return. He had even been willing to risk the terror of his father's wrath in order to have her. They would run away, he'd told her, far away where no one would ever find them.

Even now he could still hear the harsh sound of her laughter as she scorned his fervent proposal. "Are you crazy?" she had asked. "Why would I go away with you? You're a seventeen-year-old boy with *nothing!* I have a husband, and a home, and everything I always wanted."

"But you don't love him!" Sam had argued.

"I don't love you, either," she had replied.

Hurt and furious, Sam had threatened her. "I'll tell him about us! He'll throw you out without a cent!"

"I'll say you're lying. He'll believe me because he'll *want* to believe me, and he'll *kill* you!"

Sam wasn't afraid, but when he said so, she had countered with the most awful threat of all, the one so terrible Sam still shuddered to recall it, even after all these years. That threat had succeeded in silencing him, and Sam had sealed away his pain and humiliation forever.

His love for Adora had soured into bitterness and hate, and for the second half of his life he had kept careful guard over his heart. Since then he had never met a woman worth risking such pain for again.

Until now.

But Catherine wasn't Adora, he reminded himself sternly, and he was no longer a seventeen-year-old boy. And the situation with Cat was different. Cat would be expecting a proposal of marriage from him. In fact, she should be grateful for one, especially if she'd started worrying about being pregnant.

Unfortunately, Sam couldn't allow himself to feel too confident. He had the uneasy feeling Cat might not react to the situation the way most women would. She certainly wasn't like any of the women he'd ever known in most other respects, what with all that talk about nudity and posing for art classes and *nipples,* for God's sake.

Resolutely, he swung out of his saddle, leaving his horse ground-hitched, and started for the school, where a light still burned inside in spite of the late hour.

Catherine waited tensely, willing herself not to look out the window again lest he see her watching for him. Her vigil had seemed hours long, although it was only a little past ten o'clock. He'd waited just until he was certain the townspeople were abed. Catherine, however, was not abed. She sat on one of her chairs, fully clothed in her usual dark skirt and white shirtwaist. If Sam Connors thought to find her in her nightdress again, if he thought she'd throw herself into his arms again, he was going to be disappointed.

His boots echoed hollowly on the stoop and his knock made her jump, even though she'd been anticipating it for hours. Forcing herself to move slowly, she went to the door and opened it.

As always, the sight of him startled her, making her nerves tingle and her heart flutter. He seemed enormous, looming in the doorway, his hat in his hand, his face carefully expressionless.

After what must have been a full minute, he said, "Can I come in?"

Wordlessly, she stepped aside so he could pass. The scent of soap and hair tonic wafted from him, disguising somewhat the musky maleness she remembered so well from the other night. She held her breath for a second or two, until he had passed.

He stopped and turned back to face her, looking impossibly huge in the small room. She let the door swing shut so they would at least be assured of some privacy, although she stayed there beside it in case she felt the urge to escape.

They stared at each other across the narrow expanse of floor separating them. Aware of his gaze, she let her own roam over him, recalling all the details she hadn't allowed herself to notice yesterday—his height, the breadth of his shoulders, the crinkles beside his eyes, the way his ebony hair swept back from his forehead, and the white band of skin where his hat blocked the sun.

As if uncomfortable under her scrutiny, he shifted slightly, and then she noticed the splash of color in his hand, purple and scarlet, the flowers that blanketed the prairies.

Seeing her surprise, he lifted the makeshift bouquet and held it out.

Catherine could hardly believe her eyes. Although she'd been half expecting it, the incongruous sight of Sam Connors holding a fistful of flowers took away her breath, and for a moment she couldn't speak, couldn't even move.

Sam looked at her startled face and then back at the flowers. They were pathetic, scrawny and wilted. No wonder she looked like he'd offered her a snake. "They're not much," he muttered, tossing them on the table in disgust and wiping his hand on his pant leg.

What had possessed him to bring her weeds? She must think him a fool. The thought triggered an avalanche of unpleasant memories, and he grew defensive. "Why didn't you tell me you'd never been with a man?" he blurted, knowing instantly he had said exactly the wrong thing.

She stiffened visibly, and spots of color appeared in her cheeks. "What made you think I had?" she demanded haughtily.

"All your talk about posing naked," he replied, still defensive. "A woman who'd stand up in front of a bunch of men naked would do anything."

"I never posed for *men!*"

"But you said—"

"I said I posed for students, *female* students."

Sam needed a moment to comprehend the implications. "But all that talk . . . the things you said to me when I brought you the painting . . ."

"I was trying to shock you, to put you in your place."

He stared at her in silence, weighing her words.

"I guess you expect me to marry you."

Catherine gaped at him, hardly able to believe her ears. Of all the pompous, arrogant, boorish bastards she had ever met, he was the worst! Was this supposed to be some sort of proposal? Grudgingly offering the protection of his name? Fury stiffened her spine, and she glared at him with all the contempt she could muster. "Why should I expect anything from you?"

"Well, after what happened the other night . . ."

"Do you think I was trying to trick you into marrying me?" she asked incredulously.

"No, I never—" Sam frowned, unable to figure out why she was so mad. "If you didn't want me, why did you let me in?"

Catherine froze. Why *had* she let him in? Oh, she'd been worried about David, but that didn't explain her wanton behavior. "You forced your way in," she replied defensively, unwilling to admit her own part in it. "I asked you to leave, but you ignored me."

Sam felt his face heating at her accusation. She thought he was a rapist. No wonder she'd scorned his proposal. No wonder she'd scorned *him*. The pain of old wounds opening twisted in his gut. "Well, you won't have to ask me tonight." He started for the door, shoving his Stetson back on.

Catherine scrambled out of his way, since he didn't seem inclined to stop. As she moved, she caught sight of the flowers lying scattered on the table and felt a pang. For a moment there she'd glimpsed the warm, sensitive man she had come to love, then somehow they'd started yelling at each other again. How had things gotten so far off track? Nothing was settled and now he was leaving! "Sam, wait," she cried.

He stopped, his hand on the latch, but he didn't turn to look at her. Her mind went blank. What on earth could she say? How could she open subjects so sensitive she didn't even want to think about them? "I . . . why did you go to the Redferns for dinner yesterday?"

Slowly, he turned to her, his expression wary. "Why do you think?"

"I don't know. That's why I asked."

He let his hand drop from the latch. "I guess I hoped maybe at the Redferns' house we could talk without fighting."

Could they talk without fighting? Catherine was willing to try. "Opal thought you were courting me, and so did David," she ventured.

"He's probably jealous about it, too. I guess that's the real reason he wouldn't let me out of his sight last night."

"Then you *were* coming to see me last night." She noticed he hadn't denied her charge that he was courting her.

206

"Yes, I was," he admitted, softening in response to her obvious relief. He took a step closer. "I wanted to come Friday, but then I remembered you'd be staying at somebody's house, and Davy didn't know whose and—" He shrugged.

"And when you found out, you begged an invitation from poor Opal."

He raised his eyebrows in surprise. *"Poor* Opal? She loved every minute of it."

"Yes, she did."

"And how about you? Did you like being the center of attention of all those men?"

She thought he sounded jealous, but perhaps that was only wishful thinking. "No, I found it unnerving, especially—"

"Especially what?"

"Especially when you—you touched me under the table."

He drew a ragged breath. "You're lucky that's all I did."

Every one of her nerve ends leaped to life. "What else did you want to do?" she asked, knowing she was leading him on and not feeling the least bit guilty.

"This," he replied, reaching for her as she had known he would. His mouth was warm and hard and demanding. He parted her lips with his tongue, forcing his way past her teeth in an intimate invasion she didn't even pretend to resist.

His body felt wonderful against hers, hard and strong and vibrant. His hands moved feverishly over her, stirring the embers of the passion he had awakened. He couldn't get enough of her. Surely, he cared for her. He *must!*

His kiss went on and on, until the need for air forced

them apart. They clung, breathless and gasping, his hand still cupping her breast.

"Cat, we shouldn't," he whispered.

"No, we shouldn't," she agreed, touched by his concern. She stroked the smooth curve of his jaw and noticed a tiny knick where his razor had slipped. He had shaved before coming. The knowledge made him infinitely more dear to her.

"You make me crazy," he said against her mouth.

He made her crazy, too. How could she be melting in his arms when nothing was settled?

"I say things I don't mean . . ." he murmured, sealing her lips with his own.

What things hadn't he meant? she wondered vaguely. His hand came up and stroked her throat, and she smelled the acrid scent of wildflowers. The memory of them undid what was left of her resolve. She knew she was insane to even consider what she was considering, but she loved him so much, and the only time they weren't arguing was when they were making love. . . .

"Stop me, Cat," he begged.

"I—I can't," she said, meaning "I won't," pressing herself more closely against him. They could talk afterward. This time she wouldn't be afraid to face him. This time, in the afterglow of their love, they would be able to open their hearts.

She found where his shirttail had come lose and slipped her hand beneath, touching heated skin. He groaned her name, pulling her closer as his mouth found hers again.

Her breasts swelled, straining against him, and little shivers danced over her, warming quickly into flickers of desire. He pulled her shirtwaist loose, but he encountered the unyielding barrier of her corset. Frustrated, he sought the buttons at her throat, unfastening them with little regard to their future usefulness. Her hands were busy with buttons, too, seeking the furred expanse of his chest.

He jerked her shirtwaist open, yanked down the thin fabric of her chemise, and brought her to him, flesh to flesh.

"Do you want me to stop?" he asked breathlessly.

"No," she whispered, exploring the velvet textures beneath his shirt.

Her "No" unleashed a tiger. In a frenzy of need, they undressed each other, frantically stripping away garment after garment, struggling with buttons and hooks and ties and boots and shoes and garters, until they stood before each other with nothing to hide.

Lamplight turned their skin to gold. Catherine thought she had never seen a more magnificent male body. Hard work had honed him to perfection, sculpting each muscle into bold relief. She admired the way the dark hair swirled on him, providing stark contrast to the whiteness of his skin where the sun had never touched.

Had she thought herself familiar with male anatomy? She realized now a woman knew nothing at all until she had seen the man she loved aroused by the sight of her.

His languorous gaze moved over her like a loving hand, stirring her like a physical touch. Had she ever been self-conscious about her body? Had she ever thought her slenderness less than feminine? All such doubts fled before Sam's fierce approval.

He murmured her name in reverence and then scooped her up into his arms.

"The lamp," she said as he swept down the covers and laid her on the bed.

"No, I want to see you this time."

He lay beside her, pulling her close, enveloping her in his warmth. This time she knew what to do, and she wrapped her arms around him, returning his kisses with equal fervor.

With a groan, he rolled over on his back, carrying her with him so she lay sprawled full length upon him. His hands explored freely, finding the curve of her hips and the fullness of her bottom.

"You're so soft," he breathed against her breast.

She shivered as his callused palms grazed her tingling flesh. Kneading his powerful shoulders, she replied, "You're so hard."

For some reason he laughed, a breathless, gasping sound. "God, yes, always when I'm with you." He captured a rigid nipple in his mouth and suckled avidly, sending shock waves coursing through her.

Her hips churned instinctively against his, urged by his eager hands. Beneath her, the swell of his manhood was hot and rigid, tempting and torturing her with the promise of fulfillment. An aching void formed within her, swirling and pulsing, a void only he could fill.

"Sam?" she whispered against the smooth curve of his jaw. He spread her thighs, abrading the sensitive inner skin with the roughened pads of his fingers. "Sam!"

This time he heard her, and in the next second she was on her back, bearing his weight and clinging to him, mouth to mouth, breast to chest. His hands still cupped her buttocks, and he lifted her to him. This time no barrier blocked his way, and he sank easily into her welcoming depths.

Her name rumbled from his chest, an agonized cry that might have come from pain, but Catherine knew otherwise. Her body cried out, too, but silently. A roar of pleasure filled her head and heart and soul as Sam had filled her body. He moved, and the roar reverberated until she trembled.

Clinging desperately, she met him thrust for thrust. The tumult within her grew and swelled, echoing back upon itself and redoubling into a resounding crescendo. Catherine gasped and panted, her nails scraping his back as she fought against what she most desired.

But she had no choice. The roar exploded into sunbursts of joy that tore the very soul from her body and sent it soaring into the light. Still quaking, she absorbed his shudders of release, hearing his groan as if from far away.

"Sam," she whispered or thought she did, holding onto him with all her strength because she was slipping off into the realm of oblivion.

He clasped her to him, murmuring her name, but he couldn't keep her. The inexorable darkness closed around her.

Sam shifted his weight, afraid of crushing her now that he was too wrung out to support himself anymore. Blessing the lamplight, he stared down into her sleeping face. She looked like a wanton angel with her golden hair spilling across the pillow and her lips red and swollen from his kisses. Her dewed skin glowed, as sleek and shimmering as satin.

"You're mine now, Cat," he said, knowing it wasn't completely true, knowing only too well it took more than physical possession to truly make such a claim.

Catherine's eyelids flickered but remained closed. He

envied her the exhausted, blissful sleep of contentment. Although his body was sated, he was far from content and would not be until Cat truly did belong to him, until she lived in his house and slept in his bed and called herself by his name.

Longing sliced through him like a shard of glass. Surely, now, she'd marry him. In fact, she'd probably demand his compliance.

Sam smiled as he imagined her doing so, the way her blue eyes would flash and her chin would lift, defying him to refuse. He shook her, anxious for the confrontation. "Cat? Wake up."

She murmured something and snuggled closer to him, seeking his warmth but not awakening. "Cat?" he tried again. She didn't even stir.

He sighed in frustration, wondering how long he would have to wait until she woke up. Minutes ticked by, five and then ten. He tried to rouse her again but got only unintelligible mutterings. Finally, he had to admit she was out for the night. Of course, he could curl up beside her and be here first thing in the morning when she awakened.

Sam grinned at the thought, knowing he didn't dare risk such a thing. He'd already endangered her reputation enough by coming here in the dead of night. If anyone saw him leaving at dawn . . . No, he'd have to wait until tomorrow night for his answer.

Slipping reluctantly from the bed, he took a long moment to look at her, drinking in the sight of her alabaster body. Reminding himself how late it was, he resisted the urge to climb back in beside her. Instead, he pulled the sheet over her and resolutely turned away to collect his clothes from where they had been scattered in the haste of passion.

When he was dressed, he returned to her. Brushing the hair away from her face, he pressed a kiss to her mouth. Her eyelids lifted a fraction of an inch. "Sam?"

His heart leaped. "We need to talk, Cat."

She murmured a sleepy agreement that made him smile. He stroked her cheek, and she nuzzled his hand like a fawning kitten. Unfortunately, she fell instantly asleep again. Sighing his disappointment, he turned away, blew out the lamp, and left, consoling himself with the knowledge he would return tomorrow to claim her for his own.

Amos Pettigrew cursed softly as his horse picked its way along the almost invisible trail. In spite of the warmth of the spring evening, he was sweating like a pig, starting at every rustle of the wind.

Damn those Taggerts, anyway. Why in the hell couldn't they have chosen a more civilized time and place to meet him? Riding around this country in the dark was dangerous enough, but he also knew those two would murder their own grandmother for two bits. At that thought, he touched the gun he wore under his coat, verifying that it would be close at hand if he needed it.

Of course, even mongrel dogs didn't bite the hand that fed them, so Pettigrew figured he was pretty safe— at least until he'd paid them off.

Suddenly, his horse's ears flicked up, and Pettigrew reined to a halt. "Who's there?" he called into the outcropping of rock up ahead toward which his horse was looking.

"That you, Pettigrew?"

"Yeah, it's me. That you, Taggert?"

Taggert didn't deign to reply. Instead, Pettigrew

heard two horses shuffle into motion, then they materialized out of the shadows. The brothers each carried a Winchester propped on his thigh. Pettigrew's sweat chilled instantly.

"You boys sure picked the darkest night of the year," he said, trying to sound amiable. "I like to never found this place."

"Don't worry. We'd of found you," Will Taggert said, and his brother giggled stupidly. "You got the money?"

Pettigrew reached into his coat pocket and drew out an envelope, which he held out at arm's length. Will Taggert nudged his horse a few steps closer, so he could reach it, then snatched the envelope from Pettigrew's hand.

Taggert struck a match and examined the contents of the envelope. "I oughta charge double," he said when he had shaken out the match. "Connors shot my brother, you know."

"Yeah, that's right," Floyd said, sounding aggrieved. "Hurts like hell, too. We oughta charge double."

"You should have told me," Pettigrew said, shifting nervously in his saddle and wondering if they were crazy enough to shoot him down in cold blood because he hadn't read their minds and brought more money. "Connors claimed he'd hit one of you, but nobody knew for sure. I don't have any more money on me now, but I can—"

"Shut up. We just want to know what you want us to do next."

"I—" Pettigrew stared at them in dismay, hoping they couldn't read his expression in the dark or smell his fear. "I really didn't want you to do anything except cut Sam's fence. I told you before, I only wanted you to make Sam mad enough to turn against the small ranchers.''

"Well, now, Mr. Pettigrew," Will said silkily, "are you telling us we're fired?"

"I'm telling you I don't have any more work for you." Pettigrew could hear the fear in his voice and cleared his throat. "Things are going to get pretty hot for you boys around here. Connors recognized you, and if you so much as show your faces, you're liable to get strung up."

"We don't mind a little heat, do we, Floyd?"

Floyd giggled again. The sound made Pettigrew's flesh crawl.

"In fact," Taggert continued, "we like it real fine around here. We've got ourselves a hideout nobody'll ever find, so we can just keep on doing little jobs for you until we get tired of it, can't we, Floyd?"

"Sure can," Floyd snickered.

Pettigrew felt the sweat pouring down his ribs, and he shifted in his saddle. "But I don't have any more jobs for you to do."

"Then we'll have to think up some of our own, won't we, Floyd? See, Pettigrew, we've got a score to settle with Connors now, so we're gonna keep on pestering him till we figure we've got it settled. And you're gonna keep on paying us to do it."

"Now see here—" Pettigrew began, but caught himself just in time. He had to remember how tenuous his position was. They could kill him right here and no one would ever know. "I . . . why should I continue to pay you?"

"Because if you don't, we'll let Connors know it wasn't Nylan's bunch who cut his fence. I don't think he'll be too happy when he finds out you turned on him, and besides, you've got fences of your own to worry about. Long as you're paying us, they'll be safe.''

Pettigrew stared at the two men in horror. He was being blackmailed, and there wasn't a damn thing he could do about it. If the community found out he'd hired the Taggerts to cut Sam's fence in order to force Connors to take a stand, they'd all turn against him, and if he refused to go along with Taggert's scheme, his fences would be ruined.

"How—how much do you want?'' he asked hoarsely.

"Well, now, let me just think about it for a minute,'' Taggert said smugly.

A few minutes later, when Pettigrew had disappeared into the shadows again, Will Taggert turned to his brother. "You in the mood for some fun tonight?''

Floyd cackled. "I always am. What you got in mind?''

"Connors has got him a bull he's mighty proud of. What say we pay it a little visit?''

Floyd's laughter echoed in the night.

Lulie Nylan awoke with a start, knowing instinctively one of her children needed her. She lay awake, listening to the sounds of the darkness but hearing no cry. Puzzled, she slipped out of the bed, taking care not to disturb her husband, who snored in contented oblivion.

The main room was empty but the front door hung open, so Lulie looked outside. Jessica stood on the porch, wrapped in a shawl and staring up at the sliver of moonlight.

Lulie took her own shawl from the hook on the wall and joined her daughter outside. "What're you doing up at this hour?"

Jessica jumped. "Ma, I didn't hear you."

"You shouldn't be out here in your nightdress. What if one of the men was to see you? He might think you was offering something you're not."

Jessica sighed impatiently. "Maybe I was hoping one of them would."

Lulie grapped her arm and gave her a shake. "You mind your tongue. You're talking to your mother, don't forget."

"I can't forget," Jessica snapped, jerking free of Lulie's grasp. "You remind me all the time." She sighed, brushing aside a lock of hair the wind had teased into her eyes. "I'm so sick of this place I could scream."

Lulie made a rude noise. "At least you got a chance of getting away. All you gotta do is find yourself a man."

"I already found him. Problem is, I gotta get him to marry me, and he don't seem too interested just yet."

"Davy's still young," Lulie said wisely. "Give him a little time."

"I don't want to wait! I'm sick and tired of taking care of babies and wearing rags and never having any fun. I want to get married *now!*"

"Getting married ain't that much fun," Lulie reminded her sharply. "And what makes you think you won't have babies of your own to take care of?"

Jessica laughed derisively. "Davy'll hire me a nurse. I'll have somebody to cook and clean for me, too. When I'm living in that big house, I won't ever have to turn my hand. All I'll have to worry about is keeping him happy in bed . . .''

Lulie grabbed her daughter with both hands this time and shook her violently. "Where'd you learn to talk like that?"

"None of your business," Jessica said, wrenching away. "But maybe you'd like to know where I learned to keep a man happy . . . and from who."

Lulie gasped, clutching at her heart. "You ain't been with no boys, have you? What if you get yourself a baby? Davy Connors won't have nothing to do with you then."

"I'm not stupid! I don't let 'em put it *in* me."

"They! You been with more than one?"

"I'll never tell," Jessica simpered, feigning shyness.

"You'll burn in hell, girl!"

"Hell's a long way off. Right now I'm worried about where I'm gonna spend the next fifty years, and I sure don't want to spend 'em with somebody like Pa. I want a husband who'll amount to something."

"Your pa's a fine man," Lulie insisted.

"Sure, fine and poor, dirt poor. Once I leave here, I'll never be poor again."

Lulie stared at her daughter, unable to believe the bitterness in her young face. "You might've set your sights too high. Chances are, Davy'll find himself some rich girl to marry."

"Not if I get him first."

"And his brother won't want him marrying into our family," Lulie said with bitterness of her own.

"He won't have no choice if I'm carrying Davy's baby."

"Jessie, you wouldn't!"

"Wouldn't I? That's how you got Pa, isn't it?"

Her mother gaped, aghast.

"You didn't think I knew, did you?" Jessica charged. "I saw the dates in the family Bible, and I figured it out. Like they say, like mother, like daughter."

"It wasn't what you think, Jessie. Your pa and me, we were in love. We planned to marry anyway."

"Then you were a fool. You should've held out for somebody important."

"You can't just—" Lulie made a helpless gesture.

"Can't I? You haven't seen the way Davy looks at me. I can and I will, and I'll get him before he can even think about other girls. And Sam Connors won't have a word to say about it!"

Catherine awoke slowly, only gradually becoming aware of who and where she was. Even more slowly did the memories return, and when they did, she reached instinctively for Sam, but the bed beside her was empty.

"Sam?" she called, sitting up and squinting into the predawn darkness. But he was gone, as she had known he would be. She sighed in frustration and lay back down, trying to remember everything from the night before. Their conversation came back to her in bits and pieces—his grudging proposal, her heated reply, her absurd accusation, him storming out or starting to, the flowers. . . .

The flowers! Catherine jumped up from the bed, heedless of her nakedness, and found the flowers lying on the table where Sam had tossed them. They were limp and lifeless now, their vivid colors a mockery in death. She gathered them lovingly and lifted them to her nose.

They still bore the faint scent of wildness she had first noticed on Sam's hand.

The memories came flooding back then—his hands, his lips, his body moving in hers, and . . . nothing more. Good heavens, she had fallen asleep! So much for her intentions of talking to him afterwards. She had a vague recollection of Sam kissing her before he left, but perhaps it had only been a dream.

Why hadn't he awakened her? She tried to think of a logical explanation, but nothing reasonable occurred to her. Instead, she had visions of him slipping silently, carelessly, away into the night. Why should he awaken her? He'd gotten what he came for, after all.

Had all his protests been pretense? Was he so sure of her response he would allow her to make the first move? Had she been a fool to think he truly cared for her?

Tears stung her eyes, but she blinked them away. She wouldn't cry. If Sam did think so little of her, she wouldn't humiliate herself any more by weeping over him. And if, by some miracle, there was an explanation for his leaving without a word, she didn't want to waste her tears.

Still holding the flowers, she climbed back into bed and inhaled Sam's scent from the pillow where he had lain. Love throbbed painfully in her heart, and she wondered how she had come to such a pass. Her friends in Philadelphia would laugh at her, prudish Catherine surrendering at last to an uncontrollable passion. Sensible Catherine taking a lover who wooed her with wildflowers and arguments.

Lover. She turned the word over in her mind and examined it, trying to make it fit Sam Connors. He wasn't at all the way she had imagined a lover to be, but if a lover was the man you loved and the man with whom you made love, then Sam fit the description.

Would he ever be more? She remembered his words, "I guess you expect me to marry you." Catherine felt certain no woman had ever received a more ungracious proposal of marriage, yet she could not forget the wary expression on his face when he had offered it.

Sam must feel as uncomfortable at the thought of marriage between them as she did. Passion wasn't everything, after all. She knew—or at least she had been told—that it faded quickly. Truly successful marriages depended on deeper feelings, common interests, compatible natures.

Compatible natures? Catherine laughed aloud at the thought, then sobered as she recalled her parents' marriage, their mutual devotion, the quiet love that radiated so constantly in their home Catherine hadn't even been aware of its presence until it had died with her father. She and Sam could never have such a relationship, and Catherine wanted nothing less.

Suddenly, she realized she still held Sam's flowers. Slowly, deliberately, she laid them down on the pillow he had used. No, she had no future with Sam Connors, whether or not he truly cared for her, whether or not he had meant his grudging proposal. She had been a fool to surrender to her physical desires, and she would be crazy to continue the relationship.

Pulling the sheet tightly against her, she reminded herself of the dangers—pregnancy, ruin, humiliation. No man was worth such sacrifice. She must end this now, before things went any further, before she fell even more deeply in love with him. She must never see Sam Connors again.

The tears she had controlled before sprang up anew, and this time she did not fight them.

Sam squinted in the morning sunlight and cursed eloquently as his horse ate up the miles between him and the circling vultures. He had outstripped the other men in his eagerness to see what feast the birds had found, so he was the first to discover the carnage.

For a merciful moment, he couldn't make out the animal's markings for all the gore. The birds flapped and fluttered and danced reluctantly away from their prize, screaming their protest. Sam ignored them, not slowing his horse until he had reached the bloody mound of hide.

Then he saw the white face and recognized Sir Herald, the purebred Hereford bull he had bought last year. Sam sat and stared, numb with shock at the way the animal had been butchered, sliced from end to end. The vultures had dragged the entrails free, and flies swarmed in a pulsing, humming cloud. Sir Herald's blood soaked the ground, forming a black shadow around the carcass.

Fury boiled up in Sam like a red-hot tide. He was swearing slowly and methodically when the other men caught up and reined in around him. Sam had ordered the bull directly from England, having him shipped over and sent by rail the rest of the way. He'd met the train himself and escorted Sir Herald back to the ranch in easy stages so the bull wouldn't be too tired to do his duty when he arrived at the Spur.

Sam had set aside a pasture just for Sir Herald's use and had brought him the youngest, healthiest cows. The bull's blue blood would upgrade the herd until, in a few years, they were running only Hereford cattle, the heaviest, beefiest, most gentle cattle alive. Then they would no longer have to worry about droughts or blizzards or other natural disasters. They would keep the herd like pets, fenced in and protected from every calamity, and the owners of the Spur would be secure. *Davy* would be secure.

Now Sam's dreams lay in a bloody heap on the prairie.

"Shot him right through the eye," Black George remarked, spitting a stream of tobacco in disgust.

Sam nodded, having already noticed the darkened socket. At least the poor beast hadn't suffered. Sam struggled with his rage, wishing he were angry because of the fortune he had tied up in Sir Herald or the trouble of setting up the breeding grounds. Instead, all he could think about was how heartbroken Davy would be to learn the magnificent animal was dead. And what the loss would mean to Davy's future.

With a mighty effort, Sam got a grip on his temper and forced himself to think of more practical matters. "Careful there," he called to the other men. "Don't mess up the tracks. Maybe we can follow them this time."

Sam swung down from his horse and began his examination, making a slow circle around Sir Herald. He found the trail easily enough. They had made no attempt to hide it, at least not in the beginning.

"Two men," he said, feeling his fury hardening into resolve. "My guess would be the Taggerts were mad because I took a few potshots at them the other night." Sam designated some men to go with him after the Taggerts and some others to see Sir Herald properly buried. He couldn't just leave him for the vultures, he reasoned, not asking himself why Sir Herald in death was any different from any other member of his herd.

"At least they waited until Herald had a chance to service most of the cows," one of the men said.

"Yeah, Sam. We oughta have us quite a crop of whitefaces this year," said another. "Some of 'em have already dropped."

"If we got any bulls, we better gather them up before the Taggerts figure out they can do me more harm." Sam climbed back into his saddle and gave Sir Herald one last, long look. He had his anger under control now. It was like a hard, cold lump beneath his heart. He'd get those bastards if it was the last thing he did, and damn their souls, he'd get them before sundown so he could see Catherine tonight.

Catherine heard about the killing of Sir Herald from Twila Shallcross, who came over to the school as soon as the children had been dismissed to suggest David go straight home.

"There's been more trouble?" David asked in alarm. "Sam's not—?"

"Sam's fine, but the Taggerts were out doing mischief last night. Sam'll want you home right now."

David mumbled an apology to Catherine as he gathered his things and raced out the door. When he was gone, Catherine released the breath she hadn't realized she'd been holding and turned to Twila.

"Did you tell him the truth? About Sam not being hurt?"

"Yes, I did," Twila assured her, laying a comforting hand on Catherine's arm. "My goodness, you look like you've seen a ghost."

"I . . . I'm just concerned after . . . I mean, he's been shot at several times now."

"Well, you needn't worry. This time it was his bull that got shot at."

"What do you mean?"

"I mean he's got this bull, or rather, he *had* this bull. He sent all the way to England for it. Prettiest thing you ever saw, if you can imagine a pretty bull. Anyways, last night somebody shot it dead and gutted it."

"How awful!"

"Worse than awful if you ask me. Losing any bull is bad, but this one cost Sam so much money, I can't even bear to think about it. He was going to build a whole new herd with Sir Herald—that was the bull's name, cute, ain't it?—but now I reckon it'll be years before he can afford to get another one like it, too."

"Poor Sam," Catherine said before she could stop herself. She knew she shouldn't let Twila see how much she cared, but she couldn't help herself.

Twila smiled slyly. "I guess Opal is right about you two."

"Opal?" Catherine asked reluctantly, almost afraid to hear what the woman had said.

"She says Sam's crazy about you and that you're pretty interested yourself."

"That's ridiculous," Catherine insisted, trying not to feel too elated over Opal's opinion of Sam's feelings. "I barely know the man, and all we've ever done is quarrel over David."

"Sometimes it starts with fighting, you know."

"*What* starts with fighting?"

Twila batted her eyes coyly. "Romance."

"Twila, really," Catherine scolded, knowing her burning cheeks betrayed her.

"No need to be embarrassed. Anybody'd think you were doing something wrong."

Catherine's heart jumped to her throat. "What do you mean, 'something wrong'?"

"Oh, I don't know," Twila replied, oblivious to her friend's rampaging guilt. "You act like Sam was married or something, and you didn't have any right to him. I'll tell you one thing: I've never known a more eligible bachelor than Sam Connors. It's long past time some woman set her sights on him. And we'd all given up hope he'd ever find a woman to suit him. Ever since I've known him, he's never cared about anything except that ranch and that boy. He acts more like a doting father than a brother, if you ask me. He needs a family of his own to distract him, especially now that Davy's growing up."

Catherine's stomach fluttered alarmingly as she considered the possibility she already carried the seed of Sam's "family."

When Twila was gone, Catherine sank down into her chair, too weary for the moment to begin closing up the classroom. She had been right in her decision not to see Sam anymore. People had already sensed the attraction between them and were bound to wonder why Sam did not take their relationship to the altar.

And why should he? A man doesn't buy the cow if he gets the milk for free. The crude aphorism reverberated in her mind until she could stand it no longer and forced herself to get up and close the schoolroom windows.

Catherine slept poorly that night, half listening for the sounds of Sam's horse approaching while the other half of her worried about what she would do if he did come.

Of course, common sense told her he was out hunting for the Taggerts. He couldn't leave his ranch at night, not after what had happened to his bull. She was relieved he couldn't come.

Wasn't she?

David didn't show up at school the next day, confirming her theory that the search for the Taggerts was going strong. Some of the children told her their fathers were helping Davy and his brother scour the hills for the Taggerts' hideout.

In the afternoon, when she would otherwise have been tutoring David, Catherine got out her sketchbook and drew Sam Connors from memory, drew him the way she had seen him the other night, naked and magnificent and thoroughly aroused. She stared at the sketch for a long time afterwards, until tears blurred her eyes.

Then she burned it. Having such a picture around could be dangerous, she told herself, touching a match to one corner and watching Sam's figure crinkle and blacken and disappear. If someone happened to see it, she would be ruined. Besides, she didn't need a picture of Sam Connors. His image had been burned into her memory by the heat of passion, and she knew she would be able to draw it just as clearly fifty years from now as she had today.

David came to school on Thursday morning, looking tired and apologizing before he was even off his horse because he couldn't stay for his lesson that afternoon.

"Sam made me come to school, but I don't like to be away too long in case anything happens," he explained.

"He . . . you haven't found the Taggerts?"

"No, and I don't reckon we will unless we come on

227

'em by accident. They've got themselves a hidey-hole *nobody* can find. Sam says they must be in—'' He caught himself and blushed furiously.

"What does Sam say?'' she demanded.

"He says they must stay down in h—e—l—l,'' he replied, lowering his voice so the younger children wouldn't hear.

It sounded so much like something Sam would say that Catherine smiled in spite of herself, feeling warmed somehow. Knowing she was being foolish, she tried to change the subject.

"I'm sorry about the bull you lost.''

David's face fell. "I wish you could've seen him, Miss Eaton. Sir Herald was beautiful.''

"Beautiful?'' Catherine asked incredulously.

"Oh, yes, ma'am. He was red with a white face and his hair curled all over and he had a great big—'' David broke off, flushing furiously. "I mean, he was a bull and all . . . you know.''

Catherine thought she did but decided not to say so. "Did you ever paint a picture of him?''

"No,'' David said with a sigh. "I sure wish I had, but I'm not too good with animals yet and I figured I'd wait until I was better. Now it's too late.''

Catherine tried to console him, but before she could do more than mutter a few words of comfort, Jessica came running over.

"Oh, Davy, I heard about your bull. I'm so sorry. He was about the most elegant-looking bull I ever saw.''

Catherine stared after them in wonder as Jessica led him away. Elegant? she thought with a puzzled frown.

After a few minutes, she called the children in to begin class. As the day progressed, Catherine found herself thinking less and less about Sam Connors. Perhaps simply being away from him would be enough to cure her, she thought with a secret smile as she dismissed the children for the day.

As usual, David stayed behind but only to help her with the windows, since he wasn't going to have a lesson today. Catherine was straightening the books on the shelf when the hairs on the back of her neck prickled in warning. Even before she looked up she knew Sam stood in the doorway, staring at her with those eyes that haunted her dreams.

David saw him at the same instant. "What're you doing here?" he asked, delighted as always to see his brother.

"We needed some supplies, so I thought I'd come by and ride back out to the ranch with you," he said, never looking at David but keeping his gaze fixed steadfastly on Catherine, who forced her quivering legs to unbend so she could rise to her feet.

"Great. I just need to get this last window, and then I'll be ready to go." David slammed down the window, and Catherine heard the sound as if from far away.

Sam hadn't come for David at all. He had come for her. She knew it from the way his chin jutted out in determination. She also knew she should refuse whatever demands he planned to make.

"You need anything else before I go, Miss Eaton?" David asked.

Catherine shook her head, finding the motion required a conscious and concerted effort. "No, thank you. I'll see you tomorrow." Still, Sam's eyes held hers as if some irresistible force had paralyzed her.

David headed for the door and paused on the stoop, puzzled, when Sam made no move to follow him.

"Go ahead. I'll catch up," Sam said. "I want to talk to Miss Eaton a minute."

Looking past Sam, Catherine saw David's chin jut out with the same Connors determination. "What do you want to talk to her about?"

"Not you, squirt," Sam said, finally shifting his disturbing gaze to David. "We've got some private business, so run along."

David hesitated, and for a moment Catherine thought he would refuse, *prayed* he would refuse. Then he turned away, trudging down the porch steps with the unmistakable tread of reluctance.

Slowly, Sam's gaze swung back to her. He reached up and pulled off his Stetson, using his other hand to smooth his hair in an oddly self-conscious gesture.

Catherine folded her hands in front of her, clasping them so they wouldn't tremble as he approached, his long strides closing the distance between them much too quickly for her peace of mind.

Her breath caught when he was an arm's length away, when she thought he wasn't going to stop. But he did, teetering on his toes as if he were only just able to hold himself back.

For a long moment he simply looked at her. Close up, she saw the dark circles beneath his eyes. He looked haggard, and she imagined he had slept very little in the past few days. Even though she tried to feel nothing, her heart ached for him.

"How are you?" he asked at last.

"I—I'm fine," she lied, thinking she might well faint if any more blood rushed from her head. "I heard about what happened. I'm sorry." She felt like Jessica, mooning over an "elegant" bull, but she couldn't seem to stop herself.

"We didn't have much time to talk the other night," he said. "You—you fell asleep after—"

Now the blood was back in her head, scalding her cheeks. "Did I?" she asked inanely.

His lips quirked as if he might smile. "Yeah, I tried to wake you up, but you were out like a poleaxed steer . . . uh . . ."

He gestured apologetically, and she saw his dismay at his choice of words. This time *her* lips twitched, even though she would have sworn she couldn't possibly smile in his presence.

"You didn't even wake up when I kissed you good-bye."

It hadn't been a dream! The heat in her cheeks spread inexorably, scorching over her body and settling into the pit of her stomach. "I—I wanted to talk to you."

His fingers flexed restlessly, crushing the brim of his hat. "I know. Listen, I still can't get away at night. We're trying to set a trap for the Taggerts. Where'll you be this weekend?"

She thought frantically, then sighed in disgust. "With the Nylans."

"I don't suppose Lulie'll invite me to dinner," he said with a self-mocking grin.

"No, I don't suppose she will." Catherine felt a flash of anger at the woman's unreasonable dislike for Sam.

"I guess we'll have to wait then."

"Yes, we will."

Vaguely, Catherine realized she had consented to see Sam again, the very thing she had vowed never to do, but somehow that no longer mattered.

"I—" He hesitated, glancing over his shoulder to see if David was in sight. He wasn't, and Sam's hand came out to touch her cheek. His dark eyes flared with desire, and an answering flame licked through her.

"Oh, Sam," she whispered, forsaking all her intentions.

His face came down to hers. "Cat—"

"Sam? Are you coming or not?"

They jerked apart, glancing guiltily toward the door, but David was still not in sight. Sam muttered an imprecation and turned back to her.

"I'll come as soon as I can," he promised, and she nodded her assent. They stared at each other for another heartbeat before he grabbed the back of her neck and pulled her mouth to his for a quick, hungry kiss.

It was over almost before it began, and then he was gone, hurrying across the room and not looking back. Lifting a hand to cover her clamoring heart, Catherine knew he didn't dare. If their eyes had met again, she wouldn't have been able to let him go.

Chapter Eight

Catherine had dreaded the weekend with the Nylans, but she managed to at least appear enthusiastic about her visit. Luckily, Lulie had plenty of gossip to convey and seemed unaware of Catherine's lack of enthusiasm.

Late in the evening, after the younger children had been put to bed and the adults were sitting out on the front porch, Catherine found an opportunity to bring up a topic that had been bothering her for quite some time.

"Mr. Nylan, I want to tell you how much I appreciate your not mentioning who told you Sam Connors and his men were coming to visit you."

Gus looked a little surprised. "I didn't reckon you'd want your name mentioned. I was a little worried the womenfolk wouldn't be able to keep it a secret, but so far they've done all right." His gimlet eyes flashed a warning at Lulie and Jessica, who were sitting with them.

Jessica frowned, obviously unhappy with her father's mandate, but Lulie tossed her head haughtily. "I can keep a secret when it's *important,*" she said. "Seems like Miss Eaton would be proud of what she did, though."

Catherine almost choked. "Proud? Two men got shot because I meddled. I could never be proud of that!"

"Wasn't your fault they was shot," Gus insisted. "A man's got to expect trouble when he goes riding up to another man's house in the dead of night."

"Served Sam Connors right," Lulie muttered. "Who gave him the right to lord it over the rest of us, anyways?"

Catherine's stomach twisted, and she bit back the sharp reply trembling on her lips.

"He's got money," Jessica replied bitterly. "That gives him the right to do anything he wants."

"Jessie!" her father chastened.

"It's true!" the girl insisted.

"Jessica, apologize to Miss Eaton and go to bed!" Gus said.

The girl glared at them all, jumped to her feet, and flounced inside without another word.

Gus rose as if to follow, his hands clenched into fists and his face twisted in fury, but Lulie grabbed his arm. "Let it go, Gus. You know how she is. You could beat her black and blue, and she'd never back down."

Catherine watched apprehensively as Gus Nylan regained control of his temper and sank down in his chair again.

"I'm sorry you had to see that, Miss Eaton," Gus said wearily. "I hope she don't talk back to you at school."

"Oh, no," Catherine hastily assured him. She was beginning to realize how lucky she had been to have Jessica's cooperation. For whatever reason, the girl must be determined to put up a good front in front of the other children, a front she didn't feel compelled to maintain at home. Catherine didn't need much imagination to figure out the reason: Jessica wanted David Connors to think well of her. "Jessica is a model student."

Lulie sniffed derisively. "You don't have to lie to us."

"I'm not lying. I—I—" Catherine searched for a possible explanation she could give the Nylans. "I'm sure most children behave much better in public than they do at home."

"Ours don't usually," Lulie said tightly.

Catherine had to agree, at least about the little ones, but she decided not to say anything. An awkward silence fell, and Catherine tried in vain to think of some way to change the subject.

"Does Jessie chase after Davy Connors?" Lulie asked at last.

"Chase?" Catherine echoed carefully, knowing she was on dangerous ground.

"What're you asking?" Nylan demanded. "You think Jessie's been doing things she shouldn't?"

"Oh, no," Lulie replied hastily. "It's just . . . she's always liked Davy, and he's the only boy her age at school. . . ."

"They're friendly, of course," Catherine offered, certain she shouldn't mention her conversation with Jessica on the subject of David Connors. "And they're both very helpful to me in managing the younger children."

"Does Jessie act like a lady when she's at school?" her father wanted to know.

"She always behaves properly," Catherine said, as

honestly as she could. Flirting wasn't exactly unlady-like, after all, and they were so young that surely a little flirting couldn't be considered improper.

"I don't like it," Nylan muttered. "Sam Connors wouldn't let his brother have any truck with Jessie, not if he knew. So where does that leave Jessie?"

Catherine breathed a sigh of relief. If Jessica's father put a stop to this "romance," she would no longer have to worry about it. "Perhaps you should point that out to Jessica," she ventured.

"So you think Jessie isn't good enough for him, either, is that it?" Lulie snapped.

"Why, no, I—I didn't mean that at all," Catherine stammered, knowing instantly she had touched a sensitive spot with Lulie. She should have been more careful, knowing how much Lulie despised Sam.

"Well, she's good enough for anyone, even Davy Connors," Lulie said, jumping to her feet and storming off into the house, much as Jessica had done.

"Oh, dear," Catherine whispered, wondering how to make amends.

"Don't worry, she'll get over it," Gus sighed. "I know you didn't mean nothing and so does she. Sometimes she just. . . . I don't know, she just don't think straight when it comes to the Connors boys."

"I've noticed," Catherine said without thinking.

"But I don't want no more trouble with Connors," Nylan went on, as if he had not heard. "He thinks it was the Taggert brothers what killed his bull, and folks are saying I put them up to it."

"I haven't heard anyone saying that!"

"Well, they are just the same, and those who aren't are thinking it. I swear to God, Miss Eaton, I fired those Taggerts the day Connors brought the coffin out

236

here to the ranch after his fence was cut the first time. I ain't seen hide nor hair of 'em since. If somebody's still paying 'em, it ain't me."

"Have you told Mr. Connors this?"

Nylan shifted uncomfortably in his chair. "We ain't exactly sociable just now."

"I'm sure if you told him, he'd believe you," Catherine promised rashly. "You could offer to help them in the search for the Taggerts."

Nylan laughed mirthlessly. "I don't expect Sam wants my help with anything."

"He needs all the help he can get right now. From what David tells me, he has half his men guarding his cattle in shifts and the other half combing the hills for the Taggerts. I saw Sam the other day, and he looks as if he hasn't slept in days."

Too late Catherine realized she had called Sam by his first name, but Nylan didn't seem to notice. "He might think it was some kind of trick. If I knew where the Taggerts was hid out, I could make sure they went off in another direction."

"I doubt Mr. Connors would let you *direct* the search," Catherine pointed out logically.

"Guess you're right," Nylan said, rubbing his chin thoughtfully.

Lulie's shadow appeared suddenly on the porch as she stepped into the lamp-lit doorway. "You ain't going to help Sam Connors. How can you after he came here to murder your children in their beds?"

Catherine's jaw dropped, and Nylan made a snarling noise. "Shut up, Lulie. You don't know what you're talking about."

"I most certainly do! He didn't know you'd sent me

and the kids away. Him and his rowdies rode up here in the middle of the night—"

"It wasn't even ten-thirty."

"—with their guns drawn, shooting at everything in sight . . . ."

"*Lulie!* For God's sake, how many times do I have to tell you: *We* was the ones fired the first shots."

"It don't matter *who* fired first! He came here to cause trouble, and he did!" she shrieked.

Catherine flinched, but no one noticed her reaction.

"Why in the hell can't you leave it alone?" Nylan rose ominously from his chair, his fists clenched again as if he would beat some sense into his wife.

Catherine's breath lodged in her chest, and she waited for what seemed endless minutes for Lulie's answer. But the answer never came. Instead, Lulie turned on her heel and disappeared into the house again.

Nylan muttered something incomprehensible and stood where he was, while Catherine let her breath out in a long sigh. The sound seemed to startle him. "Oh, God, Miss Eaton, I plumb forgot you was here. You must think we're all crazy."

"I . . . oh, no, of course not," she managed, rising slowly from her chair. "Lulie has every right to be upset. Any woman would be if her home were in danger," Catherine babbled, beginning to back toward the door. Suddenly, even Jessie's company seemed preferable. If she were lucky, the girl would already be asleep or at least pretend to be. Catherine didn't think she could stand one more confrontation over the Connors brothers tonight. "It's getting late. I'll say good night now."

He let her go without a protest, and to Catherine's great relief, Lulie seemed to have retired to her own room. Jessica hadn't bothered to leave a light on for Catherine, so she undressed in the dark and crawled into the bed, lying with her back to her companion.

The girl wasn't asleep but she did not speak, so neither did Catherine. In the dark stillness, Catherine closed her eyes and saw Sam's face, his chin lifted stubbornly. Would he really believe Mr. Nylan about the Taggerts? Then she pictured his face as it was when he was making love to her, all traces of anger and obstinacy gone, and tried to imagine him greeting Gus Nylan with the same expression. The effort made her smile.

No, if Mr. Nylan did work up the courage to face Sam, he wouldn't see a glimpse of softness in the rancher. But Sam didn't have to be soft, he only had to believe. Maybe she would speak to him about Mr. Nylan.

The thought came so naturally that for a moment Catherine didn't realize how revolutionary it was. Why did she think she would have any influence on Sam's opinions? Just because they were lovers didn't mean he would care what she thought. And why should he trust her after the way she had betrayed him to Nylan in the first place?

Catherine sighed. He shouldn't, of course, any more than she should even think of seeing Sam again. But she would, because she had no other choice. Perhaps he would listen to her for the same reason.

Catherine endured the rest of the weekend only through dogged determination. Every time Sam's name came up—and Lulie managed to work it into every conversation—Catherine simply stared at her hands and then excused herself as soon as she possibly could.

If they found her behavior odd, no one commented. After church, she gratefully accepted Twila's invitation to Sunday dinner and made her escape from the Nylans.

Twila and Catherine started walking toward her house, leaving Mathias to visit with his friends in the churchyard. "You look a little sad today, Catherine. Are you worried because Sam wasn't in church?"

Instantly, Catherine went on guard. She couldn't let people know exactly how much she cared about Sam's welfare. "Oh, no, I'm sure he's still out looking for the Taggerts. I'm just a little tired. I didn't sleep well last night."

"Did Lulie and Gus keep you up with their arguing?"

Catherine stared at her in surprise. "They didn't argue," she lied, but Twila simply rolled her eyes.

"Don't bother trying to protect them. We all know they fight like cats and dogs. It makes a body wonder how they ever got all them kids."

Catherine had wondered the same thing herself, and her face heated guiltily.

"Sorry, I didn't mean to embarrass you," Twila said with a mischievous grin, making Catherine smile in return.

"I'm not embarrassed. I was just thinking about something Mr. Nylan said. He wants Sam Connors to know he fired the Taggerts. They haven't been working for him since Sam's fence was cut the first time."

"*Sam* is it?" Twila teased, and Catherine vowed to be more careful in the future. "Well, maybe you ought to mention it to *Sam,* seeing as how Gus and him probably ain't on speaking terms at the moment."

"I thought I would," Catherine replied, ignoring Twila's knowing grin.

They were just passing the Shallcrosses' store on their way to the corner when a buckboard lumbered into view. Both women stopped by mutual if unspoken consent to see who might be coming into town on a Sunday after church was already over.

Catherine stared in growing disbelief. Surely this was someone's idea of a joke, and from the way the driver of the buckboard was grinning, he was in on it. The "team" he drove consisted of a swaybacked nag and a mule. The pair pulled not so much in tandem as in mutual distrust. They actually leaned away from each other in their harnesses, keeping as much distance as possible between them.

Their brisk pace seemed to indicate an effort to put even more distance between themselves and the rickety conveyance they pulled. The wagon clattered and shuddered at each bump, giving every indication it might break apart at any moment.

A monotonous hum rose above the racket. Catherine soon identified it as the unskilled efforts of the buckboard's second occupant to produce a tune on a harmonica. The mournful whine of the mouth organ was a perfect complement to the two men who looked more like beggars than anything else.

Now that she was used to seeing men wearing frayed jeans to church, Catherine would have thought nothing could shock her, but these men looked almost ostentatiously bedraggled in their rags and patches.

The driver brought the buckboard to a precipitous and noisy halt in front of the store, and the harmonica ceased with a plaintive squawk.

"Good morning, ladies," the driver called, lifting

his sorry hat and nodding politely. "Is this Crosswicks?"

"It certainly is," Twila said, making no effort to hide her astonishment at their appearance.

The driver turned in triumph to his companion. "See, Skeeter, I told you it was."

Skeeter grinned vacantly and shrugged at the women. "How come the store's closed?"

Twila blinked but recovered quickly. "Because it's the Sabbath."

"Is it now?" the driver said in astonishment. "I reckon we've lost track of the days."

Catherine looked up at the sound of boots hurrying along the sidewalk. Mathias Shallcross had caught sight of the new arrivals and was making his way over to them. "Welcome to Crosswicks, gentlemen," he called as he approached, eyeing the buckboard and its occupants askance. He introduced himself as the mayor and shook the men's hands.

"This here is Skeeter, and folks call me Bones," the driver informed him. Catherine couldn't help thinking the scrawny man was aptly named, being all knees and elbows, yet she also found herself questioning the evidence before her. Something about these men simply did not ring true.

"May I present my wife, and Miss Eaton, our schoolteacher." Mathias said, giving the women a wink to tell them he understood the absurdity of introducing them to two such social nonentities.

The men tipped their hats again, and Bones said, "We're right pleased to make your acquaintance."

"Were you looking for someone in particular?" Twila asked.

The two men exchanged a glance. "Nobody special," Bones replied. "We sure would be obliged if you could tell us where we could find a job, though."

"What type of work are you looking for?" Mathias asked.

"Farm work, I reckon. We can work cows, too, but we had to sell our horses and gear a while back." Cowboys were expected to provide their own saddles and at least one horse. Mathias made some suggestions about where they might go to look for jobs, and in a few minutes the men bade them farewell and drove away.

Mathias watched them go, shaking his head at the drone of the harmonica drifting behind them. "Did you ever?"

No longer able to contain herself, Twila tittered and then giggled and finally surrendered to full-fledged laughter. She caught Catherine's eye, apparently expecting to find her friend overcome with amusement, too. Instead, Catherine frowned thoughtfully as she watched the buckboard vanish from sight.

"I can't believe they're dangerous, can you, Mathias?" Twila asked, misunderstanding Catherine's concern.

"Not at all. Just a couple of harmless, simpleminded drifters," Mathias said, but Catherine disagreed.

"They aren't simpleminded. Didn't you look at their eyes?"

The Shallcrosses certainly had looked at their eyes and had found nothing remarkable.

"But didn't you think they were a little *too* ridiculous?" Catherine insisted. "And their teeth were too good."

Twila plainly thought she was making no sense. Catherine sighed in frustration.

"Men as poor and stupid as they were pretending to be don't have good teeth, but did you notice the set on that fellow Skeeter when he grinned at us?"

"The only thing I noticed was how badly he played the harmonica," Twila said, waving away the subject of the two drifters. "Come on, let's get over to the house so I can get dinner started before Mathias faints from hunger right here in the street."

Catherine followed obediently, but she couldn't resist one last, long look at the buckboard, which had shrunk and disappeared into a cloud of dust as it drove off down the road. She was certain she was right about those men. They'd let their beards grow for several days, their hair hung in greasy strings to their shoulders, and their manner bespoke a limited intelligence, but Catherine wasn't fooled.

Perhaps her training as an artist enabled her to see beyond the obvious. Her father had taught her the lines on a person's face revealed character. Stupid people spent little time in contemplation, so their faces remained smooth. The faces of the men she had just met bore the unmistakable marks of thoughtful consideration, and the blank stares could not disguise eyes that saw far more than the casual observer would suspect. They had fooled the Shallcrosses and would probably fool most everyone they met.

How could Catherine change people's perceptions of them? And why should she even try? The Shallcrosses seemed to think the men were harmless, and Catherine had no reason to believe otherwise, at least not yet. But what if they weren't? Shouldn't she warn someone? Shouldn't someone be watching them, just in case?

At least she should warn Sam. Surely he would take

her warning seriously, and if anything needed to be done, he would do it.

But Sam didn't come to her that night, and David explained to her the next day how frustrating the search had become. Sam was starting to believe the Taggerts had fled the area completely, but he didn't dare drop his guard in case that was exactly what the two gun-wielding brothers were waiting for.

Lost in her own concerns, Catherine paid little attention to what her students were doing during the lunch break. David sketched pictures of the children while they argued over who would be next. Jessica stood behind him, admiring the work over his shoulder. When Catherine called the children in at last, Jessica lingered while David collected his things.

"You've never done my picture, Davy. I'm starting to think you don't like me," she pouted.

"That's not true," he said, rising defensively to his feet, but then he saw she was only teasing him. "I'd be glad to do your picture. How about tomorrow?"

Jessica shook her head. "Not during school with all the others around. I want something real nice, something you take your time on."

She stood close to him, so close her breasts almost brushed his arm, and his breath caught. He shifted his weight just a bit, closing the small space so his sleeve and then his arm touched the pillowy softness of her.

To his surprise, she did not pull away. Instead she smiled, a slow, sensuous smile, full of promise. "We could go somewhere after school today, just you and me," she whispered.

His mouth went dry. He knew he should refuse. Sam had warned him about Jessie, after all. Instead he said, "All right, after school today."

"David? Jessica? Didn't you hear me?" Catherine called.

David jumped away guiltily and headed for the school in a lope. Jessie followed more slowly, savoring her victory.

That afternoon, after the other children had gone, David approached Catherine. "Miss Eaton? I've changed my mind about taking my lesson today. I think maybe I'd better get on home in case Sam needs me . . . that is, if you don't mind."

"Of course I don't mind. If Sam needs you, you should be home." Catherine smiled, making David feel even more guilty, but he managed to smile back. When he had helped her close the windows, he hurried out, knowing Jessie would be annoyed at having been kept waiting.

At least she'd had the good sense to wait for him down the road a ways, where Miss Eaton wouldn't see her. Davy reined up beside her.

"Would you like to ride with me or do you want me to walk?"

"I'll ride," she said, and allowed him to pull her up into the saddle behind him.

He tried not to notice the flash of bare ankle when she swung up, but he couldn't ignore the way she slipped her arms around his waist and pressed her soft, cushiony breasts into his back. She was soft everywhere. Inanely, he remembered Miss Eaton's explanation of women's body fat.

Davy flexed his hands into fists as he resisted the urge to reach around and touch her. Instead, he drew a deep breath but only succeeded in inhaling her womanly scent.

He shifted in the saddle to ease the sudden constriction in his jeans, and Jessie laughed knowingly. "Go down the road a ways. I'll tell you where to turn off."

He kicked the horse into motion, holding himself rigid in her arms, but he couldn't stop his body's reaction to her touch. At least she was behind him and couldn't see the bulge in his crotch. He figured she probably knew it was there all the same, though. The thought made him hot all over.

Jessie directed him to a quiet spot in a clump of scrubby live oaks. The shade was a welcome relief, and so was getting out of Jessie's grasp. Davy slid down and helped Jessie out of the saddle, touching her as little as possible. She laughed at his caution, but he turned abruptly away and began to unpack the sketchbook he had stuck in his saddlebag.

"Where do you want me to sit?" she asked, wandering aimlessly around.

Davy studied the possibilities and pointed to a place beneath one of the trees. "How about right there?"

Jessie cleared away the debris of sticks and stones, then sat, folding her legs beneath her and spreading her skirts. "What should I do?" she asked, clasping her hands in her lap and looking up expectantly.

"Just—just look natural," he said, finding a place nearby and sitting down with his sketchbook.

"Should I look at you or away?"

"Uh . . . away," he decided, not liking the idea of Jessie's knowing eyes upon him while he drew.

She posed as if she had been doing so all her life, and Davy wondered if she had practiced for this moment. Pushing the thought away, he began to sketch in the general outline of her head. The lines flowed easily, effortlessly. On some level, he realized her face wasn't nearly as interesting as Miss Eaton's. In fact,

247

she was rather plain except for her eyes, which could, for some inexplicable reason, scramble his reason with just a glance.

She wasn't looking at him now, though, so he had no trouble concentrating on the job at hand. Before long he was adding the finishing touches, but when he stopped, he realized he had left the bottom third of the page blank, as if he had intended the portrait to include more than just her face.

He had, of course. He wanted to include her shoulders and those enticing swells beneath her bodice. After a moment's hesitation, he continued the line of her neck and outlined her shoulder. Then he paused, feeling almost indecent but delighting in the surge of excitement his guilt caused. It was like doing the nude painting, except this time he had a real live woman— or girl—here with him. Quickly, before he lost his nerve, he sketched in the curves.

Too quickly, he realized instantly. Oh, God, he'd made them too big, or at least one of them was. He stared at it in horror for a moment, then crumpled the page in frantic disgust.

"Davy, what's wrong?"

"Nothing. I made a mistake. I'll do it over." He tucked the wadded paper beneath his thigh and prepared to start again, but his model was descending upon him.

"What did you do wrong? Let me see." She crawled over to him and reached for the discarded drawing.

Davy grabbed her hand. "No, it's terrible. Don't look at it."

"I don't believe you." She was laughing now, wrestling with him. His sketchbook slipped to the ground as he used both hands to keep her from the drawing.

She twisted and turned, sprawling across his lap and tumbling him over backward. When he fell he released her hand, and she snatched up the paper. He made a grab for it and missed, and then it was too late. She had seen.

"What . . . ?" she asked, staring at it for a moment in puzzled silence. Jessica still lay half across his body, and she straightened slowly as comprehension dawned.

She grinned, delighted. "Well, looks like you don't draw *everything* perfect."

He pulled the picture out of her unresisting hands and wadded it up viciously again. She sat back on her heels and watched. Then, still grinning, she looked down at her chest. "Or do you draw what you see? Am I really that lopsided, Davy?" she taunted.

His face felt like it was on fire. He picked up his sketchbook and righted it in his lap.

"You didn't answer my question, Davy," she insisted.

"No, you're not lopsided," he mumbled, not daring to look up. He couldn't seem to find where he'd dropped his charcoal.

"There it is," Jessie said, reaching for it.

Davy jumped as her hand darted between his legs, grazing his crotch. Smiling innocently, she pulled out the stub of charcoal and presented it to him. He took it gingerly, his breath coming in quick gasps.

"How come you couldn't draw my tits right, Davy?" she asked.

Davy gaped at her. "I—I don't . . . I can't . . ."

"You can't what?" she prompted provocatively.

He swallowed, debating whether or not to tell her the truth. She was so close that he found it difficult to

249

breathe. Why not? he thought. Why shouldn't she be as uncomfortable as he was?

"I can't draw what I've never seen." His face flamed again, but Jessie didn't seem the least bit shocked.

She leaned forward slightly, her eyes twinkling. "Would you *like* to see them?"

Davy's heart hammered its way right up into his throat. He could only nod.

Swiftly, before he even realized what she was doing, she unbuttoned her bodice and pulled it open. His breath lodged in his chest and he watched, mesmerized, as she tugged down the top of her chemise above her corset, revealing the creamy white orbs.

The sketchbook slipped unnoticed from his hands, and he drew a rasping breath.

"Do you want to touch them?"

His whole body felt like it was on fire. He nodded vigorously.

"Go ahead, then," she offered, spreading her dress wider.

He lifted his hand and suddenly realized he still held the charcoal. He dropped it hastily and wiped his blackened fingers on his pant leg, then lifted his hand again.

He saw a dozen things at once: the stark contrast of his sun-darkened flesh against the milk-white smoothness of hers, the way her nipple tightened when his fingers grazed it.

"No, like this, silly," she chided, taking his wrists and laying his palms full against her.

"Oh, God, Jessie," he groaned, closing his fingers convulsively over the yielding flesh.

"You can kiss me if you want," she whispered, lifting her face to his.

Tentatively, he touched his mouth to hers, once and then again. She released his wrists and grabbed his head, pulling it closer and opening her mouth. Soon she'd shown him exactly how to do it and they were rolling on the ground, mouths mating hungrily while his hands groped inside her bodice.

When she was assured of his cooperation, she did some groping of her own, finding the bulge between his legs and cupping it eagerly.

"Jessie!" he cried, but he could not have said if he meant the word as protest or encouragement. No one had ever touched him *there* before, and the burst of sensation sent the air rushing from his lungs. His head spun, and he croaked her name again.

Her fingers swiftly disposed of the buttons on his pants and then closed hotly around his swollen shaft.

"Have you ever done it, Davy?" she whispered.

He shook his head.

"Do you want to?"

He couldn't speak, couldn't even think. He was throbbing with need. She took her hand away and for a minute he could breathe, but then she grabbed his wrist and guided his hand up under her skirt. Her thigh was as soft as her breasts. He squeezed, and she shivered. "Oh, yes," she murmured. "Do it, Davy. Do it."

She flipped her skirt up over her hips, and Davy stared down at her, stunned. Two thoughts collided irrelevantly in his brain: She wasn't wearing any drawers, and women had hair down there the same as men.

What should he do now? he wondered frantically, having no idea how to proceed. Ignorance and need paralyzed him.

"Come on," she urged, grasping him like a handle and pulling him closer.

"I . . . wait!" he cried as her fingers tightened around him and he felt the warning surge. "No!"

But it was too late. His body convulsed in release wrenching a groan from his chest.

"Damn you, Davy Connors," she shrieked, throwing up her hands and scrambling away. "What's wrong with you? Don't you know *anything?*"

He collapsed on the ground where she had been, weak and trembling as the shudders rippled through him. After what seemed like a long time, he finally caught his breath and managed to struggle up on one elbow.

Although Jessie smiled, Davy could see she was annoyed with him.

"I . . . I'm sorry," he said, although he wasn't quite sure that was appropriate.

"Don't worry," she said with forced lightness. "We'll try again in a minute." She'd pushed her skirt back down, but her bodice still hung open, giving him tantalizing glimpses of the swelling flesh beneath. "Just as soon as you're able."

She glanced down significantly, and Davy realized he was completely exposed. Shamed, he hastily adjusted his pants, clumsily forcing the buttons into their holes.

"No need for that," she said, trying to stop him, but he shook her hands off and turned away, suddenly realizing what he had almost done. Good God, Sam had warned him about Jessie. Why hadn't he listened? Why hadn't he been more careful? What if they'd actually done it and she'd told her pa? What if she'd gotten a *baby?* Davy shuddered and jumped to his feet.

252

"We better go now," he said, snatching up his sketchbook.

"Not yet," she protested, grabbing for his hand.

He shook her off, refusing to look at her.

"What's wrong with you, Davy? I thought boys liked it. Don't you want to—"

"Shut up, Jessie. It's wicked. Don't you know what can happen?"

"What's wrong with you?" she asked angrily.

"What's wrong with *you?* The girl's the one who's supposed to say no."

"You son of a bitch!" she cried, jumping to her feet. "Are you saying I'm cheap?"

Davy looked at her now, taking in her rumpled clothes, her disheveled hair, and her flushed cheeks. She certainly didn't look like a lady, and she hadn't acted much like one a few minutes ago, either. And how had she known how to touch him and get him so excited? "Your ma'll be wondering where you are" was all he said, turning away and starting for his horse.

He heard the rustle of cloth as she did up her bodice and furiously brushed the dirt off her clothing. Davy waited by his horse, knowing he would have to give her a ride home and dreading the ordeal of feeling her arms around him again.

"Don't bother waiting for me," she snapped. "I wouldn't ride with you if you were the last boy alive."

Davy knew he should have insisted. He hated leaving a girl all alone like this, but he couldn't wait to get away. Just the sight of her made him ashamed. Stuffing the sketchbook back in his saddlebag, he swung up into the saddle and kicked his horse into motion.

"Damn you, Davy Connors," she screamed again.

"I hate you! You're not a man at all! You're just a big baby!"

He rode faster, wanting to cover his ears but not wanting her to know how much her scorn hurt him. Was she right? Was he a baby? He hadn't even known how to do it, after all. His uncovered ears burned long after he was too far away to hear her taunts.

When he got back to the ranch and turned his horse loose in the corral, one of the men told him Sam was inside taking a nap. Davy entered the house quietly, too miserable to face his brother just yet. He had almost made it to the sanctuary of his room when Sam stepped out of his own room and saw him.

"Hey, Davy, what're you doing here? I thought you'd be taking a lesson after school today."

"I . . . uh . . . I decided to come on home in case you needed me for anything," Davy said, hoping he sounded more natural than he thought he did.

"I told you not to worry about—" Sam had been coming closer, and now he stopped, eyeing Davy suspiciously. "Is something wrong?"

"No, what could be wrong?" To Davy's mortification, his voice cracked and he flushed scarlet.

"Something *is* wrong. Is it Catherine?"

Davy blinked in surprise. Why would he think Miss Eaton was involved? Then he remembered the nude painting and flushed more deeply. "No, not her."

"Who then?" he insisted. "You didn't run into any trouble on the way home, did you?"

"No, not—not exactly."

"Then what exactly?"

"Nothing! Why does something have to be wrong, for God's sake?" he protested, knowing even as he did so he was protesting too much. Now Sam was even more suspicious.

"Come here," Sam said, pulling Davy into his bedroom and closing the door. "Now, spit it out. What happened?"

"Nothing, I told you," he tried, but Sam's expression held a warning he couldn't ignore. "All right, I gave Jessie Nylan a ride home."

Sam's gaze swept over him, pausing at the grass stains on his jeans. After a moment, he reached up and brushed a leaf from Davy's shoulder. "Was a ride home the only kind of ride you gave her?"

"We didn't do anything," Davy insisted defensively. "She wanted me to draw a picture of her, so we stopped and then she—"

"She what?" Sam prompted, crossing his arms in a gesture that told Davy he was prepared to wait all day, if necessary, for the answer.

"She let me touch her—her chest and kiss her and then she—she pulled up her skirt and said I could do it . . ."

"God Almighty, Davy," Sam shouted, grabbing his brother by the shoulders. "Didn't I warn you about that girl?"

"Nothing happened!" Davy insisted, shaking loose. "At least, not what you think."

"Well, what *did* happen? Tell me the truth now."

Davy looked down, mortified at having to make such a confession to the brother he idolized. "She said—she said I could do it, but before I could, she touched me and—and—"

"It was over before it started?" Sam guessed.

Davy nodded miserably, unable to meet his brother's eye.

"Thank God," Sam breathed. Before Davy could even react, Sam's arms were around him in a bear hug. Davy couldn't remember the last time Sam had hugged him, but it felt good, even though he knew men didn't carry on like this. As if he suddenly came to his senses, Sam released him abruptly and clapped him awkwardly on the shoulder. "I guess you were kind of disappointed. Not exactly the way you thought the first time would be, was it?"

Surprised at Sam's insight, Davy shook his head.

"Well, considering the girl, you'd better be glad things happened the way they did. Otherwise, you can bet Gus Nylan'd be on our doorstep waving a shotgun."

"He'd shoot me?" Davy squawked.

"Not unless you refused to marry Jessie."

"*Marry?* We're not old enough to get married!" Suddenly, he was glad it was true.

"If you're old enough to bundle, you're old enough to marry—or at least that's what Gus would say. He'd probably be happy to get Jessie off his hands, too."

Davy muttered a curse, staggered over to his bed, and sank down on it, too overwhelmed by the implications to stand another minute.

"I tried to tell you before, but I guess I didn't make things clear enough. Girls like Jessie Nylan only got one thing on their minds. They want to land themselves a husband. You may only be a kid, but you've got half the Spur, and I guess Jessie's tired of living under her mother's thumb."

Davy stared at Sam numbly as he realized the narrowness of his escape.

"And don't forget, if a woman'll spread her legs for you, she'll do it for anybody. That ain't the kind of woman you want for a wife, now, is it?"

Davy shook his head vigorously. He wasn't even sure he wanted a wife at all, but if he did get married, it wouldn't be for a good long time yet and he sure as hell wasn't *ever* going to marry Jessie Nylan.

Sam left him to his thoughts. Outside in the hallway, he breathed a sigh of relief. Thank God Davy's inability to control himself had prevented a disaster. Briefly, he considered taking the boy out of school and thereby removing the temptation of Jessie Nylan's nubile young body. Catherine would be furious, of course, but surely she'd understand when he explained his reasons.

On the other hand, she'd also help him keep them apart if she knew the situation. Yes, that's what he'd do. He'd explain things to her and ask for her help. And, damnit, he'd do it tonight. Why should he waste another night looking for the Taggerts when any fool could see they'd vanished into thin air?

Catherine had already prepared for bed and was brushing her hair when she heard him ride up. Her stomach and heart reacted as they always did, churning and thumping in anticipation. Even as her common sense called her a fool and reminded her of her earlier vows never to see him again, she ran to the window to verify what her ears had already told her.

Was she crazy? her mind screamed at her. The man had bedded her twice and never mentioned marriage— or at least not in a serious way. He'd never said he loved her, never even hinted at any tenderness.

But he'd brought her flowers, her heart argued. And she wasn't even sure she *wanted* to marry him. Marriage was such a permanent state, and did she really want to bind herself permanently to Sam Connors? As a lover he was magnificent, but she still couldn't imagine them growing old together the way her parents had.

All she knew for certain was that she wanted to be with him *now*, tonight. Other women took lovers, women who didn't want the restrictions of marriage. Why should she deny herself the pleasure he brought her? She well knew how little pleasure life generally offered. To refuse it when it came seemed wasteful, somehow.

And Catherine was certainly strong and sophisticated enough to deal with the consequences of a love affair, whatever they might be. Having Sam Connors couldn't hurt her, she decided as she heard his footsteps approaching.

Sam paused outside, wiping damp palms on his pant legs and feeling like a hypocrite. Hadn't he warned Davy about women who surrendered their virtue before marriage? "If a woman'll spread her legs for you, she'll do it for anybody,' he'd said, but he knew it was a lie. Cat was his and only his.

He'd seen the flash of fear in her eyes when he'd come to the school last week. She was worried and rightly so. Tonight she'd demand to know his intentions; she'd probably even refuse to kiss him until things were settled between them. In spite of himself, he smiled. Her demands would be a relief, settling their relationship once and for all. The future stretched out before him, a continuous stream of glorious days brightened by Catherine's presence in his life.

Feeling more confident, he strode up to the school and knocked on her door. It opened at once, and Cat stood there in the circle of lamplight, looking like an angel in her white nightdress with her golden hair spilling over her shoulders.

Wordlessly, she stepped aside and allowed him to enter, closing the door behind him. For a moment they simply stared at each other. He tried to read her thoughts, judge her feelings, but she kept her face carefully expressionless.

She seemed small and fragile, and he ached to hold her close. "Cat?" he whispered.

He never knew who made the first move, but in the next second she was in his arms, warm and soft and vibrant. Her mouth opened beneath his and he swooped in, devouring her essence as his hands caressed her through the thin fabric of her nightdress.

Yes, yes, he thought, she wanted him as much as he wanted her. Her delicate hands clung fiercely, her body pressed his urgently. So much for his plans to settle things before taking her to bed. He had no other rational thought before he reached down, lifted her high against his chest, and carried her to the bed.

She helped him strip away his clothes and then held her arms up while he removed her nightdress. Her body was even more perfect than he remembered—the tiny pink-tipped breasts, the gentle curve of her waist, the nest of golden curls on her flat belly, the long, slender legs.

"Cat, you're so beautiful," he murmured as he lowered himself to her.

Her embrace was tentative at first, her hands cautious as they stroked his back and shoulders, but he knew how to turn her into a tigress. He nipped the sensitive cord of her neck and found the swell of her breasts. Satin-soft beneath the callused tips of his fingers, they swelled as if yearning for his touch. He captured one pebbled tip in his mouth, laving it until she moaned her pleasure.

Her fingers tightened on his shoulders, and joy welled up inside of him. Driven by the need to make her want him, he worshiped her with hands and lips, paying tribute to every part of her, her wrists and ankles and the tender curve behind her knee, until her center was a moist, molten core and she called his name in blatant need.

Only then did he surrender to his own desire, sheathing himself in her heat and warming himself with her fire. "Dear God," he murmured in awe as he sank into her and saw his own amazement in her eyes. He wanted to tell her how he felt, how wonderful she was, how much he adored her, but he could no longer speak. Instead he showed her with his body, stroking her, loving her, coaxing forth the purring sounds of her pleasure until she quivered beneath him, trembling on the brink of ecstasy. He drove into her then, his own needs forgotten as he watched her face.

Her eyes grew large and larger still. Her sweet breath rasped through parted lips, fast and faster. She called his name again, and her whole body arched as the spasms of her release shook them both. Sam cried out his own release, burying himself and his seed in a fury of abandon.

After many minutes, his breathing slowed to normal and he lifted his weight up on one elbow. "Cat?"

"Mmmm?" she replied drowsily.

"Don't go to sleep," he cautioned, giving her a little shake.

Her eyes flew open obediently, making him smile. He slid the upper half of his body off hers but kept their legs entangled. "We need to talk," he said.

She stared up at him, her blue eyes searching his as

if she could read his mind in them. "Yes, we do," she replied.

The heat of their passion seemed to cool instantly, leaving them separate again. He rolled away to lie beside her on his back, close but no longer touching. For a long minute he let the night breeze dry his damp body as he searched for the proper words.

He cleared his throat. "Cat, how come you've never married?"

Surprised by his question, Catherine studied his face, trying to understand what he was really asking. But he gave her no clue. "I suppose I never found a man I respected as much as I respected my father," she said carefully. His eyes narrowed, but she saw no other reaction and went on. "My father was an extraordinary man, a genius. My mother and I adored him, and my parents had a very special relationship. I suppose I decided if I couldn't have a marriage like theirs, I wouldn't marry at all."

She waited, but he said nothing. He lay, staring up at the ceiling for several minutes, his jaw clenched. "Why haven't *you* ever married?" she asked at last.

He laughed mirthlessly, almost bitterly. "Never had the chance. Maybe you've noticed there aren't many single women around here. The only one . . . *ones,*" he corrected, "I was interested in were already married."

Fighting an irrational surge of jealousy over the unnamed *one,* Catherine bit back her instinctive reply. She wanted to remind him *she* wasn't married, but pride forbade such a blatant hint. Besides, she'd already decided she didn't want to marry him, hadn't she? She only wished he would at least give her the satisfaction of refusing his offer.

He continued to stare up at the ceiling, then raised his hands to his face, rubbed it briskly, and pushed himself up to a sitting position. "Well," he said in an odd voice, "I reckon I'd better get going." He swung his legs over the side of the bed and reached for his pants.

"Sam, wait," she said, suddenly panicked. How could he leave when they still had so many things to say?

He turned, looking at her over his shoulder, and suddenly she felt naked, exposed. She snatched up the covers and pulled them to her breasts. "I—I thought we were going to talk."

"What do you want to talk about?" he asked stiffly.

Us, she wanted to say, but of course she didn't. She cast about for some other subject and recalled one. "The Nylans."

Sam swore. "How'd you find out already?"

"Mr. Nylan told me," she said, puzzled by his anger.

"You mean that little bitch told her father? Well, nothing happened. Davy didn't do anything to her, no matter what she said. . . ."

"What are you talking about?"

"Davy and Jessie, this afternoon. Isn't that what you meant?"

"No. What happened this afternoon?"

Sam sighed, running a hand through his hair. He shifted so he was facing her, laying his pants modestly across his lap. "Jessie asked Davy to draw her picture this afternoon, and then she got real friendly and offered to let Davy have his way."

"Oh, no!"

"Oh, yes," Sam corrected, still furious. "Luckily,

Davy . . . well, he didn't know what to do and nothing happened—at least not this time—but I don't trust the girl. She'd like nothing better than to get her claws in Davy.''

"But they're so young," Catherine protested, knowing the excuse wasn't valid. She remembered Jessie's jealousy over Catherine's friendship with Davy, and she knew Sam was right.

"They're old enough," Sam said acidly. "What I want to know is if you'll help me keep them apart. I thought about taking Davy out of school. . . ."

"Oh, please, don't do that!"

"I already decided not to, but you'll have to make sure they don't go off together when he's supposed to be with you."

"I'll do what I can," she promised, knowing she couldn't prevent Davy from doing whatever he wanted. She *could* talk to the boy, though, and she would, at the first opportunity.

"Good," Sam said. An awkward silence fell as Catherine once again became aware of the intimacy of the situation, of her own nakedness and of Sam's, of his bare chest looming above her and his heavy thigh so close she could have touched it without releasing her hold on the sheet.

The musky scent of their lovemaking drifted around them, and the very air seemed to vibrate in the stillness. Finally he said, "What did you want to tell me about the Nylans?"

"Oh!" she said, grateful for the reminder. "Mr. Nylan wants you to know he fired the Taggerts the day you brought the coffin to his house. He hasn't seen them since, and he doesn't know who they're working for now."

"You must've had quite a little talk with him," Sam said, sounding annoyed.

"I spent the weekend there," she reminded him. "He doesn't want any more trouble with you, Sam."

"No, I'm sure he doesn't." Sam turned away again and began pulling on his pants.

"He wants to help with the search," she persisted.

Sam laughed again, a bark of derision.

"Can't you at least go talk to him?"

He stood up, buttoning his pants, and whirled to face her. "I *did* go talk to him once, and this is what I got for my trouble!" He pointed to the livid red scar on his chest where the bullet had carved away a goodly chunk of flesh. Catherine winced, but she didn't give up.

"Then send him a message, have him come to you," she tried.

"What's it to you, anyway?" he asked angrily. "It's not your fight."

She bit her lip, wanting to tell him her love for him *made* it her fight, but she couldn't say such a thing. "I just . . . you don't need any more enemies. Why not make peace if you can?"

She saw she'd made a point, but he refused to acknowledge it. He reached down, snatched up his shirt, and shrugged into it. Helplessly, she watched as he finished dressing with short, angry motions.

What had gone wrong? she wondered. Why did they always end up in an argument? She already knew the answer, of course. They argued because they were too different, not suited for each other at all. This proved she shouldn't even consider marrying him.

The knowledge gave her no satisfaction, however. Instead, it formed a cold, painful lump in her chest as she watched him strap on his gunbelt. He had settled the Stetson on his head and started for the door before she found her voice.

"Sam," she called, not even certain why she had stopped him.

He turned back slowly, cautiously. "What?"

Swallowing against the dryness in her throat, she cast about for something to say to make things right again, but no magic words occurred to her. Finally she said, "Be careful."

His anger softened and for one single moment he looked infinitely sad. "Sure," he replied, and then he was gone.

The lump in her chest twisted, sending waves of wrenching agony coursing through her. Had she thought loving Sam Connors couldn't hurt her? She had been so terribly wrong.

Chapter Nine

Sam swore viciously as he rode away from the school. What in the hell was wrong with him? Why was he doomed to fall in love with the wrong woman?

He might no longer be a seventeen-year-old boy, but he wasn't the man Catherine Eaton wanted, either. No, ignorant Sam Connors didn't even come close to meeting her standards. She wanted a man who was extraordinary, a genius, for God's sake.

And what was wrong with *her?* Didn't she know he'd ruined her? Didn't she know she could be carrying his bastard child? Was the thought of marriage to him more horrible than scandal and disgrace?

Apparently so.

The pain he'd sworn never to feel again assaulted him, the agony of rejection, of being judged and found unworthy. The wind whistling in his ears became a woman's scornful laughter, echoing into the night. Catherine hadn't laughed, but then, he hadn't given her the chance. This time he'd had the good sense to protect himself, salvaging his pride if not his heart. It was small comfort.

* * *

Catherine wasn't sure whether she felt more stupid for having surrendered yet again to Sam Connors or for having decided ahead of time she was going to. How could she have been such a fool? How could she have forgotten the kind of man he was? How could she have thought herself strong enough to handle the pain of his rejection?

She began the next day with a splitting headache, which worsened the instant David arrived, thus reminding her she had promised to help Sam keep him away from Jessica. However, when the Nylan children arrived, Jessica was not among them. According to Tommy, Jessica had decided she was too old for school and wouldn't be coming back.

Catherine's gaze immediately sought David's. He looked guiltily away, but she saw the relief he could not hide. Catherine shared his relief. Still, she decided it wouldn't hurt to talk the situation over with him. Maybe she could spare him some of the same kind of pain she was experiencing.

That afternoon they began their lesson by mounting canvases, one of the more physically demanding tasks an artist must master. David's wiry strength was more than equal to the job, and Catherine stood back, admiring how tautly he stretched the fabric.

"How did Jessica's portrait turn out?" she ventured after a few minutes of watching him in silence.

His eyes widened in shock, and he flushed scarlet. "Who told you?"

Oh, dear! How could she explain the circumstances under which she came by this information? "Your brother is very concerned about you," she tried.

Fortunately, David was too mortified to wonder

267

when Sam had spoken to her. "Nothing happened, Miss Eaton. Didn't Sam tell you?"

"I believe Sam is worried about what may happen in the future."

"Nothing," David said emphatically. "Sam already warned me about girls like her, but I . . . well, I guess I forgot, but I won't forget again."

"What do you mean, Sam warned you about 'girls like her'?" Catherine asked apprehensively.

David blushed again, concentrating on tapping in a tack at exactly the right spot. "I . . . well, he said if a girl will . . . you know, with me, then she'll do it with anyone. A man doesn't want a wife like that, now, does he?"

David's earnest expression sent the heat rushing to Catherine's own cheeks. So that was what Sam thought! No wonder he hadn't made a proposal. He didn't think she was worthy of marriage. Of course, he knew he had been her first and only lover, but apparently that made no difference. Now Catherine felt doubly a fool and totally humiliated. Why, he probably thought he could come to her any time he pleased now. He probably thought she was his *mistress*.

"I'm sorry," David was saying, seeing her reaction. "I didn't mean to embarrass you."

"I'm not embarrassed, and Sam's right, of course. You're entirely too young to be thinking about marriage. You have to plan for your education first."

David's hand froze, the tack hammer raised to strike. His robin's egg eyes were bleak when they met hers. "What education do you think I'm going to get after this?" he asked, gesturing to include the one-room school.

For a moment Catherine had no answer. In Philadelphia, David's talents would have been encouraged, and he would have been given every opportunity to improve them. Even if his family did not value art, he would have been sent somewhere to improve his mind. But here things were different. Here a boy learned the skills he needed from the back of a horse, not from books. David already possessed more academic knowledge than he would ever need to manage the Spur. And of course Sam had long ago informed her he had no intention of furthering David's education.

"What would *you* like to do?" she asked the boy.

He stared at her thoughtfully, lowering the hammer and straightening from his task. "I'd like to go to the school where your father used to teach."

Oh, yes, she thought, and that would be just the beginning. Then he should go to Europe, to study with the masters. And then . . . She couldn't let her imagination go any farther. She had already raced past the possible in dreaming of David at the Pennsylvania Academy. A few months from now, David would be a full-time cowboy, browned and toughened by the sun and wind, all dreams of artistic achievement forgotten.

Except they wouldn't be forgotten, as she well knew. They would remain, stifled and frustrated, souring in his heart until he grew bitter long before he grew old. How could she let it happen?

"David, have you told Sam what you want to do?"

He shook his head, raising the hammer and assaulting the tacks again. "You know what he'd say."

"Maybe he's changed his mind. I mean, he didn't think you could learn to draw any better than you already did, but look at how much you've improved. If you told him how you feel . . ."

269

He looked up hopefully. "Maybe *you* could talk to him."

"Me?"

"Sure. He—he likes you," David said reluctantly, plainly unhappy with the idea. She knew Sam had been right when he had guessed David was jealous of his brother's attentions toward her. She only hoped David never learned the full extent of those attentions.

"I'm sure you're mistaken about Sam's feelings for me. Besides, I've already meddled enough. He's hardly likely to appreciate any more suggestions from me on how to handle you. Remember, you were the one who convinced him to let me give you lessons in the first place. If it will help, you can tell him I have friends in Philadelphia with whom you could stay, any one of several families who would watch over you like a son. He wouldn't have to worry about your being alone so far from home. And the classes aren't so very expensive. . . ."

David was shaking his head. "It won't matter. None of it matters. He doesn't want me to go away at all. The Spur is our home, it's all we've got, Miss Eaton. He wants me to love it as much as he does."

"And do you?"

David shrugged, avoiding her eyes. "It'll always be my home."

"But you love painting more, don't you?"

David drew a deep breath and let it out on a shaky sigh. "Sam could never understand."

Common sense told her he was right, but against her will, she recalled times when Sam had surprised her with his reasonableness and good judgment. Perhaps there was still hope. "David, Sam loves you very much, and he wants you to be happy. I think if he

270

knew how important this is to you, he might change his mind.''

''Are you just trying to make me feel better?''

''No, of course not! Your brother is a reasonable man, and he's kind and—'' Her throat constricted, and she could not go on. If only Sam were as perfect as she made him out to be. Fortunately, David was too lost in his own thoughts to notice her distress. When she had control of her voice again, Catherine said, ''When you're finished there we'll mix some paints.'' David nodded absently.

The next day Catherine asked David if he had spoken to Sam. The boy explained Sam had been as grouchy as a bear with a sore paw ever since Sir Herald had been killed. David was waiting until his brother was in a better mood before broaching the subject. Catherine agreed this was a good strategy.

Meanwhile, she instructed David on the methods of mixing oils and delighted in his unorthodox creations. At night she slept poorly, afraid Sam Connors might try to see her again.

And, as much as she hated to admit it, afraid he wouldn't.

She spent the weekend with the Tates now that Alice's mother had recovered from her miscarriage. They lived on a ranch not too far distant from town, so Catherine accompanied them back in for their Saturday shopping.

The main street was crowded with horses and wagons. Drivers called greetings to each other or shouted warnings to pedestrians. Catherine found herself searching the busy sidewalks for Sam's familiar figure, telling herself she only wanted to avoid him. When she failed to find him, she could not explain away the pang of disappointment she felt.

Twila waved at her when she entered the store but she was busy with a customer, so Catherine wandered down the aisle toward the rear of the cavernous building, leaving Mrs. Tate to wait at the counter until Twila was free to fill her order.

Catherine was examining some dress goods when she noticed the two strangers she had seen last Sunday come in. If anything, they looked even more disreputable than before, but Catherine could not shake the feeling they were not what they seemed. She waited, and sure enough, they finally wandered down near where she was standing.

"Good morning, gentlemen," she said, catching them by surprise. They obviously never expected a lady to address them.

They each tipped their hats and the one called Bones sketched a little bow. " 'Morning, ma'am. Miss Eaton, ain't it?"

Catherine nodded.

"We better mind our manners, Skeeter. This here's the schoolteacher," he said with mock solemnity.

Skeeter smiled his vacant grin, showing those marvelous teeth. In the confines of the store, Catherine couldn't help but notice that neither man gave off an overly offensive body odor. Apparently, they weren't as slovenly as their ragged clothes indicated.

Determined to learn what she could about them, she returned Skeeter's grin. "Where are you gentlemen from?"

"Oh, here and there," Bones said.

"Mostly there," Skeeter added. Catherine caught

the twinkle in his eyes, eyes that held the light of more intelligence than his demeanor indicated.

"Have you found a job yet?"

"Yes, ma'am. We went to the farm like Mr. Shall-cross said, and we got jobs right away. Planting was mostly over, but we'll be here for the harvest. That's when a farmer needs help most," Bones informed her.

"So I've heard," Catherine replied wryly, noticing a twinkle in his eye, too. Close up she was able to see details about them she had missed at their first meeting. Bones's lankiness did not equate to clumsiness. His awkwardness was studied, intentional. Behind Skeeter's grin lay a fine bone structure, firm chin, and high forehead, denoting character.

And underneath the straggly beards, both men were actually handsome, something they had taken great pains to conceal. In Catherine's experience, attractive, intelligent men didn't go around in rags. These men were undoubtedly trying to disguise their true selves, and Catherine had no trouble discerning why. Her only concern now was on which side these men were secretly working.

"I hope someone has warned you about the men who are cutting fences," she said pleasantly.

The two exchanged a look, a habit Catherine had observed before. Were they deciding on an answer or merely expressing their amazement at her question?

"We heard about it," Bones said, "but folks are saying the ones who done it have hightailed it out of the country."

"So they say, and I'm afraid that if more fences are cut now, people might suspect any newcomers to the area."

Skeeter's grin grew broader, and Catherine saw a

flash of admiration in his eyes. Bones chuckled outright. "Now, Miss Eaton, you wouldn't be trying to scare us, would you?"

"I have a feeling you two don't scare very easily. It would take more than a warning from a schoolteacher to run you off, wouldn't it?"

"Yes, ma'am, it would," Bones said. " 'Specially since we ain't causing nobody any trouble. We got ourselves some good jobs here. Why should we leave?"

"Why should you come here in the first place?" she countered.

For a second, Catherine glimpsed the cunning in Bones's eyes and warning prickled down her spine. If these men were working with the Taggerts, she was courting danger.

Then Bones was smiling again, all traces of concentration gone from his expression. "We come here 'cause we thought we might find work, and when the work's done, we'll be on our way again. Don't bother yourself none about us. We ain't going to get in any trouble. Come on, Skeeter, we got to see Mr. Shallcross about some supplies."

They tipped their hats again and hurried away. Catherine released her breath in a long sigh. Good heavens, she really must be losing her mind. First she carried on like a madwoman with Sam Connors, and now she was confronting men who might very well be dangerous. As Sam had pointed out to her, this wasn't even her fight. When would she learn not to meddle in other people's business?

Still, she could not resist asking her hostess if she had noticed anything peculiar about the two men with whom she had been speaking. Nadine Tate, a slender, attractive woman only a few years older than Catherine, stared after them thoughtfully.

"A hundred-dollar saddle on a forty-dollar pony," Nadine murmured.

"What?"

"Their guns," Nadine replied. "The men look like they've seen hard times but their guns are awful nice."

Catherine recalled the scarred leather of their holsters and disagreed. "Somebody probably wore those gunbelts in the war," she said, thinking they must be at least twenty years old.

"Not the gunbelts, the *guns*. Didn't you notice how new they were?"

No, she hadn't. Her trained eye had failed her for once, but perhaps that was because she still felt uncomfortable at the thought of men going armed and refrained from examining the six-shooters virtually every adult man wore. "What is odd about their wearing new guns?"

"If they can't afford decent clothes, why would they have such expensive weapons?"

Once again Catherine felt the prickle of warning. "Do you think they might be hired gunmen?"

Nadine shook her head. "Why would hired gunmen get jobs shoveling manure?"

"To disguise their identity," Catherine suggested.

"They could get jobs punching cows just as easy and keep themselves just as secret. Why swallow their pride?"

"But if they were hired by the farmers to fight the fencing, it would be most logical for them to work for a farmer, wouldn't it?"

Nadine waved away the argument. "I don't know. Maybe we're both being silly. Guns or no guns, those two fellows don't look any more dangerous than a baby. Come help me pick out some fabric. Alice needs a new dress for school.''

Catherine tried to forget the two men, but she couldn't shake the feeling of impending disaster. Last Sunday she had decided to tell Sam what she had noticed about them, but she had completely forgotten. Considering the circumstances of her last meeting with Sam, this was understandable. Now, in spite of that last meeting, she felt even more compelled to warn him, but the likelihood of having an opportunity to do so seemed quite remote.

Or at least it did until Nadine Tate took a hand. The next morning both Sam and David attended church. David greeted her warmly as she walked by with the Tate family. Sam nodded without speaking. Not wanting him to guess the way her whole body quaked at his nearness, Catherine did not meet his eye.

When the service was over, Catherine and Nadine joined a group of ladies in the yard. Catherine let the gossip drift around her, barely aware of the subjects under discussion as her nerves tuned themselves in to follow Sam's every move. Surely he wouldn't dare approach her here, not in front of all these people. And why should he approach her at all? They really had nothing more to say to each other.

Apparently, Sam agreed. He kept his distance, and after a while, Catherine began to relax. Suddenly, she realized the subject of the gossip had changed and *she* was the new topic.

''. . . all your suitors,'' Twila was saying slyly.

''What about them?'' Catherine asked, wishing she had been following the conversation more closely.

''Some of them have already managed to get Nadine

to invite them to dinner today, but not the most important one," Twila explained, still looking smug.

The other women tittered, and Catherine grew uncomfortably warm. She took solace in the assurance that Sam was not trying to continue the pretense of courtship, however. At least she would be spared that humiliation.

But only briefly. Opal gave Nadine an elbow to the ribs and pointed to draw her attention to where Nadine's husband stood talking with Sam Connors. Giving Catherine a wink, Nadine excused herself and wandered over to them.

Feeling a little faint, Catherine closed her eyes and prayed Sam would refuse to cooperate in this obvious attempt at matchmaking.

"I think we can quit looking for them Taggerts now," Al Tate was saying to Sam. "They just wanted to get even with you for shooting at them before they lit out."

Sam opened his mouth to reply, then noticed Nadine Tate coming to take possession of her husband. He touched his hat brim and wished her good morning.

" 'Morning, Sam. Nice day, ain't it?" she asked, taking her husband's arm. "Al, we'd better be going along home. We've got some guests coming for dinner. Seems Miss Eaton draws a crowd wherever she goes."

She barely glanced at Sam, but he knew the remark was for his benefit. He'd been the victim of enough matchmaking attempts in his life to recognize a hint a mile away, and he responded exactly the way she wanted him to: Jealously blazed hotly in his gut at the thought of those other men sniffing around Cat. Which of them would she take to her bed next?

Rage flooded up in him like a crimson tide, and for

a moment he didn't even hear what Nadine was saying.

". . . you and Davy'll join us for dinner." She smiled expectantly, and Sam realized he had been issued an invitation.

He knew he shouldn't go. He'd have to be crazy to subject himself to the pain of seeing her with other men and watching her pick her next lover, but he heard himself say, "Much obliged. Me and Davy'll be glad to come."

Nadine's smile grew conspiratorial. "You know, Sam, somebody'll have to bring Miss Eaton back to town this afternoon. If you came out in a buggy, you could offer to do it and spare Al the trip."

"Where would Sam get a buggy?" Al asked, obviously confused by all this plotting.

"Mathias Shallcross would lend him his, I'm sure," Nadine said confidently. "We'll see you later, Sam," she added, turning her husband and leading him away.

Sam cursed silently. He'd be a fool to borrow that buggy. Cat might well refuse to go with him. Besides, what would be the point? They could hardly exchange two words without fighting.

But if she were with him, she couldn't be with anyone else, now, could she?

Catherine couldn't believe this was happening. How could she have allowed herself to be tricked into allowing Sam Connors to take her home from the Tates?

All afternoon she had successfully avoided him, helping Nadine with the cooking and serving, finding a place at the table as far from him as she could get, and keeping David by her side as a buffer.

Just when she'd been congratulating herself on her

success, Nadine had asked if she wouldn't mind letting Sam take her home and saving Al the trouble. How could she refuse without sounding ungracious?

Consequently, she now found herself riding with Sam Connors alone, in a buggy. David was nearby, of course, riding his horse and not very happy about the arrangement. She thought again of his jealousy and felt a pang, but it was minor compared to the fury she felt at her own predicament.

She sat as far away from Sam as she could get, which wasn't far enough, she realized with dismay. Although he was being as careful as she to avoid any physical contact, his mere presence was overwhelming in the enclosed vehicle. Memories of earlier intimacies teased at her consciousness. She hugged herself tightly and kept her eyes straight ahead.

"This wasn't my idea," he said as the Tate ranch buildings receded from view.

She glanced over in surprise. "Whose idea was it, then?"

"Nadine's. She told me to borrow Mathias's buggy so I could take you home."

"You didn't have to do it," she pointed out, wondering how he could expect her to believe he didn't relish having her at a disadvantage.

"If you didn't want me to drive you home, you should have said so," he snapped, more annoyed than he had any right to be.

"How could I refuse and ask Mr. Tate to make a special trip?"

His expression reminded her he had faced the same problem. She looked quickly away, unwilling to feel any sympathy for him. She'd be safer if she could hold onto her anger.

Casting about for a neutral subject with which to fill the looming silence, she settled on his brother. "David is doing remarkably well with his painting."

"I've noticed."

"You have?" she said in renewed surprise. So far David had left all of his oils with her.

Sam shot her another annoyed glance. "I may not be a *genius,* but I can tell good work when I see it."

What on earth did he mean he wasn't a genius? Deciding not to inquire into what was obviously a sensitive subject, she asked, "When have you seen his work? Except for the nude woman, I mean."

"He's got half-a-dozen pictures in his room."

"Really? I had no idea," she cried, forgetting her inhibitions for a moment. "What is he doing?"

Sam shrugged. "Tress and scenery."

"Landscapes."

He frowned at her correction, but she hardly noticed.

"And you say they're good?"

"They look fine to me, but of course, I'm no fancy artist."

Fancy artist. The words brought back a rush of memories of their first night together. *"I'm not one of your fancy artists, but I'll make you happy,"* he had said. Of course, he hadn't said how long the happiness would last. What she couldn't understand was the bitterness behind his words. Anyone would think *he* was the one who had been used so shamefully.

But she couldn't point all this out to Sam Connors. "One needn't be an artist to appreciate art," she said tactfully, remembering David wanted to go to Philadelphia. Before he could Sam would have to be placated and convinced. "Your brother is extremely talented, talented enough to impress anyone."

His eyes narrowed, even though he didn't look at her. "You've done a good job of teaching him."

He didn't sound as if he appreciated her efforts. "I only give him a little guidance. If he could study with the men who taught me, he could learn so much more."

Sam's dark gaze turned to her suspiciously. "Why would he need to do that?"

Catherine's heart lodged in her throat. She had gone too far. Hadn't she told David she was not the proper person to discuss this with Sam? Judging from the flinty gleam in his eye, she had been right. "He wouldn't *need* to, but I'm sure he'd enjoy it," she said with forced lightness, turning away to admire the scenery, as if the matter were of little importance.

She held her breath, but Sam did not pursue the subject. She tried to think of something to distract his thoughts. After a few minutes of silence, she recalled the two strangers she had wanted to warn Sam about. She glanced over at him, trying to gauge his mood. He'd probably think she was meddling again, but why should his opinion matter anymore?

"Have you seen those two new men who're working out on Shultz's farm?"

He looked at her sharply. "What two men?"

"They call themselves Skeeter and Bones. Have you seen them?"

He studied her for a long moment. "No, I haven't."

"There's something strange about them."

"What do you mean, strange?"

"They're . . . well, they're not what they pretend to

281

be. Their clothes are ragged and they look like down-at-the-heels drifters, but they aren't.''

"What makes you think so?"

Catherine hesitated, remembering how Twila and Mathias had laughed off her observations. Sam would be even more skeptical, but she plunged ahead. ''I noticed details about them that don't fit. They seem to be poor, yet the guns they wear are expensive.''

His eyebrows lifted. ''You know a lot about guns, do you?''

Fighting a surge of irritation, she said, ''Of course not. Nadine made the observation.''

"I thought you said *you* noticed the details."

Biting back a sharp retort, she went on doggedly, ''They're teeth are too good.''

"Their teeth!" he echoed incredulously.

"Yes," she insisted. ''Men who labor for a living usually have poor teeth—broken, missing, discolored. These men have good teeth. And they're nice-looking, too. Attractive men usually take more pride in their appearance than these two do.''

Sam's expression hardened. ''I guess you noticed just about everything about them, didn't you?''

The question sounded like an accusation, so Catherine did not bother to respond. ''They pretend to be stupid, but they aren't. You can see it in their eyes. They're cunning and they're smart, and they're up to something.''

"And just what do you think they're up to?"

"I was hoping you'd know, but if they aren't working for the big ranchers, they must be working for the other side. The Taggerts were stupid and vicious, and look how much trouble they caused. These men are capable of much more, and that makes them even more dangerous.''

Sam's steady gaze was unsettling, but she refused to look away. He had to understand how serious she was. At last he responded, shaking his head in wonder. ''You're a piece of work, Catherine. Next thing you know, you'll be seeing boogies behind every bush.''

''These men aren't boogies!'' she exclaimed in frustration. ''At least meet them yourself before passing judgment.''

''I intend to.'' He turned back to driving the horse. ''I doubt I'll be as impressed as you were, though. From what I've heard . . . from other *men* . . . the worst damage these two might do is shooting themselves in the foot.''

Catherine glared at him, but her fury was wasted since he didn't deign to notice it. How dare he make fun of her? How dare he imply a man's opinion was more reliable than hers? It would serve him right if these fellows cut every foot of his fence into bite-sized pieces!

Fuming, she scrunched herself into her corner of the seat and stared off into the distance, willing the miles to pass quickly. For a long time, neither of them spoke. Just when she was beginning to regain her composure, he said, ''Cat?''

Her nerves sprang to attention, responding instinctively to the nickname that had become almost an endearment between them. Resisting her body's reaction, she hugged herself even tighter and turned to him disdainfully.

His dark eyes were guarded beneath the shadowed brim of his hat. ''Why did you tell me about those men?''

"Because I thought you might be interested in averting any more trouble before it starts."

"Why do you care?"

The question stung. Why *did* she care? What difference did it make if Sam Connors lost everything he owned? Or if he were ambushed some dark night? Pain twisted her stomach, and she bit her lip. It made all the difference in the world, but of course she couldn't say that.

"I . . . I'm concerned for the community. When you . . . when you were shot at the Nylans' house, parents were afraid to send their children to school. Heaven only knows what would happen if real violence broke out. More people would be hurt, and the children—" She looked away, unable to hold his intense gaze.

Could he see her love? Had he guessed he was the one about whom she was most concerned? Did he sense how tenuously she held her emotions in check? How humiliating it would be to have him guess her true feelings for him, feelings so strong even his cruelty couldn't kill them.

"The children?" he prodded. "That's all you care about?"

"I care about everyone in the community," she snapped. What did he want, a profession of her undying devotion to him?

Fortunately, he did not press, although she could sense his growing displeasure. The atmosphere within the confines of the buggy grew more tense with each passing minute, and Catherine greeted the sight of town with relief. Soon this ordeal would be over and she would never have to be alone with Sam Connors again.

They were approaching the schoolyard when he

turned to her and said, "Have you chosen a replacement yet?"

She blinked at the hostility of the question. "A replacement for what?"

"For me. Have you picked a new lover yet?"

Catherine gasped in outrage.

"Is that why you were mad I brought you home? Did you have other plans for the afternoon? Who were you going to meet?"

"You bastard!" she cried, remembering only too clearly what he had told David about women who let a man have his way. "For your information, I have no intention of replacing you. Unlike some people, I learn from my mistakes, and you were the biggest mistake of my life. Stop this wagon right now and let me out!"

Sam was already reining to a halt. Quickly, she gathered her skirts and sprang from the buggy. She would have run for the sanctuary of the schoolhouse, but she had only gone a few steps when she saw David was waiting for them in the yard.

He waved a greeting and sauntered over, leading his horse. She blinked away the tears of fury and managed a semblance of a smile. Behind her she heard Sam retrieving her carpetbag from the back of the buggy. If she could hold herself together for just a few more minutes, it would all be over, she told herself.

"Davy, will you take the buggy back to Mr. Shallcross?" Sam asked. "I'll bring your horse and follow in a minute."

Catherine's stomach turned over. Her apprehension must have shown on her face, because David frowned uncertainly. "I can wait for you."

"I'd like to talk to Miss Eaton alone."

David's expression hardened, and for a moment she

glimpsed the Connors stubbornness. "You talked to her the whole way out from the Tates."

Sam came up beside them, carrying the carpetbag. She didn't look at him, but she felt his presence with every fiber of her being. "We're not quite finished. We need a few more minutes."

The brothers stared at each other for what seemed a long time. David made a silent resistance, but he was no match for Sam.

"You'll be right along?" the boy asked.

"Yes," Sam replied, and David surrendered.

Catherine knew a cowardly urge to beg him not to leave her, but she resisted it, stiffening her spine. She'd prove herself a match for Sam Connors and his filthy accusations.

"See you tomorrow, Miss Eaton," David called as he hurried off to the buggy. Neither she nor Sam moved a muscle until they heard the buggy clatter into motion.

"Cat—"

"I have nothing more to say to you, Mr. Connors," she declared, whirling away. She'd only taken one step when he grabbed her arm and jerked her to a halt.

"Cat, wait—"

"Don't touch me!" She swung without thinking. The crack of flesh against flesh stunned her, and for a moment she did not realize the hand that had struck his face was hers. Then she felt the sting and saw his shock and knew the horror of it.

"Oh!" she whispered, clasping the guilty hand with the other and clutching it to her breast as if to hide it.

His black eyes flared, and for a moment she trembled with terror lest he strike her back. Fearing even to breathe, she watched the play of emotions across his face as he fought for control of his temper. Slowly, the anger drained away, leaving only a strange sadness. "I shouldn't have said what I did."

"No, you shouldn't have," she said, furious to hear her voice shake.

He drew a ragged breath. "I told you before, you make me crazy. I say things I don't mean."

"Oh, you meant it, all right. David told me what you think about women who—" The words strangled in her throat, and she stared up at him helplessly, fighting tears.

He reached for her but she flinched, so he dropped his hand, looking as helpless as she felt. "Maybe we both say things we don't mean," he tried.

"I don't!" she said bravely, lifting her chin in defiance. "I never want to see you or speak to you again." This time when she fled, he made no move to stop her.

She slammed the door behind her, leaning against it. For several minutes she stood there, panting as if she had run a mile. Then she heard the horse clopping out of the yard, and she ran to the window. Yes, he was leaving!

But instead of relief, she felt only despair. The tears she had fought began to flow now, and she lifted her hand to stifle a sob. He was an awful, horrible man. How could she still love him so much?

Sam glanced back once. He thought he saw the curtain move, but perhaps it was only wishful thinking. Why would she be watching him leave? And if she were, it was only to make sure he was gone.

He swore roundly, cursing his own stupidity, and realized he'd been doing that a lot lately. This time he'd really put his foot in it, though. He must truly be losing his mind.

Good God, what had ever possessed him to accuse her of having another lover? Hadn't he seen the way she had avoided *all* the men this afternoon, hiding behind Davy as if he were a shield? The only thing Sam couldn't figure out was what had made her so standoffish. She was acting as if he'd seduced and abandoned her, as if *she* were the one who had been rejected.

Hell, hadn't he offered for her? Hadn't he . . .

Realization came like a lightning bolt. No, he *hadn't* offered for her, not really. He'd been so sure she didn't want him that he hadn't given her a chance!

Sam reined to a halt in the middle of the street and looked at the school again. He should go back right now and confront her. What in the hell was he waiting for?

"Sam!"

The sound of a running horse brought his head around, and he saw Davy galloping toward him. The horse skidded to a halt, and Davy's blue eyes met his in challenge. "What are you and Miss Eaton fighting about?"

"That's none of your business."

"I'm making it my business. You got no right to treat her bad. What did you say to make her look so scared?"

"Scared?" Sam repeated in amazement. "She wasn't scared."

"She sure as hell was, and I want to know why. You didn't try anything, did you? If you ever laid a hand on her—"

"Whoa! Hold up there!" Sam said, lifting his hands in surrender. "I know Miss Eaton's a lady." The words echoed in his head, and he recognized his own conviction. Cat may have surrendered to him, but she'd never do such a thing lightly. There was more to it for her than simple lust, just as there had been more to it for him, too. "What makes you think she was scared of me?"

"The look on her face, the way her eyes were kind of wild. If you didn't try anything, why did she look that way? What did you say to her?"

"I—" Sam hesitated, wondering what explanation he could give. "I was . . . Catherine is a fine-looking woman, Davy. You've noticed, too. Hell, you're in love with her yourself."

Davy opened his mouth but nothing came out, and Sam saw the truth dawning on him. "You . . . you . . ." he stammered at last, "you're in love with her, too?"

Sam nodded grimly and watched despair claim his brother. "But she doesn't feel the same way," Sam said. "That's what we were fighting about. I guess I thought I could force her to, but women don't take kindly to forcing—or at least she doesn't."

Davy's despair mollified somewhat. "She don't like you then?"

"I'd say so," Sam admitted reluctantly, fearing it was an understatement. He glanced back at the schoolhouse again.

"Leave her alone," Davy warned, and Sam figured he was probably right. Better to let things calm down a little before trying to talk to her again. Besides, Davy would never let him near her again today.

Sam kicked his horse into motion. "Come on, let's get on home."

As they rode, Sam brooded over what had happened

between him and Cat, thinking back to the very beginning and replaying every conversation they had ever had.

How could he have been such an idiot? The woman had given herself to him, made love with him, made him feel pleasure he'd never dreamed existed, and he'd acted like a jackass. He'd imagined her rejection without ever giving her a chance, and then he'd been too much of a coward to risk asking her. God, no wonder she hated him! And how could he ever change her mind?

The next afternoon Catherine had David set up the easel outside so she could watch him paint. Although she had forced herself to forget most of her conversation with Sam, she did remember what he had said about David's painting.

She was dying to see the work he had done in private, but she also knew if David had *wanted* her to see it, he would have shown it to her. At the very least, he would have told her he was working at home, too, so she must assume he wanted it to be a secret.

"Sam is very impressed with the improvement in your work," she remarked, giving him an opening if he wanted to use it.

"Did you two talk about me yesterday?"

"Not very much," she assured him, seeing his concerned frown. "I just commented on how pleased I was with your progress, and he agreed. I'm afraid I did mention your going to Philadelphia—it just slipped out, I'm sorry—but I only said it was a shame you couldn't go."

David nodded absently. He laid a few brush strokes

on the canvas, then turned back to her. "You don't like Sam much, do you?"

"What do you mean?" she asked in surprise.

"I mean, do you like him or don't you?"

Like was far too neutral a word to describe any of her feelings for Sam. "We don't seem to get along very well," she allowed.

David smiled smugly. "He told me what you two were arguing about yesterday."

"He did?" Catherine asked in alarm.

"Yeah, but you don't have to worry. I think he'll leave you alone from now on. He's figured out he can't *make* you fall in love with him."

Catherine stared at him blankly. Surely, she must have misunderstood his last statement. "Make me fall in love with him?"

"Yeah, he's—"

David paused when they heard someone calling Catherine's name. Twila Shallcross was hurrying over to where they were seated beneath the willows. "Have you two heard the news?"

"What news?" Catherine asked apprehensively as she rose from her seat on the ground.

"There's been more fence cutting, the worst yet. Davy, your fences was cut, and so was Tate's and Price's and Pettigrew's. Either they've got themselves an army, or somebody didn't get any sleep last night."

"Was there a lot of damage?" David asked.

"Luckily, not much. Seems like they just wanted to hit as many ranches as possible."

"I'd better get on home." He gave Catherine an apologetic look.

"Yes, go ahead," she urged, although she realized

their very provocative conversation would not be completed now.

He gathered up the easel, and Catherine told him not to worry about the rest of the things, that she'd take them in.

Twila sighed as she watched him go. "Seems like I'm always bringing that boy bad news."

"At least no one was hurt this time." Catherine's hands trembled slightly at the thought, and she closed them into fists.

David disappeared into the school and quickly reappeared without the easel. He gave the two women a hasty wave before he mounted his pony and rode away.

Twila patted Catherine's arm. "Don't look so worried. This is really the best thing that could've happened."

"Are you serious?"

"Sure. So long as the troublemakers was laying low, nobody could do anything. Now they've started up again, they're bound to get themselves caught. Then maybe life can get back to normal."

"Normal? Catherine couldn't even remember what that felt like.

The sun hovered on the horizon by the time Sam and his men arrived at Pettigrew's ranch. Amos Pettigrew stood on the porch, his stocky figure silhouetted in the open doorway. "Get down and come in, Sam. Your men can get something to eat over at the mess house if they're hungry."

"Thanks, but Mrs. Tate fed us. Boys, rest your saddles while Pettigrew and me have a palaver."

Pettigrew's house was little more than a cabin and boasted none of the amenities of the Spur. The front room held a motley collection of crude homemade furniture, which bore the scars of countless spurs and cigarettes.

"Whiskey?" Pettigrew asked when they were inside.

"Sounds good," Sam replied, slumping wearily down into the only comfortable-looking chair in the room.

Pettigrew went to a battered sideboard and poured two generous glasses. Sam gratefully accepted one of them, taking a large swallow and savoring the soothing warmth.

"How bad did Tate and Price get hit?" Pettigrew asked, putting a chair closer to where Sam sat.

"The cutters were in a hurry, I'd guess. They cut every piece of fence between fifteen or twenty posts on each ranch. Seems like they just wanted us to know they were back."

"Then you think it was the Taggerts?"

Something in the way Pettigrew asked the question warned Sam it was more than idle curiosity. "Who else could it have been?"

"*Anyone* else," Pettigrew said too quickly. "I mean, maybe Nylan did it, or one of the farmers, or how about those two strangers who're working for Shultz? Nobody knows anything about them, and we do know we haven't been able to find hide nor hair of the Taggerts. They *must* have left the country by now."

"Maybe they came back."

Sweat had beaded on Pettigrew's forehead even though the room was comfortably cool, and Sam noticed his skin had turned an unhealthy shade of gray.

When he did not reply, Sam asked, "Amos, do you know something about all this?"

Pettigrew stiffened, already preparing a denial, but Sam could see the inner battle he waged with himself. At last his shoulders slumped in defeat. "Sam, I want you to know, I didn't have anything to do with them killing your bull. If I'd known they were planning to—''

"Are you saying the Taggerts work for you?" Sam bolted up from his chair, knocking his glass to the floor with a crash.

Pettigrew lurched to his feet, hands raised defensively. "I didn't mean for things to go this far, Sam. Please, let me explain."

Trembling with rage, Sam fought for control of his temper. "I'm listening," he said tightly.

"I . . . God," he murmured, running a hand through his thinning hair. "I can't believe I did it now, but it seemed like the right thing."

"Just spit it out," Sam snapped.

Pettigrew drew a ragged breath and sank back into his chair as if his legs could no longer hold him. Sam sat down, too, perching on the edge of his seat.

"When Gus fired the Taggerts, I hired them. I only wanted them to do one job, and then I'd let them go. I told them to cut your fence again." Pettigrew flinched at Sam's hiss of fury, then continued carefully. "I figured if you got mad, you'd help me clean out all these free-grassers once and for all."

"A real smart plan, Amos," Sam said sarcastically.

"I'm not proud of myself, especially after what happened later."

"And what was that?"

"I went to pay them off, and they told me if I didn't keep paying them, they'd cut my fence. They would've ruined me, Sam," he wailed, but Connors offered no sympathy. "I was even afraid they'd kill me if I refused, so I agreed. What else could I do?"

"Did you pay them for killing my bull?" Sam asked through gritted teeth.

"No! I never gave them another dime, not after that, I swear! I expected to hear from them, but when I didn't and you couldn't find them, I figured they'd run off."

"And now they're back."

"You don't know it was them," Pettigrew was sweating profusely now. "Why'd they come back? And they haven't contacted me. If they was around, they'd be wanting more money, wouldn't they? And why would they cut *my* fence?"

"I don't know. I'll ask them when I find them," Sam said, rising to his feet again. "I guess I'll be going now, Amos. Suddenly, I don't like the smell in here."

"Sam, I'm sorry," Amos cried, following him to the door. "I never thought—"

"Then you should have," Sam replied coldly. "You lost a good friend tonight, Amos."

"You won't tell anybody it was me, will you?" he begged. "I'll be ruined. Nobody'll ever speak to me again."

Sam didn't answer. He had no intention of spreading the ugly story, but he also felt no need to put Pettigrew's mind at ease. "Come on, boys," he called as he stepped outside. "Let's head on home."

As they rode, Black George fell in beside Sam. "Did Pettigrew have any ideas who it might've been?"

"He thinks it's somebody new, maybe those two fellows Shultz hired."

"What do you think?"

"I think I'll find those fellows and see what they have to say for themselves."

Chapter Ten

Sam rode slowly, listening to the night sounds, alert for any signal he was not alone. His horse's ears pricked, sensing something Sam had missed, and he stopped, waiting.

Up ahead a horse snuffled. "Connors?" someone said.

"Yeah, it's me."

"Come on."

Sam directed his mount toward the voice. Suddenly, a match flared and a man's face appeared. The match touched the end of a cigarette, then passed to illuminate another face and light a second cigarette.

"You boys look like you've seen hard times since we last met," Sam said, grinning.

The man called Skeeter shook the match, plunging them into darkness again.

"We thank you kindly," Bones said, amusement thick in his voice. "We worked right hard on these outfits. Had to roll a couple of bums."

"Where'd you get the wagon I've heard so much about?"

"Some farmer was about to bust it up for firewood."

"You should've let him."

"Now, Sam, don't make fun."

One of the animals made an odd noise. "Oh, God, don't tell me one of you is riding the mule."

Skeeter chuckled. "He's a good-natured son of a bitch."

"I'll just bet." The silence stretched for a few moments, and at last Sam drew a deep breath, inhaling the scent of his companion's cigarettes. "I wasn't sure you'd get my letter. It's good to see you boys again. It's been too long."

"That it has," Bones agreed. "We're glad you sent for us."

"With everybody else hiring guns, I didn't have much choice."

"No, you didn't, and I don't guess we've got any excuse not to start work now, do we?"

"No, I reckon either the Taggerts are back or somebody new is on the job."

"Any idea who it might be?"

"Pettigrew thinks you two might be the ones."

"Which means he don't have any idea."

"That's what I figure," Sam said, reaching for his own tobacco. "Although he did tell me something real interesting. Seems he hired the Taggerts after Nylan fired them. He told them to cut my fence again so I'd be mad enough to help Pettigrew."

Skeeter whistled his amazement. "Pettigrew's a damn fool, ain't he? How come him to tell you?"

"I reckon he's scared, thinking they've come back. See, when he tried to pay them off, they decided they still wanted to work for him. They threatened to cut *his* fences if he didn't keep paying."

"I reckon those two aren't as stupid as we thought," Bones said.

"They was smart enough to lay low when things got hot," Skeeter observed.

"But now they're back with a vengeance." Bones took a draw on his cigarette and the tip glowed orange in the shadows. "We'll heat things up again, see if we can't catch 'em in the act."

"Just be careful," Sam warned. "A couple people are already suspicious."

"You mean Pettigrew?"

"He was just grabbing at straws, hoping it was somebody besides the Taggerts, but the schoolteacher warned me about you the other day."

Bones laughed aloud. "Miss Eaton? What'd she say?"

Fighting an irrational surge of jealousy, Sam said, "How'd you know her name?"

"Shallcross introduced her to us when we first hit town," Skeeter said. "What'd she say?"

"She said your teeth are too good," Sam told him sourly.

"She likes my teeth?" Skeeter said in delight.

"I didn't say she *likes* them; I said she thinks they're too good. She noticed a lot of little things about you that didn't add up." Sam couldn't bring himself to say Catherine thought they were handsome. The knowledge burned in his throat, though, and made his next words slightly hoarse. "She thinks you're in disguise, and she's got you figured for hired guns."

"Well, I'll be," Bones exclaimed. "A pretty woman who's smart, too."

"Don't get any ideas about her," Sam said sharply. "She's a lady."

"Never doubted it. Seems like she's spoken for, too, wouldn't you say, Skeeter?"

"Seems like," Skeeter agreed.

"Just don't forget it," Sam said.

"If we do, I reckon I know who'll remind us." The two men chuckled knowingly, and something twisted painfully in Sam's chest. He only wished he could openly lay claim to Catherine, and he wondered what she would say if she could hear him defending her to these two ragged drifters.

"Like I said, keep your heads down. No telling who else has noticed you're not as dumb and worthless as you pretend to be. What have you got planned?"

"Sure you want to know? You'll have to act surprised when the time comes."

Sam considered for a moment. "Tell me."

When they did, Sam swore in admiration. "I knew you two would stir up the soup, but I didn't figure you'd cause a twister."

"You want this stopped, don't you?" Bones asked.

"Yeah, and I figure this is probably the only way."

The men talked for a few minutes, decided on the time and place of their next meeting, and bade each other farewell. As Sam rode away, Bones called, "Give that pretty little schoolteacher a kiss for us, eh?"

Sam laughed perfunctorily. "I'll do that."

And one day, he promised himself, he really would give Cat a kiss for Bones.

Catherine had decided she'd probably never sleep soundly again. Lately, the slightest noise woke her. She knew it was only nerves, nerves and the fear that Sam Connors would try to force his way back into her life.

The mere thought made her tremble, although she

could not have said if the tremor came from fear or longing. As much as she detested him while she was awake, he haunted her dreams, coming to her with kisses and caresses until she woke again, aching with the needs he had stirred in her.

Tonight the dreams had been particularly bad. Ever since David had made the remark about Sam wanting to force her to fall in love with him, her mind had been in constant turmoil. She hadn't had the courage to raise the subject again or to ask David what he had meant. Perhaps she had simply misunderstood him. She only wished her heart didn't flutter every time she considered the possibility he had been telling the absolute truth.

But Sam Connors didn't have a romantic bone in his body. Why would he care whether she loved him or not? He'd gotten what he wanted from her, after all. Unless . . .

She could hardly bear the thought, but common sense warned her it was probably the truth: If Sam knew she were in love with him, he'd have a power over her. Would she be able to resist that power?

Before she could decide, a loud boom sent her bolt upright in the bed. The building shook, and the lamp beside her bed clattered.

"What in the world? . . ." she wondered aloud, scrambling out of bed and snatching up her robe.

By the time she got outside, she could hear the faint sounds of the townsfolk stirring in reaction. She waited, listening for something else, something to explain the strange explosion, but in the distance all she heard was silence.

Soon Mathias Shallcross's voice called to her. "Catherine, are you all right?"

"Yes, I'm fine. What was it?"

He came hurrying toward her out of the night shadows, wearing a nightshirt hastily stuffed into pants. "Sounded like some kind of explosion. Shook the whole house."

"It shook the school, too. Where do you suppose it was?"

"Someplace nearby, although I don't see any fire. Are you sure you're all right? First thing Twila says to me is, 'Go see if Catherine is all right.' "

"I'd feel a lot better if I knew what had exploded and why." She stared blindly off into the distance again, hoping to see some sort of sign.

The sounds of activity from the town grew louder. "I reckon some of the men are going out to see what they can find. I should probably go with them. Why don't you come over to our house and keep Twila company?"

Grateful for the excuse to escape the lonely confines of her room, Catherine went inside and gathered some clothes to take with her.

By the time they reached the Shallcrosses' house, men and horses were milling in the street. "Wait for me, boys. I'll be out as soon as I get my gun."

Twila stood on the porch, wringing her hands. "I was so worried about you, dear," she said as Catherine came up the steps.

"I'm fine, just a little shocked, like everyone else."

"What a strange thing," Twila murmured, staring off into the night as Catherine had done, as if she could see through the darkness to the explanation.

They waited on the porch until Mathias reappeared, fully clothed and armed. "Be careful, darling," Twila

301

urged. Mathias patted her shoulder and then hurried away to join the others.

"They'll never be able to find anything in the dark," Twila murmured.

"I don't suppose they could just sit here waiting for morning, either, though," Catherine replied, thinking how very much she wanted to go along with them. All she could think about was Sam out there somewhere. Had he been looking for the Taggerts tonight, or was he at home, asleep? Had he simply heard the explosion, too, or had he been closer? She shivered with dread.

"You're cold," Twila observed. "Let's go inside. I'll make some hot cocoa to keep us occupied while we wait."

Catherine picked up the bundle of clothes Mathias had carried over for her and followed Twila inside.

Dawn was painting pink streaks in the sky when Sam heard the gunshots. Three in a row and then silence. Someone had found the source of the strange disturbances. He and the men with him turned their horses in the direction of the shots.

By the time they arrived at the scene of the explosion, a large crowd had already gathered. Sam slowed his horse to a walk and approached cautiously, taking in the sight of the crater and struggling against the delighted smile twitching on his lips. By the time he had dismounted and walked over to the edge of the newly turned earth, he had control of his expression again and managed to sound thoroughly outraged when he asked, "What in the hell happened here?"

Several men started to explain at once, and when

they fell silent, Mathias Shallcross said, "Looks like dynamite, wouldn't you say?"

Sam studied the gaping hole where a section of Amos Pettigrew's barbed wire fence had once stood, and he nodded. "Seems kind of strange somebody'd *blow* a hole when he could've just cut one, though."

Amos Pettigrew made a disgusted sound. "That's what I been saying." He paced up and down, glaring at the hole, his face an alarming shade of purple.

"We figure it was a booby trap . . . ," Mathias explained. "Didn't you see those contraptions hanging on the fences?"

"No, what contraptions?"

Mathias motioned for Sam to follow him, and they walked down the length of fence where it picked up at the edge of the hole. Sam spotted the odd-looking device immediately. Hanging from a strand of barbed wire several hundred feet away, it swung lazily in the wind.

"Don't get too close," Mathias warned when they had come within twenty feet.

"What is it?"

"Dynamite," Mathias explained unnecessarily. The sticks were plainly visible, bound together with wire and several pieces of wood.

"But dynamite won't explode unless it's lit," Sam pointed out.

"We figure they've got it rigged some other way, some way none of us knows about. We've seen these things all over the place today, hanging on everybody's fences. Nobody knows who put them there, or at least nobody's saying if they do."

"What're they for?"

"Probably to keep the fence cutters away," Mathias

explained patiently. "Don't you see? Nobody's gonna go tromping around in the dark cutting fences with these things hanging everywhere. If one of 'em was to go off in your face . . ." Mathias shook his head ominously.

Sam managed to hold his solemn expression in place. "What do you think set that one off?" he asked, gesturing toward the scene of the disaster.

"I hope it was a jackrabbit. If it was a man, there wasn't enough left of him to find."

Sam ran a hand over his beard stubble to hide his twitching lips. He could easily imagine Skeeter and Bones laughing uproariously as they lit the fuse last night, knowing full well the speculation and consternation their audacity would cause.

News of the booby traps reached town within a matter of hours. A weary Mathias told the tale to Twila and Catherine, who listened incredulously.

"Are you sure nobody was hurt in the explosion?" Twila asked when he had finished.

"Nobody we could find. We think it went off by accident."

"Or maybe whoever put those things out set one off just to get everyone's attention," Catherine suggested.

"That's what Sam thought, too," Mathias said, leaning back in his chair. The three of them were sitting around the table in the Shallcrosses' kitchen. Uncertainty over the source of the explosion had kept all the children at home, so Catherine had spent the morning with Twila. "At least, that's what we hope. Sam doesn't think those things'll blow up from just touching them, but nobody's willing to try out his theory."

"I should hope not," Twila said, rising to get the

coffee pot from the stove. She refilled Mathias's cup and offered Catherine some more.

Catherine shook her head. "Does anyone know who is responsible?"

"Some folks think it was the Taggerts, but I doubt they're smart enough to come up with an idea like this. Besides, we figure whoever put these things out was trying to *stop* the fence cutting."

"Where would they have gotten so much dynamite?"

Mathias shrugged. "We haven't sold any in a while at the store. It must've come in from outside."

"Maybe those two new men brought it," Catherine said, looking from Mathias to Twila and back again.

"Skeeter and Bones?" Mathias scoffed.

"They did have a wagon," Twila reminded him. "Seems like it was loaded down, too. They *could* have brought it in."

"So could anyone else who owns a wagon," Mathias pointed out. "I doubt those two would know what to do with dynamite."

"Maybe they're working for someone else," Catherine said, "someone who *does* know what to do."

"It's possible," Mathias said. "I never thought of that."

"Maybe you ought to go out and have a talk with those two fellows," Twila suggested.

"Maybe I should," Mathias muttered, "but not today. I need a little sleep before I do any more investigating." He rose and stretched, yawning hugely.

"I suppose I should be running along," Catherine said, rising also. She thanked Twila for her hospitality and took her leave.

On the way home, Catherine allowed herself a small

smile of satisfaction. At last she'd managed to convince someone those two strangers might be dangerous. At the thought, her smile vanished. She only hoped Mathias was careful when he approached them.

Catherine need not have worried. Mathias delayed his trip to the Shultzes' farm until Friday, when he carried Catherine out for the weekend. The two Shultz children, Inge and Gretchen, squeezed between them on the buggy seat, giggling at the treat of riding with their adored Miss Eaton. Their antics kept Catherine's mind off the confrontation ahead.

The Shultz farm was a prosperous-looking place, with a comfortable house and well-kept outbuildings. Mrs. Shultz greeted Catherine warmly. Most of the young matrons whom Catherine had met were either pregnant or nursing, and Heide Shultz's plump figure gave every indication there would soon be yet another Shultz baby. Her husband, as blond and blue-eyed as the females in his family, might have been her brother, so similar were they in appearance. Equally as plump as his expectant wife, Walter Shultz stood only an inch or two taller than she.

As soon as she arrived, Catherine had to meet the remaining Shultz sister, the one too young for school, so she missed Mathias's conversation with Mr. Shultz. The two men disappeared for almost an hour, during which time Catherine gave only half her attention to the children and their mother while she worried over what was happening with Mathias.

At last he returned, and to her relief, he was smiling. He drew her aside, ostensibly to bid her good-bye, and he whispered, "You don't have to worry about those two fellows. They're straight."

Before she could ask exactly what *straight* meant, Mathias was gone, calling his farewells to the Shultz family.

What on earth had he meant? Had he learned something new about them, or had they managed to fool him once again? Unfortunately, she had no opportunity to ask.

She hoped to get some feel for what Mathias had learned when she saw the two hired men at supper. When they did not join the family, Mr. Shultz explained they had already left for town to celebrate the extra day off he had given them in honor of her visit. Disappointed, Catherine allowed the Shultz children to distract her from her concerns.

The next morning Catherine and the family piled into the wagon for their weekly shopping trip. Actual purchases might be no more than a sack of coffee or candy sticks for the children. The main purpose of the trip was to see and be seen. Mr. Shultz turned the females loose at the mercantile and went off in search of his own friends. Catherine and Heide visited with the ladies gathered around a new display of dress goods and the children found their peers for a run in the alley.

"Have you heard what happened last night?" Opal Redfern asked. "Three of Sam Connors's calves were killed."

"Killed? How?" Nadine Tate asked as Catherine felt the familiar pangs of apprehension.

"Somebody cut their throats. Bull calves they was, too. Sam's men was guarding 'em special since he lost Sir Herald. Luckily, one of his men heard the ruckus before they got all of them. He's got two or three left, but this'll hurt him bad."

"I don't suppose they caught the men doing it," Catherine said.

Opal shook her head. "Sam is fit to be tied. Everybody thought those dynamite booby traps would scare the Taggerts off. They aren't cutting fences anymore, but they're still bound and determined to get even with poor Sam."

"Poor Sam?" Sam Connors's voice mocked.

Catherine jumped and her heart lodged in her throat. Slowly, she turned to face him, bracing herself for the impact he always had on her emotions. This time it was worse than usual because he was smiling, a cocky half smile that made him look like David. Catherine could barely breathe.

"You know what I meant," Opal defended herself. "It's a sin the things those devils have done to you."

"I couldn't agree more, but don't mark me down as the loser yet. This thing isn't over."

No one had ever looked less like a loser, Catherine thought, staring up at his imposing height. Relaxed and grinning, he seemed capable of overcoming any obstacle.

With studied nonchalance, he swung his dark gaze down to her, and her breath stopped completely.

"Good morning, Miss Eaton," he said softly.

Every nerve in her body sprang to attention. "Good morning," she replied through a constricted throat.

One of the other women coughed discreetly. "I guess I've got errands to run."

"So do I," someone else said. Catherine didn't bother to sort out the voices. In another moment, she and Heide Shultz were the only two women left standing with Sam.

308

"Miz Shultz, would you mind if I came by this evening and paid a call on Miss Eaton?"

"A call?" Heide echoed, sharing a conspiratorial smile with him. Catherine heard the words only faintly over the roaring in her ears. What was he up to now? "I'm sure we'd be glad to have you for supper, too. But why tonight? Aren't you going to call after church tomorrow?"

Sam's grin broadened. "Sundays with Miss Eaton are getting awful crowded. I thought I'd try to do my courting a little more privately if I could."

Courting! What in heaven's name was he talking about? What in heaven's name was he *thinking!*

"Sounds fine to me. I'm even willing to feed you supper, but maybe you'd better ask Miss Eaton first," Heide said slyly, then strolled casually away.

Sam's dark gaze touched Catherine again, and her chest tightened as if a steel band were squeezing it.

"What *does* Miss Eaton think about the idea?" he asked.

"I think you have a lot of gall!" she whispered furiously. "I told you I never wanted to see you again."

Something flickered in his eyes, something remarkably like pain. His jaw clenched with a determination she recognized. "Cat, I'm sorry for what I said the other day."

Catherine gaped at him.

"I'm not really the rotten son of a bitch you think I am," he continued doggedly. "Will you give me a chance to prove it?"

This was a dream, she knew it was. Sam Connors couldn't possibly be standing in the Shallcrosses' mercantile, apologizing and asking permission to court her.

Because this wasn't really happening and her answer wouldn't make any difference, she nodded.

His broad shoulders sagged for just an instant, as if in relief. "I'll see you tonight then," he said, and smiled.

His smile stopped the few vital functions her body was still managing to perform. His black eyes glittered, promising sweet, tender things that she knew Sam Connors did not feel, *could* not feel. He only wanted her body, didn't he?

But if he did, why hadn't he come to the school all week? And why was he making such a production out of wanting to see her in a well-chaperoned situation?

When she didn't respond, his smile faded just a bit, but he reached out and touched her arm, giving it a little squeeze. "Tonight," he said, tipped his hat, and walked away.

Sam showed up early for supper, freshly shaved and barbered and sporting what appeared to be a new shirt and string tie. He brought candy, too, but it turned out to be licorice whips for the children.

To Catherine's surprise, the girls took to him immediately, although he was a virtual stranger to them. While Catherine watched through the window, he allowed them to pester him into pushing them on their swing and giving them piggyback rides.

Over supper he was the model guest, complimenting the food and making polite conversation. Catherine watched him closely, trying to make some sense of all this, but his carefully neutral expression revealed nothing.

After the meal, the men went outside to smoke while the women cleaned up. At last Catherine had no further excuse for avoiding him, and she accompanied Heide out to the front porch.

The setting sun cast long shadows in the yard, and the scent of tobacco was heavy in the air. Walter Shultz sat on the porch swing and Sam sat on the steps. He rose when the women came out. Heide took the vacant seat beside her husband on the swing, and Catherine stood uncertainly, knowing she couldn't sit on the step beside Sam and somehow not wanting to take one of the chairs that would place her far from him, either.

"Maybe you'd like to walk off some of your supper, Miss Eaton," he said after a long moment of awkward silence.

Common sense told her she was a fool to go off alone with him, but she was also dying to know exactly what his purpose had been in coming here tonight. What better opportunity would she have? They needn't go far from the house, and surely Sam wouldn't try anything untoward with help so near at hand. Of course, he might be thinking she wouldn't resist, but if so, he would be surprised.

"All right," she said. He held out his hand to help her down the steps, but she ignored it. He fell in beside her as they started aimlessly across the yard.

Almost immediately, Catherine realized she had made a mistake. Although she knew she detested this man, his physical presence still had a profound effect on her. Her body was vitally aware of his, of the careful way he avoided even brushing her arm when all her nerves were screaming for his touch.

"That was a terrible thing they did to your calves," she said to fill the vibrating silence. The subject had come up at supper, but Sam had quickly dismissed it.

311

"Oh, please," he said just as quickly. "If you say *poor Sam*, I just might break down and cry."

"Well, it *was* a terrible thing," she insisted. "Didn't anybody put dynamite on *your* fences?"

"Not enough to scare the Taggerts, I reckon. But maybe they're the ones put it out in the first place, so naturally they wouldn't be scared."

"Why would they want to stop the fence cutting?"

"Why do they do anything?" he countered. "All those two are interested in is causing trouble. I don't imagine they care too much who gets hurt in the process."

"So long as it's you."

Sam shrugged. "They haven't been too fond of me ever since I put a bullet in one of them."

Mention of the shooting that had been one of Sam's close calls made Catherine shiver. She changed the subject. "Did you ever talk to those two men, Bones and Skeeter?"

Sam looked at her sharply. "Yes, I did."

"Well?"

"Well, what?"

Catherine sighed in frustration. "What did you think of them?"

"They're straight."

"What does *that* mean?"

"It means they didn't kill my calves."

"Did they hang up the dynamite?"

"They aren't likely to admit that to me, now, are they?"

Catherine supposed he was right, but she didn't feel inclined to say so. "Do you think they did?"

"Cat, why are you so worried about all this?"

They stopped in the shadow of the barn and looked

at each other. From here, they were out of sight of the house. The evening stillness settled around them, punctuated by the hum of insects and the plaintive calls of birds.

"I—I told you," she said. "I'm worried about the community."

Her breath caught when she saw him reach for her, but he must have seen her reaction and let his hand drop. "Damn it, aren't you a little worried about *me,* too?"

"Why should I be?" she challenged, wrapping her arms protectively around her.

He drew a ragged breath, and she saw his inner struggle reflected in his eyes as he decided how to answer her. "Because of what happened between us."

"You forced me!" she cried defensively, but he wouldn't let her get away with her lie. He grabbed her arms and shook her slightly.

"The first time, maybe, but what about the other times? I didn't force you then, did I? I even asked you to stop me, but you couldn't could you?"

She shook her head, tears of humiliation burning her eyes.

"Why, Cat? Why?"

"Stop it!" she begged. "You've already gotten what you wanted. Can't you leave me alone?"

Her words startled him and he froze, staring down at her incredulously. "Do you think all I wanted from you was a roll in the hay?"

Pride forbade her from answering, so she simply lifted her chin defiantly.

He read her expression, and his lips curved into a smile. "You're wrong, Cat," he said as his grip on her

313

arms gentled into a caress. "I want a lot more than that. I want *you,* all of you, forever."

Stunned, she did not resist when his mouth claimed hers in a kiss of fierce possession. Some distant part of her brain recalled David's words about Sam wanting to make her fall in love with him. But why?

Too numb to decide, she passively accepted Sam's kiss. When at last he broke it, he held her to his heart in a cherishing embrace. A tremor shook him, and he whispered, "God, I've missed you, Cat."

She'd missed him, too, or at least she'd missed the loving they had shared briefly. His body felt warm and strong, as if he could protect her from every evil in the world. In his arms, she could almost forget it was Sam Connors from whom she most needed protection.

Reluctantly, she recalled her suspicions about him. Perhaps he did want her to love him, but he had said nothing about loving her in return. He wanted her to think well of him, but why?

"Sam, don't," she said, pushing out of his arms.

He released her immediately, stepping back and cramming his hands into his pants pockets. Desire burned in his eyes, but he would not force her.

Feeling oddly bereft, she hugged herself again. "Sam, I—I don't understand any of this. What do you want from me?"

"I want you to feel the same way about me that I feel about you," he said boldly. "I know that might never happen, so I'll settle for just having you. I'm not a very patient man, but I can wait when I have to. I'll wait for you to change your mind about me, and in the meantime, I'll do everything I can to *make* you change your mind."

Catherine didn't know what to say. For one wild instant she considered telling him she already loved him, but she quickly rejected the idea as insane. She still didn't know exactly why he wanted her to love him. "If you think you can come to my room anytime you want—"

He shook his head vigorously. "No, Cat, we got things a little backwards before, but they're straight now. I won't come again until you ask me."

Ask him? Was that his plan? To woo her into becoming his voluntary mistress? The outrage she tried to muster foundered under the weight of her fear as she realized how weak her love for him made her. Even at this very moment, she yearned to be in his arms again. How long could she resist a concentrated assault on her emotions?

But why not simply surrender right now? Hadn't she once decided a love affair with him was the wisest course? She didn't believe a marriage between them could work, did she?

"I'm going to court you, Cat. If you've got any objections, you'd better make them right now."

She stared up at his implacable expression and felt her own helplessness. At least his ridiculous plan would give her some time to sort things out and decide on a plan of her own. "I have no objections."

He seemed relieved. He drew a long breath, let it out slowly, and said, "I reckon we'd better get back before they start wondering where we are. I don't want any gossip."

He offered his arm and she took it, not trusting her legs to function properly after the shock she had just sustained. The man who had seduced her was worried

315

about her good name! She wondered if she would ever understand him.

Sam showed up at the Shultzes again on Sunday, along with half-a-dozen other bachelors, so Catherine had no opportunity to speak with him alone. No one could mistake the way he looked at her, though, as if he already owned her. Heide remarked on it, amused at the dampening effect it was having on Catherine's other suitors.

In spite of his promise, Sam didn't stay completely away from the school. On Tuesday and again on Thursday, he stopped by just as David was finishing up his lessons. Under David's suspicious observation, she and Sam exchanged pleasantries. Sam's conduct remained exemplary, yet the look in his eyes could have burned a hole through a brick wall.

Each night Catherine lay awake until the wee hours, certain Sam would come to her and not really relieved when he did not. Then, on Friday morning, she found a package on her doorstep when she started out to the privy.

She glanced quickly around, half expecting to see him standing under the willows, but of course he wasn't there. She tore open the package and found a bouquet of roses . . . *silk* roses.

Common sense told her anyone could have left them, but she remembered the night Sam had brought her wildflowers and how ashamed he had seemed of the poor offering. It would be like him to make amends. He would have no way of knowing how she treasured those wildflowers or that she had pressed them in a book.

Where on earth had he found silk flowers? Someone must have made them for him. With a smile, she realized she would probably find out who on Sunday, if not before. Surely, none of the Crosswicks matrons would be able to keep this secret for long.

She carried the flowers inside and laid them on the table. They certainly were lovely, she thought, knowing she was foolish to be so sentimental, knowing she was playing right into his hands and not caring one bit. In his attempts to make her love him, he was making her love him more, but so long as she kept her love a secret from him, what harm could it do?

Only a few children had arrived that morning when Eli Redfern came dashing up. "Miss Eaton! Miss Eaton!"

"Slow down, Eli," she chastened, catching him as she stooped down to eye level. "What's wrong?"

"There's been a robbery. Somebody broke into the Shallcrosses' store last night."

"Who was it? Do they know?"

"Mr. Shallcross says it was the Taggerts, but nobody saw 'em, so they don't know for sure."

"Oh, dear," Catherine murmured, wondering what she should do. Her instinct was to go to Twila, but she had her students to worry about. Just then David rode into the yard. She explained the situation to him, and he readily agreed to watch the children for her.

Most of the townspeople had gathered in the street outside the mercantile. Everyone started talking at once when she arrived, explaining what had happened. Unable to make sense of the jumble, she sought Mathias and Twila, who were in the middle of the crowd.

"Twila!" she called.

Twila saw her and waved, and Catherine fought her way over. "What on earth happened? Eli Redfern said the store had been robbed."

"Somebody broke in overnight. They took some

food and a couple blankets, but mostly they took ammunition. Not even any guns. I guess they already have all the guns they can carry."

"You think it was the Taggerts?"

"Who else could it have been? Anyone else could have walked in and bought whatever they wanted."

"What will you do?"

"We've sent for Sam Connors. He's the best tracker in these parts, and Mathias found where they left a trail. If anybody can find them, Sam will."

"He's tried before without much success," Catherine reminded her. Part of her hoped Sam wouldn't find them this time, either. To do so would mean gunplay, and the thought of Sam being shot again made her weak.

To Catherine's relief, the search for the Taggerts was once again a failure. The posse rode back into town late that evening, weary and defeated. David had long since left for home, and Catherine was keeping Twila company when the men returned. Sam followed Mathias into the Shallcrosses' house.

"I invited Sam to stay for supper," Mathias explained.

"Catherine, you'll stay, too, won't you?" Twila asked, and did not wait for a reply. "We'll have something ready in no time."

The men ate silently. Sitting across from Sam in the Shallcrosses' dining room, Catherine tried unsuccessfully to resist the feelings of tenderness the sight of him stirred in her. Dusty and trail-worn and discouraged, he seemed very much in need of love. She was grateful for their chaperones, whose presence prevented her from offering him any comfort.

They hadn't quite finished their meal when they heard shouts coming from the center of town.

"What now?" Mathias muttered, rising from his chair. The four of them hurried outside and down to the main street, where once again a crowd was gathering, this time around the newly arrived stage.

"Good heavens," Twila said as they ran. "In all the excitement, I never noticed the stage was late today."

Sam and Mathias pushed their way through the crowd to the driver.

"What happened?" Mathias asked.

"Two fellows held me up. They shot the lead horse, and the whole shebang almost went over. Don't know what they was after. I wasn't carrying anything but mail and a few passengers. They had the passengers turn out their pockets, and they took my watch and then they hightailed it."

"What did the men look like?" Sam asked.

The driver and the two passengers, a cowboy and a drummer, gave descriptions that sounded very much like the Taggert brothers.

"Their faces were covered, but I'd bet money it was them all right," the cowboy said.

Sam and Mathias exchanged a look. "Feel like going for another ride tonight, Sam?" Mathias asked.

"It's almost dark. We'd best wait till morning."

Mathias nodded his agreement and instructed the other men to meet them at first light.

"There's no use in you going all the way home tonight, Sam," Mathias said. "You can stay with us." Sam nodded absently, his gaze scanning the crowd for sight of Catherine.

She was waiting for him, her stomach churning in renewed apprehension at the thought of Sam going af-

319

ter the Taggerts again tomorrow. The Shallcrosses went on ahead to their house, and Sam and Catherine followed more slowly.

"Why would they rob the stage?" Catherine asked as they walked.

"I reckon they thought they'd get some money. They aren't real smart."

"If they're so stupid, why haven't you been able to catch them?" she snapped.

"Ouch," he said, grinning sheepishly and rubbing his chest as if she'd given him a blow to the heart.

She sighed in exasperation. "I'm not trying to insult you, Sam. I'm just worried."

"About the *community?*"

Catherine bit her lip and silently debated the wisdom of telling him the truth. "No, I'm worried about you."

He stopped dead. They were in the middle of the street, in front of the Shallcrosses' house.

"Mathias!" he called, stopping his friend on the porch steps. "I'll walk Catherine over to the school."

Mathias waved his reply and went on into the house. Before he had even turned away, Sam had Catherine by the arm. He walked so fast she stumbled trying to keep up with him, and she began to regret her confession. Why was he in such a hurry? Did he think her concern meant she was willing to go to bed with him again?

The instant they reached the privacy of the far side of the school, Sam hauled her into his arms. Her name rumbled from his chest as he crushed her to him, and instinctively, she hugged him back, putting all the love she felt into the embrace. They stood, clinging, for long minutes as Catherine fought the tide of emotions swelling in her.

He sighed apologetically. "I must smell like a horse."

She shook her head against his shirtfront. He did, of course, but she didn't care.

He stroked her hair and kissed the top of her head. "Why are you so worried about me, Cat?"

She drew a shaky breath. "I don't want you to die."

He pulled away, cupping her face in his two huge hands and turning it up so he could read the expression in the fading light. The desperation in his dark eyes took her breath away. "Do you care about me just a little, Cat?"

"A little," she admitted as a tear spilled down her cheek.

He caught it with his thumb and looked at it in wonder. "You're crying."

She tried to cover her face, but he wouldn't let her. His hands tightened on her head, holding her still for his inspection. "Why are you crying, Cat?"

"I told you, I'm worried."

"I know. You don't want me to get killed."

"I don't want *anyone* to get killed," she insisted.

"Are you crying for *anyone* or are you crying for me?"

She closed her eyes and pressed her lips together against the words straining to break free. She couldn't tell him. She couldn't give him that power.

"Please, Cat, I have to know!"

Her eyes flew open, and she saw his anguish and his pain. Dear heaven, he was suffering as much as she! "For you," she whispered.

The sound he made was part groan and part laugh. He crushed her to him again, and she reveled in the thunder of his heartbeat against her ear. His hands moved over her back and shoulders with what could only be described as reverence, and he murmured her name over and over.

Never had she felt so cherished or so adored. At last she understood his compulsion to have her love him. *He loved her, too.* Perhaps he wouldn't call it that. Perhaps he thought of his feelings in terms of physical possession. Hadn't he said he wanted to have her forever? But whatever he named it, she knew how he felt because she shared the same desperate longing.

After what seemed a long time, she said, "Aren't you going to kiss me?"

He made a startled sound, but when he looked down at her, he was grinning. "I'd probably tear your skin off with these whiskers."

"Do you think I'd care?"

"Oh, Cat," he breathed, lowering his face to hers. He was infinitely careful, at least at first, touching her gently with lips and tongue, merely tasting, until she captured his head in her two hands and opened her mouth.

His whiskers were vicious, but she welcomed the pain. Wrapping her arms around his neck, she rose up on tiptoe, offering him every part of her. The kiss went on and on until they were both gasping and he finally let her go, sliding her slowly down his body until she stood on her feet again.

"I have to go," he said hoarsely. "Twila and Mathias will wonder where I am."

She smiled smugly. "I didn't ask you to stay, did I?"

He smiled back. "No, you didn't. Do you want to?"

Feigning outrage, she gave him a playful swat. He caught her hands and pulled them up around his neck again. "Maybe I can convince you to," he said, grasping her bottom and moving his hips against hers.

"Conceited man!" she cried, so full of joy she could have wept. "Maybe I can make you *beg* me!"

In the ensuing battle, Sam lost his hat and Catherine's hair came tumbling down around her shoulders. When she finally surrendered, she was pressed, helpless, between the schoolhouse wall and Sam's desire. Laughing and panting, they kissed between breaths.

"Do you . . . want me . . . to stay?" Sam gasped.

"I'll never . . . tell!" she replied coyly, squirming wantonly in a phony attempt to free herself.

At last, in self-defense, he pushed himself away, still holding her against the wall so he could regain his self-control. "You're a witch, Miss Eaton. No wonder all your students are in love with you."

"Not all of them are. I don't think Jessica Nylan cares for me at all."

"Then she's the only one. You oughta be locked away somewhere, for the good of the *community*."

"And where would you suggest locking me away?"

His eyes glittered wickedly. "Anyplace, so long as I was your only guard."

"Oh, Sam!" she cried, struggling against his hands to embrace him again, but he called upon reserves of strength and resisted the temptation.

"I have to go, Cat," he reminded her regretfully. "Mathias is liable to come looking for me."

She surrendered with a sigh, and suddenly reality came rushing back. Whether Sam loved her or not, tomorrow he was going after the Taggerts again. Tears stung her eyes. "Be careful," she said.

He straightened, dropping his hold on her. Reaching

up, he lightly stroked her cheek. "I have a reason to be now, don't I?"

She nodded, unable to speak.

Desire kindled in his eyes, but he took a step back, allowing her room to escape. "Get on inside now while I can still let you go."

Leaving him was the last thing she wanted to do, but she knew he was right. She certainly didn't want Twila or Mathias to find them in bed together, and if he stayed another minute, she was going to drag him inside herself.

She walked slowly toward the door, backward so she didn't have to tear her gaze away from him just yet. "Good night," she said when she reached the door.

"Good night," he replied.

She gave him a tentative wave.

He lifted a hand in silent salute.

"Come back to me," she said.

"I will."

Chapter Eleven

"Please, Jessie, let me do it, just this once!"

Jessica Nylan pushed the cowboy away and scrambled off the bunk. "Are you crazy? I don't want no babies!" she said, pulling her skirt down as she stood.

"You won't get a baby from just one time," he argued.

Jessica laughed scornfully. "How stupid do you think I am, Johnny Fitzpatrick?"

"Now don't get mad. Hey, where're you going?"

She had wandered over to the door of the tiny line shack where they had met for their assignation and was looking out at the line of barbed wire fence that had made shacks like this one obsolete. Before fencing, a cowboy would be stationed here for months on end, his job to ride the ranch's boundary line each day and drive back any cattle that had drifted onto the neighbor's property.

"This sure is an ugly place. Ain't nothing pretty for miles and miles," she said half to herself.

She heard Johnny rising from the bunk, but she didn't bother to look at him. He came up behind her

325

and slipped his arms around her waist. "Too bad there ain't a mirror in here. I'd show you something pretty."

In spite of herself, she smiled. Johnny had a glib tongue. He was handsome, too, with dark curly hair and a rakish mustache. Unfortunately, he was pretty worthless otherwise. Jessica had set her sights a lot higher than a thirty-a-month cowboy, especially one who worked for Sam Connors.

His hands were wandering, sliding up to cup her breasts. He nudged his erection against her buttocks coaxingly. "Come back to bed, Jess. I won't make you do nothing you don't want."

"You bet your life you won't," she said, turning in his arms. "You've got a lot of nerve, you know that, Johnny?"

"Aw, Jess, you let the other fellows do it. Why won't you let me?"

"I do *not* let the other fellows," she said angrily, pushing him away again. "Who told you a nasty lie like that?"

His surprise was almost comic. "Just some of them," he hedged. "Billy, I think. . . ."

"Billy's a damn liar! He's the *last* fellow I'd do it with. I never even let him put his hand up my dress."

"Gosh, I'm sorry, Jess. I didn't mean anything."

Jessica turned away in a huff, crossing her arms over her heaving bosom. Damn them. Damn them all.

"Jessie?" He put his hand on her shoulder, but she shook it off.

"Don't touch me, you stupid cowboy! You think I'd spread my legs for the likes of you?"

Stung, he lashed out at her. "You think you're too good for me, do you? I'd of thought you learned your lesson when Davy Connors jilted you."

"Jilted!" she screamed, whirling on him. "Who told you that?"

"Everybody says so," he informed her smugly. "You made a fool of yourself, going off to school everyday, but he's sweet on that teacher."

"Liar! Liar!" She lunged at him, but he caught her hands, grinning broadly.

"What happened, Jess? Didn't he want what you've given every other man in the county?"

"Oh, he wanted it all right," she cried, jerking free of his grip. "Or at least he claimed he did, but when he tried, he couldn't do anything, not anything at all."

Confused, Johnny stared at her for a few seconds. "You mean he couldn't . . ." Words failed him.

"Couldn't get it up, and you know why? 'Cause he don't like girls, that's why. He only likes *boys!*"

"The hell you say." Johnny backed up a step, thoroughly shocked.

"That's what *he* said. He said, 'I'm real sorry, Jessie. I figured if any girl could help me, you could, but it seems I can only get excited about other boys.' "

Johnny blanched, and Jessie smiled evilly. "And you know what else he said? He said he liked *you* best of all!"

Johnny swore and started for the door, but Jessica grabbed his arm. "Where're you going? Oh, don't tell me!" she said, feigning shock. "You like boys, too, and you're going after him right now."

"You bitch!" He grabbed her arms and shook her, but she only laughed.

"That's better," she said. "Be a man. I can't stand it when you beg."

"I'll be a man," he growled, dragging her toward the bed.

327

She put up a token struggle, but in the end she let him push her down. He threw up her skirt and rubbed himself against her urgently.

"Now, Johnny, now," she said, struggling with the buttons on his pants.

In another moment he was free, and he plowed into her viciously. She shrieked in pain, but he didn't stop. He plunged into her again and again, heedless of her cries, and just when she thought she would tear apart, he convulsed in release and was still.

"Get off! Get off!" She pushed and struggled until at last he moved, releasing her from his weight. "You bastard!"

To her horror, she was crying. What had she been thinking? Johnny Fitzpatrick, of all people! He was nothing but a poor cowboy.

"Hey, Jess, don't cry," he said in alarm, trying to draw her into his arms. "I didn't mean to hurt you, but it always hurts the first time for a girl. Next time, it'll be better."

"Next time!" she snapped, reluctantly letting him hold her. She hated him now, but if somebody didn't hold her, she was liable to fly into a million pieces. "What makes you think there'll be a next time?"

" 'Cause you like me, Jess. I know you do or else you wouldn't have let me. I know now you never let none of the others. They were all lying, but you let me, so that must mean you like me best."

What a fool she was! She tried to hold back the tears, but the next thing she knew she was sobbing against Johnny's shoulder. Totally bewildered, he wasn't much comfort, but at least he was there.

* * *

When Sam rode up to the schoolhouse that afternoon, he looked as thoroughly beaten as Catherine had ever seen him. Dust coated his clothes, and two days worth of stubble darkened his chin. Black circles shadowed his eyes and the expression in them was utterly weary.

"You didn't find them," she guessed as he swung down from the saddle. David stood beside her on the front steps, so she could only stand and watch instead of running into his arms.

He shook his head. "There's this one rocky patch where we always lose them. I keep thinking we'll be able to find the place where they come out of it, but we never do."

"Damn," David said, and then remembered Catherine's presence. "Oh, I'm sorry, Miss Eaton. I just get so mad when I think of those two varmints. . . ,"

"I know, I get mad, too," she said. "What are you going to do now?" she asked Sam.

He ran a hand over his face, and Catherine's heart ached. She wanted to take him inside and help him get a bath and lie down beside him on the bed and then . . . But none of that would happen, at least not today.

"I'm going to call a meeting," he said. "I told all the others to spread the word. Davy, I want you to go out to Shultz's farm and tell his two hired men I need to see them right away."

"Those two?" Catherine said. "Why?"

Sam's dark eyes were apologetic. "You might say they're working for me."

"*Working for you?* All that time I was warning you about them they were *working* for you?" she demanded.

"I couldn't tell anyone," Sam said. "Even Davy didn't know."

"Why couldn't you at least tell *me?*" the boy asked, even more annoyed than Catherine.

"Because their lives would've been in danger if the wrong people found out who they are."

"And what they were doing," Catherine guessed. "They made those bombs, didn't they?"

"They aren't bombs. They can't explode without a fuse. Bones set off the one that did explode, just to scare everybody."

"That's the most horrible thing I've ever . . . *David!*"

David was laughing, although he tried to control himself when he saw Catherine's disapproval. "There's no reason to get so riled, Miss Eaton. They're on *our* side."

"Perhaps they are on your and Sam's side. *I* do not have a side in all this. My only concern is—"

"—for the community," Sam finished for her, beginning to look somewhat annoyed himself. "We know. Look, I just came by to get Davy, not a lecture. Come on, kid, we've got some riding to do."

He looked so worn out and depressed that Catherine's heart instantly softened. "Sam, wait," she called when he started to mount.

David was already moving toward where his own pony grazed nearby and he stopped, watching curiously. Both Catherine and Sam stared at him until, shamefaced, he was forced to continue his quest.

Momentarily without an audience, they looked into each other's eyes. Catherine clasped her hands together to keep from reaching for him. "You look awfully tired."

"I am."

"Are you going straight home?"

330

"I have to stop at a few ranches on the way first."

"Sam, why didn't you tell me about those two men?"

He grinned unrepentantly. "Because I liked having you worry about me."

Grateful for the excuse to touch him, she gave him a token swat, which raised a small cloud of dust from his shirt.

"I'd like to take you inside and show you how much I've missed you," he whispered.

Catherine's face grew hot, and the heat spread inexorably all over her body. "You're awfully bold, Mr. Connors. Aren't you forgetting your promise?"

"Oh, I think you'd invite me in if you could."

She didn't bother to deny it, not even in fun. Surely, he could see the truth in her eyes.

"I'll be here tomorrow night for sure," he said after a moment.

David had mounted his pony and was almost upon them. "Tomorrow?" she replied breathlessly.

"Yeah, I—" his grin was sheepish, "I told everybody to meet at the school."

"Oh," she said, too disappointed to care how much her disappointment had pleased him.

This time she didn't stop him when he mounted. "We'll see you tomorrow night," he called.

She smiled sadly and returned their waves. Tomorrow seemed very far away.

Catherine and Twila claimed front row seats at the meeting. At least fifty people had gathered in the school to hear what Sam had to say. Catherine glanced over to where Skeeter and Bones stood lounging against the side wall. They no longer looked like penniless drifters.

Tonight even the most casual observer would know them for what they were.

Skeeter caught her eye and grinned, pointing to his teeth.

Catherine gasped. He knew what she had said about him! Just wait until she got Sam Connors alone again. Blushing furiously, she turned her attention back to Mathias, who was calling the meeting to order.

" 'Evening everybody. As you all know, we're here to figure out what we're going to do about the Taggerts. So far they've robbed my store and held up the stage. We've also learned that several ranches have had their supplies pilfered over the past few weeks, so we figure they're the ones responsible for that, too. Up till now we haven't been able to find out where they're hiding out. Sam here has a plan for catching them."

Mathias stepped back to make way for Sam. Catherine felt a sense of pride at the way Sam took control of the meeting. She clearly remembered another such meeting weeks ago, the one on which she had eavesdropped. That night he had encountered some resistance to his ideas. Tonight the crowd seemed more cooperative.

"You all know I've got more reason than anybody to want the Taggerts caught, and you also know how much time I've spent trying to do it. What you don't know is I've had some help."

Catherine winced, hating the thought that Sam had hired gunmen to do his dirty work.

"I told some of you I was thinking about sending for the Rangers, and that's what I did."

A murmur of surprise swelled in the room, and Catherine stared at the two strangers with new eyes.

Texas Rangers! No wonder they had seemed so competent in spite of their disguises.

"You folks know them by other names, but this here is Ted 'Skeeter' Smith and Al 'Bones' Blalock. We rode together back when Quanah Parker was still on the loose," Sam explained, naming the last great Comanche war chief.

The two Rangers gave the crowd a careless salute, and Catherine thought she would have more than a few sharp words to say to Sam when she finally did get him alone.

"First off, they want to tell you about the dynamite."

"Bones" Blalock had the grace to look embarrassed as he strode up to the front to stand beside Sam. "Those things we hung on the fences are dummies. They don't even have powder in them, so you don't have to be afraid they'll blow up. We set the explosion that went off the other night 'cause we wanted to scare whoever was cutting the fences."

"That was a terrible thing to do!" Lulie Nylan exclaimed above the crowd's roar of disapproval. "You scared folks half to death!"

"Shush, Lulie," her husband said sternly, startling Lulie back to silence.

"You're right, ma'am, it was a terrible thing to do, but cutting folks' fences ain't exactly friendly, either. You gotta remember, we didn't know but that the Taggerts were long gone and all the recent trouble was being caused by neighbors."

"He's right," Gus Nylan said, rising to his feet from where he sat near the center of the room and silencing the continued protest. "I was pretty mad myself when Sam brought these two fellows by to see me today, but

333

the main reason I was mad was because they thought *I* might've been the one cutting fences. Once I got over that, I realized they did the right thing. What we gotta remember is nobody got hurt and the Taggerts don't know them things they hung up is harmless.''

Catherine listened in amazement. Sam had certainly made Gus Nylan a convert, although she could tell by the expression on Lulie's face that she was far from convinced. Of course, Lulie would be influenced by her acute dislike for Sam.

"Thanks, Gus," Sam was saying as Nylan sat back down. "This trouble might've started with cutting fences, but it's gotten a lot more serious now. Near as we can find out, the Taggerts aren't working for anyone. They've gone renegade, and none of us is safe anymore. If we hope to stop them, we've got to work together.

"To start with, we're going to get up a reward. Mathias and I have each kicked in fifty dollars to get things started, and the rest of you are welcome to contribute whatever you can. Skeeter and Bones have some ideas on how to catch these varmints. They'll explain what they want us to do."

Catherine only half listened to the plan Bones described, in which he was going to form search parties to comb the hills in search of the Taggerts' hideout. When he had finished, he turned to her with a grin. "Miss Eaton, would you take down the names of everybody who wants to help?

Resisting the urge to tell him exactly what she thought of his high-handed methods, Catherine smiled sweetly and went in search of pencil and paper. When the meeting broke up, a line formed in front of Catherine's desk as she took down the name of virtually every man in the room and made a note of how many hands he could supply for the search efforts.

Only a few people remained in the room when the last person in line stepped up to the desk. "Sam Connors," he said.

Catherine glanced up to meet his laughing gaze. "Texas Rangers," she said in disgust. "You must've had quite a laugh at my expense."

"Oh, no, ma'am," Bones insisted, coming up beside Sam. "We was mighty flattered you thought we was dangerous outlaws. Sam here, he told us to stay away from you, though, 'cause he figured you're smart enough to figure out who we really were if you had half a chance."

"Bones," Sam warned, but his friend ignored him.

"Although, just between you, me, and the fence-post," Bones added, leaning closer, "I think he just didn't want two handsome fellows with good teeth hanging around his girl."

Totally flustered, Catherine flushed hotly. "He told you I thought you were handsome?" she blurted without thinking.

Bones blinked in surprise and shot Sam a speculative look. "Well, no, he didn't." He turned the speculation on Catherine. "Do you?"

Catherine did think he had fine bone structure, but she didn't believe it would be politic to say so. Instead, she smiled her artificial smile and handed him the list. "Here are your volunteers."

"Much obliged," he replied with a knowing grin. "Sam didn't tell me how many men he would supply, but I assume he'll give you as many as you need."

"As a matter of fact, we only need him. Since he's

335

our best tracker, we're gonna be running him ragged.''

Catherine's gaze sought Sam's, and she saw her own disappointment mirrored in his eyes. ''You'll be pretty busy, I suppose,'' she said.

He only nodded, although his eyes said much more—how sorry he was, how much he wanted to be with her, how much he *wanted* her.

Bones cleared his throat. ''Well, now, I reckon Skeeter and me'll wait outside for you, Sam.''

Only then did Catherine realize everyone else had gone. Her face grew hot again as Bones and Skeeter bid her good night. Finally, she and Sam were alone.

''Where'll you be this weekend?'' he asked.

''With the Millers,'' she said, naming a farming family. ''After tonight, I'm sure you'd be welcome for Sunday dinner. Mr. Miller promised to send all his hired men to help with the search.''

He smiled sadly. ''I doubt Bones'll give me any time off for courting. We've got some outlaws to catch.''

''Maybe you'll catch them before Sunday.''

''God, I hope so.''

Catherine tried to draw a breath and found it took a great deal of effort. Her heart seemed to have swelled in her chest and she felt an irrational urge to cry. She knew she was being silly. She should be *glad* she couldn't be with Sam. Every minute she spent with him brought her more firmly under his spell.

But he was falling under her spell, too, if the longing in his eyes was any indication.

He swallowed loudly. ''I'd like to kiss you.''

''Why don't you?'' she asked over the thundering of her heart.

336

He glanced toward the door. "They can probably see us."

"I don't care."

And she didn't. She didn't care if everyone in town saw them. If Sam Connors didn't kiss her right this minute, she would probably die.

And when he did kiss her, she was sure she would. Afterwards, he held her close, pressing his mouth worshipfully to her cheeks and forehead.

"Oh, Sam, please be careful."

"I told you before I would be."

"The Taggerts hate you. I know they'd like nothing better than to—"

"Hush. I'm not going to give them a chance. You know," he said, pulling back so he could see her face, "a man might think you were sweet on him the way you carry on."

"And a woman would be crazy to make you any more conceited then you are," she told him with the semblance of a smile.

He sighed. "If I had more time, I'd *make* you tell me how you feel."

"Oh, you would, would you?"

"Yes, I would," he promised wickedly. "And I will, just as soon as Skeeter and Bones have carted the Taggerts off to jail."

"Then you'd better get busy looking for them, hadn't you?"

"I guess I'd better," he replied regretfully.

They stared at each other for a long moment, then he bent down and kissed her, hard and fast. Before he lost control, he pulled away and started for the door. This time he was the one who walked backward so he could keep her in sight as long as possible.

When he reached the door, he paused. For an instant she thought he might come back, but then he was gone. Outside, Bones made some teasing remark, and she heard the rumble of Sam's reply. She blinked quickly, waiting, waiting, until at last the horses left the schoolyard.

Then she sank down into her chair and let the tears come. Whether she was crying over Sam's danger or her feelings for him, she didn't bother to decide.

The Taggerts proved as elusive as ever, even though they held up the stage again the following Wednesday. On Thursday, David came to school smiling as if he knew a wonderful secret. At first Catherine thought Sam had finally caught the Taggerts, but she was quickly disabused of that notion.

She had to wait until David's lesson to discover what had made him so happy. "Do you know where you're going to spend the weekend?" he asked when she insisted on an explanation.

"What does that have to do with anything?"

"You'll see. Do you know?"

"Yes," she said with exaggerated patience. "I'll be with the Stones."

"No, you won't. You'll be with us."

"Us? You mean you and Sam?"

He nodded smugly. "They've called off the search for the time being so the men can get some rest, and Sam convinced Mrs. Stone to let us take their turn."

"How did he do that?" she asked, not really caring. She and Sam would be together all weekend!

"I don't know. I think he said something about not being able to court you with so many other men around. But you don't have to worry. I won't let Sam

338

bother you, and we can spend the whole weekend painting just like we'd planned the last time.''

Catherine stared at him blankly, wondering what on earth she should say. She'd somehow forgotten David was infatuated with her, and obviously, he did not realize her feelings for Sam had changed. "Yes, that'll be fun," she managed, with a feeling of foreboding. She only hoped Sam would have a talk with David tonight and explain how things were.

The next day David rented a buggy from the livery with which to take Catherine out to the ranch. Judging from David's cheerful mood, Sam had not fulfilled her hopes. How awful to have their beautiful weekend spoiled by David's jealousy. But she couldn't blame Sam for not warning him. He loved the boy and couldn't bear to puncture his dreams any more than Catherine could.

This time Catherine saw the Spur through new eyes. Every tree, every building, every post took on a different dimension because they belonged to the man she loved.

"That's new, isn't it?" she asked as they pulled into the ranch yard, pointing to a watering trough near the front porch.

"Yeah," David said with a mischievous grin. "Remember when the Taggerts cut our fence and left a coffin?"

"Oh, yes! I'd forgotten."

David grinned proudly, as if the idea had been his. But Catherine knew whose idea it was, and she smiled at Sam's audacity.

Then she saw Sam. He stood on the porch, hands in his pockets as if he were casually awaiting an ordinary visitor. He spoiled the effect by bouncing anxiously on the balls of his feet, however, and he reached the bottom of the porch steps even before the buggy stopped.

"Whoa!" David called, reining in.

"What took you so long?" Sam demanded.

"Nothing," David replied, bewildered. "We came straight here as soon as school was out."

Catherine bit back a smile as she watched Sam restraining his eagerness. He turned to her and bowed politely. "Welcome to the Spur, Miss Eaton. May I?"

He offered his hand and Catherine took it gladly, rejoicing in his touch. Her hand wasn't nearly enough, though. The instant she moved to descend from the buggy, Sam dropped her fingers, caught her around the waist, and lifted her to the ground.

Breathless, she stared up at him for a few seconds while his hands lingered on her sides.

"Sam, you promised," David said sternly, and Sam released her at once.

"Sorry," he said unrepentantly. "You better put the buggy away. I'll take Miss Eaton inside."

Before David could refuse, Sam took her elbow and conducted her up the porch steps.

"We're going to have a problem with him," Sam whispered.

"I know. I didn't know what to tell him."

"I didn't, either. It's not like we're—" he hesitated, as if uncertain exactly what to say, "like we're engaged or anything."

Obviously, Sam wouldn't mind if they were. Catherine bit her lip, not knowing how to reply. She still did not know how she felt about marrying him. Perhaps their time together this weekend would help her decide.

Inside, Inez greeted her and asked if she wanted to freshen up before supper.

"I've been dreaming about a bath in the famous Spur bathtub ever since my last visit," she admitted.

Sam's expression said he'd like very much to join her, but he allowed Inez to spirit her away. In a few minutes, David brought her bag to her room and Catherine retired to the bathroom, where she luxuriated in Adora Connor's pride and joy.

She emerged from the bathroom a half hour later wearing a lavender lawn gown, which she had selected for its form-flattering style. She was the first to admit her figure lacked an abundance in feminine curves, but what curves she did possess were shown to best advantage in this dress.

Both David and Sam awaited her in the parlor, and to her delight, both were wearing suits. David looked achingly young with his golden hair pomaded down, and Sam looked every inch the rogue with his glittering dark eyes and raven hair. She wondered if anyone except her saw the remarkable likeness between them, but perhaps the likeness was only visible to one who loved them both.

Sam offered her sherry, which he served in a delicate crystal glass. They made small talk, acutely aware of David's presence. Sam explained that the search had been called off because their persistence had driven the Taggerts underground. Now they would have to wait for the outlaws to strike again and create a fresh trail.

Sam looked as if he'd lost weight and dark circles under his eyes revealed how tired he was, but her presence seemed to imbue him with new vitality.

At supper, which Inez served on the good china again, Sam allowed David to take the conversational

341

lead. Only Sam's eyes spoke to her, but what they said made her heart race and her nerves tingle with anticipation.

After the meal, they all adjourned to the porch while Sam smoked. When he had tossed away his cigarette, he turned to his brother with a mischievous grin. "Why don't you show Miss Eaton the pictures you have in your room."

David flushed scarlet and gave Sam an ugly look, which didn't faze the older man in the least. "You aren't ashamed of them, are you?" Sam taunted lightly.

Catherine decided to intervene, knowing how sensitive an artist could be about exposing his work to criticism. "If you'd rather not, I'll understand, although Sam tells me your work is quite good."

"He did?" David asked suspiciously. "When did you talk about it?"

"I . . . uh . . ." She glanced at Sam, trying to remember and hoping it would be a meeting of which David was aware. "Oh, yes, he told me when he drove me home from the Tates' house."

"Oh," David said, making no move to comply with Sam's suggestion.

"Show her the one with the calf in it," Sam prompted.

"That one's terrible!"

"Then show her one of the others. She's not going to bite you if she doesn't like them."

David glared at Sam, who only grinned in reply. Once again Catherine witnessed a battle of wills between the brothers, and as usual, David lost. After another moment, he rose and stomped into the house.

Catherine would have called him back if she hadn't

been dying of curiosity to see David's creations. "You shouldn't have forced him to show me the pictures," she chastened Sam.

"He would've refused if he didn't want you to see them."

"You shamed him into it. He didn't have a choice."

Sam shook his head. "He *let* me shame him into it. That kid's got tricks you never dreamed of, and he never does anything he doesn't want to do. Take my word for it. I practically raised him, and there's nothing I don't know about him."

Catherine bit her tongue, thinking there was at least one thing Sam didn't know or at least couldn't understand, and that was David's burning desire to paint.

"Come on," Sam added. "Let's go inside for the show."

Sam took her arm and led her into the house. The parlor was empty and they paused, listening for the sounds of David's arrival. Hearing nothing, they turned to each other, alone for the first time since her arrival. Catherine saw her own desires reflected in Sam's dark eyes, and in the next instant she was in his arms.

His mouth took hers in a hungry kiss. He tasted of tobacco and Sam Connors, and for a moment she simply lost herself to sensation. But only for a moment. Conscious of David's imminent return, they broke regretfully apart. Sam led her to the sofa, leaving her there with eloquent if silent regret.

When David returned carrying an armful of canvases, Sam was leaning negligently on the mantel while Catherine sat in solitary splendor nearby. A little surprised to see them there, David hesitated before setting down his burden. He was very careful to position the

343

paintings so Catherine couldn't see them. He glanced warily at her, and she gave him back what she hoped was a reassuring smile.

After some deliberation, he selected a canvas from the group and pulled it out. "I reckon this one's my favorite," he said, holding it up.

Catherine could only stare. Where on earth had David gotten this picture? Surely he couldn't have . . . But then she looked more closely. Yes, he had painted it, all right. She recognized his style. But that was all she recognized.

Unconsciously, she rose to her feet and walked closer, studying the brush strokes, the technique, the use of color. Then she stepped back again to reaffirm her initial impression of the overall effect.

Earth, sky, trees. Sam would have called it "scenery." Catherine had no words for it at all. The painting blurred, and David's voice came to her. "Miss Eaton? What's wrong? Is it really terrible?"

She shook her head, blinking furiously and willing herself not to cry. "No, of course not! It's wonderful, David. The best thing you've ever done. I—I just can't understand why you've never painted like this for me."

His cheeks reddened. "I didn't know . . . I mean, this isn't the way you taught me. I broke a lot of rules and—"

"David, the rules are made to be broken. You learn them so you have a starting place, and then you do what seems right to you."

"I was afraid you might get mad if you saw these."

"Mad?" She laughed in delight. "Show me the rest, quickly. I want to see all of them."

Sunlight glistening on water. A hawk soaring majestically. Trees turning their leaves before a storm. A barbed wire fence silhouetted against the setting sun. Each painting spoke a message too profound for words.

Only in the face of David's genius could Catherine admit her limitations as a teacher. She had taught him all the basics, but she hadn't taught him this. She hadn't even known how to explain this to him. But he had done it instinctively, breaking free of the bonds to find his own style.

He held up the last one, a cow and a nursing calf protected by a barbed wire fence. "This one is Sam's favorite, but it's not very good. I couldn't seem to get the animals right."

"I told you, you need to do some dissection," she said, absently noting how appealing the animals were even though they were not physiologically accurate. "Oh, David, I don't know what to say. You don't really need me anymore. There's nothing else I can teach you. You simply *must* go to Philadelphia. I'll write my father's old friends. When they see your work—"

"Wait a minute," Sam said sharply.

Catherine jumped, having forgotten he was there. How could she have been so careless?

"What's all this about Philadelphia?" he asked.

Her gaze met David's for an instant. He had gone pale, but she recognized the Connors determination in the set of his chin. "Miss Eaton thinks I should go to the art school there to study."

Sam's eyes narrowed dangerously. "Oh, she does, does she?"

"Yes, I do," she said, but he ignored her.

"We already talked about this, Davy," Sam reminded him. "You said you'd take lessons from Catherine until school was out, and then you'd come to work on the ranch."

"That was before I knew what it was like."

"What what was like?"

"Painting. Sam, I can't explain the way it makes me feel. I *have* to do it!"

"Nobody's trying to stop you!" Sam exclaimed in exasperation. "You can paint right here. You already do it."

"I can't study right here, though," David replied. "You heard Miss Eaton. She can't teach me anymore, and there's so much I want to learn. . . ."

"What in God's name for? What good'll it ever do you? You're a rancher, Davy. Nobody ever earned a living painting pictures."

"I don't expect to earn a living."

"Then what *do* you expect? Do you expect I'll run the Spur alone so you can go off to the big city and draw pictures of naked women?"

Catherine covered her mouth to hold back her protest. Sam really did understand David, and with his understanding came the knowledge of how to hurt him. Catherine knew perfectly well Sam wouldn't mind supporting David for the rest of his life, if necessary, so long as he was doing something of which Sam approved.

Unfortunately, David could not see through the ploy. His blue eyes blazed as he glared at his brother. "You don't know anything about it. The only thing you understand comes out of the back end of a cow!"

"David!" Catherine cried, realizing Sam wasn't the only one who knew how to hurt. "Stop it, both of you! You don't mean any of this!"

"Mind your own business, Catherine," Sam said. "If you'd done that in the first place, we wouldn't have a problem."

346

"You're probably right, but this *is* my business now. I've caused trouble between the two of you, and I—"

"Stay out of it, Miss Eaton." David's voice held a warning, which she ignored.

She went to Sam and took him by the arms. "Sam, listen, what harm can it do if David goes to Philadelphia?"

He stiffened at her touch, and when she looked into his eyes, she saw not the anger she had expected but a strange, desperate fear. "Because once he goes, he'll never come back."

She gasped at the agony in his voice. Behind her David was protesting, but neither of them listened. They stared at each other, and for one horrible moment Catherine plumbed the depths of his pain. She'd known he loved David, but not how much, not how obsessively.

It was wrong, so terribly wrong, but how could she presume to tell him so? "Sam, don't," she tried.

He shook himself slightly, as if awakening from a dream, and instantly all expression vanished from his face. He pulled free of her grasp and straightened his jacket. "Please forgive me, Miss Eaton. We've been rude to drag you into our family squabbles."

"I don't . . ." she tried, but he cut her off.

"Davy, entertain Miss Eaton. I have some business."

"Sam, wait!" she said as he headed for the door.

"Sam!" David called, but he ignored them both.

David went after him, but Catherine knew it was no use. In a few minutes David returned, looking as dejected as she had ever seen him.

"Why would he think I'd never come back? This is my home."

Catherine shook her head sympathetically, but she understood Sam's fears and knew he was probably right. Once David had been to Philadelphia, he wouldn't be satisfied until he discovered Paris. Someone with his talent would be swallowed up into the world of art, and what attraction would Crosswicks, Texas hold for him then? He would never even look back.

But surely Sam didn't think he could keep the boy with him forever, in any case. It was only natural for brothers to grow apart as they grew older, to make their own lives. True, Sam probably felt more protective of David than most brothers because of the difference in their ages and the fact that he had been a surrogate father to the boy. Even still, his attachment to David was too intense, his possessiveness abnormal.

Realizing she couldn't hope to figure it out without Sam's help, she turned her attention back to David. "I suppose Sam feels very protective of you."

David snorted in derision. "He taught me how to swim by throwing me in water over my head."

"I'll bet he stood nearby, though, just in case you didn't learn fast enough."

"He doesn't have to stand by anymore. I'm a man now."

Catherine chose not to argue.

"Was what he said true, about not being able to earn a living by painting?" he asked after a minute.

"I'm afraid so. Usually the artists who stick with it are those from wealthy families who can support them. The rest get tired of starving in garrets and eventually get a job or return home to their families."

"I don't guess it would be fair to ask Sam to support me. He hasn't said anything yet, but losing Sir Herald hurt us real bad. Things'll be tough for the next couple years."

"You needn't be a drain on Sam. You could probably find work in Philadelphia and study, too. A single man can live very cheaply."

David frowned. "Are you trying to convince me to go or convince me not to?"

"I'm not sure," she admitted with a smile. "I know how difficult it will be for you, but I also know how much you need to try."

He sank down on the sofa and buried his face in his hands. Catherine sat down beside him and laid a comforting hand on his shoulder. "You don't have to make any decisions tonight. Give Sam a chance to calm down and talk with him again, only next time try not to insult him."

David lowered his hands and grinned in spite of himself. "I was pretty rough on him, wasn't I?"

"He was rough on you first. You just can't let him get you angry. Sam truly wants you to be happy. You have to convince him going to Philadelphia is the best thing for you."

"Maybe he's right. Maybe I really shouldn't go."

Catherine sighed. "Maybe he is, but that should be your decision. And remember, you're only fifteen years old. If you don't go this year, there's still plenty of time."

"I'll be sixteen next month."

"There's *still* plenty of time," she repeated with a smile.

His answering smile was slightly sad.

"Now," she said with forced brightness, "didn't Sam say something about entertaining me? How about a game of checkers?"

David won every game easily, since Catherine's attention tended to wander as she listened for Sam's return. At last she could think of no more excuses for keeping David up and Catherine retired to her bedroom.

As she undressed, she considered how differently she had expected the evening to turn out. She had even debated whether or not she would allow Sam to seduce her. What better opportunity would they ever have for being together than in his own house? Of course, she knew she was being foolish to even consider such a thing, but somehow she couldn't stop her body from longing for it all the same.

When she lay in the big bed Sam and David's parents had each shared, she stared up at the darkness and tried not to think how glorious it would be to have Sam here beside her.

She rose early the next morning after a fitful night, but not early enough to catch Sam at breakfast. David waited for her, eager for the lesson she had promised him. When she had eaten, she suggested they take a stroll around the ranch yard in search of a good prospect.

Catherine hoped for a glimpse of Sam, but he was nowhere to be found. Instead, they encountered one of the cowboys driving a wagon into the yard.

"Hey, Johnny, what've you got in there?" David called, loping over to the wagon.

"An old cow broke her leg last night. Had to shoot her," Johnny said. He tipped his hat when Catherine approached and grinned beneath an elegant mustache, showing even white teeth. Catherine noted what a good subject he would make for a portrait.

"What will you do with the poor thing?" she asked, peering over the side of the wagon at the carcass.

"Mr. Connors said to butcher it. Reckon we'll have steak for dinner, although it'll probably be tough," he added with a flirtatious smile at Catherine.

She smiled back. "Do you suppose David and I could cut on it a little first?"

"Cut on it? What do you mean?" he asked suspiciously.

"Dissect, although I don't suppose you know what that means."

"No, ma'am, I don't."

"We want to skin it and look at the muscles and bones. David needs to know how the cow is made underneath the skin so he can draw it correctly."

Plainly, the whole idea appalled poor Johnny. "*You* want to do all that?"

"I've done it many times before, although usually with horses."

"Come on, Johnny," David urged, obviously enthusiastic over the project. "We won't hurt the meat any. You have to skin it anyways. We can do it in the barn."

"Well, I reckon, If Mr. Connors don't mind . . ."

"He won't," David said confidently. "Come on, I'll help you get it skinned."

"I think I'd better change my clothes first, and so should you," Catherine told David.

"Yeah, I guess you're right," he agreed, looking down at the natty outfit he had apparently worn to impress her. "We'll be right back," he promised Johnny, and hurried Catherine off to the house.

"I'm afraid I didn't bring any old clothes with me,"

Catherine said as they walked. "Do you have a shirt I could use?"

"Sure, and some britches, too," he said wickedly.

"A shirt will be fine," she assured him, ignoring his grin.

When Catherine arrived at the barn a short while later, David and Johnny were already stripping the hide from the carcass, a laborious job that Catherine was prepared to simply observe.

When they had finished, she instructed them to lay planks across some sawhorses to make a table of sorts, and after much grunting and groaning, they managed to drag the carcass from the wagon bed onto the table.

Johnny paused to catch his breath, dubiously eyeing the bloody mess. "You sure you want to do this?"

"We're sure, all right," David said. "Would you like to watch?"

"Not on your life," Johnny assured them, and beat a hasty retreat.

"Oh, dear, I hadn't counted on all these flies," Catherine said, brushing one away from her face. "I usually dissect inside so it isn't a problem."

"Just ignore them," David suggested, sending a slew of them droning off the carcass with a wave of his hand."

"I suppose we'll have to, won't we?" she replied gamely.

Catherine had appropriated some sharp knives from the kitchen and proceeded to give David his first lesson in dissection. At first he couldn't control his grinning delight at seeing the proper Miss Eaton elbow-deep in blood and gore, but soon his natural curiosity overcame his mirth and he was listening raptly to everything she said and even taking a hand with the knife himself.

"What the hell is going on?"

Sam's voice startled them both. They looked up to find him looming in the barn doorway, staring incredulously at them. "What are you doing?"

"I'm showing David how a cow is made so the next time he paints a picture of one it will look right."

If anything, Sam was even more appalled than Johnny had been. His expression told her they must be a sight. David looked as if he had just participated in some heathen ritual, and she supposed she looked equally bad.

"Next time I paint you a picture of a calf, you'll expect it to jump out and lick your hand," David informed him.

Apparently, the idea did not appeal to Sam at all. He came closer, moving cautiously as if afraid of being corrupted by whatever insanity had possessed them.

"In order for an artist to accurately draw a living thing, he must understand how it's made," Catherine explained, watching his caution with amusement.

"Yeah, you told me all that before. Hearing about it and seeing it are two different things, though." He eyed her bloodstained clothing with distaste. "Your father let you do this kind of thing?"

"He taught me how," she informed him.

Sam shook his head in wonder.

"Would you like to stay and watch?" she asked.

"Yeah, Sam, stay," David urged.

"No, thanks. Just cut off a couple good steaks for dinner before the flies get it all." Shaking his head again, he strode out of the barn, but Catherine noticed he didn't go far. She kept catching glimpses of him as he passed by outside and she wondered if he were trying to eavesdrop.

She continued with her lecture, but her mind was no longer on the lesson. Vitally aware of Sam's presence, she yearned for some time alone with him. She told herself she only wanted to find out if he was still upset from the scene last night, but she had to admit she wouldn't mind tasting his kiss again, either.

Outside, Sam paced around the yard, trying to think of tasks that would take him near the barn. Damn her, anyway. No matter how angry she made him, no matter how she turned his life upside down, he couldn't forget her, not for a minute.

Until last night, he'd actually begun to think they might have a future together, but now he was no longer certain. Had she only been nice to him the past few weeks because of her plans for Davy? She wanted to send him off to Philadelphia, but she couldn't do it without Sam's cooperation. What better way to make him cooperative than to play on his feelings for her? Why else would prickly Catherine Eaton suddenly turn warm and sweet and willing?

He stomped past the barn door again and allowed himself a glance inside. God Almighty, what a sight! And how could she stand the stench? She must be far more cold-blooded than he'd ever given her credit for being.

Inside the barn, David gave a shaky sigh. "You know, the idea of steak for dinner isn't real appealing anymore."

Catherine noticed he looked a little pale. "You get used to it after a while."

"Doesn't this bother you at all?"

354

"Oh, no, I . . . is it getting hot in here?" she asked, feeling suddenly warm.

"Maybe. The sun's getting high."

Catherine's vision blurred a bit and she blinked, trying to clear it. Perspiration broke out on her face. She lifted a hand to wipe it off and saw the crimson stains and clinging clumps of raw flesh. The sickly sweet stench of death roiled up, and a cloud of buzzing flies swooped onto her head. Her stomach clenched.

"Miss Eaton?" David said.

The barn tilted dangerously.

"Cat!" Sam called just as everything went black.

Chapter Twelve

David caught her as she fell, and Sam was beside them in an instant.

"What happened?"

"I think she fainted," David said, struggling with her weight.

Sam took her limp body from him, lifting her into his arms. "No wonder. The stink in here would choke a buzzard."

He was already out of the barn and heading for the house with his bloody burden.

"She was fine, really," David insisted, running along beside him. "I was the one starting to get sick, and then all of a sudden she just keeled over."

Sam looked down at Catherine's white face, and his heart constricted. If anything happened to her . . . *"Inez!"* he shouted as they approached the house. "Inez!"

She came scurrying out of a back hallway just as they entered the parlor.

"Madre de Dios!" she exclaimed, crossing herself. "Is she dead?"

Sam glanced down at Catherine again and realized how all the blood must look to poor Inez. "No, this isn't *her* blood. She and Davy were cutting up a cow, and she fainted."

"Cutting up a cow?" Inez echoed in complete bewilderment.

"I'll explain later. I think we'd better get Miss Eaton to bed."

"Not to bed!" Inez protested, looking askance at the gore. "Take her into the bathroom." Then she noticed David hovering nearby. *"Dios!* Outside with you. Go to the pump and get clean!" She shooed him out as Sam made his way down the hall to the bath.

At the door, he waited for Inez to catch up.

"Put her in the tub," Inez instructed. "I will take care of her there."

As gently as he could, Sam placed Catherine into the claw-footed tub. She moaned once, softly, and his heart wrenched again. "Cat?" he said, but she did not respond.

Inez shouldered him out of the way and knelt down beside the tub. "Did you say she was cutting up a *cow?"*

"She was teaching Davy a lesson in anatomy."

Obviously, Inez had never heard the word *anatomy* before. She muttered something under her breath and started to unbutton Catherine's shirt. Sam hurried to the other end of the tub and pulled off one of Catherine's shoes.

"Mr. Sam, what are you doing?" Inez demanded in outrage.

Sam dropped the shoe as if it had burned him. "I . . . I'm sorry, I forgot myself for a minute. I'll leave you alone now," he added, backing out of the room.

What would Inez think? What had *he* been thinking to start undressing Cat like that? He looked at her again. She seemed so small and fragile. "Will she be all right?"

"If she only fainted, yes," Inez said impatiently.

"I . . . uh . . . holler if you need anything." He closed the door very firmly behind him.

By the time he got back to the parlor, David was just coming back inside, shirtless and dripping from a drenching under the pump. "How is she?"

"Still out. Tell me exactly what happened."

"We were talking, and I said something about not being able to eat dinner today, and she asked me if it was getting hot. Next thing I knew, she was falling."

"Damn fool woman," Sam muttered.

"She told me she's done this lots of times and she never got sick before."

Sam only grunted. "Better tell Johnny to get that carcass salted down before the maggots take it over."

"Sure." David hurried out.

"Damn fool woman," Sam muttered again.

Catherine heard someone calling her name, but she didn't want to wake up, not yet. Then she heard something strange. Was it water splashing? Yes, water splashing on *her.*

She forced her eyelids open but snapped them shut again when she saw all the blood. It couldn't be! Why was she lying in a pool of blood?

"*Señorita* Eaton? Can you hear me?"

Catherine lifted one eyelid. "Inez?"

"*Sí,* you are awake?"

"Sort of." She ventured another glance and saw Inez pouring a pitcherful of water over her naked body, or more accurately, over her scarlet arms and hands, which were lying across her naked body. "What happened?"

"Mr. Sam says you and Davy were cutting up a cow," Inez explained, not bothering to conceal her contempt for such a lie. "You must have fainted."

"Oh, no!" she groaned, closing her eyes again as the whole scene came back. Then another thought occurred to her. "How did I get here?" she asked, looking around in alarm, half expecting to find Sam lurking in a corner.

"Mr. Sam carried you in."

She looked down at her nakedness again. "Like *this?*"

"No, I took your clothes off . . . *after* he left." Inez gave her a knowing smile. "Would you like me to run some water for a bath now? I have cleaned off most of the blood, and if you can get out, I will scrub out the tub."

"Of course," Catherine said, attempting to rise.

She found the effort more difficult than she had expected, however, and she needed Inez's assistance to get to a nearby chair. Inez wrapped her in a towel and left her there to begin cleaning the tub.

"I can't imagine what happened," Catherine murmured. "I've done dozens of dissections and I've *never* fainted."

Inez paused in her scrubbing and shot Catherine another knowing look. "When a woman carries a child, she will often faint."

Still woozy, Catherine could only stare stupidly. What on earth did she mean? Catherine wasn't carrying a child.

Or was she?

"Inez, what did you mean?" she asked.

This time Inez didn't even look up. "I think you must be careful now that you carry Mr. Sam's baby, or you will faint all the time."

As one in a daze, Catherine watched Inez finish cleaning the tub, run her a bath, and fetch her clean clothes. It couldn't be true, she told herself over and over. Surely she would have known. Surely she would have sensed the changes in her body.

But of course she *had* sensed the changes. She had simply ignored them, unable or unwilling to accept what they meant. How long since she had last menstruated? Not since her first night with Sam, certainly. Had she felt queasy in the mornings? Yes, and she had blamed it on nerves and worry over Sam.

When Inez left to get her clean clothes, Catherine opened the towel and looked at her body with new eyes. Still she saw no change, nothing to indicate the momentous secret Inez had guessed. How could she have known?

By the time Inez returned, the tub was full. Inez shut off the water and came to help Catherine into it. Catherine accepted her ministrations without protest, and when she was settled comfortably in the warm water, she ventured the question. "Inez, what makes you think? . . ."

Inez smiled conspiratorially. "A woman's body changes, here and here." She pointed, and Catherine blushed. "My mother is a midwife, so I know these things. When Mr. Sam started to help me undress you, I think to myself, 'This is something a husband would do, something my Patrick would do for me, not something a man would do for a woman he hardly knows.' It was not hard to guess who your man is."

"You didn't tell him, did you?" Catherine asked in alarm.

She shrugged. "I thought he might know already, and Mr. Sam does not like others to know his secrets."

Catherine had noticed this character trait, but she made no comment.

"You will have to tell him," Inez said. "Tongues will wag when the baby comes early, so you must be married as soon as possible."

"Yes, you're right," she agreed hastily. "But in the meantime, promise me you won't say anything to him."

Inez looked offended. "It is not my place."

"Thank you," Catherine mumbled, unable to bear Inez's scrutiny another moment. "You don't have to stay with me anymore. I'm feeling much better."

"I will stay nearby in case you cannot get out by yourself. You will call me if you need help?"

"Yes, I will."

Seemingly satisfied, Inez left Catherine alone with her crisis. Oh, dear heaven, a baby, *Sam's* baby! What on earth should she do?

She should tell him, of course. He had a right to know.

Or did he? She remembered what she had seen in his eyes the previous night when he had refused to let David go to Philadelphia. If he were so obsessive with his brother, how would he feel about his own child? What if her son inherited her father's genius? What if he were even more talented than David? Could she bear to watch Sam crush his hopes and dreams, too?

But she loved Sam. Could she bear to leave him and to take his child?

Before she even realized it she was sobbing, overwhelmed by the burden of responsibility she bore to the child she carried. How could she even hope to know what was right?

Quickly, before Inez heard her and came to investigate, Catherine smothered her sobs and dashed water on her face. Then she scrubbed herself mercilessly, as if she could wash away the problems facing her. When she was finished the water was faintly pink, but all traces of blood were gone from her hands and arms.

Feeling somewhat numb, Catherine maneuvered herself out of the tub and toweled off. She could have used Inez's help, but she couldn't face anyone just yet. She struggled into the clothes Inez had laid out for her and then peered out of the bathroom. Seeing no one, she stole down the hall to her room. Someone had very thoughtfully closed the shutters against the noonday sun, and Catherine stretched out on the bed, feeling unutterably weary.

She must have slept because she woke with a start and saw a pair of jean-clad legs in front of her. She looked up to find Sam Connors.

"I didn't mean to wake you," he said, his dark eyes filled with adoration. "I just wanted to make sure you were all right. How do you feel?" He reached out and touched her cheek so tenderly that her eyes filled with tears.

"I'm fine," she said, glad to hear how firm her voice was. "There's no need to be concerned."

"No need!" he replied in exasperation. "Look at you! You pass out cold on the barn floor, and then you come in here and sleep for two hours. What in the hell is wrong with you?"

"Nothing's wrong with me," she insisted in alarm,

struggling to a sitting position. Had he guessed already? Had Inez told him?

"Nothing's wrong?" he asked in mock amazement. "I call being out of your mind having something *seriously* wrong, and you, lady, are totally crazy! Cutting up dead animals in the heat and the stench with the flies buzzing around you like—"

"Sam, don't!" she cried, feeling faint again.

"Oh, God, what am I doing?" he whispered, instantly contrite. "I'm sorry, Cat, I didn't mean . . . You scared me to death and now *I'm* acting crazy." He ran a hand through his raven hair, and she could see from how mussed it was that this was not the first time he had done so.

"I didn't mean to scare you," she managed around the tightness in her throat. He really did look frightened and incredibly dear, and she was afraid she might cry again.

He glanced uneasily at the door that he had closed, presumably to keep this totally improper visit a secret. "I'd like to—" He stopped and drew a ragged breath.

"What would you like to do?" she asked, wishing he weren't so far away, wishing he were here on the bed beside her.

"I'd like to hold you. Just hold you, Cat, just for a minute . . ."

"Oh, Sam," she cried, reaching for him.

He came to her with a groan that sounded almost like agony, and his arms closed around her.

"Tighter," she urged when he tried to be gentle.

She buried her face in the curve of his neck and inhaled the musky male scent of him. She loved him so much she could hardly bear the thought of it, and once again she had to fight the tears.

He gave a shuddering sigh and pressed his lips to her temple. "Are you sure you're all right? The nearest doctor is in Dallas, but Inez's mother is a midwife and she takes care of most of the sickness. . . ."

"No, I'm fine," she hastily assured him, knowing she couldn't face a midwife right now. "I didn't sleep very well last night and it was hot in the barn and . . . well, the combination of everything was just too much."

He pulled away so he could see her face. "Why didn't you sleep well?"

"I was worried about the fight we had last night."

"*We* didn't have a fight. Davy and me had a fight."

"I was there, too, and as you pointed out, I'm the one who caused the problems in the first place."

"We'll get things settled, Cat. It's not your lookout."

"I hope you're not going to tell me to mind my own business again," she said acerbically.

He gave her a grudging smile. "I guess you really are feeling better if you're ready to pick a fight with me."

"I'm not picking a fight," she began, but caught herself when she realized she most certainly was. She returned his smile sheepishly.

"I reckon I know a way to take your mind off all this, and if you weren't feeling so poorly, I'd show it to you."

The wicked glint in his eyes heated her blood, and she wanted to tell him she wasn't feeling *that* poorly, but common sense intervened. Making love would only complicate an already hopelessly muddled situation.

"Not to mention that Inez might come in any minute to check on me," Catherine reminded him. "She's already scandalized because you tried to undress me."

Sam winced at the memory. "I only took off your shoe. You looked so helpless, and I wanted to do something. . . ." His voice trailed off, and his eyes told her how much he cared for her, perhaps even loved her. Her heart ached as she fought the urge to confess her own feelings. It was still too soon, and she was still too unsure of so many things, especially now that she knew about the baby.

His hands moved over her back, gentle and possessive. "Are you sure you don't want me to send for Inez's mother?" he asked.

Catherine shook her head. "I'm fine, really, except I'm starving!" she suddenly realized.

"I'm not surprised. You slept right through dinner. I'll have Inez bring you a tray."

"Oh, no! I'm not an invalid. I can go to the kitchen."

"If you're sure . . ."

"I'm sure."

Sam studied her expression for a moment before surrendering to her will. Reluctantly, he released her and rose from the bed. He looked as bereft as she felt.

"I suppose I could use a strong arm to lean on, though," she allowed.

He seemed relieved. "You can have either one of mine."

"Just give me a minute to pin up my hair," she said, realizing it was still loose around her shoulders.

"I'll wait outside."

When Catherine looked into the dressing table mirror, she almost cried out in dismay. No wonder Sam was so worried about her. She looked absolutely terrible, pale and drawn, with her hair a wild tangle and her eyes haunted by secrets she dared not reveal. She looked only slightly better when her hair was pinned up again. Pinching some color into her cheeks, she practiced a few carefree smiles with questionable success. Well, she decided, it was probably better if Sam did think she was ill. At least he wouldn't be wondering what else could be wrong with her.

He was waiting in the hall for her, leaning against the wall. He snapped to attention the instant she appeared. "Are you sure you want to try this?"

"Yes. I just realized poor David must be worried sick, too. I suppose I fainted right in front of him."

"Right into his arms, just like in a book," Sam informed her with a grin as he tucked her arm through his. "But I was the one who carried you into the house. Davy's knees were knocking too hard to make the trip."

"Oh, dear," she murmured.

They found Inez in the kitchen. "Look who I found wandering around loose," Sam said, presenting Catherine. "She says she's hungry, though I wouldn't offer her a steak just yet."

Inez muttered all sorts of disapproving imprecations as she seated Catherine at the kitchen table. "I have made some soup. You will feel better when you have eaten," Inez assured her.

Sam nonchalantly went to the stove and poured himself a cup of coffee, but Catherine soon realized he was using it as an excuse to remain there with her while she ate. Feeling absurdly cherished, she allowed Inez to coax her into finishing the entire bowl of soup and several slices of bread.

"Her color's coming back, don't you think?" he asked Inez.

Inez nodded, and Catherine saw the speculation in the housekeeper's eyes as she wondered whether Catherine had told him about the baby yet.

"We should find David and put his mind at ease," Catherine said briskly to distract them both.

Sam walked her back to the parlor, where he left her ensconced on the sofa while he went in search of his brother. In a few minutes she heard the sound of running, and David came charging out of the hallway that led to his room. "Miss Eaton, are you all right?"

"I'm fine," she assured him as he skidded to a halt in front of her. "And I'm afraid I owe you an apology."

"What for?"

"For fainting. I've never done that before, and I wanted you to know how sorry I am I frightened you."

"You did, for sure," David said, looking at her more closely. "Are you really feeling better?"

"She says she is," Sam said, entering the room behind him at a more sedate pace. "But you know how stubborn she is. I don't expect she'd tell us if she was dying."

"I am most certainly not dying," she informed them both. "And I'm feeling well enough to give you the art lesson I promised."

"You don't have to—"

"I *want* to. In fact, I insist."

"Well, all right," David agreed, unable to disguise his pleasure. "What would you like to do?"

For all her bravado, Catherine knew she shouldn't risk going out into the sun again. "Why don't we find something inside to sketch and then you can do an oil of it later."

"Like what?" he asked, scanning the room thoughtfully for a subject.

Catherine looked, too, and her wandering gaze snagged Sam's. To her surprise, she saw disappointment. "I reckon I'll get out of your way, then," he said, and started for the door.

"Sam, wait!" she called, realizing he saw her offer as a desire to exclude him from her presence. "David, wouldn't you like to do a portrait of Sam?"

Both brothers were equally surprised at the question. David's surprise quickly turned to delight, however, while Sam remained dubious.

"I've been wanting to, but I can't never get him to hold still long enough," David said.

"He's much too polite to refuse a guest, though," Catherine told David with a wink. "Sam, would you sit for us please?" she asked sweetly.

He tried to look put-upon but without much success. "I've got work to do," he offered perfunctorily.

"Please?" she repeated with a smile.

"You can't turn down a guest," David said, already grinning triumphantly. "Where should we have him sit, Miss Eaton?"

Sam never did agree, but a few minutes later he was posed beside the fireplace, looking uncomfortable but pleased at having been included in their afternoon's activities.

Catherine took up her sketchbook, too, glad for the opportunity to have Sam as a model. She didn't allow herself to think about why she wanted a picture of him or why she might need one.

"I'm not real good at painting people yet, Sam, so this might not turn out looking much like you," David remarked when they had been sketching for a while.

"I just don't want to hear any jokes about skinning me to learn how to draw better," Sam replied.

"I wouldn't do it in front of Miss Eaton, anyways," David said with a grin.

"And I don't want to hear any more jokes about my fainting," Catherine informed them both.

Sam's dark gaze softened and grew speculative—or at least Catherine imagined it did. Perhaps her secret made her see things that weren't there. He couldn't possibly know she was pregnant.

But he could guess, an inner voice told her. Surely he knew all about the birds and the bees and where babies come from. She could also imagine how thrilled he'd be at the prospect of a child. He wouldn't care about the gossip, nor would her own hesitancy over their suitability for each other stop him from sweeping her to the altar. How well she understood Sam Connors's indomitable will and her inability to resist it. If she decided she shouldn't marry Sam, her only choice would be not to tell him about the baby at all.

How could she be so cruel to him?

"If Sam doesn't like to sit for you, you should find yourself another model," she said to distract herself from her thoughts. "That boy who helped us this afternoon would be a good subject."

"Johnny?" David said. "Yeah, I guess he would."

Sam rolled his eyes. "Now you're going to take my men away from their work so you can draw their pictures?"

"I'll do it when they aren't working," David assured him with a grin.

Sam and David kept up a steady banter all afternoon and over supper, so Catherine had no further opportunity to worry. Afterwards, Sam decreed Cathcrine needed entertainment, not work, and invited Inez and her husband to join them for cards. No one would have ever known from Inez's attitude that she shared Catherine's secret, and the evening passed cheerfully.

It wasn't very late when Inez said, at the end of a hand, "Miss Eaton should go to bed now."

"Not yet," Catherine protested.

"You fainted today," Inez said, and her eyes gave a silent reminder of the child she carried.

"I suppose you're right," she admitted grudgingly. "Although I hate to spoil everyone's fun."

"Oh, I'm kinda tired myself," David said gallantly.

"Yeah," Sam agreed, straight-faced. "Cutting up livestock'll wear a fellow out."

David made a face and Catherine excused herself, wishing everyone a good night. Did Sam's eyes linger on her as she left the room? Probably she was imagining things again.

In her room she prepared for bed, then listened as the house slowly grew silent. By now everyone would have retired, she thought as she carefully brushed her hair one hundred strokes.

In another wing of the house Sam paced in his own bedroom. More than once he started for the door and caught himself. Was he some kind of animal? The woman wasn't well, she'd actually fainted today, but all he could think about was holding her in his arms again and tasting her sweet lips.

And putting his seed in her, he admitted. Oh, he wanted to make love to her until she cried out in joy and clung to him as if she'd never let him go, but even more than that, he wanted to get her with child.

The whole time he had waited for her to wake up this afternoon he had considered the possibility she might already be pregnant. She'd said she had never fainted during dissections back in Philadelphia, so maybe her weakness came from another cause. He knew how sickly expectant women could be. Adora had swooned practically every day when she was carrying Davy.

If Cat were pregnant, she would have no choice but to marry him. The hope burned white hot within him. He should go to her and give her the opportunity to tell him.

And if she weren't already with child, he should go to her in hopes of giving her one.

The thought of Cat belonging to him was a stronger lure than passion had ever been. Desire boiled up in him, hot and strong and compelling. True, she had been ill, but he would give her a chance to say no. And if she said yes . . .

Catherine laid the brush down on the dressing table and began to braid her hair for sleep. Her hands slowed as she reached the end of the braid, and she realized she didn't want to finish because she didn't want to go to bed just yet. Feeling rested from her nap, she knew she would only lie awake, tortured by thoughts of Sam and worries for the future.

For one silly moment, she entertained the fantasy of slipping out of her room and through the darkened house to where Sam slept and creeping into his bed and . . .

But she could never be so bold, not even if she were going for the sole purpose of telling him about their child, which she had absolutely no intention of doing.

Absently, she picked up the ribbon to bind her braid when someone knocked on her door. Suddenly, every

one of her nerves came to life with a burning anticipation. "Who's there?"

The door opened and Sam came in. He shut the
door carefully, silently behind him but made no move
to come farther into the room. Her heart hammered
so loudly that she could hardly hear him when he said,
"If you want me to leave, just say so."

Her breath caught somewhere in her chest, so she
could only shake her head. The ribbon slipped from
her fingers, and she reached out her hand to him.

He was beside her in an instant, lifting her to her
feet and lowering his face to hers for the kisses she had
craved, one after another, quick and sweet and urgent.
He clutched her hips, holding her to him, while her
own hands grasped his head so the kisses wouldn't stop.

"Oh, Cat," he murmured on a rasping breath. "It's
been so long."

"Yes," she replied, wondering how she could ever
bear to leave him. Never to hold him or kiss him again?
What a fool she was to even consider it. No matter
how they fought, they belonged together. He worshiped her, she knew. He would never hurt her or their
child.

Sam loosened the tie of her robe while she struggled
with his shirt buttons. They inched their way toward
the bed, leaving a trail of clothing in their wake.

"Where are your shoes?" she wondered as he
stepped out of his pants.

"I didn't want Davy to hear me," he explained,
lifting her nightdress over her head. "He'd probably
shoot me if he saw me going into your room." He bore
her backward onto the bed.

"You should have told him how things are."

"How *are* things?" he asked.

"That—that we're lovers," she replied.

"You think I should've told him we're *lovers?*" He cupped her breasts with both hands, using his thumbs to abrade the tips into tight, aching buds.

"N . . . no . . ." she said breathlessly. "I guess . . . not. . . ."

"Cat, stop talking." He lowered his mouth to hers, and she had no choice but to obey.

His hands worked their magic, stoking the embers of desire until they glowed and her breath came in ragged gasps.

"Touch me, Cat," he said, guiding her hand downward to grasp the heated shaft.

When he groaned his pleasure, she glimpsed the power she had over him, twin to the power he exercised over her body. She stroked him tentatively, earning another groan. Emboldened, she nuzzled his chest, finding his flat nipple and teasing it with her tongue.

"My God, you're a witch," he murmured hoarsely, withdrawing defensively and removing her hand to a place of safety. "Do you know what you're doing?"

"Teasing you?" she replied.

"I'll show you teasing," he growled in mock fierceness, and rolled her flat onto her back, pinning her there with his weight.

When he had kissed her senseless, he began to work his way down her body, lavishing attention on her breasts until they throbbed, then moving lower until he reached the nest of golden curls on her belly.

Gently but inexorably, he spread her legs so she was completely exposed. When he lowered his mouth, she cried out in surprise.

"Sam, what are you? . . ." The rest of her question lodged in her throat, smothered by the sensations building within her. Desire blossomed beneath Sam's mouth, growing and spreading, tangling through her like a silken vine. It crept over her breasts and belly, and curled between her fingers and toes, and wrapped itself around her soul.

When she was completely in thrall, Sam claimed her, sliding into her welcoming depths with a sigh.

"Is the . . . teasing over?" she managed to ask before he claimed her lips again, and she saw at once he intended to torture her further as he moved in her with excruciating slowness.

But she knew her power now and would have none of his domination. When his mouth left hers, she nipped his throat and scraped her nails along his lean flanks. Reaction shuddered through him, but she gave him no time to recover. Wrapping her legs around him, she opened her lips against his and plunged her tongue into his mouth.

His restraint crumbled, and suddenly his hips thrust against hers with frantic urgency. Mouths devoured, hands clutched, and breaths mingled until neither could have said where one body left off and the other began. United, they strove for the goal, churning, panting, groping, lunging, on and on until they spiraled out of control, collapsing into one another in the feverish convulsions of ecstasy.

A long time later Catherine roused herself, conscious of the burden of Sam's weight still crushing her into the bed. She pushed ineffectually on his shoulder. He murmured a complaint and then rolled away, carrying her with him so she lay on top of him.

Still too weary to speak, they lay together for a time. Sam raked his fingers through her hair, undoing the last of her braid and spreading the silken strands out into a golden curtain across her back.

At last Catherine found her voice. "I had no idea teasing could be so—so interesting."

"*Interesting?*" Sam said, lifting one eyelid and glaring at her in disapproval.

"Didn't you think it was interesting?" she inquired innocently.

"Oh, yes," he replied, reaching down to position her hips so she could tell just how interested he still was.

"Oh, my," she said with an impish grin, while his fingers traced erotic trails up the back of her thighs and over her bare bottom.

Nearly intoxicated with happiness, Catherine pressed kiss after kiss onto his beloved face, across the jaw that still bore the dark traces of his beard in spite of a recent shave, on the strong, straight nose and the broad forehead. Then she closed his dark eyes with more kisses as she tunneled her fingers into his thick black hair.

"Mmmm," he said contentedly. "Imagine what it would be like if you lived here all the time. Every night, in this bed . . ."

"You sneaking down the hall in your sock feet?" she taunted.

His eyes flew open, and she saw he wasn't really teasing. "If you were my wife, I wouldn't have to sneak in to see you."

For one second her heart stopped as she recalled all her old fears, but only for a second. Sam wanted to marry her. Given the slightest encouragement, he would ask her right now, and when he did, she would say yes.

And then she would have to deal with her doubts. Why

spoil the moment? Later, there would be time for confessions and plans and explanations. Later, but not now.

She made a pouting face. "How boring that will be. You'll come in here every night and pull off your boots and hang up your clothes and put on a nightshirt—"

"a nightshirt!"

"—and forget to shave and you probably snore and—"

"I do not snore!"

"How do you know?"

"I—I just do, that's all," he insisted. "And I never wear a nightshirt."

She feigned shock. "Not even in the winter?"

"Not if I have somebody to keep me warm."

"And who's been keeping you warm up until now?" she wanted to know.

"Nobody, which is why I'm looking forward to having a little blond schoolteacher to snuggle with."

His hands were doing delicious things to her body, and she had to admit she was looking forward to cozying up with Sam this winter, too.

"What will you tell David?" she asked, unwilling to let him get too comfortable with his daydreams.

He sighed dramatically. "Maybe I'll have to ship him off to Philadelphia after all, just so we can be alone."

She laughed with delight. "Oh, Sam, I knew you'd let him go!"

His gaiety vanished. "I was only joking. I'm not going to let him go. Davy belongs here."

"I—I thought—"

"Well, you thought wrong."

"Sam, can't you see how much this means to him? Don't you want him to be happy?"

"Of course, I want him to be happy. I know what happens when you take someone out of his rightful place. His mother *died*, for God's sake."

"That's hardly the same thing. David won't die from going to Philadelphia, and you have no right to make this decision for him. You aren't his father!"

Sam's eyes narrowed dangerously, and for an instant she thought she had gone too far. For a few seconds he fought for control of his temper and won. His face smoothed out again, all traces of irritation gone from his expression. "And you aren't his mother, Cat. You aren't even a blood relative," he pointed out reasonably. "You have no rights at all."

"I—I love him as much as you do," she tried.

"I doubt it," Sam said, but he smiled, telling her he wasn't angry any longer. He sighed again, wearily this time. "Remember what I said this afternoon about there being only one way to shut you up?"

She nodded smugly. "Too bad you've already used it."

In the next second she was on her back beneath him. "I used it *once*, and I can use it again."

"Again?" she echoed in amazement, feeling the evidence of his claim pressing against her thigh.

"And again and again, as often as I have to," he bragged, touching her the way he knew she liked to be touched. "If this is the only way we can keep from arguing, we should have a very interesting life together."

Vaguely, Catherine realized she had tacitly agreed to become Sam's wife, but the knowledge was lost in the swirl of passion that followed. Once again she and Sam rode the crest, higher and higher, until they plunged together into the vortex of release.

When it was over she lay limp and replete, draped across Sam's chest. "Do you still want to argue?" he asked softly.

"About what?" she inquired just before sleep claimed her. She thought she heard him chuckle, but perhaps it was only a dream.

She awoke to someone pounding on her door. Sunlight flooded the room.

"Miss Eaton? Are you awake? We've got church this morning."

David! she thought in panic, but to her relief the bed beside her was empty. Sam had left sometime during the night.

"Yes, I'm awake. I'll be ready in a minute," she called, falling back against the pillows.

"A minute?" he taunted cheerfully. "Should I start timing you?"

'Don't you dare!"

After her shock, she found her body reluctant to bestir itself again, so she needed even more time than usual to get washed and dressed. When she was at last ready, she made her way out to the parlor, where she found her two hosts awaiting her.

Both David and Sam rose as she entered the room. David beamed a greeting. Sam was more circumspect, although no less happy to see her. His smile warmed her to her toes, and she realized she no longer felt any reluctance to become his wife. Things would never be placid between them, but the joys would more than equal the trials if last night was any indication of what Sam had in store for her.

David offered his arm to escort her into breakfast.

She cast Sam an apologetic look to which he responded with a wink.

Catherine found she was ravenous and ate two helpings of flapjacks.

"Looks like you worked up an appetite last night," Sam remarked guilelessly.

"How could she work up an appetite sleeping?" David scoffed, frowning when he saw Catherine's blush.

"I'm sure I don't know," Sam replied, not looking up from his plate.

Catherine made a great effort not to choke on her pancake.

The ride into town was pure torture as she sat wedged in the buggy between David and Sam. The two of them exerted themselves to keep her entertained, but Catherine felt unaccountably irritable, perhaps because Sam seemed unaffected by their proximity while she could hardly breathe. The mere brush of his elbow sent her heart skittering in her chest.

She recalled her conversation with Sam last night about how boring marriage would become. At the moment boredom seemed quite attractive. She would have to set a wedding date soon if she hoped to maintain her dignity.

When they arrived at church, the women closed ranks around her, pretending to scold her for being brazen enough to spend the weekend at Sam's ranch but really curious to learn how their relationship had progressed. Catherine hinted broadly about future plans but revealed nothing.

The Reverend Fletcher had just rung the bell when a cowboy came racing into town. He reined up so quickly that his horse reared, but everyone heard his shouted message. "Amos Pettigrew was killed last night!"

The men surged forward to hear the rest of the message while the women gasped their horror.

"Killed? How?" Sam demanded.

"Shot down in the road. One of the men found him this morning. We went looking when we realized he hadn't come home last night."

"Any idea who did it?" Mathias Shallcross asked.

"The tracks showed two riders. Looks like they met, maybe even had a few words. Mr. Pettigrew's gun was still in his holster, so he couldn't of been expecting trouble."

"The Taggerts," Sam said.

"But why would he have let them ride up to him like that?" someone asked.

"Maybe it was dark," Mathias suggested.

"The Taggerts were working for Amos," Sam explained reluctantly. "He hired them after Gus fired them. He only wanted them to cut my fence so I'd get mad enough to fight, but they didn't want to quit. They told him he'd have to keep on paying them or else they'd cut his fences . . . or maybe even kill him."

"How do you know all this?" Gus Nylan asked.

"Amos told me. He begged me not to tell anybody, but I don't guess it matters now."

Bones Blalock stepped out of the crowd. "I reckon there'll be a trail to follow."

"I reckon so," Sam agreed. "We'll need some men to ride with us."

Every man present wanted to go, so Bones selected half-a-dozen while Sam sought out Catherine.

"I'm sorry," he said.

"I am, too," she said, fighting the fear that was

380

turning her breakfast into a sickening lump. She laid a hand on his arm. "Please be careful."

He gave her his cocky grin. "Nothing's going to happen to me now." He glanced around and found his brother. "Davy, see that Miss Eaton gets home, will you?"

"They can both come home with me," Twila declared. "I've got a roast on and nobody to eat it, with Mathias running off chasing killers. We can wait together."

The next week dragged by as Sam spent most of his time once again scouring the hills in search of the Taggerts. David kept her informed of their progress—or lack of it.

"Sometimes Sam swears he can almost smell the Taggerts, he's that close, but they're like weasels. They go to ground and don't leave a trace."

"How can they disappear so completely?"

"It's rough country out there, with lots of hidey-holes. They must be smarter than we thought, too, or at least they know how to cover their trail so even Sam can't find it."

"But don't they leave tracks?"

"On the ground, yes, but not on rocks and in water. They use every trick in the book to hide their trail. Sam can even follow somebody across rock, usually, because they leave other signs, like broken twigs or scuff marks or even animal droppings, but the Taggerts don't leave nothing behind. He thinks they cover their horses' hooves with something."

Catherine laid awake far into each night, picturing Sam riding into an ambush the way Amos Pettigrew had. Her blood ran cold when she thought of losing him before she even had a chance to tell him how much she loved him.

Why had she hesitated when she had the chance? Why hadn't she agreed to marry him and told him about the baby? Why had she let her foolish doubts rob them of the joy they could have shared?

When her thoughts got too bleak, she had to remind herself Sam was still alive and well and probably would remain so. They had many years ahead during which to share every scrap of joy due them. In her more reasonable moments, she tried to figure out how she could have grown so despondent and decided it must be one of the inexplicable results of her pregnancy. Or perhaps she was simply losing her mind from the tension of waiting.

Thursday morning, David reported that Sam and the Rangers had once again given up the search, and Catherine breathed a sigh of relief. Surely, Sam would come to her tonight and they could finally settle things between them.

Too excited to concentrate on David's lesson, she sent him home early, pleading that she had to make plans for the commencement exercises that would be held the next week. At least she and Sam wouldn't have to wait any length of time for school to be out before getting married. As Inez had said, they were already late and couldn't afford any protracted delays.

When David arrived home, the men hadn't come back from their day's work yet. He unsaddled his pony and turned it loose in the corral. He was heading for the house when he heard the sound of wood being chopped. Looking for a little conversation, he made his way around the back of the house, where he found

Johnny Fitzpatrick working the ax with little enthusiasm.

As the newest man on the Spur, Johnny often got stuck with the less desirable jobs. No cowboy liked doing anything that couldn't be done from the back of a horse.

"Hey, how's it going?" David called, knowing Johnny would be happy for any distraction.

"Just fine," Johnny replied sarcastically. The heat and labor had plastered his shirt to his body, and he paused to wipe his dripping forehead on his sleeve.

David noticed with an artist's eye how picturesque the setting was—a young man with an ax, the stacks of wood and piles of chips and sawdust. Then he recalled what Catherine had said about finding himself a model. Of course, serving as a model would hardly seem attractive to a cowboy.

"I was just wondering if you'd like to make a few extra dollars," David began, thinking he would offer a little incentive.

Johnny frowned, lowering the ax. "Doing what?" he asked suspiciously.

"Nothing much, just sitting around mostly. See, I'm learning to paint people, and I need someone to practice on and—"

"You want to draw my picture?" he asked, suddenly furious. He dropped the ax and clenched his fists. "Like you did Jessie's?"

"Well, yeah," David said, bewildered by his anger. "You just have to sit there and—"

"You son of a bitch!"

Before David could react, Johnny swung. The blow glanced off the side of his face. "Hey, wait a minute. . . ."

Johnny swung again, and the next thing David knew they were rolling on the ground. At first he only tried to ward off the blows, but soon his own anger was roused at the unprovoked attack and he began to hit back.

"I know what you want!" Johnny panted. "Jessie told me all about you!"

The words made no sense. In the distance, David heard Inez shouting. He landed a blow, and Johnny grunted.

"Goddamnit, what's wrong with you?" David shouted, grappling.

"What the hell's going on?" Sam's voice demanded, and strong arms pulled the two boys apart.

David fell back gratefully but Johnny resisted, struggling until Sam was forced to wrap his arms around him and subdue him.

"Now, what is this all about?" Sam asked, as angry as Johnny had been.

"I don't know," David said. "He just came at me for no reason."

"No reason!" Johnny's face was red and his breath came in savage gasps. "He wanted me to—to—"

"To what?" Sam insisted when he hesitated.

Johnny clamped his lips together, refusing to reply, so Sam looked to David for the answer.

"I asked him to pose for me is all. I even offered to pay him."

"*Pay* me, you son of a bitch! What do you think I am, some kind of whore?"

"Whore? What in God's name are you talking about?" Sam asked, releasing him and turning Johnny to face him.

"Yeah, whore! Jessie Nylan told me how he couldn't

do nothing with her because he only likes boys. I know what he wanted. He wanted to get me off alone so he could—''

"Liar!" David screamed, lunging for him.

Sam caught him just in time.

"Why would I make up something like that?" Johnny asked Sam. "She told me all about it."

"She's a liar!" David yelled.

"Shut up!" Sam shouted, shaking him until he stopped struggling. "Exactly what did she say?"

Johnny took a deep breath, looking at David, who strained against Sam's hold again. Satisfied Sam held him securely, he said, "She told me how Davy took her off alone to draw her picture and they started . . . you know, fooling around and—and he couldn't do anything because he said he only gets excited with boys."

David roared with rage and fought ferociously to free himself. "She's a lying little bitch! She said that because I wouldn't do it with her. She's nothing but a cheap little whore!"

Johnny backed up a step, but he stuck his chin out belligerently. "That's my girl you're talking about!"

"Then you know she's a whore!"

Sam released David and grabbed Johnny as he lunged. "Stop it, both of you!" When Johnny was still, Sam released him, too. "Davy, go to your room. I'll deal with you later."

"But, Sam—"

"Go, *now!*"

Reluctantly, resentfully, David started for the house. Sam turned to Johnny. "And you, come with me."

Sam followed David into the house, leading Johnny through the cavernous rooms to his office. Sam closed the door behind them and crossed his arms over his chest.

"You made a big mistake, Johnny. Jessie told you a lie and you believed it."

"Now wait a minute!"

"I don't expect you to believe me, but I do expect you to keep this story to yourself. Have you told anybody else?"

"No, sir. The fact is, I didn't believe it myself at first, but anybody who draws pictures all the time has to be a sissy, and when he asked me to—"

"All right," Sam snapped. "Just understand this: If you tell this lie to another living soul, I'll kill you."

Johnny's eyes grew large and Sam noticed his fighting flush had drained away, leaving him chalk-white. "I won't say nothing, but I can't speak for Jessie."

"I'll take care of Jessie," Sam informed him.

Johnny swallowed loudly.

"I'm going to make it real easy for you," Sam continued. "I'm going to pay you off and I want you out, clean out of the county. I never want to see your face around here again."

Sam went to the safe, opened it, and pulled out a drawstring bag. From it he took several gold coins. He rose and handed the coins to Johnny.

"You've got one month's wages coming, but I'm giving you a hundred dollars. That should take you just as far as you want to go. Tell the cook you're leaving. He'll give you some grub to carry along. I want you out of here before the rest of the men come back."

"Y . . . yes, sir." He left the door hanging open in his haste to be gone.

Literally trembling with rage, Sam sank down into

his desk chair and buried his face in his hands. Johnny's words kept ringing in his ears: "Anybody who draws pictures all the time has to be a sissy."

How many others were doubting Davy's manhood, even without Jessica's lies to give them ideas? His worst fears had come true.

And it was all Catherine's fault. Damn her and her high falutin ideas! It wasn't bad enough she wanted to send him off to Philadelphia, she wanted to take away his masculinity, too.

Sam had made a terrible mistake, letting his attraction for Catherine color his judgment. It was fine for a child to draw pictures but not for a man, and Davy was a man now. Sam had indulged them both for too long. Now he'd have to put a stop to it.

Catherine wouldn't like it, he knew, but if she was going to be his wife, she would have to learn to obey him, and she would have to start now.

His anger had carried him halfway across the ranch yard before he realized he was on his way to confront her.

Chapter Thirteen

The Nylans were just sitting down to supper when Johnny Fitzpatrick rode into the yard and called for Jessica. In spite of her mother's protests, Jessica went outside to greet him.

"You going somewhere?" she asked when she saw the gear tied to his saddle.

"I gotta talk to you, in private," he said, glancing past her to where her parents and several of her siblings hovered in the doorway.

Not bothering to seek permission, she strolled down the porch steps and out into the yard where Johnny sat his horse.

"Invite the boy for supper, at least," Lulie called in annoyance.

Johnny swung down from his saddle as Jessica approached.

"What's so gosh-awful important?" she asked without much concern.

"I got fired."

"Fired? What on earth for?"

"For fighting with Davy Connors. He asked if he

388

could draw my picture, and I remembered what you said about him and—"

"You didn't *tell* him, did you?" she cried in alarm.

"Well, yeah, I had to when Mr. Connors broke us up. I couldn't let him think I lit into Davy for no reason. Besides," he added righteously, "he oughta know what his brother is."

"Goddamn you, Johnny Fitzpatrick, if they put your brains in a jaybird, he'd fly backwards!"

Johnny flushed, but he refused to retreat. "I know I got you in trouble, too. Connors said he'd kill me if I ever told anybody else about Davy, and he said he'd take care of you, too."

"What'd he mean, he'd 'take care' of me?"

"I don't know, and I don't reckon we wanna find out. That's why I come by. He paid me a hundred dollars, Jess. We could go off together, to Dallas or someplace. Maybe even New Orleans. Whadda ya say?"

Jessica thought fast, weighing the possibilities. Any chance she had with Davy was gone now. If she stayed around here, her future would hold only another cowboy like Johnny and Sam Connors's wrath. In a city, there would be lots of men.

"All right, only I can't go now. My folks'll kill me if they find out. I'll meet you someplace tonight after they're asleep."

They had barely settled on a rendezvous when Gus Nylan called to Jessie to hurry up.

" 'Bye for now," she whispered, backing away. "Good-bye, Johnny. I'll miss you," she called for her parents' benefit. She waved as he rode away.

"What did he want?" her father demanded.

"Sam Connors fired him and he came to say good-bye."

"Why didn't he ask me for a job, then?"

Jessica shrugged. "I reckon he's tired of Crosswicks." She wandered back into supper, already deciding what she would take with her when she went.

Catherine had just finished her meager dinner, too excited over Sam's expected visit to eat much, when she heard a horse out in the yard.

"Catherine!"

She started at the sound of Sam's voice, instantly realizing he was upset. He certainly wouldn't have come so early unless something were amiss. She hurried outside to find him approaching her door with determined steps. "What's wrong?" she asked, stepping aside so he could enter her room and following him back inside.

"Davy got into a fight today with Johnny Fitzpatrick."

She flinched from Sam's accusing glare, wondering why he seemed so angry with her. "A fight? What about?"

"Jessie Nylan told Johnny that Davy is one of those fellows who only likes boys."

"Oh, no!"

"Oh, yes. I see I don't have to explain it to you. I guess they have lots of those fellows in your art school. And of course Johnny believed it, because everybody knows only sissies draw pictures."

"Good heavens, is that what he said?"

"You're damn right that's what he said, and that's what a lot of other people are thinking, too, which is why Davy's not going to Philadelphia and why he's finished with drawing and painting and all the rest."

"Sam, you can't mean it!"

"The hell I can't! I let Davy take lessons from you so I could get on your good side, but I can see now I was a fool. You've wasted his time and filled his head full of crazy ideas, and now people are starting to think he's strange. Now it's going to stop."

Catherine fought the rage building inside her, knowing they would accomplish little if they were both angry. "Don't you think that should be David's decision?"

"I've let him and you make the decisions so far, and look what happened. From now on, I'll be in charge. If you're going to be my wife, you'd better get used to it."

"I'm not your wife yet," she reminded him furiously. "And even if I were, I have no intention of obeying you or any man. As for David, you know Jessica only said those things out of spite. No one else thinks David is 'strange,' and you have absolutely no right to ruin his life. . . ."

"Ruin his life!"

"Yes, ruin his life by forcing him to give up art. He's only your brother, Sam, he's not your son!"

"But he *is* my son!"

The words hung between them in the deadly silence for a long moment while Catherine stared at him in horror, trying to make sense of his claim. "Your— your son? But how? . . . You and Adora? . . ."

Suddenly, she glimpsed the pain she had seen before, the hurt he usually kept so carefully hidden, but he covered it quickly with righteous indignation. "I can see you've already decided I was the villain. After all, what kind of man would seduce his father's wife? Well, you're wrong, Catherine. I was seventeen years old, not much older than Davy is now, when my father brought her home.

"He'd gone to New Orleans on business. Adora was some kin to my mother's family, a cousin or something. Her parents were dead and her brother had gambled away the family fortune. She was twenty-one—already an old maid—and they were thrilled to find somebody who'd take her without a dowry.

"I'd never seen a woman so beautiful. I could barely remember my mother, and I'd hardly been around any women at all. Naturally, I fell in love with her, and she encouraged me. My father was a busy man and couldn't pay her the attention she thought she deserved."

"But you didn't have to—to—"

"No, I don't suppose I did, but then, neither did she. My father went away on another trip. He was gone over a month. It was summer, and Adora made me take her on picnics so we could be alone. I'd never been with a woman before, so I didn't really know what was happening the first time. I figured she'd stop me before things went too far, but she didn't want to stop me.

"Afterwards, I felt terrible for what we'd done to my father, but she said she loved me and somehow that made everything all right. I started thinking we'd run away together. It never occurred to me she would refuse, but she did. My father was due home soon, and I told her we should leave before he got back.

"She laughed at me, told me she didn't want a penniless boy when she already had a rich husband. I was furious. I told her I'd tell my father everything, but she wasn't afraid. She said she would deny it, and then she told me she was carrying my child. If I told, my father wouldn't believe me, but he'd throw me out and I'd never see my son. If I kept her secret, I could stay. Even though I could never claim the child, at least I could be with him. So I stayed, and when they both were dead, Davy was all mine."

"Oh, Sam!" she cried, hardly able to bear the pain she saw in his eyes. How had he borne it all these years? How had he watched his own child growing up without once acknowledging him?

"I've kept him safe for fifteen years, and I'm not going to let you ruin him, now, Cat. You see, I *am* his father, and I know what's best for him, and I have the right to protect him. That means he stays here and becomes a man."

For a moment, Catherine had wanted to throw her arms around Sam and comfort him, but his cold belligerence wiped all such desires from her mind. Instead, she felt her fury building again. How could he be so unreasonable?

"Have you told David your decision?" she asked as calmly as she could.

"Not yet, but he won't argue, not when I tell him what Johnny said. And you won't mention Philadelphia or painting or anything like that to him ever again. Do you understand?"

Catherine had never been so furious in her entire life. Quaking from the force of her anger, she could barely speak. "I understand perfectly, and I want you to leave my house this instant."

He seemed surprised. "Cat, this doesn't change things between you and me."

"It most certainly does!"

"I thought you'd understand when I told you the truth," he said, obviously puzzled by her anger. "You always claimed I didn't have the right to make Davy's decisions, but I do."

"No one has the right to make the *wrong* decisions for *anyone!*"

"This isn't the wrong decision!"

"Yes, it is!" she cried, but quickly regained her control. "However, as you have pointed out to me, I have no right to make decisions of any kind where David is concerned. But I do have the right to decide whom I shall marry, and nothing on this earth could induce me to marry you!"

"Cat!" he protested, reaching for her.

"Don't touch me!" she fairly screamed, raising her hands defensively and backing away. "Get out of here, right now!"

"Cat, listen to me. I didn't mean—"

"I can't force you to leave, but if you don't, I'll start screaming," she said, her voice less than steady. "People will hear me, and I'll tell them you broke in here and tried to attack me. I swear I will."

Something in her face must have convinced him she was telling the truth. "All right, I'll leave, but I'll be back when you've had a chance to calm down so we can talk things over."

"There's nothing to talk over," she insisted.

"I think there is," he said infuriatingly. He turned on his heel and left.

Catherine held herself together until she heard his horse leaving the yard, then she collapsed onto the floor and surrendered to her tears. Huge wracking sobs shook her and tears poured down her face as she called Sam Connors every name she knew. He was the most overbearing, domineering, insufferable, cruel, and hateful man she had ever met, and she despised him to the depths of her soul.

Slowly, inexorably, time passed and exhaustion overcame her. Her sobbing stilled to an occasional hiccup, leaving her mind free to analyze what had happened.

Sam was David's father. This explained so much that she had no cause to doubt it. The truth appalled her, but she also remembered Sam's pain and knew he had suffered for whatever sins he had committed. She thought about what Johnny had said and wondered if David knew the terrible lies Jessica had told. How shattered he must be to bear the shame and know his love for art had caused it. She wanted to go to him, to comfort him, certain Sam would never dream of offering him solace. No, sympathy wouldn't fit in with Sam's very narrow view of manhood. He would force poor David to conform to his own standards and crush every instinct for creativity the boy possessed. How could Sam be so cruel to his own son?

His son. And Catherine carried his second child. Had she thought Sam incapable of hurting his own child? What a fool she was! She had allowed her love to blind her to his faults, but she was blind no longer.

And she knew her only hope for protecting her child from Sam's domination was to escape.

"Catherine, come in," Twila said in delight, finding her friend at the back door. "Mathias and I were just finishing supper. Won't you join us?"

"No, thank you. I've already eaten."

"Is something wrong? You look a little . . . Have you been crying?"

Catherine gave a nervous laugh. "Of course not, but I suddenly realized how foolish it is of me to stay alone at the school at night with these killers on the loose."

"Oh, my! You're absolutely right! I never thought—"

"So I was wondering if I could sleep in your spare room until the term is over."

"Yes, of course. You'll be staying with us all summer, anyway, and—"

"No, I won't."

"Won't?" Twila echoed in confusion, then her eyes brightened. "Don't tell me you and Sam—"

"No!" she said, too quickly. "I mean, Sam and I have decided we don't suit. I'm afraid I'll be going home at the end of the term."

"Home? You mean to Philadelphia?"

"Yes," Catherine said, thinking the city wasn't her home any longer but knowing of no other suitable destination. At least she had some friends there.

"Oh, my!" Twila said again, obviously at a loss. "I can't understand . . . I mean, I thought for sure . . . Oh, my!"

"Please don't tell anyone just yet. I don't want to spoil the commencement festivities."

"I won't tell a soul. Oh, Catherine, I don't know what to say. Have you told Davy? He'll simply die when he hears."

"I'll break it to him as gently as I can," she promised, knowing Twila's prediction wasn't much of an exaggeration. On top of everything else, her leaving would seem like desertion to him, but she couldn't allow herself to think of David's pain. As Sam delighted in reminding her, David was not her responsibility, and she had her own child to consider.

"Well, come on in. We can at least tell Mathias, can't we?"

"Not yet, please," Catherine said, softening her refusal with a smile. "The fewer people who know, the easier it will be to keep the secret. I'll go back to the school and get my things."

"I'll send Mathias to help you carry them, then."

While Catherine waited for Twila to fetch her husband, she sagged wearily against the door frame. At least she wouldn't have to worry about Sam coming to her at night and trying to convince her to change her mind. As soon as school was out every day, she would come over here. She wouldn't be alone for a minute, not until the stage carried her away from Crosswicks forever.

Sam reined up when he came to the turnoff to the Nylan place. Maybe he should confront Jessie right now, before she could do any more damage, but the very thought of seeing her repelled him. Besides, he was still far too angry and couldn't trust himself not to do her physical harm for the lies she'd told about Davy. No, he'd come back tomorrow, when he'd had time to cool off.

As he rode on toward the Spur, his thoughts drifted once again to Catherine. He'd done little else since leaving her except try to figure her out, but with no success.

What did the woman want, anyway? She'd known from the beginning Davy was a rancher. Couldn't she see what a waste of time it would be to send him off to school?

And when he remembered what Johnny Fitzpatrick had said, the red haze of fury engulfed him again and he wondered how he had managed to restrain himself from beating the words back down the boy's lying throat.

But no one else would tell the lie and no one else would even think it, not once Davy packed up his paints for good and took his rightful place on the Spur.

All Sam had to do now was deal with Cat. He supposed she was just spoiled, like a lot of women, used to getting her own way. She didn't like being thwarted, and Sam couldn't blame her. On the other hand, he couldn't let her have her way in this, either. She'd have to learn who was the boss.

Of course, he realized now he'd been too straightforward with her. Like with a high-spirited filly, the use of force only made her more stubborn. She'd have to be broken with gentleness. He'd have to humble himself and apologize and sweet-talk her, but he didn't mind. Remembering the way she felt in bed beneath him, he knew no sacrifice was too great to win her back.

When he reached the ranch, he found Davy brooding in his room.

"Where'd you go?" the boy demanded when Sam appeared in the doorway.

"I went to see Catherine. I thought she oughta know what happened."

"Oh, God! You didn't tell her what he said, did you?" he asked in horror.

Sam sighed wearily, knowing how humiliating this was for him. "I had to, Davy. This is all her fault, filling your head with strange ideas and making people think—"

"It's *not* her fault! It's Jessie's fault! She's the one who—"

"Yeah, Jessie told the lies, but Johnny believed her because he said that only sissies draw pictures."

"Oh," Davy murmured miserably.

"I paid him his time. I told him I'd kill him if he ever told another soul, and I told him I never wanted to see him around here again."

"But Jessie'll tell!" he wailed.

"I'll have a few words with her and with her folks tomorrow. She won't say anything to anybody."

Davy covered his face with both hands and groaned.

Sam felt his agony and laid an awkward hand on the boy's shoulder, wishing he knew a more effective way to comfort him. "I already told Catherine you aren't going to take any more lessons. You don't even have to go back to school if you don't want to."

"Sam?" he said in a muffled voice.

"Yeah?"

"I'd like to be alone."

Sam swallowed the lump in his throat and said, "Sure." He gave Davy's shoulder a squeeze and walked to the door. "Did you get any supper?" he asked before he left.

"I'm not hungry."

Sam nodded. He wasn't hungry, either.

Two small children were playing in the dust outside the Nylans' house when Sam rode into the yard the next day. They ran as he approached, darting into the house like frightened rabbits, and soon Lulie Nylan appeared in the doorway, holding a baby on her hip. The two little ones clung to her skirts and peered at him cautiously.

"What do you want?" she demanded before he could even call a greeting.

Sam reined up and glanced around. Except for Lulie and the kids, the place seemed deserted. "I'd like a word with Jessie, if you don't mind."

"She ain't here." Lulie's eyes were cold and hard, almost accusing.

"When'll she be back?"

"I don't reckon she *will* be back," Lulie spat. "She ran off with that Johnny Fitzpatrick, and it's all your fault!"

"How do you figure that?"

"Because he come by here last night after you fired him and told Jessie to meet him somewhere. If you hadn't of fired him, he wouldn't of left, and if that snooty brother of yours didn't think he was too good for a girl like Jessie, she wouldn't have run off with a no-account cowboy, either!"

Sam felt a small surge of relief to realize Jessie was no longer a threat to Davy and had evidently not shared her lies about the boy with her folks. "I'm sorry, Miz Nylan. I had to fire Johnny because he got in a fight with Davy over Jessie. I reckon I should've come by last night. Maybe if you'd known, you could've watched her closer. Did Gus go after them?"

"Of course he did, but he won't catch them. They got too good a head start."

Although Sam had no desire to see Jessie return, the rules of neighborliness compelled him to offer his assistance. "Maybe I could help with the tracking. . . ."

"We don't need your help, Sam Connors. We don't need nothing from you and your kind."

"My kind?"

"Yeah, you big ranchers who think you're so high and mighty you can run right over the rest of us. You've hated us since the day we first come here. You

400

think because we ain't as rich as you, we're trash!"
The baby on her hip began to squall, and she bounced
it absently.

"Wait a minute," he tried, but she wasn't listening.

"I've seen the way you look at me and mine, like
we wasn't no better than the dirt under your feet. Well,
my Gus is worth ten of you any day, and I'm glad he
brought those Taggerts here. I hope they kill every head
of cattle you own!"

The baby howled and the other two children began
to cry.

Feeling the heat crawling up his neck, Sam turned
his horse. As he rode away, she flung more invectives
at him but the children drowned them out. At least he
need feel no obligation to help bring Johnny and Jessie
back.

When David didn't come to school on Friday, Catherine was frantic. Surely he hadn't bent so totally to
Sam's will that he had given up school, too.

She announced to the children that the following
Wednesday would be the last day of classes and began
drilling them on the recitations they would give when
their parents came to commencement. The day
dragged, and Catherine developed a splitting headache.

When the children had finally gone, she quickly
gathered up her things to go to Twila's house. Envi-
sioning a cool rag across her throbbing forehead and
Twila fussing over her, she had started for the door
when she heard a horse in the yard.

For one awful moment, she thought Sam had come
back, but when she saw David through the window,
she cried aloud with relief.

"David!"

He stopped in the doorway, looking miserable and defeated. "I'm sorry I missed school today."

"I was afraid you weren't coming back," she said, going to him.

"Sam said I didn't have to, but that's not why I didn't come. I wanted to talk to you first."

"Oh, David." She wanted to take him in her arms but settled for taking his hand in hers. "Sam told me what happened, and I want you to know he's wrong. No one thinks you're . . . strange."

"Johnny did. Do you know what he said about me?"

"It doesn't matter. He only believed Jessie because he likes her."

"They ran off together."

"*What?*"

"Sam went over to the Nylans today to warn Jessie to keep her mouth shut, and she was gone. Johnny went by her place before he left last night. They talked about something, and this morning she was gone. Her folks think they ran off together."

Catherine sighed. "Then you have nothing to worry about. Now no one will ever hear those horrible lies."

"Sam wants me to give up painting anyway."

Catherine's throat constricted at the sight of his agony, and she could not speak.

"He says—" he swallowed loudly, "he says folks think I'm strange because I draw pictures."

"No one thinks you're strange."

His blue eyes filled with tears. "I don't want to quit, Miss Eaton."

"Of course you don't," she said, succumbing at last to the urge to embrace him. Although he towered over

402

her, she took him in her arms and patted his back as if he were a child.

He refused to surrender to his grief, however. After a moment, he straightened, pulled away from her. "I want to go to Philadelphia to school."

"Then you should talk to Sam. Tell him—"

"No, he'll never let me go, not now, but if I don't ask him, I can just go. . . ."

"You can't run away!"

"Why not? I've got some money saved up. Sam pays me wages out of my half of the Spur. It's the only way, Miss Eaton."

He was probably right, but as much as she supported David's desire to paint, she couldn't encourage him to run away from his home.

She grasped him by the arms. "At least give Sam one more chance before you do anything so desperate, and wait a while, until you've both gotten over what happened yesterday."

David nodded, but she wasn't sure if he really agreed or if he was simply placating her. After a minute, he drew a ragged breath and said, "Aren't you going to somebody's house this weekend?"

"I've been staying with the Shallcrosses at night lately. I decided it was too dangerous to stay alone at the school and I didn't feel much like visiting, so they're keeping me this weekend, too."

"I'll walk you over to their house, then."

Twila invited him in for freshly baked cookies, and by the time he left, he looked much less miserable. "I'll be at school on Monday," he promised as he bid them farewell.

Pleading a sick headache, Catherine went to bed early that night and spent most of Saturday in the

Shallcrosses' spare room, having instructed Twila she would not be receiving visitors. Twila came up soon after the noon meal to inform her Sam had been by, asking to see her.

She could tell from Twila's disapproving look that she thought Catherine should give him another chance, but of course her friend had no idea what their fight had been about or how irrevocable their differences were. Since Catherine couldn't tell her, she stoically resisted the guilt Twila tried to make her feel.

When Sam approached her after church the next day, she turned away and asked Mathias to escort her home, saying her headache had returned. Only three more days, she told herself, and then she would leave Crosswicks and Sam Connors forever.

David returned to school on Monday, as he had promised, and helped her with the preparations for the final celebration. The children all drew pictures with which to decorate the walls and took turns practicing their "pieces."

If Sam came to the school at night in an attempt to see her, she never knew, but he stayed away during the day until Wednesday, when all the parents came to see their children perform.

The school was packed with mothers and fathers and younger siblings. Each student came forward in turn and recited, exhibiting varying degrees of nervousness. David had selected Longfellow's "Children," feeling himself justified by his advanced age in saying the lines, " 'In your hearts are the birds and the sunshine, In your thoughts the brooklets flow, But in mine is the wind of Autumn and the first fall of the snow.' "

Catherine found the last lines the most poignant.

" 'For what are all our contrivings, And the wisdom

of our books, When compared with your caresses, And the gladness of your looks? Ye are better than all the ballads That ever were sung or said; For ye are living poems, And all the rest are dead.' "

She couldn't help remembering what Sam had said about his father and Adora: "When they died, Davy was mine." David was his living poem, and all the rest were dead. She glanced at Sam, but his face revealed no emotion whatsoever. Did he sense that David was slipping away from him no matter how hard he tried to hold him?

When the program was over, the children served cookies and punch to their visitors. Catherine avoided Sam by chatting enthusiastically with some of the mothers. After a few minutes, however, David's voice rose above the noise of the crowd.

"Attention, everyone. We have something special for Miss Eaton."

All eyes turned to the front of the room where David had propped a cloth-covered canvas on her desk. Catherine felt eager hands urging her forward and she walked toward David, wondering what on earth he had painted for her. For one awful moment, she thought it might be the portrait of Sam she had encouraged him to do, but then she recalled that David had no idea she and Sam had been lovers. The very last thing he would give her was a portrait of his brother.

Forcing herself to smile, she stopped beside David and eyed the covered canvas.

"I painted this, of course," David explained to the assembly, "but all the kids pitched in to buy the canvas, so it's a present from all of us."

He whipped off the cover to reveal a portrait—not of Sam at all, but of *her*. She stood in a very authoritative pose in front of the school, and Catherine realized this must be the way she looked when she was summoning the children to class.

A bittersweet pang clenched her heart as she realized how much she would miss the school and the children. To her mortification, her eyes filled with tears and she had to cover her mouth to keep from crying.

Recognizing her distress, Mathias Shallcross rescued her. "Don't it look just like her?" he asked of the crowd.

A murmur of agreement arose from the parents.

"Yes," Twila supplied. "She'll have something to remember us by when she goes."

Catherine froze. She barely heard Opal Refern's laughing reply. "Where do you think she's going, Twila?"

"I . . . uh . . ." Twila cast Catherine a look of despair. She knew she'd broken her promise, and she was helpless to repair the damage.

The crowd immediately sensed the truth, and Catherine knew it must show on her face. She cleared the tears from her throat and gave them all a sad smile, glad for the moisture still clouding her eyes so she did not have to see Sam Connors's expression too clearly. "I'm afraid Twila is right. I'm going to be returning to Philadelphia soon. I . . . there's sickness in my family and they need me at home," she improvised.

Not daring to look at Sam, she turned to David instead. She had expected to see the shock of betrayal, but instead his eyes shone with satisfaction and triumph. Oh, dear! He thought she was going back to Philadelphia because of *him!* She had no opportunity to speak with him, however. Instantly, the women surrounded her, lamenting her departure and asking ques-

406

tions for which she had to invent answers. The next time she looked around, Sam was gone. She didn't know whether to be relieved or alarmed by his departure.

After what seemed an eternity, the crowd began to disperse. Plans had been laid for a farewell party for Catherine on Saturday night, and each departing couple said they would see her there.

At last only she and David remained at the school. He smiled conspiratorially. "You couldn't stand the thought of me going to Philadelphia alone, could you?"

"David, you mustn't run away," she insisted. "I know Sam will change his mind. Just give him some time."

"But if he doesn't, you'll be there to help me, won't you?"

"I'll help you in any way I can," she promised, although she knew she wouldn't be able to keep her pregnancy a secret from him if he followed her. She would have to disappear from his life and keep her promise by watching over him through her father's friends.

Together they finished straightening the room while David chattered about his plans. Catherine barely heard him as she considered her own plans. She would have to leave soon, immediately after the party. Every day she stayed posed a danger that Sam might be able to contact her and shatter the fragile defenses she had built around her heart. Although she was certain she had made the right decision, she wasn't sure she possessed the strength of will to resist him.

"Do you want me to walk you over to the Shallcrosses?" David asked when they were finished.

Catherine shook her head, knowing she needed a few

minutes alone before facing Twila's abject apologies for having revealed her secret. "I have a few more things to do. Thank you anyway."

"I'll see you soon," he said with a grin. "We need to make arrangements to meet in Philadelphia."

She barely managed a coherent reply, and when he was gone, she sank down wearily into a nearby chair. Poor David would be so hurt when she vanished from his life. Even knowing he would soon forget her gave Catherine little comfort. Oh, why did every one of her choices involve hurting someone?

After a few minutes, she gathered the strength to return to her room. Perhaps she should begin packing so she would be ready to go when the time came. As she walked toward the door between the classroom and her bedroom, she thought of all the things she must still do. She was already through the door when she saw him.

"Sam!"

He stood in the middle of the room, his arms crossed in silent challenge, his eyes glittering with suppressed rage. "Sick relatives, Catherine? You told me and Davy you didn't have any family left."

She fought down the wave of panic. He wasn't going to hurt her, after all. She had nothing to be afraid of. She lifted her chin defiantly. "I couldn't very well say I was leaving to get away from you, now, could I?"

Something flickered in his eyes, and she wondered if she had hurt him. If so, he gave no other indication. "Are you leaving me or are you running away with Davy?"

"Don't be ridiculous!"

"I heard you in there, making plans."

"You heard *David* making plans. Didn't you hear me tell him he should talk to you first?"

Sam laughed mirthlessly. "Oh, yeah, I heard you all right. 'I'll help you in any way I can,' " he mimicked.

Heat scorched her cheeks, but she refused to be intimidated. "If you don't allow him to go, he'll run away, Sam, and then you really will lose him forever."

This time she did hurt him, but he recovered quickly. "So what am I supposed to do? Stand by and smile while both of you run off to Philadelphia?"

"It's really none of my business what you do. David is no relation to me, as you have often reminded me, and you and I—" She shrugged eloquently, hoping she looked more calm and collected than she felt.

"What about you and I?" he insisted, moving closer.

She felt it, that fatal weakness he always inspired in her, the desire to surrender to him, but she fought it. "You and I are finished."

"Are we?"

He moved like lightning. One second he was across the room, and the next he took her in his arms. She struggled, but he was too strong. His mouth found hers, his lips hungry and demanding. Love tore at her heart, shredding it, until the pain brought tears to her eyes. She went limp in his arms, resisting the overwhelming urge to kiss him back.

When at last he lifted his mouth from hers, his face twisted in fury. "Damn you! What's the matter with you? Don't you know you could be pregnant?"

"What?" she croaked, pushing out of his arms.

"Pregnant. Surely you know you could be carrying my baby right now. What would you do with a bastard child in Philadelphia? What would you tell your friends, or won't those people care?''

Fear clogged her throat and she could barely breathe. All she could do was shake her head in silent denial.

"You hadn't thought of that, had you?" he accused. "Well, you'd better think of it. Adora cheated me out of one son, and I won't lose another. You're mine, Cat, whether you like it or not, and I keep what's mine, no matter what the cost.''

He doesn't know! she kept telling herself. *All you have to do is placate him a little so he'll leave before you blurt out the truth.*

She hugged herself, trying to still the trembling. "You . . . you're right. I hadn't thought . . .''

His expression softened instantly. "Cat," he whispered. This time his arms were gentle when he pulled her to him.

Absurdly grateful for his comforting embrace, she relaxed against him, squeezing her eyes shut against the tears burning to escape.

"I didn't want to scare you, but you didn't give me any choice,'' he breathed against her temple. "You won't be sorry. I'll take good care of you, you'll see.''

A sob escaped her, and his arms tightened protectively. "I love you, Cat.''

Her control shattered and she dissolved into tears, weeping against his shirtfront while he whispered endearments and pressed tiny kisses to her face.

He loved her! And she loved him. Dear God, why couldn't things have been different? Why couldn't *he* have been different? Because as much as she loved him, she still couldn't let him destroy their child the way he was trying to destroy David.

Slowly, determinedly, she pushed out of his embrace

again. Brushing the tears from her face, she looked up at him, and the adoration in his eyes almost broke her resolve.

Almost.

"Sam, I can't—"

"Can't what?"

"I can't . . . marry you."

Stung, he reared back, his dark eyes narrowed in fury. "You don't have any choice."

"I most certainly do. I'm not with child and—"

"How do you know?"

"A woman knows these things," she hedged, hoping he wouldn't be bold enough to ask for details. "But if we married, we most likely *would* have children and—"

"And what?" he demanded.

"And I don't want them to go through what David's going through."

"Davy's not 'going through' anything!" he shouted. "You've put some fool notions into his head, but he'll forget about them in time."

"No, he won't!" she shouted back. "And I'm not going to see my children go through the same thing. I won't marry you, Sam!"

"Maybe you won't have a choice!"

This time she fought like a tigress, struggling and kicking, but her blows fell unnoticed as he dragged her over to the bed and forced her down. His eyes were wild, and the metallic taste of fear strangled her.

"Sam, no! I don't want this!"

"I can make you want it," he said, and she knew he was right. Her body was already responding instinctively as he ran his hands over her. "If you don't have a baby yet, I'll give you one."

411

Her breath came in terrified sobs, but she didn't realize she was crying until he went still. His hands stopped, and his eyes, so crazed just moments before, cleared, as if he were seeing her for the first time. He touched her cheek and gently wiped away the moisture. "Cat?" he said softly.

She was quaking too badly to speak.

He glanced down at where his body pinned hers to the bed, at where his knee had forced her legs apart. "Oh, God, what am I doing?" he murmured. Carefully, he levered himself off her, rising up and collapsing against the footboard. "Cat, I'm sorry."

She scrambled upright, pulling her knees to her chest and clutching them protectively. Sobs convulsed her, and she scrubbed ineffectually at the tears streaming down her face. "Get out of here," she gasped. "This time . . . I won't have to . . . lie when I say . . . you tried to attack me!"

He reached for her, but she flinched away. "Get out of here! *Now!*"

Slowly, wearily, he rose from the bed.

He'd lost his hat in the tussle, and he scooped it up from the floor. "Cat, I . . . please believe me. I don't want to hurt you."

She closed her eyes against the pain, praying that he wouldn't try to reason with her. "Just go," she whispered.

He drew a ragged breath and let it out in a sigh. Then he left, closing the door softly behind him. Catherine hugged her knees more tightly, fearing she might fly into a million pieces if she let go.

Past tears now, she stared dry-eyed at the door through which he had gone. She'd reached the limits of her endurance. She couldn't face him again. There was a stage first thing in the morning. She would be on it.

Knowing he didn't dare broach the subject of Philadelphia with Davy, Sam avoided the boy for the rest of the day. That night he lay awake, alternately cursing himself for being a fool and cursing Catherine's obstinacy. What had possessed him to attack her? And why couldn't she see how wrong she was about Davy? He was certain of only one thing: He couldn't let her go.

At last morning came, and Sam made his way, bleary-eyed, to breakfast. After giving the men their instructions for the day, he returned to the house, knowing he would have to confront Davy sooner or later. Yesterday had not seemed like a good time, but he couldn't let the boy go on thinking he could run away to Philadelphia.

Hearing Davy's voice, he followed it into the dining room where he was having a conversation with Inez.

"She is *leaving?*" Inez was saying in disbelief.

"Yeah," Davy reported. "She's going back to Philadelphia. That's where she's from."

"You are sure? She told you this herself?" Inez insisted.

"She told everybody at the school yesterday. You can ask her yourself on Saturday night. They're having a good-bye party for her."

"Dios," Inez murmured as Sam came into the room. "Mr. Sam, do you know Miss Eaton is leaving?"

"She's not going anywhere," Sam said with more confidence than he felt.

Davy frowned, but Inez laid a hand over her heart and sighed with relief. "Ah, good! Then she told you."

"Told me what?"

Now Inez frowned. "She did not tell you she—?" Inez hesitated and glanced uncertainly at Davy.

"She what?" Sam prodded.

"I—I cannot say."

"What is it?" Davy asked, concerned by her obvious distress.

"I—I cannot! I promised!" she wailed, backing up in the face of Sam's determination.

"You know something about her," Sam accused. "What is it?"

She shook her head desperately, but Sam had already figured it out.

"She's pregnant, isn't she?" he asked triumphantly, and saw the answer on Inez's face. Joy sluiced through him, but his happiness was short-lived.

Davy made a strangled sound, and Sam glanced at him, horrified to realize he had forgotten the boy was there.

"You—you—" Davy sputtered, rage splotching his face. *"You son of a bitch!"*

He launched himself at Sam, catching him in the chest and carrying them both to the floor in a heap. Davy's fists flailed, landing with surprising force as he shrieked a stream of profanity. Sam threw up his hands to ward off the blows, but with little effect. Finally, he had to fight back, catching Davy's hands and throwing him over onto the floor.

Sam used his superior weight to hold the boy down while Davy continued to rant in frustration. "You bastard! You raped her, didn't you? Is that what you meant by 'forcing her to fall in love with you'? I hate you!"

"Stop it! Listen to me!"

414

"I wouldn't believe a word you said, you dirty, rotten—"

"Listen to your brother!"

Both of them looked up in surprise to find Inez glaring down at them, arms akimbo, black eyes blazing, "You are both loco over this woman, but do not be stupid, too! He did not force her."

"How do you know?" Davy challenged furiously.

"Because she told me."

Davy's tear-filled eyes went from Inez to Sam and back again. "I don't believe you!"

He strained against Sam's grip and broke free, scrambling away. "I don't believe either of you! I'm going to ask her myself!"

Staggering to his feet, he charged out of the room.

Sam sat down on the floor with a thump and stared after him numbly.

"You better go after him," Inez said. "She should not have to explain to him alone."

Sam nodded, overwhelmed by the sickening realization of how thoroughly he had disillusioned his son. The boy despised him now. How on God's earth would he ever win back his trust? "I'll give him a head start. He won't like it if he thinks I'm following him."

He lifted his gaze to Inez again. "Did she really tell you about us?"

"No," she replied grimly. "When she fainted, I guessed the truth."

"Then how do you know I didn't force her?"

"I can tell by the way she speaks of you. I say she must tell you soon so you can marry, and she say she will."

The pain of Catherine's betrayal squeezed his heart. He'd given her every opportunity to tell him. He'd even warned her she might already carry his child, and still she'd hidden it from him. Rage and frustration curdled inside him as he realized she intended to leave without ever telling him at all, leave and take his baby!

His baby and his *son*, he corrected as he hauled himself to his feet. She was going to take Davy, too.

Chapter Fourteen

David brought his pony to a skidding halt in the schoolyard and bounded to the ground before the animal had completely stopped.

"Miss Eaton!" he called, knowing the chances of finding her here were slight. She'd told him she was staying with the Shallcrosses because of the danger, and he wondered bitterly if Sam were the danger to which she had referred.

"Miss Eaton?" He pounded on the door and it flew open under his fist. He glanced inside and saw the bed had been stripped. All her personal belongings were gone, so he must have moved in with the Shallcrosses for the duration.

His pony had barely caught its breath when David leaped on its back again, headed for the Shallcrosses' house.

Sam came along a few minutes later. He had expected to see Davy's pony in the yard and he could easily read the sign of his passing, so he followed it into town, quickly realizing Cat must be at Twila's house.

Didn't he know only too well she hadn't been sleeping at the school lately?

The memory of his futile attempts to visit her in the dark of night made his lips purse with bitterness. Damn her to hell! How could he have fallen in love with *two* such faithless women in the course of one lifetime? Did he possess some terrible flaw that fated him to give his heart only to a woman who would tear it to shreds and who would take his child away from him?

He caught up with Davy at the Shallcrosses' house. The boy stood on the front porch with Twila.

"Sam, thank heaven you're here!" Twila called, waving him over. Although Davy had gone stiff with rage, Sam directed his horse up to the front porch.

"I was just telling Davy. I've been thinking maybe I should've sent you word, but I didn't want to meddle," Twila said, wringing her hands and looking distressed.

"Send me word about what?"

"She's gone," Davy reported venomously.

"What do you mean, 'gone'?" Sam asked with a stomach-wrenching sense of foreboding.

"I mean she up and left, took the stage out this morning, you son of a bitch!"

"Davy!" Twila cried. "What a way to talk! It's not Sam's fault—"

"It's *all* his fault! If he hadn't of—" He caught himself, flushing furiously, and contented himself with merely glaring murderously at Sam, who glared furiously back.

"I know the two of them quarreled," Twila said, "but Sam's been trying to make it up. She's the one who's been so unreasonable. I know if they could just talk things over—"

418

"Talking won't settle this," Davy interrupted, jamming his hands into his pockets.

"Maybe it will," Sam replied, holding onto his temper only through a great effort of will. "I'm going after her."

"Thank heaven," Twila murmured.

"The hell you will!" Davy shouted. "I'll kill you first!"

"Then you better get started," Sam said, turning his horse. Davy called after him but Sam ignored his shouts, spurring his horse into a gallop the instant he hit the road.

"Come back here and leave her alone!" Davy screamed, and jumped on his own pony.

Sam's larger, heavier mount quickly took a commanding lead, and after a while, he forgot Davy was behind him. All he could think about was finding Catherine and stopping her.

As the only passenger on the stage, Catherine had her choice of seats, but she vainly sought a more comfortable position on the cracked leather cushions. They'd only been on the road an hour, and already she felt nauseated and bone weary. Perhaps she should have waited another day, until she'd had a chance to get a full night's sleep, before setting out for Dallas and the railhead. Perhaps she should have eaten some breakfast before leaving.

And perhaps she shouldn't have left at all.

What kind of a woman was she to steal a man's child from him? It was amazing how a short stage ride could give a person such perspective on the situation. As unreasonable and cruel as Sam Connors could be, his only real fault lay in loving his son too much. When she thought of how he'd suffered in order to remain with David, her eyes filled with tears. Adora had treated Sam abominably, and if Catherine ran away, she would be no different from David's heartless mother. In fact, she would be worse!

At least she should have given him the opportunity to show how he would react, instead of simply assuming the worst and running away. Sam always said she made him do crazy things, and obviously he had the same effect on her. Did love always turn people into raving lunatics, or were she and Sam especially pathetic examples?

She didn't know and was too tired to guess. All she wanted to do now was to turn the coach around and head back to Crosswicks before Sam found out she was gone. The desire was so strong that for an instant she thought she had only imagined the stage was slowing down.

"Whoa!" the driver yelled, and Catherine tried to recall how long they had actually been gone. Surely it was much too early for them to have reached a relay station.

She lifted the window shade and peered out, seeing only a lone horseman in the road ahead. Dust billowed as the stage lumbered to a halt, momentarily blocking her view. Then she heard the shouted command.

"Don't go for your gun. Keep your hands high and you won't get hurt."

A holdup! Catherine's heart leaped to her throat. She didn't need to see anything to know who the bandits were, either. She shivered violently as she recalled the way Floyd Taggert had leered at her.

"You boys're wasting your time," the driver said with forced calmness. "I ain't carrying anything but mail."

"You got some passengers, ain't you? Maybe they've got something."

"There's only one lady inside, and she don't have anything worth stealing," the driver said. "Leave her alone."

"A lady!" the second bandit said with delight, and Catherine recognized Floyd Taggert's demented giggle.

Fear clawed at her stomach. *He* wouldn't leave her alone.

She could hear the sounds of a struggle as they dragged the driver down from his seat and tied him up. Now she would be at their mercy! She cast about for some sort of weapon and remembered the six-inch pin she had inserted this morning to hold her stylish hat in place. Swiftly, she withdrew the pin and removed the hat, tossing it aside and testing the point of the pin with her finger. It wouldn't be much protection against two armed men, but at least she wasn't totally defenseless.

"Let's get the lady out here and take a look at her," Floyd said when they had finished with the driver.

The door flew open and Floyd Taggert's face appeared above the barrel of a Colt .45. A filthy bandana covered the lower half of his face, but Catherine would have recognized his leer anywhere. Terror shut off her breath and stopped her heart.

'Well, well, well, lookee who we got here," Floyd said, reaching for her with his free hand.

She flinched from his touch, but she wasn't quick enough. He captured her arm and yanked, jerking her forward. She caught herself to keep from falling and, concealing the pin in her hand, allowed him to haul her from the coach.

Clutching at the door for support, Catherine managed a defiant glare although she trembled violently.

"Well, now," Will Taggert said behind his mask, "If it ain't Sam Connors's woman."

"No!" Catherine cried in horror before she could stop herself.

"Oh, yeah," Floyd cackled. "We seen the two of you together that day we robbed the stage. We was spying on the town to see what they'd do. You two was kissing, and you wasn't fighting him off, neither. We would've followed him that day and finished him off, but he stayed in town, just like he knowed we was after him."

Will nodded. "That Connors is part wolf, but even a wolf'll fight for his mate. Now we can get him to come to us."

Floyd cackled again, and Catherine felt the blood rushing from her head. "He won't come for me," she tried. "We—we had a fight and I'm leaving, going back where I came from."

"Then we'll just keep you for our ownselves, won't we, Will?" Floyd said, grabbing her around the waist and pulling her against his stinking body. "I figure Connors owes me something for that bullet I took."

She screamed and fought. The hand holding the pin was trapped between them. Floyd held her tightly, rubbing his hips against her obscenely. His laughter billowed out from beneath the bandana in fetid waves, and she felt the gorge rising in her throat.

"That's enough, Floyd," Will called, climbing back into his saddle. "Get her up here on my horse."

"Not yet," Floyd protested, stuffing his pistol back into its holster so he would have both hands free. "Let me have just a little piece of her before we go."

He grabbed her breast and squeezed viciously. Catherine screamed again and at last jerked her arm free. With no time to aim, she stabbed out blindly, catching him in the shoulder. He howled in pain, slashing instinctively at her arm. The blow sent the pin flying from her hand. Vaguely, she noticed blood staining his shirt in the instant before he slammed her against the side of the coach, driving the breath from her lungs. Then he threw her limp body to the ground.

"Bitch! Whore!" He shouted other words Catherine had never heard before as he rubbed his shoulder. "You'll be sorry you did that!"

Heaving, gasping, Catherine fought helplessly for breath as Taggert straddled her. He fumbled with his trousers.

"*Floyd!* I said no!"

She heard Will's voice from far away, but Floyd responded with another howl. "She stuck me."

"Get off her, *now*," Will shouted. "I don't want to have to tell you again!"

Just then the air rushed back into her lungs and she gave a wild cry, lifting her fists to ward him off, but he was already up and off of her, swearing in disgust. Clasping one of her outstretched hands, he jerked her to her feet.

"I wasn't gonna hurt her none," Floyd insisted.

"Shut up and bring her over here. She'll ride with me."

"Wait till later, little honey," he whispered as he dragged her toward Will's horse.

"Why can't she ride with me?" Floyd whined.

"Because I say so. Now hoist her up. You've done scared her so bad, she can't even walk."

It was true. Catherine's arms and legs were like

rubber, and all her strength was gone. Floyd threw her up onto the horse behind Will as if she were a sack of potatoes.

"Hang on to me, miss," Will said with absurd deference.

The very thought of touching him repelled her, but seeing her reluctance, he grabbed her arms and forcibly entwined them around his waist. "You'll like this better than falling, I expect," he remarked as he spurred his horse, and Catherine quickly realized he was correct.

Sam's temper cooled somewhat as he rode, allowing him to think more rationally about Catherine and her flight. While he could never forgive her for not telling him about the baby, he could at least understand why she had run away. He had behaved like a wild man the last time they were together. She must have been terrified. No wonder she had fled, and he had no one but himself to blame.

When he found her, he would have to be careful not to frighten her again or she would surely escape at the first opportunity. Perhaps the next time she would be more successful.

He was planning what he would say to convince her to stay with him when he saw the stage stopped in the middle of the road.

"*Catherine?*" he shouted, spurring his horse as he raced frantically toward the vehicle. The team shifted restlessly in its traces, but nothing else moved.

Panic welled in him. "*Catherine?*" he tried again, lunging from his saddle and peering inside the stage. "Cat, where are you?" Then he caught sight of the driver lying on the far side of the coach. He hurried over and began to untie him. "What happened?" he demanded when he had loosed the man's gag.

"Robbery," the driver croaked. "The Taggerts."

Fear roughened Sam's voice. "Where's Miss Eaton?"

"They took her."

Sam went cold with a terror more awful than any he had ever known.

"Can you untie me?" the driver prompted, making Sam aware he was staring off into space, lost in the nightmare of his imagination.

Swiftly, he freed the driver and helped massage the feeling back into his arms and legs.

"I reckon they was right," the driver said after a few minutes. "They said she was your woman, and they took her so's you'd come after her."

Sam started to ask how they had known about his relationship with Catherine but decided he didn't really want to find out. "Did they . . . hurt her?"

"The one called Floyd wanted to take her right here on the ground, but the other one made him stop. Seems like he wanted to keep her in good shape until they'd got you."

Sam swore. Cat was in danger and all because of him. If he hadn't frightened her the other day, she wouldn't have run away, and she'd be safe and sound at Twila's house right now.

"What happened?" Davy demanded as he thundered up on his pony.

Sam looked up at the boy and experienced a new wave of guilt. "The Taggerts held up the stage. They took Catherine," he explained, rising to his feet. "How long have they been gone?" he asked the driver.

'Not more'n an hour,'' he guessed, checking the position of the sun.

Sam headed for his horse. "Go back to town," he told the driver, "and get up a posse. I'll follow the Taggerts and leave a trail they can follow. Davy, you go with him."

"I'm going with you," Davy said.

One look at his expression told Sam an argument would be useless. He loved Catherine, too. Besides, the boy had a good eye and might see something Sam missed. He'd need all the help he could get. "Try to keep up, then," he said, swinging into his saddle.

David gaped for a moment before kicking his pony into motion again. "What makes you think you can follow them?" he taunted as Sam studied the trail, following it easily here on the road. "You've never caught them before."

"They never had Cat before." He glanced at Davy, not surprised to see his own terror reflected in the boy's eyes.

"Why did you call her Cat?" he asked unsteadily.

Sam shrugged. "That's what I call her when we're together."

"Liar!" he cried, on the verge of tears with his hurt and his fear.

"Davy, Catherine and I are lovers," he said patiently, remembering with a pang the discussion they had had over telling Davy the truth about their relationship. "I love her, and I thought she loved me, too. Whatever she felt, she let me make love to her. I never forced her."

"I don't believe you! Why did she run away, then?"

"You'll have to ask her yourself . . . when we find her." He didn't let himself say what was in his mind:

426

if we find her. But Davy sensed his uncertainties all the same.

"What'll they do to her?" he asked hoarsely.

Sam couldn't let himself think of that. "The driver said they knew about me and Cat. They're going to hold her hostage to get me."

"Then they won't hurt her?" he asked hopefully.

"They'd be crazy to, wouldn't they?" Sam replied, unwilling to consider any other alternative. He knew only too well how much damage they could do her and still keep her alive. He just hoped Davy wouldn't figure that out.

They quickened their pace, following the clear trail. Apparently, the Taggerts hadn't been too concerned with pursuit. They must have known the chances of anyone discovering the abduction for many hours were remote and had chosen to make some time during the early stage of their getaway.

In fact, Sam could already guess in which direction they would travel, having tracked them often enough to know where they always went to ground. He glanced down periodically to confirm his suspicions and found he was right, even guessing correctly at what point they would leave the road to travel cross-country.

After a long silence, Davy said, "What happens when we find her?"

Sam made a pretense of studying the trail. "We get her back."

Catherine's entire being was a seething, throbbing mass of misery. The jolting of the horse had pounded her body into one huge ache that seemed concentrated in her legs and buttocks. Riding astride on the back of the saddle had chafed her thighs raw and strained muscles she hadn't known she possessed, and each bounce reminded her of the tiny life she carried and the danger it was in. Pregnant women shouldn't ride horses at all, she knew. Every second she expected to feel the tearing sensation of the child being ripped from her body. Her head pounded from fear and lack of sleep and the blazing sun.

Mercifully, her sense of smell had dulled somewhat, but the stench of Will Taggert's unwashed body still made her stomach roll. He'd stopped earlier while she had a bout of the dry heaves, waiting impatiently as she tried to stop gagging. The urge to do so still burned in her throat but she fought it, swallowing carefully every few minutes.

Unfortunately, fear had dried her mouth, making such efforts more and more difficult. In addition, she had an overwhelming need to empty her bladder. She tried to tell herself it was only nerves, but she knew her pregnancy had increased the frequency of her visits to the outhouse.

For a while she debated which would be the more humiliating, asking Will Taggert to stop or wetting herself. At last she saw a clump of mesquite up ahead and knew she could wait no longer.

"Mr. Taggert?"

He grunted.

"I have to stop."

"What for?"

"I—I have to, that's all."

He turned, trying to see her face over his shoulder. She tried to look as miserable as she felt, which wasn't too difficult. Apparently, he realized her problem. "Those bushes all right?" he asked.

"Yes," she croaked gratefully.

428

He reined up, and for a moment Catherine found she couldn't move, not even to unclasp her arms from around his waist. He helped by breaking the grip of her hands and then grasping her arm as she slid to the ground.

"Why're we stopping?" Floyd demanded, wheeling his horse and coming back when he realized they were no longer following.

"The lady needs to pee," Will explained.

Fortunately, Catherine was past embarrassment. Clutching at his stirrup, she sagged wearily, trying to gather the strength to walk.

"*Pee!*" Floyd cackled. "I didn't know ladies did them kinda things. I think maybe I'll watch."

Catherine had only thought she was past embarrassment. She found herself casting Will Taggert an imploring look.

He didn't even glance at her, however. "You stay away from her, you hear?" he said to his brother.

"Looking won't hurt nothing."

"You won't stop at looking."

Floyd swore colorfully. "One little piece is all I want. I said I won't hurt her."

"Yeah, that's what you said about that squaw, too, and she *died,* for God's sake. Once we get Connors, you can do whatever you please, but until then I want this one alive."

Catherine stood frozen with horror, clinging to the stirrup as her imagination conjured up visions of what these men might have in store for her. And even worse, they planned to murder Sam! Couldn't she do anything to stop them?

"Lady, get moving," Will said sharply.

Instantly, Catherine's nerves sprang to life, and she

scurried over to the mesquite bush and its meager concealment. Only the urgency of her need compelled her to squat behind the bush. Luckily, she had worn field pants for the trip—underdrawers with an open crotch—so she didn't have to remove any garments. Still, she kept a lookout, alert to any hint Floyd Taggert might be making good his threat to observe her.

Oh, God, what was she going to do? She couldn't simply go with them like a lamb to the slaughter. As angry as Sam would be when he discovered she had run away, he would most certainly come after her when the Taggerts sent him word. And he would ride right into an ambush!

But surely he would expect a trick, surely he would be ready, and surely he would bring help.

And surely the Taggerts would expect him to, and surely they would have a foolproof plan for murdering him, anyway!

If only he could track them to their hideout first and catch them unawares, but she knew he'd never been able to do so before because the Taggerts covered their trail too well. They would vanish into the rocks without a trace, not leaving a broken stick or a scuff mark or anything to indicate which way they had gone.

Catherine stared blindly into the prickly interior of the mesquite bush. If only she could leave Sam a trail. If only she had something she could drop, like pebbles, the way the children in the fairy tale had.

And then she saw them, the dried brown beans lying scattered on the ground where they had fallen from their pods, the fruit of the mesquite tree. A hasty glance told her the Taggerts didn't seem to be paying her much attention. Swiftly, she scooped up a handful of the beans from the dust and stuffed them into her pocket. She had just gathered a second handful when Will Taggert yelled.

"Hurry it up, lady or I *will* let Floyd come after you."

Cramming the beans into her pocket with the others, she jumped to her feet and emerged from behind the bush, smoothing her skirts self-consciously. Hopefully, they would assume her nervousness came from maidenly modesty.

"Let her ride with me for a while, Will," Floyd whined. "I can't do nothing to her on the back of a horse."

"She's fine with me," Will said, grabbing Catherine's arm and propelling her toward his horse.

As obnoxious as Will Taggert was, Catherine certainly preferred him to his brother, so she went willingly. At least Will ignored her, which would make dropping the beans a little easier than it would be with Floyd, who would no doubt paw her the entire time and might even find her cache.

When they were on their way again, Catherine knew an overwhelming urge to begin leaving a trail at once, but she remembered what David had told her. Sam usually lost them in the rocks. Even Catherine could see they were taking no pains to hide the signs of their passing now. She forced herself to close her eyes and rest, leaning against the repellent man in front of her to conserve her waning strength. She wouldn't do Sam or anyone else any good if she passed out from fatigue.

"They stopped here all right," Sam concluded, going down on one knee to examine the footprints more closely. "Cat went off over there."

Davy had already raced ahead to the mesquite bush.

431

Sam went more slowly. If there were signs that Cat had been raped behind the bush, he was in no hurry to see them.

"She peed here," Davy said. "Looks like they left her alone." His expression reflected Sam's relief, and Sam realized that somewhere along the trail Davy had put aside his animosity, at least for the time being.

Sam hurried over and confirmed Davy's opinion. The spot was still slightly moist. They weren't far behind. If they could catch up before the Taggerts hit the rocks . . .

But they weren't close enough for that, Sam knew. If he couldn't find them before they went to ground, Cat would have to spend the night with those two animals. . . .

"What do you suppose she was after here?" Davy asked, hunkering down to look under the bush.

Sam went down beside him and peered beneath the twisted branches. The marks of her hands scraping something from the dust were clearly visible. "Wouldn't be nothing under here except maybe some dried-up beans and a few rocks," he mused. "What would she want with them?"

"Maybe she was hungry," Davy suggested.

Sam shook his head. "A city woman wouldn't know you could eat mesquite beans, and for sure she wouldn't eat them off the ground like that."

"Well, I reckon we can ask her when we find her," Davy said with forced bravado.

"Yeah, I reckon we can." Sam clapped a hand on the boy's shoulder, wishing for a moment he dared pull Davy to him for the kind of hugs they'd shared when he was much younger.

432

Davy's eyes seemed to hold the same yearning. "We're awful close, ain't we?"

"Not close enough to catch them before they hit the rocks."

"Maybe we can," he said, unwilling to admit defeat. He jumped up and ran toward his pony.

Needing to share Davy's hope, Sam hurried to catch up.

"Wake up, lady."

Will Taggert poked her rudely in the ribs, jarring her back to consciousness, and for an instant she didn't know where she was. Then the whole horrible nightmare came rushing back as every throbbing muscle in her body screamed in protest at being disturbed.

Oh, no! Were they at the hideout already? Had she passed out and missed her chance to leave a trail for Sam?

"Better pee if you need to. We ain't going to stop again until we get where we're going," Will said as he lowered her unceremoniously to the ground.

Once again Catherine grabbed for the stirrup to remain upright on her trembling legs. She shook her head to clear it and then scrambled away to avoid being kicked as Will Taggert dismounted.

The ground seemed to tilt and she fell, crying out in pain as the rocks scraped her hands.

Rocks! Instantly, she forgot her own pain and misery. They were in the rocks. She looked frantically around. The Taggerts were busy doing something to their horses' feet. Squinting against the glare, she saw they were tying flour sacking over the hooves.

Of course! Sam's theory about why they left no marks on the rocks was right. She struggled to her feet again, ignoring the pain in her muscles. Instinctively, she checked her pocket and found the beans she had hoarded. How should she drop them and when? Would Sam be able to see them against the rocky ground? Would he even come after her at all?

Despair claimed her as she considered the feebleness of her hope, but only for a moment. She forced herself to remember how he had forbidden her to leave him, arrogant enough to believe he could keep her with him by the force of his will. A man like that would come after her. A man like that would follow her barefoot through hell.

Tears stung her eyes at the thought of his wonderful stubbornness, and love convulsed her heart. Sam would find her, and when he did, she would never leave him again.

"Lady, if you've got something to do, you'd better do it," Will called, jarring her back to the present and reminding her she did need to answer a call of nature.

Quickly, she cast about for some measure of privacy. Finding nothing more than a large rock, she ducked behind it, searching for pebbles as she went.

Sam and Davy reined up and stared out at the expanse of rocky ground before them. Sam pulled off his Stetson, wiped his brow on his sleeve, and sighed wearily. Davy rubbed suspiciously at his eyes.

"We knew we couldn't catch them," Sam reminded him gently.

Davy nodded, not trusting his voice.

Sam swung down and began the futile task of searching for some clue. After a few minutes, he called to Davy. "Looks like they stopped here to put the sacks over their horses' feet like they always do."

"How much of a lead do you think they've got?"

"I figure they're almost two hours ahead. The tracking slowed us down some. From here we'll go on foot so we don't miss anything."

Davy climbed down from his saddle. They hadn't eaten since breakfast and the sun hung directly overhead, but neither of them thought about food.

"We'll cover the ground in zigzags," Sam explained. "You go that way; I'll go this way." Davy obediently started off, eyes trained to the ground. They would widen the zigzags until they encountered something to point them in the right direction.

If they encountered something to point them in the right direction, Sam thought dismally. Even if the Taggerts did intend to use Cat as a lure to draw him into a trap, how long would it be until they could get word to him? How long would they have her before he even had a chance of rescuing her? And what would they do to her in the meantime?

Fear churned inside him like broken glass, and frustration had made him desperate. When he got ahold of those Taggerts, he was going to cut them into tiny little pieces, just the way the Indians used to do it. He'd once thought no one deserved a death so horrible, but he had changed his mind in the last few hours.

So lost in thought was he that at first he didn't quite register the import of what his eyes were seeing. He blinked and looked again. Good God Almighty!

"Davy! Come quick!"

The boy raced over, finding him behind a large boulder. "What? . . . Oh, my God! You think she did it?"

They stared silently down at the message Catherine had left for them. An assortment of pebbles formed a

435

crude heart. Inside the heart she had placed a single mesquite bean.

"What does it mean?" Davy asked.

"Damned if I know. If you'd left it, I'd think—"

"You'd think what?"

"I'd think the heart was something unusual to catch a tracker's eye and you were telling me to look for a trail of mesquite beans, but a city woman wouldn't know anything about tracking."

"Yes, she would!" Davy cried. "I explained to her how you always lost the Taggerts in the rocks because they didn't leave any signs you could follow."

"What did you tell her exactly? Try to remember everything," Sam urged, feeling the first faint flickerings of renewed hope.

Davy thought back and recalled for Sam his conversation with Catherine on the subject of tracking, repeating for him all the information he had given her.

Sam stared down at the heart, and his vision blurred as he pictured Catherine trying to figure out what to do to make her message plain and kneeling there to arrange the pebbles.

"How could she know we were following her?" Davy asked after a moment.

"I don't reckon she did, but she knows me well enough to figure I'd come after her when I found out she was gone." She wanted him to find her, and by God, he would, if he had to walk barefoot through hell to get there.

"Come on," he said to the boy. "We'll keep making the zigzags until we find the first bean."

Davy spotted it instantly. They walked on, leading their horses until they found the second and the third and got a feel for which direction their quarry had headed. After that they rode slowly, searching the ground. Sometimes she dropped a bean, other times a pebble.

"I hope she don't run out," Davy said at one point, echoing Sam's concerns, but they could see she was being sparing, only leaving a bean where there might be some question about their direction.

"God, she's smart," Sam muttered when she led them down a ravine.

"Didn't you know that before?" Davy inquired testily, reminding Sam of the matters left unsettled between them. He wisely chose not to respond.

Catherine gave a shuddering hiccup and reached into her pocket for her handkerchief. Thinking of an excuse for loosening her hold on Will Taggert periodically had been even more difficult than figuring out how to leave a trail for Sam to follow. Luckily, the strain and fatigue had rasped her nerves to quivering rawness, and she had no trouble at all breaking into tears whenever the need arose.

Her seeking hand found only three beans left, and she resisted the urge to drop one. Instead, she pulled out the handkerchief and held it to her eyes for a moment.

"How much farther is it? I've got to rest soon," she sobbed.

Will Taggert shifted uneasily, as he had every time she had begun sobbing and made this plaintive request. "I told you to shut up, didn't I?"

"I can't help it," she wailed, letting the tears flow freely.

"We're almost there," he admitted grudgingly. "See

them rocks? There's a cave. Now stop that sniveling, or so help me God, I'll break your neck!''

He'd been issuing equally dire threats ever since she'd started weeping, without acting on them, so Catherine didn't flinch. She sniffed perfunctorily and pretended to get a grip on her emotions as she squinted into the sunlight, trying to make out the cave.

"I don't see anything," she said.

"That's the whole idea. The entrance is hidden. We can see everybody who comes along, but they can't see us at all."

Catherine's blood turned cold as she realized she had led Sam into a trap! How could she tell him to stop right here? What could she drop that would warn him away?

Her fingers clenched the handkerchief and she realized it was perfect—or would be if the stiff Texas wind didn't carry it away. She'd best drop all the remaining beans, too, just in case. Carefully, so as not to draw attention, she lowered her arm and pretended to tuck her handkerchief back into her pocket, gathering the three beans instead. Then she let them all slip from her fingers.

Breathing a sigh of relief, she let her aching body sag against Will's unyielding back. Now Sam would at least be on guard. The moment he saw the handkerchief, he would know. . . .

"What the hell?" Floyd Taggert yelled, galloping over to them. "Just what do you think you're doing, missy?" he demanded, pointing at the scrap of cloth lying so conspicuously on the ground behind Will's horse.

"Oh, my handkerchief!" she said in alarm. "I must have dropped it."

"You dropped it all right. You dropped it apurpose, right after Will told you something. What was you saying to her, Will?"

Will turned in the saddle and glared down at her. His annoyance had turned to fury, and Catherine knew she had made a terrible mistake. "I told her where the cave is and that we can see anybody who comes by."

"She was leaving Connors a warning," Floyd crowed, grinning as if he had solved a great mystery. "Reckon she figures she's smarter'n we are, eh, Will?"

"She's got a surprise coming, don't she?" Will replied, his pale eyes glittering menacingly.

Catherine swallowed nervously. "I . . . I'm sorry. It was an accident," she tried.

"Shut up," Will snapped. "Floyd, pick it up."

Floyd dropped down from his horse and snatched the handkerchief from the ground. Catherine held her breath, waiting. Would he see the beans? Would he realize what else she had done?

Lifting the handkerchief to his nose, he sniffed it, leering at Catherine over the delicate fabric. She turned sharply away and blinked furiously at the real tears burning her eyes. He hadn't seen the beans!

She had no time to dwell on her victory, however. Will Taggert angrily spurred his horse, forcing her to grab onto him or risk being thrown to the ground and crushed on the rocks beneath them.

Jouncing on the back of the saddle, she had little opportunity to study the entrance to the cave. Suddenly, rock walls loomed around them and then the sun disappeared completely. Cool darkness enveloped them, and Catherine was temporarily blinded.

"Your sweetheart won't never find you here," Floyd

439

cackled, and Catherine was very much afraid he was right.

"We're getting close," Sam reflected as they rode along slowly, watching for the next clue.

"How do you know?" Davy asked, looking around.

"I can feel it. I've been here before, almost to this exact spot. Remember I told you I could almost smell those bastards?"

Davy nodded. "They could be anywhere in these hills."

"There's caves everywhere, and Cat's in one of them."

"With those bastards," Davy added hoarsely.

Sam wasn't letting himself think of that. If they had indeed reached their hideout, Catherine had been with them for hours. A seething rage welled up in him, but he fought it back. He couldn't afford to let emotion color his judgment.

"Look there," Davy cried, pointing to the ground.

Sam jumped down instantly, beating Davy to the spot, and picked up the two beans lying together. A mistake? Had she accidently dropped a pair?

Then he saw the third lying nearby. Three beans could not be a mistake. She was telling him something. But what?

Davy had joined him, and he held the three beans out for the boy to see. "Why'd she drop three?"

Sam looked slowly around, studying the hills with their infinite nooks and crannies. "This must be the end of the trail."

"End? But what? . . ." Davy looked around, too.

"We're close, I told you. She's here somewhere. She might even be able to see us right now."

"Oh, God," Davy whispered, peering into the distance as if to see through the solid rocks.

"Let's leave the horses here and scout around."

Catherine awoke slowly, coming to wakefulness grudgingly, as if she were swimming to the top of a pool of molasses. Sleep was sticky, clinging to her limbs and weighing them down, so even the effort of lifting a finger seemed too great to contemplate. The dampness of the cave had stiffened her muscles, but if she lay perfectly still, she could keep the pain to a tolerable level. So long as she didn't feel the pain she most feared, she could bear anything.

Holding her breath, she centered all her thoughts on the tiny life within her and realized she felt not the slightest twinge to indicate the nightmare ride had injured her child. So long as her womb was secure, what did a few sore muscles matter? The only other thing even remotely important was keeping Sam safe.

Lifting her eyelids slightly, she looked around, finding the Taggerts near the opening to the cave. They sat cross-legged, taking turns scanning the area with a spyglass. Surely Sam could not have found them already. How long had she been asleep?

Almost the instant her feet had hit the ground inside the cave, she had collapsed into an exhausted heap and sunk into oblivion. At least Will Taggert had continued to keep Floyd from harming her while she lay defenseless. Now if only she could figure out some way of signaling Sam where the cave opening was.

Slowly, carefully, she scrunched her body around and pushed up on one elbow. Her hair had come loose sometime during her long ride, and she brushed it away from her face.

Engrossed in their lookout, the Taggerts didn't notice her movement. She took the opportunity to study the cave. The portion she could see, lighted only by the high, narrow crevice through which they had entered, was no more than twenty feet across, but she could tell this room opened into a larger one beyond. Somewhere nearby water trickled, and a horse stamped in the shadows. She shivered, trying not to think of the inky darkness of the interior. Any attempt to escape in that direction would be futile.

If she left the cave, she would have to go out the way she had come in. Under the Taggerts' watchful eyes, escape would be impossible, but what about a brief foray to get the lay of the land? As before, nature came to her rescue.

"Mr. Taggert?" she called.

Instantly, they turned to her. "Finally wake up, did you, missy?" Floyd asked with his vapid grin. "You sure are pretty when you're asleep. I told Will so, didn't I, Will?"

"Shut up, Floyd."

Floyd's eyes glittered wildly, and he rubbed his bloodstained shoulder meaningfully. Catherine shuddered and took a breath to steady her voice. "I need to go outside for a minute."

"You can't," Will said.

"But I have to!" she cried, knowing she was over-reacting. She mustn't let them see how desperate she was, so she forced herself to sound more reasonable. "I mean, I can't stay in here. Surely you don't . . . I mean, you must go outside yourselves."

"We can't let you out. You might try to get away," Will argued.

"Get away!" Floyd scoffed. "How the hell's she

442

gonna get away? She don't have a notion where she is, and we've got the horses in here."

"She might signal Connors."

"He ain't within a hundred miles of here. He prob'ly don't even know we've got her·yet."

For once, Floyd was her champion, and Catherine hid her revulsion. "He's right," she told Will. "I know I'd die out there all alone. I won't try to get away. I just need a few minutes of privacy."

Floyd giggled. "If she runs away, I'll go after her," he promised.

Will considered the situation for a long moment. Then he snatched the spyglass from his brother and gave a cursory look around. "All right, I guess you can go out, but only for a minute. And stay in plain sight."

Catherine considered these instructions ludicrous, considering *why* she was going out, but she refrained from expressing her opinion. Instead, she struggled to her feet and limped toward the opening. Will backed up to give her room to pass, but Floyd didn't move, leering up at her as she pulled her skirt aside so it wouldn't brush against him.

The blast of sunlight blinded her for a moment and she paused, waiting for her eyes to become accustomed to the glare. Then she examined her surroundings. An enormous mesquite tree screened the cave's opening. All manner of brush grew around the tree and covered the hillside approach.

Still limping, Catherine picked her way carefully around the mesquite and its thorns. She had hoped to find some open ground, but she saw at once there simply was none, as well as no place to arrange a signal for Sam. She kept walking until she felt the Taggerts could no longer see her plainly. Then she sank down to do her business.

For the first time she noticed her clothes. The long ride through the rough country had soiled her suit beyond redemption and her skirt hung in tatters. Even her petticoat was ruined, the lace shredded.

The lace! If her handkerchief had been a good idea, the lace would be almost as good. Still reasonably white, it would be easily visible against the colors of nature. Quickly, she tore off several strips.

But where would she leave them? To her untrained eye, the whole area seemed impenetrable. How would Sam find one tiny scrap of lace amidst all this, even assuming he could have followed her ridiculous trail of beans in the first place?

Despair brought tears to her eyes, and she didn't even have the energy to blink them away. What was the use? a tiny voice demanded. Even if Sam could find you, the Taggerts would kill him. Better only one of you should die.

Then she remembered she wasn't alone. She had her child to think of, and no matter how willing she might be to sacrifice herself for Sam, she couldn't sacrifice her child for any reason.

Even as the tears rolled down her cheeks, she carefully stuck a strip of lace onto a nearby thorn bush. Leaving two more along the way back to the cave, she casually hung one on the front of the mesquite tree before the cave's opening. The Taggerts would most certainly see it the next time one of them left the cave. They would be furious, but Catherine was past caring.

This time when she passed the Taggerts, Floyd's leer grew menacing. "Come here, little lady," he said, grabbing her hand.

"Let go of me!" She pulled away, twisting and struggling, trying to break his grip with her other hand, but he grabbed that one, too, and held on, cackling his fiendish laugh.

"How 'bout a little kiss, honey?" he taunted, pulling her down until her face was only inches from his. "Just one'll hold me till we've took care of Connors. Then you and me'll have a high old time."

"Stop it!" she cried, sobbing with terror as she fought to wrench free. His rancid breath gagged her, bringing the sour taste of bile to her mouth. "Don't touch me!"

"I'll touch you anywhere I want! I'll strip you naked and chain you up in this cave and you'll *beg* me to touch you then!"

"No!" she screamed as he pulled her to her knees.

"That's enough, Floyd!"

Will Taggert's voice rang against the stone walls, and Floyd's head came up like an animal alerted to sudden danger. "I'm just having a little fun," he insisted, not loosening his grip.

"You've had it, now let her go."

"Aw, Will—'

"Let her go!"

Like a petulant child, Floyd flung Catherine away. She cried out in pain as her shoulder struck the stone floor, but neither of them paid her any mind. "Will, she stuck me,"

"Stop acting like an animal! What would Mama say if she was still alive?"

"You ain't natural, Will. If you'd ever had a woman, you wouldn't begrudge me a little fun."

"You don't need to wallow around like a pig to have fun. I said to leave her alone, and I mean it."

"Someday you ain't gonna always get your way," Floyd said. "Someday I'll show you I ain't afraid of you."

"You do that," Will said, glancing at Catherine. "Get back inside."

She gladly scrambled back to the far wall, as far away from her captors as she could get. Her shoulder throbbed but she rubbed her arms where Floyd had gripped them, trying to wear away the memory of his hands on her. How could she bear it if he really did the things he had threatened?

Shuddering, she realized she would have to kill herself rather than endure Floyd Taggert's lust. Even the thought of her child could not dissuade her. If Floyd were as violent as his brother indicated, neither she nor her child could long survive him, anyway.

Leaning back against the wall of the cave, Catherine drew her knees to her chest and wrapped her arms around them. Her whole body shook, but whether the tremors came from chill or fright, she did not know. Time passed, as she could tell by the position of the sun, although no one said much of anything. Once Will offered her some jerky, but her stomach recoiled at the very thought. She took a little water from a tin cup and found herself hard-pressed to keep even that down.

She waited for the inevitable moment when one of the men would go out and see her tattered lace fluttering in the breeze, but she waited in vain. In fact, she felt the urge herself long before either of them stirred. When she could bear the discomfort no longer, she once again asked permission to go outside.

"Already? What's wrong with you, anyways?" Floyd asked in annoyance.

"I'm nervous," she snapped, forgetting for a moment she didn't want to antagonize him.

But he cackled, amused by her pique. "Then go make a nervous puddle outside."

She strode out without even glancing at him, hoping her terror didn't show. If he so much as touched her, her fragile facade would shatter into hysteria.

This time she didn't bother to look around. If the Taggerts with their constant vigilance had not seen Sam approaching, surely she had no chance of seeing him or any sign of him. She went to her spot, glad to see the lace still fluttered where she had left it.

Not wanting to linger for fear the Taggerts would come in search of her, she hurried, but as she stood up to adjust her skirts, something stung the back of her neck.

"Ouch!" she cried, her hand going automatically to touch the injured spot. A bee sting was all she needed, she thought in despair. Or perhaps she had been bitten by something more dangerous. She glanced quickly around, looking for some trace of her attacker, while her fingers explored her neck, looking for a wound.

Oddly, she found no trace of a bite, but before she could reason it out, something struck her in the back, smack between her shoulder blades. She whirled, prepared for anything except what she saw.

"Sam!"

Chapter Fifteen

Sam signaled frantically for silence, and Catherine clapped both hands over her mouth and glanced apprehensively over her shoulder to see if her outburst had alerted the Taggerts. When she looked back at Sam, he was motioning for her to come to where he had concealed himself in the rocks. She hiked up her skirts and ran, scrambling awkwardly over the rough ground.

Sam dragged her back into his hiding place and straight into his arms. They clung for one glorious moment.

"Are you all right? Did they hurt you?"

His whisper sounded unnaturally hoarse, and she knew how frightened he must have been for her safety. "No, they didn't hurt me. They wanted to keep me healthy until they had you."

His breath came out in a long, shuddering sigh.

"How did you find me?" she asked.

"We followed your trail. You did a good job, Cat."

"We?"

"Davy's with me."

"Oh, no! I led you into a trap! They want to kill you."

"They won't. Let's get you out of here."

He released her and started down the hill, holding her arm so she wouldn't fall. She saw he carried a rifle in his other hand. At the bottom, David materialized out of a clump of brush.

"Miss Eaton, are you all right?"

"Tired and bruised, but they didn't hurt me."

"Thank God," he breathed.

"Take her to where we hid the horses," Sam told him, "and head on back to town. You'll probably run into the posse on your way. Don't stop for anything, no matter what you hear."

David nodded, taking Catherine's other arm, prepared to lead her away, but she refused to budge. "Aren't you coming?" she asked Sam as a new panic bubbled up in her.

"If we all go, they'll just follow. I'll make sure they don't."

"Sam!" she cried in protest. She couldn't leave him.

"Don't you have a hat?" he asked sternly.

She touched the top of her head in confusion. "No, I—I took it off. I had to use the hatpin on Floyd Taggert."

Sam muttered a curse and took the hat from his own head, plopping it down on Catherine's. It covered her ears, and she had to hold it up with both hands to see his face. "I won't leave you, Sam!"

His face hardened stubbornly. "I'm not going to let them have you and the baby, Cat."

Stunned, she could only stare. How did he know about the baby?

"Come on, Miss Eaton," David urged, pulling her

449

away. "We've got to get you out of here before they come looking."

Numbly, she allowed David to lead her off into the tangle of brush, but she stared after her as long as Sam was still in sight. She had so many things to tell him, but there was no time. Instead, she forced herself to think of her baby and followed David blindly, trying not to stumble.

Sam stared after them longingly. Even with her clothes filthy and torn, her hair hanging down her back in a tangle, and her face cruelly sunburned, Cat was the most beautiful woman he had ever seen. The thought of the Taggerts even touching her filled him with unspeakable rage, and he knew he had no other choice except to kill them both.

The instant Cat and Davy were out of sight, he turned back to his vantage point in the rocks and settled in to wait for the Taggerts to realize Catherine wasn't coming back. He didn't have much of a wait.

"Lady?" one of them called after a few minutes. *"Lady?* Where are you?"

Floyd Taggert's demented giggle shimmered over the distance. "She's trying to hide from us, Will. I'll fetch her."

"No, you stay here," Will said. "I don't trust you alone with her."

Sam could hear Will coming through the brush. He lifted his rifle, bracing it on the rocks in front of him.

"Lady," Will called. "Where are you, Lady? Don't forget what we told you about getting lost out here. Now stop playing games and come out."

Will reached the spot where Sam had seen Catherine, and he paused, looking around. Then he swore, snatching the lace Catherine had tied to the bush. "Still

450

trying to leave a trail for Connors?'' he shouted. "You're wasting your time. He'll never find you here!"

"Yes, he will!" Sam shouted back.

Will whirled, drawing his gun, and before Sam could react, Taggert fired into the rocks where he hid. Sam fired back even before Will's bullet stopped ricocheting, sending up a plume of dust at Taggert's feet.

Will swore profanely, jumping backward and diving for cover. Sam's second bullet caught him in the calf, and he yelled sharply in pain.

"Will! What's going on!" Floyd called from the cave.

"It's Connors!" he replied, snapping off a shot in the direction of the rocks.

The bullet struck near Sam's head, sending up a shower of stinging splinters. This time Sam took careful aim, squinting to make out Will's form imperfectly concealed behind the scrub. He squeezed the trigger, and Will's second howl echoed the explosion.

"I'm hit, Floyd. He hit me twice!"

"How bad?" the voice thundered from the cave.

"He got my leg. I can't walk, but don't come out. He'll get you, too." Will snapped off another shot. This one went wild, but Sam had been waiting for the puff of gunsmoke so he could locate his quarry exactly.

Catherine and David stopped in mid-stride at the sound of the first gunshots. They could hear men shouting but could not make out the words. Catherine's heart lurched to a painful halt as she pictured Sam wounded or even dead.

"David, we can't just leave him alone up there!"

"Remember what he said. I was to get you away,

451

no matter what. You gotta think of your baby, Miss Eaton.''

Catherine saw the pain in his sky-blue eyes. The knowledge of her pregnancy had wounded him deeply, as she had known it would.

''Come on,'' he said, dragging her along behind him. ''You can't be of no help to him. You don't even have a gun.''

This was true, but she saw that David did. He wore Sam's gunbelt and six-shooter. Sam must have given it to the boy so he could protect her, leaving him with only a rifle.

Another quick volley of shots echoed across the hills and then silence. Was it over? Catherine quaked with fear but David didn't stop, and he wouldn't let Catherine stop, either. Her feet fairly flew across the rough ground, and David's firm grip on her arm prevented her from falling.

At last they reached the horses, who snorted in protest at their precipitous approach.

''You take my pony,'' David said, helping her to mount. ''I'll take Sam's horse.''

''What will Sam ride?'' Catherine asked in alarm. Surely, David didn't intend to leave his brother afoot.

David stared up at her bleakly. ''He'll either ride one of the Taggert's horses, or he won't need to ride anything at all.''

''No!'' she cried, covering her mouth as another volley of shots shattered the stillness.

She saw her own terror reflected in David's eyes.

''We can't leave him. I can't help him, but you can!'' she told him. ''You've got a gun. Go back!''

''But I can't leave you! I've got to get you out of here,'' he protested, obviously torn.

"I . . . is there really a posse coming?"

"Yeah, we came looking for you this morning, and when we found out you'd taken the stage, we followed. We got to it about an hour after the holdup. That's why we caught up with you so quick. We sent the driver back into town for a posse, so they shouldn't be too far behind."

"Then I'll meet them. I can go alone and follow my own trail until I do. Please, David, go back and help him!"

Any other time, she might have considered it folly to send a fifteen-year-old boy to help, but at the moment it was the only possible solution.

They heard another shot and David's head snapped around, his eyes wild with indecision.

"David, please!"

Sam aimed carefully at where he had seen the last pistol flash and squeezed the trigger. This time no anguished cry echoed the explosion and no answering shot came.

"Will?" Floyd Taggert called, but he received no reply from the thicket into which Sam had fired. *"Will!"*

Still only silence.

"Damn you, Connors!" Floyd Taggert yelled from within the cave. "You've went and killed Will!"

Not quite so certain, Sam moved cautiously from behind the rocks, anticipating a shot from Will's hiding place. When none came, he crept closer, maintaining his cover and keeping constant watch lest Floyd try to escape the sanctuary of the cave.

When Sam was within twenty feet of Will, he saw the slowly spreading crimson stain seeping out from beneath the prickly shrubs. Closer, he saw Will's lifeless hand from which his pistol had slipped. Approaching boldly now, he prodded Taggert with the rifle barrel and got not so much as a groan in response.

Pushing aside the vegetation, he saw the gaping wound right over Taggert's heart. A lucky shot, but Sam took no time to exult in his luck. He still had one more Taggert to dispose of.

Dropping to his knees, Sam worked his way closer to the cave. He lay down on his belly and spoke toward the ground so the exact location of his voice would be disguised. "Your brother's dead, Taggert. If you come out with your hands up, I won't shoot."

"Like hell! Will! Answer me, Will!"

"He's dead, I told you. Do you think he wouldn't have shot at me by now if he could?"

Taggert answered with a burst of gunfire, spraying the entire area. Sam hugged the ground as the bullets smashed through the undergrowth and kicked up dust all around him. When silence fell again, he crawled along the ground until he had a clear view of the cave's opening.

"Taggert, I've got you covered. You'll never get past me; now come out with your hands up."

"Go to hell!" Taggert emptied his pistol in the direction of Sam's voice while Connors scrambled to safety behind an outcropping of rock.

"There's a posse on the way, Taggert! All I have to do is sit here and wait."

"You're lying! If there's a posse, why ain't they with you?"

"Because I found the stage right after you robbed it and sent the driver back for help. I blazed a trail a blind man could follow, and it leads right to your front door.''

"I should've killed you when I had the chance, Connors. One day you and your friends rode right by here, and I had you right in my sights. It would've been so easy.''

"You might've gotten me, but you know the others would've gotten you.''

Sam moved quickly, correctly guessing that Taggert had been conversing in order to get an idea of exactly where he was hiding. No sooner had he shifted positions than a hail of bullets came smashing into the rocks where he had been. The whine of their ricochets echoed into the succeeding silence.

"Nice try, Taggert,'' Sam called. He didn't bother firing back. His chances of hitting Taggert inside the cave were nil, and he had to conserve the little ammunition he'd brought with him. Finding a semicomfortable spot, he settled in to wait, staring intently at the cave's opening lest Floyd Taggert try making a break.

At least he needn't worry about Catherine any longer. Davy loved her almost as much as Sam did, and he'd make certain she was safe. Soon the posse would arrive, and it would all be over.

Time crept slowly by. Insects buzzed lazily, attracted to Sam's salty sweat as the blazing sun tried to melt his body into the stones. The air shimmered in the heat, and Sam missed his hat as he fought to keep his eyes focused. Lazily swatting at flies, he rested the Winchester on the rocks, pointed at the cave's opening.

Suddenly, the hairs on the back of his neck prickled in warning. Glancing around, straining for any unusual sound, he saw and heard nothing untoward, but he knew someone was approaching. Probably it was the posse, being stealthy because they didn't know where he was.

"Hey, Taggert," Sam called to identify his location, "ain't you getting bored with all this waiting?"

"Not yet," said a voice immediately behind him.

Sam jerked around and came face-to-face with the barrel of Floyd Taggert's .45. "Sweet Jesus," he muttered, wondering how Taggert had gotten out of the cave without him seeing. Obviously, there must be another entrance. Swiftly, he tried to judge his chances of getting his Winchester up before Taggert could fire.

"Don't even think about it," Taggert warned, cackling with delight. The click of his cocking pistol sounded unnaturally loud in the eerie stillness. "You killed my brother so I'm gonna kill you, and then I'm gonna get your woman. Do you wanna know what I'll do to her? First off, I'll strip her down so I can find out if the pelt between her legs is as yellow as what's on her head, and then—"

Sam forced himself not to listen. He tensed his muscles, prepared to make one desperate lunge, when another voice hollered, "Taggert!"

Floyd's head jerked up. Sam grabbed for his rifle just as the brilliant sunlight exploded.

Rolling, spinning, Sam came up on one knee, his Winchester aimed, not even knowing if he had been shot. But his target was gone. Floyd Taggert lay spread-eagled on the rocks, a neat round hole in the middle of his forehead.

"Sam? Sam, are you all right?" Davy's voice piped from somewhere above them.

"Yeah, I'm fine! You got Taggert dead center!"

Sam kept his eyes on the body as Davy scrambled

out of his hiding place. "Good God Almighty," the boy breathed when he saw the results of his marksmanship. His young face had gone chalk white, and the pistol shook in his hand.

"You saved my life," Sam said, rising to his feet. "He had me dead to rights."

"I was scared spitless when I couldn't see you anywheres," Davy said hoarsely. "I thought maybe they already got you, and I couldn't call out in case they had."

Sam clapped a comforting hand on the boy's shoulder and drew a deep breath, trying to calm the surge of adrenaline for which he had no further need now that Taggert lay dead. "You did good." He looked around. "Where's the rest of the posse?"

"They didn't come yet."

Sam started in surprise. "Didn't come? You mean you came back here alone? Where's Catherine?"

"I—I let her go on. Sam, she made me leave her!" he said, backing up in the face of Sam's furious reaction. "She said if I didn't come, she would. I tried to tell her she wouldn't be any help but she wouldn't listen, so I told her how to find the main road in case she missed the trail we left. For sure, she'll run into the posse."

"Are you crazy? She's a city woman. She'll never find her way back alone. And what if she faints or something? Go after her! Hurry up! I'll take care of things here and follow as quick as I can."

Nodding, Davy stuffed the pistol back in its holster and trotted away, slipping and sliding in his boots on the gravel. Sam hurried off, thinking he wouldn't bother trying to drag the bodies back into the cave. If he could find some blankets inside, he'd cover them for

457

now. His first priority was locating the Taggerts' horses and getting to Catherine.

"Miss Eaton! Miss Eaton!"

Catherine roused herself, cursing under her breath when she realized exhaustion had claimed her again, sending her into a dangerous oblivion. She crept out of her hiding place in the shade of a rocky overhang to see who was calling her name.

"David," she whispered in relief, jumping to her feet and running out to meet him. "David! Here I am!"

As he turned his horse in her direction, she vainly searched for some sign of Sam behind him.

"Where's Sam?" she demanded as David approached. "Is he all right?"

"He's fine. The Taggerts are both dead. You were right to send me back. Floyd Taggert would've killed Sam if I hadn't been there."

"Oh," she said, feeling the blood rush from her head. David caught her arm as she swayed and helped her sit down on the ground.

"You look kinda peaked, Miss Eaton. You aren't going to faint, are you?"

"I certainly hope not," she replied with a semblance of a smile. "Are you telling me the truth about Sam? Why didn't he come with you?"

"He had to take care of the bod . . . of things, and then he had to find where the Taggerts hid their horses. I reckon he'll be along directly. He was mad as blazes when he found out I left you alone, so he sent me on ahead."

David paused, looking around at where she had tied his pony while she rested. "You shouldn't have stopped. What if the Taggerts had got us instead and come after you?''

She smiled grimly, not wanting to tell him she wouldn't have cared about living if the Taggerts had killed him and Sam. Nor did she want to tell him how close she had come to falling off the pony out of sheer weariness. "I knew you'd win the fight, so I decided to wait here for you.''

David glanced over his shoulder as if afraid his brother might be near enough to overhear. "Don't tell Sam you stopped, huh? He's mad enough as it is.''

She nodded her agreement. "Come over here into the shade. We can wait for Sam together.''

While they waited, David told her how he had returned to the cave and been unable to find either his brother or the Taggerts. He'd sneaked around in the rocks, waiting and listening, until finally Sam had broken the silence. By the time he'd located his brother, Floyd Taggert had a pistol pointed at Sam's head.

Catherine shuddered in horror as David described the scene.

"I killed him," David said in wonder, still not quite able to believe it. "I never killed a man before.''

"You didn't have a choice. He would have killed Sam otherwise," Catherine said, knowing she would have done the same thing in his place.

"He needed killing," David said, repeating something she supposed he had heard said.

"They both did," she replied, casting off her usual role as teacher. No moral lessons seemed appropriate today, and David certainly didn't need to feel guilty for having saved Sam's life. To change the subject, she asked him how they had found her.

"Well, when Inez told us about the baby—''

459

"She *told* you!" Catherine exclaimed, mortified.

"Well, not just right out," he admitted. His pained expression told her how difficult this subject was for him. "She got all upset when she found out you was leaving, and Sam made her tell."

Catherine understood. Inez would have stood no chance of keeping her secret under Sam's interrogation. "David, I'm sorry you had to find out that way."

"He's a bastard! I told him so, too. I know he forced you, Miss Eaton, and—" His chin quivered slightly and he looked away, blinking furiously.

"David, he didn't force me," she tried, but he wasn't listening.

"You didn't have to run away. If he wouldn't marry you, I would!"

"Oh, David," she cried, blinking at her own tears and slipping an arm around his shoulders. "That's not the reason I ran away. Sam would marry me in a minute. *I'm* the one who didn't want to get married."

"Why in the hell not?" he demanded, not even noticing he'd sworn in her presence.

"Because of the way he's treated you. I was afraid my son would be just like you—or at least, I hope he will be. What if he wants to go to Philadelphia or even Paris to study art, and Sam refuses to let him go?"

David looked at her as if he thought she'd lost her mind. "You ran off because of what you thought he *might* do?"

She winced. "I know it sounds like a stupid reason, and believe me, I realized it before the stage had gone a mile. I probably would have come straight back tomorrow."

He had no reply, so they sat in silence for a while,

460

watching for Sam to appear. Finally he said, "My offer is still good."

"Your offer?"

"Yeah, my offer to—to marry you. I know I'm just a kid, but the Spur is half mine. I could make Sam split it up so we wouldn't have to live with him or anything and—"

"Oh, David, thank you," she said, hugging him close and laying her head on his shoulder. "I'll never forget your offer, and I want you to know I love you dearly and I always will, but I love you like a brother. It wouldn't be fair of me to take advantage of you and ruin your life."

"You wouldn't ruin my life," he protested, but she cut him off.

"Yes, I would, because I'd always be in love with Sam. Think how unfair that would be to you."

"You love him?"

She nodded, feeling the tears well up again. "More than I can tell you."

"And you were still going to leave?" he asked incredulously.

She gave him a self-mocking smile. "You'll probably never be able to understand the female mind, so don't even try. I couldn't hope to explain the way I acted, in any case."

David considered the situation gravely for a long moment. "Sam's pretty mad at you," he warned.

"He has every right to be."

"I was afraid he'd hurt you. That's why I followed him this morning."

"He won't hurt me, although he'd certainly be justified after what I did to him," she admitted.

Just then Sam came into view, riding fast. David

461

jumped up and shouted, waving his arms as Catherine had done to catch his attention. Sam swerved his mount and galloped up.

"What's wrong?" he demanded, flinging himself out of the saddle.

"Nothing," David assured him. "Miss Eaton's awful tired, so we decided to rest while you caught up."

Sam pushed by David. "Cat? Are you all right?"

"I am now," she said, thinking how wonderful it was to see him safe and sound after all the danger he'd been in. "I just needed a little rest." She allowed him to help her to her feet. He took her in from head to toe, as if searching for wounds or injuries. "I'm fine, really, but I'm anxious to get someplace where I can have a bath and lay down in a real bed."

Several emotions flickered across Sam's face, but he quickly masked them all. "Let's get going then."

They mounted up, Catherine alone on David's pony and praying she could hold on for the long trip back. Except for Sam's occasional inquiries about her well-being, they rode in silence, too weary from their ordeal for conversation. They had almost reached the edge of the rocks when they saw the posse approaching, led by Mathias Shallcross, who hailed them lustily.

"Twila's going to be awful glad to see you alive and well, Catherine," he said when the two parties met.

"I'm equally glad," Catherine replied.

Mathias frowned, looking at her more closely beneath the shadow of Sam's Stetson, which she still wore. "Maybe you shouldn't try to get all the way to town tonight. The Spur is much closer, ain't it, Sam?"

Sam nodded, silently thanking Mathias for suggesting what he never would have dared. "Davy can take her straight there and Inez can take care of her while the rest of us go back to pick up the Taggerts."

Much too weary to argue, Catherine couldn't even manage a perfunctory protest and rode off with David into the setting sun. At least this way there would be no delay in her confrontation with Sam. As soon as he returned to the ranch, they would settle things once and for all.

"Where is she?" Sam demanded the instant he entered the house that evening and found Davy sitting in the front room.

"She's asleep," he replied, rising to meet his brother. "Inez helped her get a bath and then put her to bed."

"She's not sick, is she?" he asked in alarm. "The baby? . . ."

"Inez sent for her mother, and the old woman says she's fine, just exhausted."

"Thank God," Sam sighed wearily. He ran a hand through his uncovered hair, then walked straight to the liquor cabinet and poured himself a stiff belt of whiskey. When he had downed about half of it, he went over to the sofa where Davy sat and sank down beside him. The silence between them was awkward, but neither of them was anxious to broach any of the painful subjects they must discuss.

Sam chose the least painful with which to begin. "You did a brave thing out there today. I'm not saying you should've left Catherine alone, but I know how she gets, and she probably didn't give you any choice."

"She didn't."

"I figured. Anyway, I been thinking ever since how

wrong I've been about a lot of things, but mostly about you."

"Me?"

Sam sighed again. "Yeah, I've had a lot of crazy ideas about you and your pictures. Catherine tried to tell me I was wrong, but I wouldn't listen. I almost had to get myself killed before I could see the truth. Like I told you, I was afraid of you leaving here and never coming back, but that was only the half of it. I was also afraid that if I let you draw your pictures, you'd somehow be less than a man." Sam made himself look at Davy and endure the hurt he saw on the boy's face.

"That's why you got so mad about what Johnny said," Davy guessed, his blue eyes clouded with a pain Sam could barely stand to see.

"I was wrong, Davy. I was stupid and wrong."

Davy turned and started to rise.

Sam laid a restraining hand on his shoulder. "I said I was *wrong*. What you did today proved it."

"Because I killed a man?" he asked bitterly.

"No! The Taggerts killed, too. Killing doesn't make you a man. I'm talking about the way you acted. When you came back, you didn't run in like some silly kid, yelling and screaming for me. You took your time and sized up the situation. When you saw Taggert had the drop on me, you didn't panic. You acted like a man, Davy, and you saved my life." Sam made no effort to disguise his own hoarseness, and Davy turned, finally, to look at him again.

"I couldn't let him kill you," he said brokenly.

Sam managed a rueful smile and gave Davy's shoulder a squeeze. "I'm glad you couldn't."

They stared at each other for a long moment while

Sam gathered the courage to say what he most dreaded saying. "I've been thinking about this a lot since what happened today. If you still want to go to Philadelphia, it's all right. I won't have much ready cash this year, so—"

"Sam, do you mean it?"

"Hell, yes, I mean it," Sam said, pretending to be affronted. "Did you ever know me to go back on my word? Like I said, you might have to wait a year because money'll be tight, but—"

Davy jumped to his feet and walked quickly across the room, head down, hands jammed into his pockets.

"What's wrong? I thought you'd be happy."

"I am," Davy replied in a muffled voice, keeping his back to Sam.

"Then what's the matter?"

He stared into the fireplace for a long time before he replied. "She told me why she ran away."

"Catherine?" Sam asked in surprise. Davy nodded without turning around. "What did she tell you?" he asked warily, wondering just how angry she was at him and whether she was angry enough to use her knowledge of Davy's past to get back at Sam.

Davy turned just his head to look at him. "She said she was afraid you'd treat her baby the way you've treated me."

Sam went cold with dread. "What do you mean?"

"She thinks her baby'll be an artist, too. I guess she figures if you won't let your brother go study art, you sure as hell won't let your own son go."

Sam's shoulders sagged with relief. He should have known Cat wouldn't betray his secret. No matter how angry she was at Sam, she'd never hurt Davy. "I reckon she was right to be worried."

"But now you're going to let me go," Davy reminded him. "That'll prove you've changed, and then she won't want to leave you anymore."

"Wait a minute," Sam said in confusion. "Why do you all of a sudden care what she thinks of me?"

"Because she's gonna have your baby and I care what happens to *her*, that's why. We can't let her run off again to God knows where.

Chastened, Sam frowned. "She'll never believe I've really changed. She'll just think you told me what she said and I'm trying to get back on her good side." God knew he'd already been guilty of such ploys in the past, and Cat knew it, too.

"Then you've got to *show* her you've changed. Remember you told me you can't force somebody to love you? You can't force somebody to stay with you, either, and you might even make them want to run away."

"Like you were going to run away to Philadelphia?"

"How did you know?" Davy asked in surprise.

"Don't worry, she didn't tell me. I eavesdropped on the two of you. And she was right. You probably could've worn me down. I've never been able to refuse you anything you really wanted, not for long, anyways."

"And you can wear her down, too, if you try. Stop trying to force her to do what you want. Maybe if you'd ask her real nice, she'd even marry you."

Sam frowned again, still unable to make sense of Davy's drastic change in attitude. "I thought you wanted to protect her from me. What changed your mind?"

Davy smiled mysteriously. "Same reason you

changed your mind about me and my pictures: I found out something I didn't know before.''

"What?" Sam demanded. "What else did she tell you?"

"You'll have to ask her that yourself, and you'd better get cleaned up before you do. She'd probably pass out cold if she got a whiff of you right now."

No amount of coaxing or threats or offers of bribery would move Davy to reveal any more secrets, so Sam went off in search of clean clothes and a bath in preparation for his confrontation with Catherine.

When Catherine awoke she lay still for a long time, expecting to fall asleep again immediately as she had done several times already. This time, however, she remained awake. After tentatively moving her arms and legs to check for soreness, she decided she could get up and use the chamber pot if she were extremely careful not to move too quickly.

Someone had thoughtfully shuttered the windows, so Catherine had no idea how long she had slept until she pulled one open and saw the mid-morning sun shining brilliantly.

"Good heavens!" she said aloud, realizing how foolish her plans for confronting Sam as soon as he returned to the house had been. She'd slept more than fifteen hours.

Before she could think any further, the door opened and Inez peeked around at her. "You are awake!"

"At long last. Did Sam get back all right last night?"

"*Sí*, and he is anxious to see you, but I think first I will bring you some breakfast and some clothes, no?"

"Yes, please," Catherine said, looking down at the

nightdress she wore, a loan from Inez, and realizing for the first time how famished she was.

An hour later, Catherine had eaten a hearty meal and dressed in clothes also belonging to Inez. They were a little large, so Inez had pinned them up on her. Catherine left her hair loose, first of all because the effort of pinning it up seemed overwhelming and secondly because it seemed more appropriate with the richly embroidered blouse Inez had given her to wear.

Catherine studied her reflection critically, judging the effectiveness of the rice powder Inez had provided to tone down her sunburned nose and cheeks. The worst part would be when her damaged skin peeled in a few days, she thought critically.

She was wondering how best to arrange a meeting with Sam when someone knocked on the door.

"Who is it?" she asked, knowing instinctively and placing a hand over her racing heart.

"It's me," Sam said. "Can I come in?"

He was being a little more circumspect than he had been the last time, she thought irrelevantly. "Yes."

The door opened slowly, as if he were still uncertain of his welcome. He wore a red yoke-front shirt and jeans still stiff with newness. He'd shaved quite recently, and his ebony hair had been carefully combed. Holding his broad shoulders stiffly, he closed the door behind him with a snap. His dark eyes were veiled, his rugged face void of expression.

Neither of them spoke for a long minute, and Sam drank in the sight of her. She looked like an angel with her golden hair framing her face and spilling down her back. In spite of the sunburn, her skin still looked almost translucent. Only the wariness in her sky-blue eyes warned him of how human she was.

At last Catherine could stand the silence no longer. "You don't look like a man who almost got killed yesterday."

"And you don't look like a woman who got kidnapped yesterday."

Another silence fell, and then Sam said, "Inez told me about the baby."

"I'm sorry, Sam," she said, taking a step toward him as guilt twisted inside her. "I should have told you myself. I had no right to run away the way I did, and I realized it as soon as the stage left town. I would have come right back, although I don't expect you to believe that. I acted like a fool and I know I hurt you terribly, and now you think I'm no better than Adora for stealing your child and—"

"*No*, don't ever say that. You're nothing like Adora."

Catherine blinked in surprise. She felt certain he was mistaken but decided not to correct him.

"Davy told me why you left," he continued. "I reckon you had every right to be afraid of the way I'd treat our baby after the way I'd treated you."

"That wasn't why—"

He silenced her with a gesture. "I should've known I couldn't make you fall in love with me or make you stay with me if you didn't want to. When I went after you yesterday, I was going to drag you back by the hair if I had to, but you probably would've run away again, first chance you got."

"Maybe not," she tried, but he wasn't going to be interrupted.

"The reward for the Taggerts is almost five hundred dollars. Davy and I agree you should have it."

"Why?"

"Because—" he hesitated, betraying the first sign of uncertainty, "because you're going to have a baby. You'll need money."

Catherine's heart turned over in apprehension. "Are you going to send me away, Sam?"

"Don't make fun of me, Cat," he snapped as anger shattered his composure. "You're the one who's leaving me, remember?"

"But I'm back now," she pointed out, concealing her relief that he had finally revealed his true feelings. She could deal with anger.

"Only by accident. If you hadn't run into the Taggerts, you'd be halfway to Philadelphia by now."

"No, I wouldn't," she cried triumphantly, "because you were coming after me to drag me back by my hair! Why did you come after me, Sam? Was it only because of the baby?"

Fury stained his face a dull red. "You know why."

"Yes, I do. You came after me because I was stealing your baby away just like Adora tried to steal David from you."

"No, you're wrong!"

"Am I? Are you saying you don't want your baby?"

"I want you more!"

The words seemed to vibrate in the air between them. Sam stared at her, aghast at what he had revealed.

"Are you saying you love me, Sam?" she prodded.

"I already told you I did," he replied grudgingly.

"I wonder how much you love me. Do you love me enough to forgive me for running away? For not trusting you? For not telling you about the baby?"

"What are you talking about?"

"I'm talking about the future. I hurt you very badly, and unless you can forgive me, we'll go on hurting

470

each other for the rest of our lives. I don't want our child to see that, do you?''

He considered her question carefully. "I've hurt you, too.''

"So you have, or I wouldn't have been running away in the first place. What a pair we are, my darling.''

His eyebrows lifted at the endearment. "Am I really your darling?''

"Yes, you are. I love you, Sam Connors, whether you believe it or not.''

His expression softened, and for the first time she saw what might have been hope flicker in his dark eyes. "Cat? . . .''

"What?''

Sam struggled with the myriad questions in his mind to find exactly the right one. "Will you marry me?''

"Yes.''

He stared at her for a long moment, stunned by how simple it had been. Then he closed the distance between them in two long strides and caught her up for his kiss. Their lips met hungrily, sealing the commitment they had just made. The kiss went on and on until they separated, gasping.

"Why are you grinning?'' Catherine asked.

"I was just thinking that if I'd asked you that question a couple of months ago, I could have saved us both a lot of trouble.''

"But you didn't want to marry me a couple of months ago.''

"Of course I did!''

"Then why didn't you ask me?''

"Because you didn't want to marry me.''

"What made you think that?''

"You said so,'' he reminded her.

"Only because I thought you didn't want me."

Sam groaned in disgust, resting his forehead against hers. " 'What a pair we are, my darling.' "

"Am I really your darling?"

"Forever and ever."

"You never answered my question."

"What question?"

"Can you forgive me for running away and for not telling you about the baby?"

He sighed and kissed the tip of her nose. "Only if you promise to spend the rest of your life trying to make it up to me."

"And how shall I do that?"

"We'll think of something," he said, pressing his hips to hers suggestively.

Feeling the very obvious evidence of his arousal, Catherine's body responded instinctively. She smiled up at him. "Mmmm, seems like I'd better start right now."

His dark eyes glittered with desire, but he shook his head sternly and pulled away. "You've been through enough the past couple of days. You need to rest."

"I've *been* resting," she protested, sliding back into his arms. "I'm fine now, really, Sam."

"More than fine, I'd say." He grinned, running his hands over her slender body. "But the next time I make love to you in that bed, we'll be man and wife."

"My, my," she said, pressing herself against him to test her power. "You must be much stronger than I am. I don't think I can wait."

"You won't have to wait long. I'll have Reverend Fletcher out here tomorrow."

"Tomorrow!" she exclaimed in surprise.

"Or maybe this afternoon," he said as his mouth covered hers again.

472

Epilogue

Sam worried because Catherine was so small, so when her time came, he sent to Dallas for a doctor. After an amazingly short labor, Catherine was delivered of a healthy baby girl. The doctor arrived several hours after the baby did.

Sam and Catherine had been arguing for weeks over names. A boy would be named for Catherine's father, of course, but Sam insisted a daughter of Cat's should be named Kitten, while Catherine held out for something more traditional.

One look at Sam's face the first time he saw his child settled the matter, however. Joy Connors was the light of her father's life, and he doted on her the way he'd never allowed himself to dote on David.

She enchanted David, too, and as long as Catherine lived, she'd never forget the expression on Sam's face the first time David called him Papa. When Joy was no more than an hour old, David came in to greet the new arrival.

Sam sat in the new rocking chair beside the bed where Catherine lay, cradling his precious bundle, and

David grinned broadly at the sight of Sam's work-roughened hand stroking the baby's delicate cheek. "Hello, Papa," he chirped.

"Papa?" Sam echoed hollowly, stunned.

"Yeah, *Papa,* you'd better get used to it now that you are one." He winked at Catherine. "From the look on his face, it's a good thing I started breaking him in early. If the baby'd said it first, we might've lost him."

"It does sound strange," Sam managed hoarsely. He and Catherine had argued over David, too. She insisted David had a right to know Sam was his father. He would understand, she'd said.

And what if he didn't? Sam had responded each time, effectively ending the discussion. Thus, they'd kept the secret.

David gazed down at the baby in Sam's arms. "She sure is little, isn't she?"

"She'll grow," Catherine informed him wryly.

Obviously intimidated, David touched the baby's tiny fist with the tip of his finger. To his surprise, Joy grabbed it, looking up at him with Catherine's blue eyes. "Hello there," he said, and then—or so Sam and David always swore—she smiled.

Sam and David were completely smitten and began a competition to see who could spoil her more thoroughly. Catherine often observed that if Joy hadn't come to her to be fed, she never would have gotten to hold her own baby.

One afternoon when Joy was about six months old, Catherine wandered into the parlor to find out why her daughter hadn't awakened from her nap. Catherine's full breasts told her it was past time, and when she

474

peeked into the room they'd made for the baby in the corner of the front room, she knew why.

Stolen! Joy had been stolen again. Since David had left a few weeks earlier for Philadelphia—using the reward money to finance his trip—Catherine knew exactly where to look. She found Sam and his daughter stretched out on the big bed he and Catherine now shared.

Even before she opened the bedroom door, she could hear Sam talking nonsense and the baby's cooing replies.

"Aha!" Catherine cried in triumph as she threw the door open. "Thief! Kidnapper!"

Sam grinned unrepentantly, and Joy shrieked an enthusiastic greeting to her mother.

"I found her all alone in her bed, and she told me her mama was neglecting her," Sam said in defense as Catherine climbed onto the bed beside them.

"Liar," she chided playfully as she unbuttoned her bodice and offered Joy her breast. "You woke her up and carried her off."

"She didn't complain," he informed her, watching with adoration as his child suckled.

Joy released Catherine's nipple for a moment to cast Sam a flirtatious glance before resuming her meal.

"You are entirely too absorbed in this baby," Catherine informed him with mock sternness.

Sam captured Joy's bare foot and kissed her toes, eliciting a milky giggle. "I can't help it. I could never be this way with Davy, for fear somebody would guess I was his father."

"Well, you're going to ruin this poor child if something isn't done to stop you," Catherine said, maintaining her stern pose.

475

"What did you have in mind?" he asked, his dark eyes laughing at her.

"The solution is obvious: You must have more children."

He grinned wickedly. "I'm perfectly willing to do my part, but I'll need help."

Catherine sighed dramatically. "Well, since this is so important, I'm willing to make the sacrifice. . . ."

"Sacrifice!"

Joy jumped and gave her father a quizzical look, which he ignored.

"Yes, sacrifice," Catherine insisted. "I'm sure you'll need at least six or seven children to bring you into line."

"Six?"

Or seven. Maybe even more. I'll have to see how you do."

Sam frowned, no longer amused by her teasing. "You're awfully small, Cat. Don't you think—"

"You heard what the doctor said. I'm made for having babies small or not. Of course, I might get plump."

"I like you plump," he said, stroking the curve of her hip.

"So if you don't mind making the babies, I'll gladly have them. It's for your own good, Sam."

"Seems like I remember you didn't mind making Joy," he recalled slyly.

Catherine's lips twitched, but she managed to maintain her pose. "As I said, I'm perfectly willing to do my wifely duty."

Sam lunged, catching her by surprise with the fierceness of his embrace. His mouth sought hers hungrily, and for a moment they both forgot they were not alone.

"Whaaa," baby Joy wailed in protest at being scrunched between her parents.

Sam eased away, making a space for her while still holding Catherine fast. "What do you think are the chances of Joy taking another nap real soon so her parents can get on with their 'duties'?"

"Not very good," Catherine replied. "But maybe Inez will watch her while we take one."

Sam grinned. "I'll go ask her right now."

Author's Note

I hope you enjoyed Sam and Catherine's story. I based the accounts of the conflicts over fencing on actual events. Fencing began in Texas after the bad winter of 1882–83, and many abuses similar to those recounted in this book took place. Some of those whose fences were cut hired gunfighters from Dodge City to fight the range wars that resulted. The fights were often bloody, although records indicate only four men were actually killed.

Fence cutters sometimes left warnings behind such as coffins or nooses. In Navarro County in 1888, local officials were no longer able to control the fence cutting and called in the Texas Rangers. Sergeant Ira Aten and Jim King arrived in an old farm wagon drawn by a horse and a mule. They took jobs picking cotton and doing farm work. Aten bought dynamite and began making bombs to string along fences. Orders from Austin directed him to stop his work and return home, but gossip about the bombs was enough to stop wire cutting in the area.

I love to hear from my readers. Please enclose a SASE and write to me c/o Zebra Books, 475 Park Avenue South, New York, NY 10016.

THE BEST IN HISTORICAL ROMANCES

TIME-KEPT PROMISES   (2422, $3.95)
by Constance O'Day Flannery

Sean O'Mara froze when he saw his wife Christina standing before him. She had vanished and the news had been written about in all of the papers—he had even been charged with her murder! But now he had living proof of his innocence, and Sean was not about to let her get away. No matter that the woman was claiming to be someone named Kristine; she still caused his blood to boil.

PASSION'S PRISONER   (2573, $3.95)
by Casey Stewart

When Cassandra Lansing put on men's clothing and entered the Rawlings saloon she didn't expect to lose anything—in fact she was sure that she would win back her prized horse Rapscallion that her grandfather lost in a card game. She almost got a smug satisfaction at the thought of fooling the gamblers into believing that she was a man. But once she caught a glimpse of the virile Josh Rawlings, Cassandra wanted to be the woman in his embrace!

ANGEL HEART   (2426, $3.95)
by Victoria Thompson

Ever since Angelica's father died, Harlan Snyder had been angling to get his hands on her ranch, the Diamond R. And now, just when she had an important government contract to fulfill, she couldn't find a single cowhand to hire—all because of Snyder's threats. It was only a matter of time before the legendary gunfighter Kid Collins turned up on her doorstep, badly wounded. Angelica assessed his firmly muscled physique and ░ared into his startling blue eyes. Beneath all that blood and dirt ░e was the handsomest man she had ever seen, and the one person who could help beat Snyder at his own game.

Available wherever paperbacks are sold, or order direct from the Publisher. Send cover price plus 50¢ per copy for mailing and handling to Zebra Books, Dept. 2835, 475 Park Avenue South, New York, N.Y. 10016. Residents of New York, New Jersey and Pennsylvania must include sales tax. DO NOT SEND CASH.